THE NOMINEE

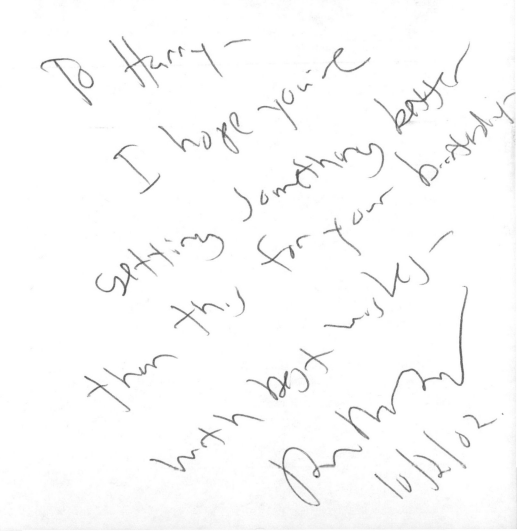

To Harry —
I hope you're
getting something better
than this for your birthday —
with best wishes —
[signature]
10/22/02.

Also by Brian McGrory

The Incumbent

THE NOMINEE

BRIAN McGRORY

ATRIA BOOKS

New York   London   Toronto   Sydney   Singapore

ATRIA BOOKS
1230 Avenue of the Americas
New York, NY 10020

ISBN 0-7434-0352-5

First Atria Books hardcover printing September 2002

10 9 8 7 6 5 4 3 2 1

ATRIA BOOKS is a trademark of Simon & Schuster, Inc.

For information regarding special discounts for bulk purchases,
please contact Simon & Schuster Special Sales at 1-800-456-6798
or business@simonandschuster.com

Printed in the U.S.A.

To Yvonne, for all the guidance and encouragement
over these many years.

THE NOMINEE

one

LANCE RANDOLPH HAD NEVER been in the White House, never been offered so much as VIP tickets for the public tour—though not for any lack of desire. It was, though, for lack of partisanship. Ever since he was elected governor of Massachusetts, the president had always been of the opposite party.

Still was, which was what was so surprising about this night, about this visit.

He sat in the passenger seat of a rented Oldsmobile driven by his chief of staff and longtime aide, Benjamin Bank, who had apparently never been there either, because at the maze of checkpoints manned by uniformed Secret Service officers, Bank kept turning to him with uncharacteristic deference and asking, "Now what?"

"How should I know? Keep driving. We drive in the wrong place, we get shot."

"Exactly."

Randolph barely paid attention. They were on the blocked off stretch of Pennsylvania Avenue staring at the gleaming, glistening building, lit up on a fragrant spring night that might well change his life. Randolph's heroes, men like Franklin Roosevelt and John F. Kennedy, lived and worked and made history in its warren of rooms and offices and hideaways, and now Randolph himself was being beckoned inside by none other than the president of the United States.

Randolph, still gazing out his side window, said, "You really think he's going to jump parties?"

Bank squinted out the windshield and replied, "Not jump parties, but abandon his party. I think he's worried that he can't win a Republican primary and he sure as hell knows he can't win a Democratic one. I think he wants to run for reelection as an Independent, and he's going to start sounding you out for your support."

Bank paused, looked over at Randolph in the passenger seat of the dark car, and added, "Time is on our side. There are eighteen months until the election. We should be able to parlay this into some federal funding for something, even without you making a definitive decision. That's some scratch we really need right about now as we start to think about your own campaign."

No one in politics ever just makes a straight shot at this level, Randolph thought to himself. Everything was always a carom or a cross-corner with a constant obsession for the leave. But it made sense, this scenario, the president pitching for his political support. After all, Randolph was one of the so-called new breed, described as such in a cover story in *Newsweek* just last year. He was young, the youngest governor in the nation, he was centrist, which was unusual considering his election and reelection in Massachusetts. He was good-looking and ambitious and smart. And right now, more than anything else, he was curious.

The two were directed to the northwest gate by a uniformed officer waving a flashlight at their car. Bank motored down both their windows and a pair of officers approached from each side, backlit by powerful spotlights shining over their shoulders from the roof of the guardshack and a nearby tree.

"Welcome to the White House, Governor," one of them said to Randolph. "Drive up toward the West Wing as far as you can go and park on the right side. It's a little crowded tonight, but we've been expecting you and saved you a space up front. Thank you."

The mechanical gate slowly slid open. Randolph saw that the driveway was nose-to-tail with limousines and dark sedans. Lights blazed inside the main mansion. The beds of red tulips glistened in the spotlights, and the dogwood trees were in full, majestic bloom—every inch, every view, as beautiful as on TV.

As they pulled closer, they heard music spilling out the main door, jazzy music, followed by a round of festive applause.

"What the hell?" Randolph said softly, as much to himself as to Bank.

Bank shrugged as he wheeled into the space. "I don't know. Maybe he's throwing you a party."

"We have the right night, right?"

"No, sir. I've completely screwed up the dates. I hope you'll accept my apologies."

Randolph ignored his aide and allowed his mind to drift again. What would it take to live here? What separated those who had from everyone else? More brains? No, Ronald Reagan did just fine. A clear vision? Jimmy Carter's presidency would indicate not. Charm? Please. Think Richard Nixon and Lyndon Johnson.

It was skill and it was luck and it was the willingness to take enormous risks, all shaken together in the most alluring of cocktails that so very few people could ever taste. Maybe he would. Maybe someday.

As they were getting out of their car on the darkened driveway, the strains of "I Left My Heart in San Francisco" wafted from the residence and drifted through the night air.

Bank said, "Tony Bennett."

"I know."

"No, I mean that's really Tony Bennett."

Randolph listened intently. It was Tony Bennett, not on a CD, but live and in person—Tony Bennett at the White House.

Randolph smiled in that sly little way of his and said, "I had the University of Massachusetts marching band at my second inauguration."

"You did, didn't you. And they were excellent."

Randolph continued smiling, but mostly to himself, as they headed toward the Marine guard standing outside the main door of the West Wing.

Maybe someday.

• • •

The two were sitting for ten, maybe fifteen minutes on a pair of royal blue wing chairs in a well lit waiting room outside of the Oval Office with a silent Secret Service officer when a self-important young female aide came through the door in a whir of motion and announced, "Governor Randolph, would you come with me."

Benjamin Bank stood up as well, until the aide said, "The president would prefer to see the governor alone. We'll come back for you." No please, not even so much as a sir. Beacon Hill this was not.

Randolph was expecting to be led into the Oval Office, but instead the attractive aide—all legs and arms, all bared—guided him through a set of French doors out into the warm Washington night, then under the columned portico that connects the West Wing to the residence. They walked quickly and in silence, with crickets chirping in the Rose Garden and moist beds of flowers gently fluttering in the springtime breeze. At the door of the mansion, a pair of well-fed Secret Service agents in navy suits waved them in as Tony Bennett sang "I've Got the World on a String." Randolph could see revelers with drinks in their hands at the far end of the hallway, but he was immediately led to an elevator and descended down one flight. They rode in silence.

Stepping off the elevator, the aide waved her hand down a long, wide hallway that ran through the spine of the building and said, "This way."

The music filtered down the stairs, though not loud, and they continued in silence until the aide, ever efficient, even clipped, pointed to a room on the right and said, "If you could just wait in there. The president will be with you momentarily." Just like that, she was gone.

"That ain't some Rand McNally."

The words rocketed through the silent room like javelins, fast and hard, causing Lance Randolph to spin around from the glass-encased map on the far wall. There in the doorway stood the president of the United States, decked out in a tuxedo and black tie, laughing so hard at his own joke that his chest was heaving like a dribbling basketball.

Before Randolph could speak, the president said, "That map you're looking at, FDR used to stick pins in it every night to follow American troop movements across Europe during W-W-Two. This was his sanctuary, where he spent hour after hour. The Map Room. Then Bill Clinton came along and held coffee klatches in here trying to shake down big-ticket contributors. You tell me whether this country is getting better or worse."

Randolph walked toward him and extended his hand. "Good evening, Mr. President."

"Clay Hutchins, son," the president replied. "Pleasure to meet you. Was a big fan of your old man's—and of yours. Boy, you do look young."

"I don't feel so young anymore, not after a few years in Boston politics."

"Well, if it makes you feel any better, I was so excited you were coming in that I put this monkey suit on just for you." He said this loud, then he let loose a deep, gravelly laugh.

In a softer, whiskeyed voice, he added, "The emir of Qatar is at the house tonight. Until about a month ago, I always thought Qatar was a planet, not a country. Now I come to find they have so much money from natural gas they could buy the state of California. If my polling doesn't get any better out there, I might well sell it to 'em.

"So I spend tonight in the company of sixty sheiks in robes while Tony Bennett sings songs none of these guys ever heard before. You seen Tony Bennett lately? He looks like he stepped out of a damned time capsule, he looks so good. The guy never changes."

"My father used to listen to him when I was a kid."

Hutchins, so caught up in his monologue, looked at Randolph blankly. Then he said, "Come sit," and guided Randolph to a pair of upholstered chairs angled toward each other. There were several other maps on the walls, and windows that looked out at ground level on the darkened South Lawn. A steward shut the heavy door and Bennett's voice was suddenly no more.

Hutchins didn't waste any time. From what Randolph read and heard and now saw, he never wasted any time—no political foreplay, no extended niceties, nothing so much as a cup of coffee and a discussion of the ongoing Massachusetts Senate race.

"Thanks for coming," Hutchins said, his voice still rough, but softer. "That's no small thing. I'm like the third rail these days. Politicians won't touch me. My own party, the bunch of stodgy old fucks, doesn't want me running again. The Democrats can't wait to take my head off in the general. For chrissakes, only the public likes me, but here in Washington, they don't seem to matter."

So Bank was right yet again, Randolph thought. The president was seeking his endorsement. He began recalling his rehearsed lines on how he couldn't at this time offer his support, but would give it every consideration as the election approached. It would make it easier to cross party lines in Massachusetts if the electorate knew that the president had been good to the state in terms of fully funding various public works and public safety projects. Hutchins would respect that kind of quid pro quo, he thought.

"I'm rambling," Hutchins said, bearing down on Randolph. "And believe it or not, I have to get back to this party before I create an international incident by disappearing on my guests.

"So here's the deal. I need an attorney general. Who the hell would have thought that Westfall would resign to become commissioner of baseball, though who can blame him? Better than dealing with all this bullshit, and you don't have to worry about some reporter crawling up your ass for taking free seats to the World Series. Anyway, I want to cross party lines with my nominee. I want to show the nation that cooperation doesn't have to be just in spirit. I want to prove that I don't give a damn about any more Democratic-led investigations. I think the only thing left to investigate about me is the size of my balls, but hell, if you decide you need to see'em, I'll show'em to you right now."

Randolph sat stunned, staring at Hutchins, who actually had his hand on the top of his fly. He thought he knew where this was leading now, but he refused to believe it, not yet, not until he heard the words.

"You were a prosecutor up there in Boston. You're a moderate. You're young and ambitious and maybe you even want to live in this house yourself someday. Here's your running start. I want you to be my attorney general."

Randolph blinked hard a couple of times, uncrossed his legs and leaned forward. Attorney general of the United States, just like Robert F. Kennedy. The most powerful law enforcement official in the nation and maybe the world.

"I've had the FBI do an expedited background check and you come up clean. Anything I need to know about you before we go any further?"

Randolph's eyes fell to the floor for the quickest flicker of a moment, then back to Hutchins. He shook his head. "No, sir."

Hutchins, ever intuitive, seemed to sense the hesitance. "You're sure? Believe me when I tell you, the press can find things out that you think are hidden away forever."

"Yes, sir."

"Good. Then you want to think this over for a while. The reason I asked you in at this odd hour on a Saturday night is so there wouldn't be any damned reporters hanging around and you wouldn't be on my official schedule. My own staff doesn't know I'm asking you. The *Washington Post* says its down to two finalists, neither of whom I like. Take it or leave it, no one knows you are here."

Randolph thought about Bank sitting over in the West Wing, how he'd want to dissect this offer five ways from Wednesday, drain the life out of it, fillet it, run it through a focus group, then go out with a poll. That's how political operatives were. They wore black socks over their pale hairy legs to the beach. You ask them what their outside interests are and they stare at you as if they don't have a clue what you mean. They're great with advice, but never, ever are they putting their own good name before the voters. When they lose, it's on to another campaign.

Sitting with the president of the United States deep in the White House, he decided to do something he rarely ever did. He'd make a decision without Bank. Bank knew a lot about him, but not quite everything.

"I accept."

"You what?" Hutchins asked this as if he was surprised, almost angry, as if he was about to counsel him not to do it.

Both men looked at each other for a long moment before Hutchins continued, his voice low again and his tone grateful, "Thank you."

"Thank you, Mr. President."

Another pause, before Hutchins broke it. "What would you say to a Rose Garden announcement Monday afternoon. We'll clang all the bells and blow all the whistles. You're going to make one hell of a great attorney general for the United States."

"That would be terrific, sir."

"Don't call me sir."

"I won't."

Randolph asked, "To help me in my home state, do you have any objections to me leaking this to the local paper ahead of time?"

Loud again. "The *Record?* I hate them. Go right ahead."

Hutchins stood up, signaling the end of the meeting. "Back to the Qataris. They're probably drilling for gas in the damned East Room by now."

After his flight back to Boston, Randolph shut his office door, settled onto a soft, beige settee, put his wingtips up on the antique coffee table and flicked the top off a bottle of Heineken. He closed his eyes and took a long pull of his beer.

Attorney general of the United States. A massive office in the Justice Department building. FBI protection. The lead in the most sophisticated, most sensitive, most sweeping investigations in the nation.

He would get constant coverage on the front pages of the *Washington Post* and the *New York Times,* profiles in the weekly news magazines, regular airtime on the networks. Someone might even write his biography, and of course, do the job well and he'd be touted as a possible Democratic presidential candidate.

It was a gimme, he told himself, an automatic. The president offers you a job like that, you don't say no. No way. He was halfway through his second term as governor, and there was a been-there, done-that quality to it all as he tried to get ramped up for his third gubernatorial campaign. The penny-ante fundraisers with the egotistical contributors who thought that by accepting their five hundred dollars, you suddenly owed them your soul. All those women with flabby arms and cat food breath who pressed against him getting their picture taken at every campaign stop. Now it was time to head to a bigger stage, Washington, DC, the Broadway of national politics. His old man, he thought, would be so proud.

He tried to smile to himself, but it came out as forced, short, stifled. He felt a pang in his stomach, then his chest. The memory again—the thundering shots, the spatter of crimson-colored blood, the screams, the inhuman look in the killer's eyes. His father, dead on the ground.

Suddenly restless, Randolph took another gulp of beer and walked toward the windows that looked out over the vast, darkened space of the Boston Common below. It was a view he had analyzed a hundred times before, sometimes by the first light of an autumn morning with the trees drenched in oranges, yellows, and reds, sometimes on a late winter afternoon when the fading sun cast a purplish hue through the bare branches over the freshly fallen snow. Now he looked at it as if he was looking at his own mind: dark and blank and uneasy.

A knock sounded at his door. Before he could answer, a State Police trooper opened it a crack and said, "Gov, Robert Fitzgerald's here."

"Thanks, Quinn," Randolph replied.

The door swung open and a tall, silver-haired man walked in, an interesting cross between patrician elegance and Irish ruddiness. He wore a navy blazer over a blue button-down shirt, casual slacks and a pair of ancient loafers. He had deep lines etched into his face, the lines of a man who has worked hard and played even harder.

"I feel like a rookie reporter," Fitzgerald said. He flashed a smile—a curious one. The skin crinkled around his eyes. "The phone rings late on a Saturday night and I take off after the story like a bat out of hell. And here I am, Jimmy Olson on the scene."

A pause, then Fitzgerald added with a warm, whimsical smile, "What the hell is going on?"

Randolph walked back across the room from the windows to the sitting area and beckoned Fitzgerald into a chair at the round antique coffee table. Only a single sidelamp with a hunter green shade lit the palatial office, giving the impression they were playing out an intimate scene on a large stage.

Randolph spoke as the two settled into facing chairs. "You've been a good friend to my family for a long, long time, Robert. You're also the best, fairest, smartest newsman I've ever met, and because of that, I wanted you to know this first."

Randolph paused, drawing a deep breath, letting the air slowly descend through his windpipe and into his lungs. Fitzgerald subconsciously fondled the pen in his chest pocket.

"I was invited down to the White House tonight by Clayton Hutchins. I met with him for about ten minutes. During that time, he offered me the nomination to be the attorney general of the United States."

Another pause. Then, "I accepted on the spot."

Fitzgerald's eyes opened wide and his brows shot upward in surprise. He reflexively brought his left hand up to slowly rub the late-night whiskers on his cheek.

After an awkward, silent moment, he said, his tone flat, "Well, I guess all I can say is, congratulations, Lance. Congratulations."

There was a pause, a sigh from the governor. He replied, "I was hoping for something more."

A longer pause. A horn sounded on Beacon Street, a vagrant on the Common screamed that Ben and Jerry were out to destroy the world.

Fitzgerald stared at the burgundy rug, his eyes still wide open, nodding his head but not speaking. Finally, he said in a methodical voice, "You'll make a great attorney general. You will. You were an outstanding prosecutor here in Boston. You're a skilled politician. It's in your blood and your genes. You'll do great."

When he finished, he stared up at Randolph, who sat looking sternly at him.

"That means a lot to me," Randolph said, his voice like ice, void of any appreciation or even emotion. "Especially coming from you."

Fitzgerald didn't respond. Randolph continued, "The announcement will be made in the Rose Garden Monday afternoon. The president's thinking in nominating me is not only a recognition of my political and prosecutorial abilities, but also to attempt to create a more bipartisan administration, and to prove to the public that he docs not fear any further Democratic investigations."

The two men locked stares again. Randolph drained his beer and said, "I'm authorized to give this to you now on a not-for-attribution basis, and would prefer you put in print that I was not available for comment. The sourcing should be an official familiar with the White House, which I guess I am now. Best that I know, the *Times* and the *Post* won't have this tomorrow. It's yours alone."

Randolph nodded at Fitzgerald, the nod being a punctuation point, a period, or in this case, an exclamation mark.

Fitzgerald said, with a resigned look on his face, "I appreciate that." It was midnight, still time to make the final edition of the Sunday paper. He stood up, slowly, and walked from the governor's office without another word, leaving young Lance Randolph alone in the dim light of the moment. His loafers clicked mournfully along the empty marble hallway and down the wide stairs until he finally reached the front door.

two

WHY IS IT THAT A SEEMINGLY inconsequential bud on an otherwise barren elm can lighten the darkest mood, or that a simple tulip, having pierced the earth on its April ascent toward the heavens, can melt the wintriest exterior and touch the coldest soul?

I pose these questions not out of any specific interest in nature or psychology, but only because rays of sunshine were suddenly caressing my pale, dry cheeks like the golden fingers of some generous god, allowing my heart to grow light and my thoughts to grow expansive. From where I was standing, the first light of morning appeared above the downtown skyline and cast a warm glow across the stately willows, the freshly filled duck pond, and the vibrant meadows of the Public Garden, in what felt like the virgin moments of a reluctant spring. Two weeks earlier, sixteen inches of snow had fallen on our quaint hamlet of Boston. The storm was followed by days of windswept rain that turned the blackened, crusty ice into deep puddles of unforgiving slush. And finally, meteorological salvation. Ah, but my benevolent mood gets away from me.

"Give me that," I said with mock seriousness, thrusting my hand into Baker's sizable mouth to pull out a muddy, slobber-soaked tennis ball.

No sooner had I grabbed it with my now-disgusting fingers than the fickle hound lost any semblance of interest, having directed his entire being toward a trio of squirrels playing in a nearby grove of trees. He stood frozen on the path, his right front leg delicately in the pointing position, casting an occasional sidelong glance my way to make sure I didn't do anything typically, foolishly human to disrupt his prey. Then he lunged toward them, sending the rodents scurrying in various directions for trees. He trotted in a wide circle, a victory lap of sorts, before walking back and taking the ball out of my hand with a half jump and a slight snort. Glad I could be of nominal use.

Rejuvenation. A renaissance, even. It was 6:30 in the morning as I peeled off my sweatshirt after a three-mile walk from the waterfront to the park and began skipping rope on an empty stretch of path. Baker roamed off in pursuit of more squirrels. My mind began wandering as well.

Things were good. Another hour of soothing sunshine and they might actually be excellent. I had moved from Washington to Boston, inarguably the greatest city in these United States. My heart was starting to feel whole again, or at least not shattered into a trillion fragments. Women seemed to find me interesting. I found myself fascinating. And I was on the verge of breaking one hell of a great story about our governor, the young Lance Randolph, lying about his prior record as a state prosecutor. Yes, good and getting better.

On about my fifth minute with the jump rope, it was either stop or die, so I caught my breath and began trotting around the pond toward the point of this Public Garden excursion, my meeting with Paul Ellis, who I could already see sitting on a wooden bench reading that day's paper.

Here, in a nutshell, is how that meeting would proceed:

Paul: "Jack, I'd like you to come over to the front office and start acting like the newspaper executive that you're destined to be."

Jack (that's me): "No thank you."

That would be followed by another temporary stalemate, which would be followed by another meeting next month. And so forth. In my mind, you string together enough temporality and you've created permanence. Or maybe not. We'd just have to wait and see, which I guess disproves the point.

Paul Ellis, by the way, is the publisher of *The Boston Record,* and as such, is not accustomed to hearing the word "No" with any great regularity, or even mild irregularity, as they describe it in all those TV commercials, especially from people like me, meaning people who work for him.

Allow me to explain. My name is Jack Flynn. I'm the senior investigative reporter for *The Boston Record*, a lofty position bestowed upon me after I wrote an exposé on a failed presidential assassination attempt a little more than two-and-a-half years ago. I was hurt in that shooting in more ways than one, and helped in other ways as well, but I'll spare you the details just now. The most important detail to keep in mind is that I'm home now.

Paul Ellis is, in the lingo of the business, my rabbi, an uncanny judge of talent who hired me at the *Record*, promoted me to my current job, gave me an equity stake in the company to persuade me from jumping ship to the *Washington Post* or the *New York Times*, and is now trying to convince me to become his heir apparent in the publisher's suite. That last bit is only partly out of respect for my abilities, more out of disdain for those of his younger cousin, Brent Cutter, currently the newspaper's president and the obvious choice to be the next publisher. That's just a theory, but my theories have a way of revolving into fact.

All of which, of course, leaves me with a choice. I could wear monogrammed custom-made shirts and dine on catered lunches as nervous vice presidents trek to my carpeted office with promises of shaving another 2.2 percent off the bottom line, or I could run around the city and its surrounding suburbs with a Bic Click and a yellow legal pad looking for news wherever I can find it, which isn't often where any normal person wants to be. So far, I choose the latter. Call me a moron, but I'm in love with words rather than numbers, emotion rather than profit. It comes down to how you want to live a life. Mine was being lived richer, but poorer, if you know what I mean.

Anyway, the Cutter-Ellis family has owned *The Boston Record* for one hundred and twenty-seven years, and over that time, has created not only one of the best family-owned newspapers in America, but one of the best newspapers of any kind. They've done it with equal parts journalistic savvy and unabashed paternalism. I'm a case in point for both.

"Hello, Paul," I said as I pulled within hearing distance of him.

Paul Ellis looked up slowly from the paper, his eyes, unusually sad, framed by uncharacteristically dark lines and grooves. His gloomy appearance stood in stark contrast to the glorious signs of spring all around us—the delicious odor of warm, fertile earth, the sun gleaming off the Hancock Tower in the near distance, the occasional self-important duck who had made his sojourn north.

"Step into my office," he said in a melancholic voice.

"My god, Paul," I said, standing over him. "You look awful. You dip into capital or something?" A little Wasp humor. Too little, apparently, because he didn't even feign a smile.

"Sit down, Jack."

As I sat, he folded up his newspaper and placed it on the bench beside him, allowing me to catch a glimpse of the banner headline: "Governor Randolph to Be Nominated U.S. Attorney General." I all but choked on my own good mood. When did this happen? Why? How did we find out? No editor had called me, and I saw nothing the prior night on the television news.

"Can I take a quick look at your paper, Paul?"

The byline was that of our star political reporter, the venerable Robert Fitzgerald. He attributed the information to "an official familiar with the White House," and the story indicated that the leak had occurred late Saturday night, which explains why I had previously heard nothing about it. The Rose Garden press conference announcing the nomination, the story said, was scheduled for tomorrow afternoon.

"Quite a hit," I said, almost to myself, as I immediately began a quick and silent assessment of my own Randolph information, calculating the potential impact on his nomination. I suddenly liked my position—a lot. And now was not the time to care about all those pesky focus groups telling us that no one give's a rat's ass about politics anymore.

I looked up at Paul, who was staring at the ground in front of him. He looked as if he was unsure what to say, or at least how to say it.

"Everything good with you?" he finally asked, his chin resting on his knuckles, his elbows on his knees.

He didn't seem to need an answer, so I replied, "They're terrific. This is a great hit by Fitzgerald today."

"Let's hope it holds up," he said absently.

Regarding Paul Ellis, he looked how an aging newspaper publisher should look, which is to say tall, perfectly manicured, and handsome in that unassuming, Jimmy Stewart kind of sixty-something way. He acted how a newspaper publisher should act, which is also to say, thoughtful, inquisitive, and confident. He was, quite literally, born to run the business, and did it quite well, inheriting the reins of a great newspaper from his cousin, John Cutter, and turning it into an even more reputable and profitable one. Best of all, he saw the *Record* not so much as a family cash cow, but as a calling, a form of public service different than politics or philanthropy, but not for one fraction of a single second any less important or noble.

He stared at me and said, "This isn't a good day for us, Jack, not for me, not for you, not for this city."

Since I have never known Paul Ellis to be even remotely melodramatic, I kept my mouth shut and my eyes trained on him, letting him continue at his own pace.

"We're facing a hostile takeover," he said, meeting my stare. "A couple of weeks back, we got what's known as a bear-hug letter. I thought we could make the problem go away, but now our lawyers and finance guys are saying they don't think we can ward it off. Minority shareholders rights' and all that—if we fight it, we could be crippled by a lawsuit from within our ranks.

"Two of the three trusts that control fifty-three percent of the newspaper were opened last year, and now the Campbell Newspaper Company has come in with an offer that none of those shareholders will want to refuse. They're offering fifty-four a share. That's ten bucks over Friday's closing, a nearly twenty-five percent gain."

I was stunned into silence as a dozen images floated through my mind, most of which involved me without a decent job and steady income. I eventually managed to say, "Doesn't Campbell Newspapers own the *Springfield American*?"

Paul replied, "And the *Burlington News* and the *Rochester Gazette* and the *Lincoln Daily Star* and two dozen remarkably mediocre small and mid-sized newspapers, all of which are incredibly profitable, and none of which have ever been known for their distinguished journalism."

"Great. Why does a chain like that want a paper like ours, and how the hell can they afford us?"

The sun was now fully up over the distant buildings. A couple of morning joggers huffed past us, and Baker lay in the nearby grass chewing hard on a stick. All I could think of at the moment were the Campbell newspapers I had read before—papers that almost prided themselves in dumbing down to the lowest feasible denominator, papers so filled with color, graphics, and gimmicks that they made *USA Today* look like the trade publication for the American Funeral Home Association.

The owner, Terry Campbell, offered me a job once, and I turned him down cold. Now it looked like he'd have me in his employment after all.

Paul replied, "My guess is that they want a flagship paper, something to give them a greater level of prestige than they now have. And I don't think money's really a problem for them. They sure as hell don't pour it back into the product."

More silence as we both sat with our elbows on our knees, looking down. It was Paul who finally spoke: "My problem is that there are so many Cutter and Ellis cousins spread all over the country, two and three and four times removed, many of whom have never even been to Boston and probably don't even read a newspaper. The *Record* doesn't mean a damn thing to them. All they see is the stock price and a way to get rich off all the hard work of the people who busted their asses to make the paper what it is today."

I said, "I don't know anything about finances, and the only family trust that the Flynns had was that my father would come home from work every day. But can you leverage the value of your trusts to outbid Campbell on the others?"

"The banks have already told me no."

He exhaled hard and looked away for a long moment. Truth is, I was worried he might be losing it. Then, to my relative relief, he said in a firm voice, "Jack, this newspaper, our newspaper, has won twenty-eight Pulitzer Prizes, including two last year. Our reporting has sent mayors to jail, had a United States senator impeached, blocked a Supreme Court nominee from confirmation, and unveiled the darkest possible secrets about the sitting president of the United States. God only knows how many other politicians stayed straight out of fear of us. God only knows how many times we've given voice to the voiceless on issues ranging from bank redlining to consumer fraud. God only knows how many times someone says to a friend or a colleague or a family member every single damned day of the week, 'Did you see that story in the *Record?*' "

He paused, then added, "And now all that's at risk. All of it." In a much softer voice, almost to himself: "Every damned bit."

And you wonder why I love the man. I mean, for chrissakes, you could have turned this speech into a television ad campaign and our circulation would go up 20 percent in a week.

Before I could say anything, he put his hand on my shoulder and looked me square in the eye.

"Jack, I've never told anyone this before, but this same jackal, Terry Campbell, tried making a run at us five years ago. We staved him off. John Cutter was the publisher at the time. I was the president. Everything was done in secret. It put so much pressure on us that John had that fatal heart attack."

Paul looked down now, his hand absently drifting off my shoulder, down my arm, and then gone. He added, his voice much lower, "At least I hope that's how he died." Then he looked at me in silence.

I replied, "You're suspicious?"

"I'm overtired and overwrought and I'm probably crazy. But this thing has been nagging at me. You know Campbell's reputation. He gets involved in bloodbaths with his unions. People have died mysterious deaths. I've started asking myself questions I probably didn't dare ask five years ago. What if he had something to do with John's death?"

There was silence between us until Paul broke it, saying, "No, I'm just talking crazy."

I said, "You want me to check it out?"

He turned to me again and nodded. "I'm not afraid, mind you. Sometimes I think that I love this newspaper so much that if I have to die for it, then so be it, and I know John felt the same way. But this battle's going to be harder than before because of the breakup of the trusts. I want to know what I'm up against."

I nodded and said, "Then I'm on it."

He gazed hard at me, his eyes moving across the features of my face. "Thank you," he said, and those two words said enough.

He pushed himself up from the bench and added, "I'm heading into the office. I have one or two ideas left to play out. Call me if you learn anything I should know about. This is all confidential, the hostile takeover and my suspicions. Right now, Brent Cutter doesn't even know."

With that, he walked across the grass in his stiff, familiar gait, past the tulip beds, past the statue of George Washington on horseback, and out onto Arlington Street, the weight of a family, of a first-class newspaper, of a city, on his shoulders. As I look back at the moment, I wish I had said something more to him, wish I had thanked him in some small way for all he had given, all he had done, and all he wanted to do. But in my current state—in fact, in any state—how was I supposed to know what was about to come?

three

I LIVE ON A HOUSEBOAT in Boston Harbor, a lifestyle not entirely congruent with the fact that (a) I hate the water, and (b) I hate boats. But best as I can tell, there was a regulation passed by the National Association of American Men that when any member of our exclusive organization goes through a divorce or particularly serious breakup, regardless of whether the split is the man's decision, mutual, or that of his mate, he must live in a virtually unbearable situation for at least the next six months, if only to give him a fuller appreciation of what he once had but will never have again. No one ever said life was easy.

Still, I don't mean to say that I hate the water as in, *I hate the water.* In truth, I like the water from the perspective of the shore, specifically, say, a powdery beach with a nice lounge chair and an Igloo cooler stocked with a 6-pack of icy cold Sam Adams Summer Ale, or the dining room of an oceanside restaurant where the grilled swordfish tastes so fresh you can probably find the captain of the boat that caught it knocking back a shot of whiskey at the bar. I did that once, went out to the bar and found him, but the union didn't prove to be quite as climactic as you might expect. Another time.

It's funny in life how too often you want what you can't have, and have what you don't want, or at least it's funny how the human mind is able to contort things to make it seem this way. As I sat on deck, my laptop computer firing up on a small table in front of me, the warm morning sun beating down on my face, I drank in for the first time the remarkable harbor vista from this little perch off Long Wharf. Gulls were floating effortlessly in the pale blue sky and alighting on the creaky wooden docks. Massive yachts bobbed in the gentle waves. And in the distance, beyond the expanse of deep blue harbor waters, jets large and small ascended from the runways of Logan Airport like words taking flight in a poem. Behind me were the towers of the city's stunning skyline gleaming in the midday light.

But another week and I'd be overboard, nautically speaking, and just as I was starting to like it. I had lived on *The Emancipation* since October, when an old college friend, retired as a hedge fund manager long before his time, headed to the Caribbean for the winter and handed me the keys as an act of charity that men bestow on each other at times of such tumult. Now, just as the weather finally made such accommodations desirable, he was due back in five days, meaning I was to be out. Another itch in the occasional rash of life.

My computer sprang to life and I logged into the *Record*'s library database. I plugged in John Cutter's name and got several dozen hits. I scrolled though the headlines until I came to one that said, "John Cutter, Longtime *Record* Publisher, Dead of Apparent Heart Attack." It ran on the front page five years ago this month.

The reporter detailed Cutter's many accomplishments, quoted various civic dignitaries about his significant contribution to the city, and provided a relatively sketchy account of his housekeeper's discovery of the body in the morning at his Four Seasons condominium overlooking the Public Garden. A Boston Police detective, a guy by the name of Hank Sweeney, was quoted on some of the particulars. There wasn't so much as a scant hint of foul play.

I pulled up another, shorter story from the next day's paper, this one headlined, "Cutter Autopsy Confirms Heart Attack." It said the determination was made by the assistant state medical examiner, Justin Cobain, who was quoted saying, "It appears to be death by natural causes."

It appears. If you're him, why couch it. Or perhaps I was simply nitpicking through the prism of time and with the prejudice of suspicion. Still, that's just what we do sometimes in the august Fourth Estate.

I plugged Cobain's name into my computer, into the library database of every *Record* for the past twenty years. The first story that popped up on my screen was his obituary from two years ago, "Justin Cobain, Veteran Coroner, at 69." So much for the old saw, "Better late than never."

When I typed Sweeney's name into the system, it spit out twenty-five stories over the last decade-and-a-half, but the most recent of them appeared nearly three years ago. I retyped his name with the keyword "Obituary," but came back with nothing, which was good news. So I called police headquarters and asked for Hank Sweeney. I heard the woman on the other end of the line type something into a computer, then riffle through what sounded like the thin pages of a directory book. Finally, she said to me, "I don't see anyone here by that name."

"How would I find out if he's retired?" I asked.

"Do you know where he used to work?"

"He was a lieutenant in homicide."

"You can try the homicide bureau. Someone up there might know." Before I could even thank her, she transferred the call.

A gruff-sounding receptionist said, "Hank Sweeney? Yeah, he's in Florida. I think it's some town outside of West Palm."

This, ladies and gentlemen, is what sometimes passes for investigative reporting, which is exponentially better than reporting about presidential stains on dresses. I thanked her and hung up.

Cops rarely—alright, never—list their telephone numbers, for all the obvious reasons. I wondered if retired cops were as private. So I was more than pleasantly surprised when I plugged his name into a phone database and retrieved one Henry Sweeney from Marshton, Florida, a town with the same area code as Palm Beach.

And here, my first key decision of the day. I decided I needed to see him, to look into his eyes as I asked him about John Cutter's death. As a reporter, whenever you visit someone, as opposed to calling them, you make it harder for them to evade you. You're standing right there in front of them, a live human being in need of information or a favor rather than just a distant voice on the phone. The actual brush-off requires more nerve and effort compared to simply hanging up the line. They have to ask you to leave their property or shut the door in your face—something that most people of even modest manners are not inclined to do, because such an act involves at least low level conflict. Humans are a breed that generally likes to please.

Decision number two: Though I was sitting with his phone number, I decided not to warn him of my arrival. Surprise, when used well, is an effective reportorial tool. If he knows I'm coming, he can think of a million reasons not to help me, then prepare and rehearse his evasive reply. If I just show up, there's a reasonable likelihood of catching him off guard, such that he may blurt out something useful or simply provide me with what I need because he hasn't had a chance to think of a reason he shouldn't. Sounds simple, but you wouldn't believe how many reporters don't get it.

As my newspaper teetered on the precipice of a catastrophic sale, tomorrow I would be in Florida, knocking on the door of one Hank Sweeney, five years late, but God willing, not too late. Even if this was the wildest of goose chases, I would do this for Paul because, truth be known, I would do virtually anything for Paul.

The sun was setting and the harbor waters were making their nightly transition from blue to black as I grabbed my well-worn Spaulding basketball, headed up the rickety wooden docks and trotted across the gravel parking lot, Baker joyfully in tow.

I was wearing a pair of warm-up pants and an old sweatshirt on what had become our nightly routine—a walk along the waterfront to the North End, the city's famous Italian enclave. There, we cut across Hanover Street, lined with bakeries, coffee shops and trattorias, and arrived in the yard of St. Mary's, a tiny parochial school with an outdoor basketball court lit by two faint floodlights.

As I walked up to the foul line, Baker settled at half-court and directed his attention to a rawhide bone. My first shot clanked off the rim. Second shot: Swish. Third shot: Swish again. Not since high school in South Boston had I played competitively, and not since a year ago had I even picked up a ball. But a funny thing tends to happen on the way toward middle age: you reach out more, and you reach back, and here I was, night after night, not so much trying to reclaim a bit of my youth, but just trying to fend off the loneliness of mortality with the familiar comfort of ability. And in my day, pardon the braggadocio, I was more able with a basketball than most.

I moved over to the corner of the foul line and began pumping jumpshots, grabbing the rebound, dribbling out to the opposite corner and shooting again. It was an act of blessed simplicity, yet one with an almost endless possibility of either error or accomplishment. You set, bend your knees, jump, flick your wrist such that your shooting hand is parallel to the ground at follow-through, then you watch the ball float through the cool, dim evening air, either to rattle off the unforgiving rim or nestle into the inviting net. Fortunately the latter was more my destiny than the former, on the court and, if you don't mind, in life.

Five, ten minutes later, my blood was pumping. Another ten minutes and I felt a nice warm sweat coating my cool forehead, then my lower back. The shots, for whatever it's worth, were falling like snow on the Rocky Mountains.

Flynn fakes right, dribbles left, stops and shoots. Bang! Fans, he's hit yet another J and the kid is on a capital-T tear.

Dribbling back to the top of the key, my mind invariably, inevitably wandered to my story on Governor Lance Randolph. What I had was compelling evidence that he had inflated his conviction rate from when he was the Suffolk County district attorney—an embellishment that helped him win his first gubernatorial campaign six years ago. He was, his campaign literature repeatedly proclaimed, the most successful prosecutor in Massachusetts, a no-nonsense, tough-on-crime, new-age Democrat uniquely able to lead the state through any stretch of unexpected tumult. Now I wasn't so sure.

Of course, when I began reporting the story, I had no idea that Randolph would be nominated as the attorney general, which elevated it to national importance. We love collecting hides in this business, and I already have some impressive ones on the wall, but it would certainly be nice to add that of a presidential appointment.

Flynn steals the inbounds pass, stops and pops at the top of the key, and swish! Folks, the guy has taken this game into his own hands and it is truly a sight to behold!

The story was now important enough that I was willing to share—an unusual accommodation for me, considering I don't usually like sharing so much as a thought. I had called friend and newsroom colleague Vinny Mongillo that afternoon with two requests: first, I wanted him to probe some of his many police sources for information about Randolph's prosecutor days, and second, in complete confidence, could he please do what we in the news biz call a scrub of Terry Campbell. I didn't tell him that Campbell might someday soon be our ultimate boss, but I would. I would.

Flynn brings the ball down court against double-team pressure, slides through two defenders, wheels into the middle and lofts a fifteen-footer toward the hoop. Bang! Ladies and gentlemen, with just two minutes remaining in a tie game, there are no words that can describe the magic going on right here on this court tonight!

I'll admit, I never had the chance to get to know John Cutter particularly well, though I do know he was a great publisher, and while he was running the paper and Paul Ellis was next in line as the company president, they were an unbeatable team. His reputation—John's—was that of a brilliant man with a dose of the family's trademark paternalism, but also subject to bouts of occasional depression. Paul Ellis, a retired army general, arrived at his family's paper to provide some balance and guidance to his older cousin. The two became famously close and John's death hit Paul hard—so hard that he even offered John's eldest son, Brent Cutter, the presidency of the company after his father's death.

With just fifteen seconds left and the championship game still tied, Flynn is dribbling out the clock, weaving in and out of his hapless opponents who haven't been able to stop him the last seven times down court. Eight seconds. Flynn fakes to the basket and pulls back. Six seconds. He dribbles around the top of the key. Four seconds. He jabs right, whirls left and launches an eighteen-footer. Bang! Ladies and gentlemen, Jack Flynn of South Boston has hit a buzzer-beating jumpshot to win this epic game!

I turned around to see Baker standing at half-court, his blond fur uncharacteristically sticking straight up on his back, staring and growling at the dark shadows of the school. To put this into context, I'd heard him growl exactly once before in his life, when I brought home a blonde with a better-than-average chest who patted him—before he growled—with an outstretched arm, like some non-dog people do. "Is he friendly," she asked, nervously.

"Not as friendly as me," I replied. And at that exact moment, the dog growled and the relationship was effectively over. I told Baker he owed me the $184 I had just spent on dinner, but he didn't seem to understand, or maybe he just didn't care.

"What's the matter, pal," I asked as I, too, probed the shadows with my eyes. I saw nothing.

Baker looked at me as if I was some sort of gold-plated idiot, then looked back toward the redbrick building. I squinted and stared harder, making out a small alley between the brick school and the sandstone chapel. Baker inched toward the dark and I called out, "Who's there?"

Silence, which is precisely what I wanted to hear. "Lie down, Baker," I said. He ignored me, so I turned toward the basket and took another jumper, then another, missing them both. When I glanced back at Baker, he was still creeping toward the dark, growling harder now, his fur still on end. I was setting myself up to take a foul shot when a voice crashed through the lonely night air.

"Does he bite?"

Unfortunately, it wasn't the blonde talking—the only thing I was sure of, because the voice was every bit a man's. I whirled toward the shadows, but still didn't see anyone. As I stared more intently, a figure emerged from the black into the hazy peripheral light, a large man wearing a baseball cap—the Detroit Tigers, as a matter of fact—slung low over his face.

"Sometimes," I replied, my tone a mix of suspicion and curiosity. Baker continued to edge toward the man, who was now standing still. I called out, "Who are you?"

"Mike," he replied. "My name's Mike. Can you call the dog off, man?"

I ignored his request and said, "What are you doing here?"

"I hang out here," he said, talking to me but staring at my dog. "Can you please call your dog off."

Not in his canine lifetime had anyone been in such fear of old Baker, who usually greets strangers by rubbing himself against their legs or dropping his tennis ball at their feet in hopes of engaging them in a game of catch.

"What do you want?" I asked him. I was standing twenty feet away, holding the basketball against my hip. The man was standing helpless a few feet from the building. Baker was somewhere between us, fixed on this man named Mike, growling up a veritable storm.

"I want you to get your dog away. Then I wanted to know if you had any game in you."

"You're going to play in those?" I asked, incredulously. The man was wearing a pair of battered work boots. Baker inched closer still.

"C'mon, the dog, man. The dog."

"Baker," I said, not very sternly, or at least not sternly enough. "Come here."

He ignored me, which didn't particularly surprise or bother me.

The man's face was dark, but I could vaguely see his eyes fixed on Baker's, who was, in turn, fixed on his. Before I found myself in a lawsuit in this overly litigious society, I stepped toward my dog, grabbed his collar, and whispered soothingly, "Sit, pal. Time to sit down." He did, but his eyes never left the intruder, or at least what we both suspected was an intruder.

"Thanks, man," he said, sounding relieved. "You got a little one-on-one in you?"

The guy emerged fully into the faint floodlight. He was slightly taller than me, probably about six foot three. He had skin pocked by acne scars, brownish hair that fell from beneath his cap in greasy strings, and a tattoo on the right side of his neck that looked to be a bird, an eagle.

"A quick one," I said.

He walked over to the side of the court and peeled off his denim jacket. He held his hands out for the ball, and when he got it, he dribbled twice, hard, and took a shot that slammed off the backboard and rim. Just from that one errant jumper, I knew he couldn't play, first because he stared at the ball while he dribbled it, and then because he surged forward when he jumped. I decided to dispatch him quickly.

"Game to five," I said, "winner's out. You start."

He took the ball, barreled toward the right and threw up a flailing layup that hit the backboard but never the rim. I rebounded it, cleared and tossed in a fifteen-foot jumper, nothing but net. One zip.

Next play, I faked right so hard that when I cut back left, he tripped over his own boots and sprawled across the pavement. I laid it in with ease. Two zip.

I stayed silent, mostly because I didn't particularly want to antagonize a tattooed guy who appeared from the shadows of the night on a lonely basketball court. Mrs. Flynn didn't raise any fools, and neither did I. Baker was usually a fine judge of character, and he didn't appreciate our new-found company one little bit. As a matter of fact, he stood at half-court intently watching every move we made. Watch dog. I liked that.

Most opponents would have said good move after that last play, but ol' Mike here didn't say a word. So I took the ball, steamed left, flipped the ball around my back, pulled up in the middle of the key and buried a ten-foot jumper. Three zip. Need I say that the crowd, ladies and gentlemen, was going wild?

He handed me the ball in silence. Not much of a talker, Mike. I took it and raced left, stutter-stepped, and faked a baseline drive. He, of course, completely went for the fake, but when I reversed into the middle, he stuck his leg out and I sprawled across the court, the ball bouncing vacantly toward the shadows of the building. Rather than apologize or offer to help me up, he trotted after the ball.

"Foul," I said when he got back. He gave me a disgusted look, then contemptuously bounced me the ball.

Just as I was about to dribble, a glint caught the corner of my eye, and I whirled around to my left to see that Baker had roamed from half-court to courtside, and was slowly walking toward me with a metal object in his mouth that was shimmering in the floodlight.

As he got closer, I saw what it was: a leather holster holding a silvery revolver, with the barrel sticking out of one side of his muzzle and the handle out of the other. Mike hadn't noticed yet. Baker's tail was wagging hard, like he was proud to show me what he had just found.

"Your gun loaded?" I asked, my voice low and even, not wanting to set off any panic.

He looked at Baker and saw what I was talking about. "Fucking dog."

"Fuck you," I said. "Tell me if the fucking gun is loaded, and tell me fast."

Granted, it's not normal for me, or for that matter, anyone I know, to threaten a stranger in the remote dark of lonely night, let alone a stranger who's packing what appears to be a Colt .45, even if that Colt .45 happens to be temporarily in the custody of my dog. But the potential for harm to Baker overcame any fear, and I was about to put my fist through this guy's greasy nose if I didn't get an answer fast.

"It's not."

I knelt down and beckoned the dog to me. "Drop it, Baker," I said, and he nuzzled against my knee, proudly looked at me and released the gun. "Good boy. Thank you."

I had done a story on the gun industry once, and had learned how to load a weapon, so I checked and realized that Mike was, in fact, lying, and that this gun held a magazine clip filled with .45 caliber bullets.

I gingerly pulled it out and placed the magazine in my sweatpants pocket. I leaned down and picked up the basketball. I dropped the gun on the asphalt pavement, the clank echoing off the nearby brick of the schoolhouse.

"Game's over," I announced as I turned and walked away, Baker at my side.

It was about twenty strides to the gate that led to the side street that would bring me to safety, and each step felt like Neil Armstrong plodding across the moon, only I think Neil felt more secure up there in his spacesuit than I did in the North End of Boston in my sweatsuit.

I heard him say—or maybe it was spit—the word "asshole," so I turned and looked back at him to make sure he wasn't loading his weapon. It was then that he flashed me a look of hatred that I didn't yet understand but wouldn't soon forget.

When we hit the street, Baker and I broke out into a healthy jog. The problem was, we didn't yet understand what we were running from.

four

THERE WAS SOMETHING INTRINSICALLY nice about the roar of the jet engines, the clouds whisking past beneath us, the slight twitches of the plane as it sliced through the sunlit sky at breakneck speed with a precise destination in mind. Nicer still was my sense—right or wrong—that I was helping my newspaper and its founding family grab hold of its own destiny. When I am a reporter, asking questions, negotiating answers, probing lies and seeking truths, I am most at home with myself, even amid the most tumultuous times. Perhaps a psychotherapist would have a field day with that, but such was not my concern right now.

Time was. My flight was scheduled to be on the ground at ten A.M. I figured it would take about an hour to disembark, rent a car, and find the home of retired Boston homicide detective Hank Sweeney in a backwater town called Marshton. I was hoping to be back at the airport for a 1:20 P.M. flight back to Logan. Missing the plane meant missing hours of valuable reporting and writing time the next day on the Randolph story, not to mention being there to help Paul at his time of greatest need. It wasn't an option.

By the way, I don't know of a nice way to say this, so I'll be direct: I hate Florida. Well, I don't mean to say I hate Florida as in, *I hate Florida.* I actually like Florida from the perspective of another state, what with the Everglades and all those nice, active retirees and the weather that's warm even when it's cold enough in Boston to freeze a tennis ball inside a golden retriever's mouth. I just hate what the state represents—the last stop before death, the constant sense of ailment, a place with so little history catering to people who have almost nothing but. Perhaps depressing is the right word.

But not today. Today it meant rejuvenation, action, and most important, today it might reveal answers to some pretty important questions. That, of course, all depended on Hank Sweeney, or perhaps my ability—never to be underestimated, mind you—to make Mr. Sweeney dependable.

The drive from the airport due west to Marshton in my standard-issue red Pontiac Grand-Am took me past the usual array of Taco Bells, Napa auto parts stores, trailer parks, and then there were the retirement communities with names like Sleepy Hollow and Shady Elms. They could have been cemeteries, these senior complexes, a thought that made me depressed all over again. I decided then that if I ever reached old age, I would retire to some temperate college town in Texas or California, wear nothing but plaid shirts and checked pants, and spend my dying days leering at young co-eds who would think me either cute or harmless—or on my best days, both.

I didn't find the drive particularly interesting, but I wondered if the gentleman behind me did. I wondered that because he had been following me in a white Cavalier ever since I left the West Palm Beach airport. He'd drift back a few cars, then catch up, fall back, get close, just like in the occasional action movie. But to paraphrase Lloyd Bentsen, Jack Flynn, you're no Bruce Willis.

I was cruising along a particularly desolate stretch of the divided road that ran ramrod straight due west from the airport when I first noticed the tail. According to Rand McNally, I was about fifteen miles outside of Marshton. I tried to think about what Bob Woodward might do in this situation. He'd probably tell his chauffeur to slow down, so I slowed down. I noticed in the rearview mirror that the Cavalier, directly behind me now, slowed down as well.

Next, Woodward would probably tell his driver to speed up, so I sped up, and sure enough, the Cavalier did as well. I slowed down, he slowed down. This was fun, as long as we remained in separate cars about thirty yards apart with no one-sided gunplay involved, which I couldn't guarantee would be the case.

Truth is, the road out here was not what you'd call congested, which wasn't good, because what I really wanted were people, under the theory that crimes were less likely to be committed in front of witnesses, mob hits in crowded steakhouses with names like Sparks being the obvious exception.

Looking back, not in my rearview mirror but in life, I can't provide an adequate explanation for my actions of the next few minutes, though an offer of temporary insanity might well fit the bill. It wasn't the smartest thing I've ever done, but hell, neither was going into the newspaper biz, what with the chronically low pay, the long hours, the high divorce rates, the lack of public esteem. But sometimes you follow your gut or your heart and you do these things anyway. And sometimes, goddammit, things turn out all right.

So I pulled off the road, right there on Highway 201 in Florida. I pulled off the road into the parking lot of one of those combination gas station and convenience marts, called, I think ConvenienceMart. Look, when you're in the American energy business, with the laws of supply and demand generally on your side, creativity doesn't have to be a strong suit. The white Cavalier pulled in as well and parked a few spaces away.

I sat in my car pretending to talk on my cellular phone. The other driver, in a baseball cap and a pair of clunky seventies-style sunglasses, got out of his car and walked up to a payphone. Sitting there, I had one overriding question: Who the hell uses a payphone anymore? Maybe I'd get the chance to ask him.

I started my ignition and he casually but quickly hung up the phone and walked back to his car. He was a lanky guy in an old tee shirt and jeans, youngish, with a hauntingly familiar look to him, but I couldn't place it. So I got out of my car, walked up to his and rapped on his window. Because of the sunglasses, I couldn't tell how surprised he was, or whether he was even surprised at all.

He rolled down his window and didn't say anything. I mean, come on. You'd think he'd just say "Hello," or "What can I do for you?"

So I asked, "You by any chance have change for a dollar for the phone?"

He replied, "Nope."

The voice was familiar as well, a little bit gravelly with what seemed to be a thick Boston accent, and I don't mean Brahmin. I said, "I can't help but notice that you've been following me since we left the airport. I hope you don't take offense if I ask you why?" I smiled at him for effect, though what effect I was going for, I'm not really sure.

"Fuck off."

Certainly not that effect. I said, "Well, have a nice day." And I walked off.

As I did, I heard his car door open behind me, and I turned and saw him striding in my direction at considerable speed. I probably should have broken for my car and tried to get away. Instead, I turned fully around and faced him.

"You want something?" I asked. I think I knew the answer already, but as my second grade teacher used to say, there's no such thing as a stupid question, though this one may have been.

I might add here that the parking lot was otherwise empty but for the two of us, and though I'm sure there was someone working in the ConvenienceMart, I had yet to see any sign of them. That's a longer than needed way of saying that out here in the God-forsaken parking lot of a seemingly barren gas station off a deserted stretch of Florida highway, I felt very much alone.

When he was within a couple of feet of me, he pulled a handgun out from behind his back and said, "Don't try anything stupid. Turn around and walk to the side of the building."

I did, or I started to anyway, but after I took about my third step, I faked right, like I was driving to the basket, and instead turned around in a swift, single motion to plow my fist into his nose. Mind you, they don't teach you these moves at the Columbia Journalism School, but more than ever, I was starting to think they should.

When I turned, it was a blur of black and pink. I saw the gun, and somewhere beyond the gun, I saw a look of shock in his eyes, and I was so close to him I saw the pockmarks in his cheeks. Before I saw his nose, I felt it on the outer edge of my fist, a perfect shot, evidenced by the explosion of blood that spattered all over his face and my wrist.

"You fucking cocksucker."

That's him, not me. He was doubled over in agony, so I took the opportunity to kick him so hard in the face that I heard him wail as he fell backward. Yet somehow he still held onto the damned gun, and writhing in pain on the ground, I saw him take aim at me and prepare to pull the trigger.

So I bolted, not toward my car, because had I gone that way I would have been fully exposed for several long strides and given him a decent shot at me. Instead I raced two steps around the corner of the building, out of his line of fire, and galloped toward the back, where there happened to be nothing more than that previously referenced marsh.

I was about to become a victim of too much open space—thank you, Sierra Club. I hesitated, then decided I had no choice but to plunge into the swamp and take refuge behind some of the brush that stuck out of the water like strands of wispy hair on the head of a nearly bald man. So I did, I did. God only knows what lived under the surface. In fact, I think I did too—poisonous snakes that would snack on my legs, exotic eels that would slither into my pants and do unspeakable things to my favorite parts, slugs that would cover all my lower extremities.

As I waded deeper, heading toward a clump of green, I heard him stagger around the corner. He still had blood gushing from his nose, across his mouth and over his chin. He was a mess, but an armed mess. I saw him take aim again from the shore, so I dove under the cappuccino-colored water. When I came up, I saw him wading in after me.

He stopped and fired from about twenty feet away. I dove back under the water, popped up just long enough to grab another mouthful of air, and dove again. From beneath the surface, I could hear the pop of gunfire, but didn't know how close it was.

I did know this: the shoulder-deep water was warm to the point of nearly being hot, rancid, filled with floating sticks and particles and leaves and other things I still don't have the stomach to explain.

Then I had an idea. I surfaced, took measure of precisely where the gunman was, and dove back under. I did the chest stroke slowly in his direction, moving my arms firmly but gently so as not to cause any surface waves. I couldn't see more than a foot in front of me as I kept pushing myself onward.

Finally, as I felt the last of the fresh air leaving my lungs, I also felt my hand graze a solid object. It was either the gunman or a tree, but I had no choice but to come up. So I thrust myself above water, saw I was right beside the guy, and slammed my left fist fully into his surprised face. I watched the gun flip through the air and splash through the skin of the swamp as his legs crumbled and he went under the surface himself.

But give him credit for resilience. From the murky depths, he grabbed my ankle and brought me down, then held me there as I flailed with my arms and legs. I must have been making reasonable contact, because he eventually let me go, and when I pushed my way up, I saw him splash toward the shore, then amble back around the building. I gave a halfhearted chase, but by the time the parking lot came into view, he was pulling out onto the highway, gone.

I limped over to my car. My hair was dripping filthy water down onto my drenched clothes. I was covered in dirt and twigs and slime, and smelled like a Delhi sewer rat on the hottest day of an Indian summer. That's when my cell phone rang. It had been sitting there on the passenger seat of my car, and it rang like there shouldn't be a worry in my little world, like I should just be able to pick it up and say, "Yeah, yeah, this is Jack. Hey, good to hear from you, thanks an awful lot for calling."

So I answered it and heard the sonorous voice of Robert Fitzgerald of *The Boston Record*, casually asking where I was and what I was doing.

When I tried to speak, to imbue him in some way with the life-and-death adventure I had just survived, my voice was surprisingly weak. So I said, "Hey, Robert, do you mind if I call you back in about ten minutes?"

"Of course not," he said. "You sound strange. Everything all right?"

"Fine," I said. "Right now, I'm just really swamped."

five

I BEGAN THIS TRIP believing I was doing little more than a favor for Paul Ellis, conducting a process of elimination, the goal here being to eliminate his suspicion of foul play. Oh, it was a process of elimination all right, only someone was trying to eliminate me. I suddenly realized I was on a life-or-death mission in search of an unknown truth.

I pulled into Marshton without the white Cavalier anywhere in sight. I jumped off the highway onto Waterview Boulevard, though the only water to view seemed to be that damned swamp on one side of the divided road. I guess you have to credit the prescient town fathers for not calling their home Swampton. A mile or so down the road, just as my MapQuest directions said I would, I arrived at a complex called Serenity Heights.

Once there, I pulled into a community of tiny, cookie-cutter houses that sat on minuscule lots tight to the street. It was, in its defense, immaculate. You could eat stewed prunes right out of the gutters—not that you'd want to, but like I said, you could.

I took a left on Pleasant Street, went through the intersection with Hereafter Boulevard—just kidding—and turned right on Tranquility Road, where I found Sweeney's house, which was just like every other house—nondescript, shaped like a box, and small. The Buick Park Avenue sitting under the carport told me he was home, or at least somebody was.

I looked at myself in the rearview mirror and saw that my hair, mostly dry, was stiff and rigid from the swamp. My face was streaked with caked crud, as if I had just been thrown out of a spa in the middle of a mud wrap because the receptionist realized I wouldn't be able to pay. My clothes, still damp, carried the odor of a men's room at Fenway Park toward the end of an extra innings game. It would be nothing short of a miracle if I could convince Hank Sweeney that, (a) I wasn't a vagrant seeking a handout, and (b) he should talk to me. In my present condition, I don't think Oscar Madison would invite me inside.

Here's what I know about homicide detectives: They spend their lives on the edge of the darkest abyss. They tiptoe across the spattered blood of freshly killed babies, kneel beside the mutilated corpses of beautiful young women, engage in idle chitchat with suspects who have inexplicably strangled the life out of the only person they may ever love. The good ones go home and coach Little League games and attend PTA meetings between telephone calls summoning them to yet another scene of still another horrific crime. The bad ones sit back night after night with a bottle of whiskey or a 12-pack of cheap beer getting shamelessly, stupidly drunk.

The best of them are the most creative members of a profession better known for regulation than invention. They can save lives and change worlds by the discovery of a single strand of hair, a microscopic fiber, or a cigarette butt discarded in a nearby sewer. They see a room forever marked by death and imagine the last pitiful moments of life. They look at a suspect, perhaps a suburban high school kid or an otherwise successful husband, and slowly, methodically, deconstruct the boundaries separating good and evil and imagine just how far over the division this creature might have passed—and what sent him over the line.

To a man, and, okay, woman, though there aren't many of those, they are more moneyed than the average cop because of all the overtime calls in the godforsaken hours of the early morning. Homicide isn't a 9–5 job. Many of them wear bespoken suits and expensive Italian ties to make certain that no one confuses them with their carefully regimented brethren cops on the street or the suspects they're so eager to throw in jail. They are at the top of the order, the fighter pilots of the police force, and they want you to know it.

I walked down the small driveway aside the perfectly neat little lawn, which, all in all, wasn't exactly what I had expected of someone who had reached such an august position. The air wasn't just hot. It was like climbing inside a pig's anus and sloshing around in his lower intestine, that's how hot and humid it was. I felt little streams of sweat carve lines in the drying dirt on my forehead. Still, his side door sat open, with only an aluminum screen door separating Sweeney from the thronging masses, which in this case, was me, so I knocked on the metal border. Within seconds, I could see the vague outline of a large black man ambling toward the door in that stiff gait that some older men have—heavy on the left side, then heavy on the right. As he got closer, I could see he was holding a newspaper in one hand and had reading glasses slung low over his nose. Maybe this is what all those consultants mean when they tell us reporter types that our readership was literally dying off.

"Yes?" he said, slowly with a hint of amusement.

It occurred to me that they probably got their fair share of traveling Bible salesmen, life insurance peddlers and snake oil con men in these parts, and given my current appearance, I probably looked like the worst of the lot.

"Mr. Sweeney?" I asked.

He kept the screen door closed between us. "That's me," he said, his amusement transforming to skepticism.

Already, from his tone and stance, I knew I could at least engage him, and if I could engage him, then chances were vastly improved that I could sway him, and possibly, eventually, move him. Far better he be like this than some by-the-numbers, just-the-facts-ma'am Joe Friday types who wouldn't tell me if my shirt was on fire unless Rule VIa., second paragraph in the Department Handbook told them that even in retirement, they were required to.

I gave him my most polite voice, shaped and sorted from years of schooling at the hands of strict nuns in the parochial schools on the not-so-mean streets of South Boston.

"Sir, you don't know me, but my name is Jack Flynn, and I'm from Boston."

He replied, "Yeah, I do. You're the writer for the *Record*. You used to be in Washington, and now you do a lot of investigative stuff. Liked your stories on the president." Real casual, almost matter of fact, like it was the most normal thing in the world that I'd show up at his house covered in swamp water to shoot the breeze. Still, the door remained shut between us.

"I am, and thank you," I said, unable not to smile at the guy. I regained my footing. "Please pardon my appearance. I just had an unfortunate incident in your town's namesake marsh. I'm hoping you might be able to help me."

Still no invitation, or even a move to open the door, which did not bode well. If he didn't shake my hand or make direct eye contact without a screen between us, it would be one hell of a lot easier for him to send me on my way.

"Me help you?" He started laughing a chesty laugh. "An old guy like me living in a swamp village in this hellish outback can help a young buck like you? I can't wait to hear this."

"It's about our former publisher," I said, calmly, sincerely. "John Cutter. Some questions have arisen, and I think you might be able to answer them."

He just kind of stood there behind that screen like a priest in a confessional.

I asked, "Is this a bad time or do you have a few minutes to talk."

"Son, I ain't got nothing but time."

The door stayed shut.

I had an idea. "I want to show you something," I said, and turned around and trotted to the car, grabbed that day's *Record* and a printout of the news clipping on John Cutter's death, and returned, hoping to bait him outside.

I'm brilliant. He pressed on the handle, turned back into the kitchen and yelled, "Mother, I'll be in the yard for a minute," and came outside. Breakthrough.

He was, indeed, a very large man, not fat, just big all over, tall with broad shoulders and a barrel chest and something of a gut that didn't look bad and almost looked good, given the enormity of his frame. He had a full head of grayish-black hair, dark and crinkled eyes, skin the color of bitter-sweet chocolate, and an expression on his face that said there wasn't an awful lot in this life that he hadn't already seen.

I shoved my dirty hand out, and he looked at it for a short moment and shook it. Then we sat on a pair of plastic, KMart-quality lawn chairs around a matching table, and he scanned the headlines.

"Used to read this damned thing every day," he said to me, slightly amused again. "Now I only see it when someone brings it down for me. I miss the Red Sox."

"Well, you haven't missed much these last couple of seasons."

He didn't reply.

I said, "I'm going to be honest with you. There are some lingering doubts, suspicions even, at the very highest levels of my newspaper that John Cutter's death wasn't from natural causes five years ago."

I stared into Sweeney's eyes, and he stared back at me, squinting a bit in the midday sun, which seemed to bother him not a whit. Me, the mud was washing down my face in rising rivers of sweat, which I kept trying to wipe off with my filthy hands.

I continued, "But the paper never asked the questions it probably should have asked back then. It never pushed the investigation as hard as it should have been pushed, maybe out of a fear of appearing too self-serving, of seeking preferential treatment.

"Probably it was a heart attack, but I just wanted to come down here and make sure that's what you really, truly believed."

Sweeney sat in silence for a moment, looking at me and then the newspaper clip in front of him.

Finally, he said, "Son, that was the last case of my career, my last day on the job, and probably the most famous victim I ever had. Everyone knew your publisher."

He paused to pull a pack of cigarettes out of his chest pocket, lit one and took a long, leisurely puff.

"Some people never forget a face. I never forget a crime scene. Sometimes that's not so good, not when you've seen the crimes I've seen—blood spattered everywhere, pretty young girls with crushed heads, kids shot dead before they ever made their First Communion, babies burned by their dads."

That last one seemed to catch him for a moment. "Some dads," he said, shaking his head and looking down.

He continued, "In this one, I think it was the old man's house-keeper who found him in the morning. Stop me if I'm wrong here. She called one of the building managers. The building manager called 911, and a uniformed officer was there within about six minutes.

"He looks the place over and it all seems fine, but then he finds out from the manager who the dead guy is and he's saying to himself, 'Aw, shit.'" He paused. "Sorry, by the way. I don't mean to make light of it."

I shook my head to show I wasn't offended.

He took another puff, blew the smoke off to the side, and continued. "He realizes that reporters and politicians are going to be crawling up our butts on this one, so he does everything by the book. He seals off the room and he calls for homicide, just in case. It's exactly what you're supposed to do in a sudden death. I'm cleaning out my desk and I get a call directly from the commissioner himself telling me to head up the crime scene. I get there, and because of who the victim is, I, in turn, do everything right by the book. I numbered every item in the room. I diagrammed the whole place—damned nice condominium, if I remember right. We pho-tographed extensively. We dusted. And I ordered a battery of tests.

"This is my way of saying, if the M.E."—medical examiner— "came back and said it was a heart attack, which obviously he did, then it was a heart attack. I supply them information. They're the ones who make determinations."

Interesting, but an extraordinarily unsatisfying answer, on multiple levels, so I asked, "Okay, but did you have any reason to believe it was something other than a heart attack?"

"Son, I'm a crotchety old man. Put a duck on the table and I'll assume it's a pigeon in disguise. It's why I don't mind saying that I was pretty good at what I did for all those years. You have to be that way in homicide. You're not dealing with the church choir."

I seemed to remember writing a story once about how a member of a church choir in Chelsea bashed his wife's skull in, but didn't see the need to raise that issue just then.

Instead, I asked, "But did you specifically see anything in that room that raised suspicions?"

He looked away at nothing in particular and grimaced, I think, reflectively, though when you're old, there's always the possibility that something actually hurts.

He said, "In this case, there were no outward signs of a struggle. There were no visible injuries on the victim. There was nothing obviously disrupted in the apartment. It comes down to what the toxicology tests say. I assume they showed no signs of a narcotic?"

He was asking me. I wanted him to tell me things.

I looked back at him and said squarely, "I don't know what the toxicology tests say. I assumed you knew. You were the investigating officer."

"But you'll remember, that was my last day. I was as surprised as anyone that they gave me the case, knowing I was on the way out the door. Those tests take a couple of days to complete. I was gone by the time they came back, which is why I assume they came back negative and that's why the M.E. determined it was a heart attack. They had to have come back negative."

I nodded. "And there was nothing else in that room that bothered you?"

"Well, there was a dead body. That always kind of bothers me." He had a nice twinkle in his eye, like he was starting to like the company, someone new to hear his old patter.

"Nothing else?"

He grimaced again and shook his head. Was he holding back? Was there some microfiber somewhere on the bed, a pillow out of place, a drop of blood on the kitchen floor? No way to know, not yet. But I would.

We sat in mutual silence for an elongated moment until I decided I had squeezed him for everything I could, at least at this sitting.

I changed the subject. "You don't mind this heat, huh?" By then, all the mud had washed down my face and onto my neck. He, meanwhile, looked like an ad for Johnson's Baby Powder, if they used old, over-weight actors.

"The heat!" He said this loudly, like I was telling him about it for the first time, like the guy was angry with me.

Then he said, "I hate the fudging heat. But what are you going to do? I'm old. This is Florida. It's where I belong, I guess."

I got up and we shook hands. He asked if he could keep the news-paper. "Homesick," he said. "Mother will want to read the obituaries."

I asked, "You mind if I call you if something comes up?"

"Go ahead," he said. Then he looked me over for a long moment and asked in a whimsical tone, "What happened to you?"

I replied, "I was chased into a swamp about fifteen miles back by a guy with a gun who had been following me from the airport."

He simply shook his head slowly as he looked straight ahead at nothing in particular. He said with a newfound determination, "Call me with the toxicology results."

And right then, I knew it wasn't a request, but a challenge. Questions were popping up all around me like August corn on a Nebraska prairie, blocking my clear view, and with it, my perspective. Right then, I knew it wasn't just a good idea to get those test results, but something I had to do.

six

As THE LATE AFTERNOON breeze turned brisk across Boston Harbor, I was somewhere far beyond thrilled to get out of the ill-fitting Wal-Mart khakis and $12 golf shirt I had bought on my way back to the West Palm Beach airport, even more thrilled to get into that cramped houseboat shower to wash the Eau de Florida Swamp off my body and out of my hair. I had sat silently in a middle seat on the USAirways flight back north, the nice gentlemen on either side leaning considerably away from me. They should be entitled to a free round-trip ticket to anywhere in the world, Envoy Class.

Oh well. I took Baker out for a quick walk with promises of a longer romp that night—though probably not back to the North End basketball court. I had seen so many guns in the last twenty-four hours that I was starting to feel like Charlton Heston and didn't need to tempt the presence of any more.

I hadn't yet reported the shooting to the authorities because I had too much work to do in Boston and didn't want to be detained any longer than necessary in Florida. I also didn't want the Florida State Police to get out in front of *The Boston Record* quite yet on a story that could have considerable impact on my newspaper, assuming that my merry gunman was in some way connected to John Cutter's death.

On the drive to work, I couldn't help but think of how change was now encompassing, if not overwhelming me. Maybe this would be one of my last forays into the newsroom, because why would I want to stay and watch the *Record*—my *Record*—sold to a cost-cutting chain and gutted like a freshly caught tuna on a deep-sea fishing boat?

But what to be at this tender age. Being a reporter is like getting a

Ph.D. in philosophy, meaning, it doesn't really prepare you to do anything else, except, perhaps, public relations, but what right-thinking person would ever want to do that? Perhaps I should be a plumber, the problem being, I don't like small places and don't actually know anything about pipes. A fireman? I don't like the heat. A carpenter? I don't own a hammer and the only thing I know about a Phillips is that it's the surname of a boarding school that would never have admitted me, and rest assured, they didn't teach carpentry. I still held hope, not to mention trust, in Paul's abilities that these would be purely hypothetical questions.

It was a little past five P.M. when, sitting in rush hour traffic, I caught a glimpse of the sun's rays doing a little two-step across the massive windows of the *Record* building, and I'll confess here and now, with Paul's warning of a possible sale still rattling around my brain, I wasn't quite prepared for the flood of memories that this familiar, even mundane, sight so powerfully unleashed.

I thought of my first visit to the newspaper. I was eight years old. My father was a *Record* pressman spending yet another weekend working another overtime shift in his dark green, ink-stained apron. I remember being entranced at the sight of the hulking machines whirling around in creation of that day's paper—the sounds of the presses, the smell of the paper, the splotches of black ink everywhere you looked.

I thought of the lede—a newspaper word meaning the first paragraph of a story—to my first front-page story, headlined "Dare Jump Death" ("Two Quincy teenagers, acting on a dare from a small group of friends, jumped sixty feet to their deaths yesterday in the frigid waters of an abandoned granite quarry"). I thought of the crackle of gunfire at Congressional Country Club a couple of years ago that led to me breaking the biggest story of my life, not to mention one of my right ribs.

I knew I had one more good one to come, at least while the paper was under Cutter-Ellis control: the embellished record of Governor Lance Randolph—a story getting better by the moment as the nice radio announcer informed me that President Clayton Hutchins had officially nominated him that afternoon to be attorney general. I had already been researching the Randolph story out for a little more than a week, and rushed back from Florida, among other reasons, to work on it.

I found myself with a cross of conflicting emotions—short-term excitement over the Randolph story, long-term dread over what was about to happen to my newspaper, and a very pronounced apprehension at who out there was trying to kill me for reasons that I didn't yet know. I was confused and a little bit disoriented. I looked forward to stepping inside the familiar environs of the newsroom at the critical deadline hour.

Pulling beyond the unmanned guard shack into the paper's side parking lot, I saw a Boston Police cruiser idling at a horizontal angle, its overhead lights flashing and its headlights pulsing, blocking the way. This was a bad afternoon for a foreign dignitary to be visiting our editorial board. I thought, too much to do, too much at stake, to be worried about the overzealous whims of the Secret Service protecting the King of Guam, though wait a minute, isn't Guam one of ours? Where the hell is Guam, anyway?

As I slowly approached the car, the young cop leaning on it gruffly waved me off and barked, "Turn around. This is off-limits."

I rolled down my window, contemplating whether to explain to the gentleman that this was a private way, owned and operated by the good people of *The Boston Record*, and he'd be best to get the hell out of the way.

Instead, I said, "Afternoon, officer. I work here. I'm just trying to get through to the parking lot."

"Did you hear me?" he said, his voice as sharp as a Swiss Army knife blade. "I said there's no traffic beyond this point."

I have already been blessed with a vital dislike, even disdain, for authority, and the idea of a rookie cop directing traffic at a newspaper was like a cat suddenly gaining entry to a mouse hole, not that I regard reporters as a bunch of mice, or even any other kind of rodent, but you get the picture.

"Did you hear me?" I asked. "I said I work here. Move your car out of my way."

That got some of his precious synapses firing.

He replied, "Hey jerk-off, turn your damned car around and get out of my sight before you end up with cuffs on in the back of this cruiser. This is a crime scene."

Finally, some information, even if unwittingly provided. I was in no position to press him further, and even in less of a position to get past him, so I quickly turned around, parked in the small front visitor's lot and hustled up the three steps into the visitor's entrance.

First thing I noticed was several men in trench coats huddled in one corner of the lobby with police radios blabbing and shrieking from their pockets. I asked the security guard, a longtime employee named Edgar, what the hell was going on.

"You haven't heard?" he said, a look of panic crossing his gray features. "Jack, it's Paul Ellis."

"What about him?" I asked, the fear in my voice surprising even me.

Edgar simply shook his head in a mix of uncertainty and anguish. So I bolted around him, through a couple of sets of industrial double-doors and into the pressroom, where the mammoth presses were silently waiting for the next day's run. I raced through the length of the room, roughly the size of half a football field, dodging some of the pressmen—old friends of my father's—as they called out my name, and slammed through a metal door that led to the side parking lot.

Once outside, with the low afternoon sun hitting me square in the eyes, I saw something that spurred a wave of nausea from my stomach to my chest and almost brought me to my knees: a white van with spare blue letters that said, "State Medical Examiner."

As I settled myself, my eyes focused on about a dozen or so men and women striding purposefully about, some carrying kits in their hands, others talking on radios and cellular telephones. Two younger men in jump-suits stood beside an empty, rolling gurney, the purpose of which I wasn't sure I wanted to know, but knew I had to learn. A helicopter swooped low over the nearby highway and hovered above an adjacent neighborhood.

I jogged toward the van, trying not to attract attention to myself, though I was sweating like a walrus.

"What do we have," I asked one of the kids by the gurney, trying to sound casual.

He nodded absently toward a row of *Record* delivery trucks and replied, "Body's over there. They're photographing it now."

I was something of a veteran of crime scenes, having spent too much time at them as a young reporter in the heyday of crack cocaine in the late 1980s and early 90s, when kids—I mean, ten-, eleven-, and twelve-year-olds—were routinely shot dead just for playing in the wrong inner-city street at the wrong time, which could have been any-time. The tone of this crime scene already felt decidedly different, more businesslike and urgent, which made me more panicked.

I began making my way across the parking lot, though headed where, I didn't know. Didn't matter. After a few steps, I stopped in my tracks at the sight of the human being I least wanted to see: Luke Travers, a Boston Police homicide lieutenant. Just to put my disdain for this jackass into proper context, I think I'd invite Saddam Hussein out to dinner before I did him.

He spotted me just when I did him. He veered in my direction and walked hurriedly toward me, then a few feet past me, yelling to a pair of uniformed cops nearby, "I thought we had this locked down. How the hell are civilians getting out here?"

He walked back toward me and I said through a clenched jaw, "What the hell's going on here?"

He stopped a few feet away, his gaze avoiding mine. To be more accurate, he refused to look me in the eye. "Has anyone told you any-thing?" he asked.

I shook my head. I wanted to make as little verbal contact with him as possible, but I needed information.

His tone became slightly softer, but still official, superior. "Paul Ellis, the publisher, is dead. He's been shot."

I couldn't speak, and even if I could, there was nothing I wanted to say to this asshole.

Travers continued, "I think you'll want to know some details. One of the pressroom guys found his briefcase sitting here in the lot an hour or so ago. *Record* security checked his office, and he wasn't there, so they called the police. A few uniformed guys did a search of the area and found him on the ground over there"—he pointed to his left—"behind one of the Dumpsters."

He paused again to study me, then continued, "He was shot in the head at least three times, maybe more, at very close range, following a struggle. I don't have the benefit of an autopsy report yet, but he appears to have died instantly from the bullet wounds. The coroner believes he's been dead at least twenty-four hours. His wife is on vacation in California, which explains why he wasn't reported missing last night. His secretary said she assumed he went out to morning meetings today that he neglected to tell her about."

I turned and walked away from him without another word. The copter still hovered overhead. The small army of investigators still combed through the area. But I felt and saw none of it, as if all my feelings, all my senses, were shrouded in some deep fog of inconsolable gloom. I kept thinking of our conversation the prior morning, of the melancholic look in Paul's eyes and the heaviness in his voice as he told me that he might lose the newspaper. I kept thinking of him walking away from me, his shoulders uncharacteristically slumped from the gravity of impending defeat.

I turned back toward Travers, who remained in the same spot. He was, I assumed, the senior detective on the case, and as such, was leading the investigation. "I want to see the scene," I said.

"Can't," he replied.

His quick response, his rigid tone, among many other factors, made me want to deck him. I think he sensed this, because he stepped away. He was wearing a perfectly pressed brown suit, a white shirt, and a solid blue necktie. His pale, puffy face was marked by a day's worth of stubble that glistened in the afternoon sun. Don Johnson he was not, though I would bet that's exactly the self-image that he had.

Another detective, a rumpled veteran named Tommy O'Brien,

came hustling over, his police windbreaker jostling against his beer gut with every step.

"I want to see the scene," I told O'Brien, an old ally of mine from long ago murder stories.

"Can't allow it," Travers repeated, emotionless.

O'Brien looked at me carefully and said, "Jack, you know we can't. You're a reporter, an employee, and a friend. Some defense attorney somewhere would have a field day with any one of those three. And believe me, I know what it looks like, and I'm here to tell you that you don't want to see it."

We were both quiet for a moment, when he added, "I could use you to identify the body, though, before they wheel it out of here. Would you do that?"

I nodded my head. Then I asked him, "Suspects? Motive? Anyone in custody?" I walked past Travers, ignoring him, as I asked the questions.

O'Brien shook his head. "No one yet, but we will, we will. At first glance, looks like a robbery. He was apparently chased from the parking lot over behind those trucks, where he caught it in the head." O'Brien cringed, stopped, and said, "I'm sorry, Jack. Where he was shot in the head. He apparently tried to fight the assailant off, and one of our forensic guys is saying it looks like the victim even hid under one of the trucks. It probably happened yesterday afternoon, so there weren't a lot of witnesses around on a Sunday. We'll have the whole scenario in a couple of hours."

As I walked toward the medical examiner's van, Travers called out to me, "We're going to want to have a longer conversation with you this evening."

I turned and looked at him, but didn't reply.

As we got close to the van, O'Brien said, "Stay right there for a minute, Jack."

I gazed around slowly as if the world was just coming back into focus. There were men and women walking alone and in small groups every which way like fish in an outsized aquarium. I saw the two guys I had talked to earlier start rolling the gurney toward the Dumpster, which sat behind a row of delivery trucks. I saw several uniformed cops stretching yellow police crime scene tape around the perimeter of the area. A couple of men in trench coats knelt on the pavement measuring tire tracks in the loose gravel. A man and a woman wearing rubber gloves poked around the inside of Paul's Jeep. In the distance, I could see the surly young cop turning back copy editors and nightside reporters trying to get to work for the evening shift.

I also noticed something missing from this god-awful scene. Here we were in the shadows of the most powerful newspaper in New England, one of the most respected publications in all of America, and there wasn't a single *Record* reporter, pen in hand, recording the scene for the next day's editions. Perhaps I should have been thankful, not worried, because any account of this murder would inevitably lead to questions over the possible sale of the newspaper—a prospect that wasn't known by anyone but a closely held few at that time. But what I really felt, along with the heartbreak, was panic. We could not be beat by any newspaper or television station on a single fact on the murder of our own publisher.

I pulled my cell phone out of my suit pocket, got the city editor on the line, and inquired in as nice a voice as I could muster whether any of our reporters might be done with their afternoon tea and scones and could wander out into the parking lot of their own newspaper to cover the murder of our publisher.

"Jack, we're trying like hell. The police have every door sealed out of the building. They're not letting us anywhere near the place."

"Pretend there's a fire—or tell the staff there's a fire sale at Armani. That will get them out the doors."

I hung up as O'Brien made his way back, gently grabbed my elbow and said, "Come with me."

I pulled back and replied, "Tommy, unless you allow a couple of our reporters out here, tell Travers that he's going to be reading everything I know about Paul's last hours in tomorrow's paper."

He looked at me surprised. "Can't do, Jack. This is the biggest murder of the year. We're not risking anyone—anyone—trampling evidence or mucking around the crime scene. I don't care if it happened right in your own newsroom."

I said, "Two reporters, outside the police tape, briefed by you, or we go right over your heads and cooperate only with the State Police."

"Wait here," he said, aggravated but not angry. He hustled toward Travers, consulted for a minute, and came back. "Okay, but they're under escort the whole time."

As he pulled out his radio, he muttered, "You're some piece of work."

He talked to the uniforms on his radio. I called the newsroom on my cell phone.

"You ready," O'Brien said when we both got off.

I nodded. He pulled back the cloth and there was Paul, barely distinguishable as a human being, let alone as my friend and publisher, for the massive holes in his forehead. I felt my stomach heave. I fixed on what was familiar—the perfectly formed nose, the ruddy cheeks, the pursed mouth. I pushed the sheet further down and saw the same blue shirt he had on in the Public Garden the prior morning. As my nerves steadied, I let my gaze remain on his face for a time, on his chin, around his neck, then looked up at O'Brien and nodded slowly, my eyes now closed.

Before I could even open them again, I heard the van doors yanked open, and the gurney lifted inside. When the doors slammed shut, I walked over to the side of the building, put my palms firmly against the bricks, hunched down and vomited on the ground.

A truly great man and, beyond that, a great newspaperman was dead. And my life was already changing in ways I couldn't even begin to imagine—none of them, I already knew, particularly good.

seven

Two HOURS EARLIER GOVERNOR Lance Randolph sat in the Cabinet Room of the White House, his chin in his palm, staring out the windows at the technicians and crew of advance men setting up the Rose Garden for his upcoming event. His mind wandered half an hour ahead to the speech he was planning to give.

He would accept this nomination to be the attorney general of the United States with enormous pride in what he accomplished in Massachusetts, with an unyielding belief that now more than ever he could have an impact on a national stage, and with strong conviction that by crossing the partisan divide, he could play a role in helping the two parties end their festering name-calling and constant bickering and work together toward common, crucial goals.

He nodded to himself, liking the key phrases, the lines, the message. He brought his gaze around the Cabinet Room, across the polished wood table, at all the leather swivel chairs in a perfect line, at the original paintings that hung on the walls. Someday soon he would be sitting here in a cabinet meeting, listening to the president, providing his own insight, the lone Democrat helping to guide the government of the United States.

His top aide, Benjamin Bank, paced back and forth at the far end of the room yammering into his cellular telephone. Finally, he hung up and walked back toward Randolph, taking the seat right beside his boss.

"You're all set, you know your lines, you're comfortable?" he asked.

Randolph looked at him and nodded.

Bank said, "You should know, I just got word from Leavitt"—Boston Police Commissioner John Leavitt—"that *Record* publisher Paul

Ellis has been found dead this afternoon, possibly killed. No further details known."

Randolph exclaimed softly, "Holy shit. We should offer the state cops and the FBI crime lab."

Bank nodded. Randolph looked at him absently. His closest aide had a thick mop of constantly unkempt brown hair. Aside from that, he was almost painfully ordinary, neither handsome nor ugly, neither fit nor fat, but always somewhere in between, the type of guy you meet and then forget twenty minutes later.

He was, though, one hell of a political strategist, and a ruthlessly loyal friend, and for that, Randolph thought, he would offer him the job as his chief of staff at the Justice Department and hope that he was willing to expand his horizons beyond Boston and make the move.

Bank broke his silent musings and asked, "Tell me about Fitzgerald. The story came out well. We couldn't have asked for anything better. But did he seem happy for you?"

"You know the old guy," Randolph responded. "He's brooding. He's always got another question. And even though he's an old family friend, he always makes you feel like you're not giving just the right answer."

Randolph paused and asked, "Any word from any of our friends on whether Jack Flynn is still nosing around on that bullshit story?"

At that moment, the door to the room clicked open, and a short, bald presidential aide, recognizable to both men from so many appearances on national television, walked into the room. He shut the door behind him, extended his right hand and said, "Governor, I'm Murray Ferren. A pleasure to meet you."

Before Randolph could barely respond, Ferren shook Bank's hand and said, "I just want to give you the quick lay of the land here. The event will obviously be covered by the entire White House press corps—a notoriously fickle crowd. I'm going to take you in to see the president right after we finish here. You'll chat with him in the Oval for about ten minutes, then the two of you will walk out his private doors, across the veranda, and into the Rose Garden.

"The president will speak for approximately six minutes. He'll discuss your record in Massachusetts, and his hopes for the future. He'll stress that, by selecting a Democrat, he is opening himself up to further investigation, and by doing that, is hopeful of putting any hint of further scandal behind him.

"Then he'll turn the podium over to you. I've seen the faxed copy of your remarks, which are quite good. The president would appreciate it if you would linger for a while on the point about crossing party lines. Plan on talking for about four minutes, then we'll open it up to questions.

"It may get a little tricky at that point. You're an unknown to the White House press. The story was broken by a Boston paper. They're not happy about any of this. So you might sense something of an attitude out there. On television, that's going to play to your favor—the outsider comes to Washington and takes on the establishment. Just stay calm and collected. And also be prepared, they might be asking the president about a change in our Iraq policy. That's not because you're not an interesting story, but because this is his only public availability of the day."

Ferren, one of President Clayton Hutchins's closest aides, paused and looked long and hard at Randolph.

"You were a surprise choice, governor," Ferren said. "And when I say that, I mean that the choice surprised even me, and I'm not surprised much in this White House. I make it my job not to be.

"Now because of this, you did not undergo our typical, rigorous vetting process. So I want to ask you this, and this is the only time I'll have the opportunity to do that. It will also be the last time you have the chance to save the president and yourself from any sort of colossal embarrassment, if there is anything in your record, or in your past, that might prove embarrassing. Now is there?"

He asked the question as he stared across the shiny table into Randolph's pale eyes. Ferren thought to himself how young the governor looked, how inexperienced, and he wondered if he was prepared for the onslaught of national publicity to come, some good, some invariably, inevitably bad.

In a long moment of awkward silence, Randolph stared back, then let his eyes fall to the table. He thought about his father, felled by gunfire, the smoke, the burst of red, the sickening feel of his still flesh. He thought about Fitzgerald's reaction two nights before. He wondered what Jack Flynn might ask in the next few days.

Then he thought about his future, his destiny, the speech he was prepared to give in the Rose Garden of the White House to the most seasoned, most famous reporters in the world.

"Nothing that comes to mind," Randolph replied at last, his gaze again fixing on Ferren.

Ferren slapped the table with his palms as he stood up. "Good. Then it's almost show time. Come with me. The president would like to see you for a few minutes before we head out."

Bank clapped Randolph on the back. Ferren flicked open the door. At this moment, Randolph should have felt elated. But what nagged at him was a sense that he might have just lost all control.

eight

I ALL BUT STAGGERED into the newsroom, my mind soft and my body weak, drifting past one messy metal desk after another, every frantic reporter in a state of deadline panic, until I finally arrived at mine. I stripped off my jacket and slumped deep into my chair.

I put my head in my hands and took a quick assessment of my situation, trying to add structure to a life that was whirling out of control. Not to sound too selfish here, but I was pretty much in the process of losing just about everything I had of any value, including not just my job, but my life. Add to this the fact that we didn't have a natural successor to the publisher's office at a time when we needed one most. This may explain why Paul had spent so much energy trying to recruit me to the executive suite. To say the very least, things were not good. In fact, I couldn't picture them being any worse, unless, of course, I was the one who was dead.

I was flailing away in this deep pool of self-pity when I felt a presence along the edge, and looked up to see the rather rotund figure of Vinny Mongillo standing beside my desk, no doubt ready to throw me a lifeline.

He wrapped his arm, all damp and beefy, around my neck and jerked my head against his heaving stomach, saying in a determined, monotonic voice, "We're going to get that cocksucker, Jack, and when we do, we'll string him up by his shriveled balls."

I pulled my head away, politely so, not wanting to offend him. This was Vinny's version of a condolence call. The Irish bring a casserole and say the Rosary. Wasps offer a handshake and a sympathetic grimace. Italians like Vinny vow to rip people's private parts off. Right now, I think I liked his approach best.

Regarding Vinny, he's my best friend in the building, pure and simple, a veritable olive-colored mountain of a man with a constant sheen of perspiration on his brow and the forever odor of a well-made pepperoni pizza emanating from parts of him that no decent-thinking person ever wants to see. I actually think he steps out of the shower sweating.

Which is fine, because he's also one of the best reporters ever to grace the pages of *The Boston Record*. He sits in a custom-built, extra-wide chair at an impeccably neat desk in the heart of the newsroom, working a pair of side-by-side telephones, hanging up one only to take a call on the other, always asking, "What's new? What d'ya have? What can you tell me? C'mon, you're fucking with me," the receiver tucked between his flabby cheek and his puffy neck while his fingers furiously dance across the computer keyboard with information, insight, or gossip from yet another well-placed source.

His is not the quiet work of documents and musty records. No, it's all based on human relationships, on the spoken word, the little nod, the off-the-record guidance. People tell him things because people tell him things. If they don't, they believe someone else will, and they figure it's better to leave their own mark. Fear, and the exploitation thereof, is one of the most unheralded tools of the journalism trade.

If I were ever to become editor of this paper, assuming there's still a Cutter-Ellis paper here to become editor of, I'll pay him a king's ransom just to spend the rest of his career doing exactly what he does now, because his is the kind of work that's impossible to teach others to do. You either have it or you don't. No one taught Secretariat or Seabiscuit how to run.

Anyway, he rested his enormous girth on my desk. His plaid shirt was opened at the collar and rolled up at the sleeves, showing a fleshy neck and forearms that resembled flank steak wrapped in brown butcher's paper. He wore a wrinkled pair of sturdy, brown pants that he buys at a specialty store for large-sized tradesmen.

"Justine"— Steele, the editor in chief—"held a quick staff meeting and gave us the basics. I've made some calls," he said, his big brown eyes probing my blue ones. "I talked to Leavitt about ten minutes ago, and he assures me up and down that he has every possible detective on this thing, all his best and brightest. Right now, they're leaning toward robbery, but they have a team going door-to-door in the area to see if anyone saw anything. Every detective is pressing every one of their informants to find out what they know. They're going to canvass the neighborhood, track down anyone who might have been walking a dog, maybe even set up a roadblock to find out if anyone saw absolutely anything at all. He says they're sparing no expense."

I nodded. Truth is, the flow of information almost felt like intravenous medicine, making me feel slightly, slowly better, even if I couldn't explain why.

Vinny knew my relationship with Paul. As a matter of fact, he had dedicated no small amount of time giving me shit about it, calling me the teacher's pet and the like. He could see, or at least sense, that he was helping, so he continued, still monotonic, like a Pentagon briefer hinting at distant troop movements on the eve of a war, "I also talked to Randolph today after he arrived in Washington." The governor.

He paused, then said, "Randolph says he's put state cops on the case, their major crime squad, and he's personally made a call to the mayor and to Leavitt guaranteeing cooperation and promising there'll be none of the usual turf battles or glory grabs."

Another pause, as Vinny's eyes fell on mine. He added, "And Randolph also says he talked to the FBI director, and the feds are prepared to play an active role in this. They'll make their laboratory available, their databases, their agents, profilers, whatever we need, all on an expedited basis. All they need is a phone call asking their help."

We looked at each other for a moment, two inherently, intrinsically different people tossed together into this crazy business of news and words, and now friendship and tragedy. "Jack," he said in that convincing, reassuring way of his, "this thing's going to get solved."

I nodded my head again and absently ran my fingers through my hair.

"I loved the guy," I said. He nodded. "I can't picture what this paper is going to be like without him." He kept staring at me, his face growing sad as he considered what I was saying.

I thought about telling him about yesterday morning's meeting, about the possibility that the paper would no longer be under family control. I felt like I needed to tell someone. But I held it in, mostly because I know Mongillo well, which means I know that as a good reporter, he might trade my information for more information from his sources, even if I told him in the strictest confidence. He wouldn't be able to help himself.

So what I said was, "We need some answers to this thing, fast."

We both sat there in a stultifying silence, the room coming to life all around us but the air between us dead.

I looked up at him looking down at me. Usually our conversations existed at no higher plane than the utterly banal—quips and insults and jabs and jokes. As a matter of fact, I think this is the longest exchange that didn't involve him calling me "Fair Hair," which was probably testament to what we really had between us, the battles we had fought together, the places we had both been.

"You and I have to get to the bottom of this thing. We can't just count on the cops and we can't sit idly by while the paper is transformed above us. Paul had asked me for my help, and now I'm asking you for yours."

He placed his massive hands, the size and color of catchers' mitts, on each of my shoulders, and I could feel the dampness of his palms soak into my previously crisp white shirt. What are you going to do?

"How many times have I saved your sorry ass before?" he asked.

I said, "Have you begun scrubbing Terry Campbell?"

"Just barely, but I assume you want me to put that aside for now."

I replied, "Just the opposite. Look at him harder than ever. I'll explain why very soon."

With that, he pushed his face toward mine. I quelled any vague notion of panic and allowed the scene to unfold. He pressed his enormous lips against my temple, his oily skin causing my hair to mat against my scalp. And he kissed me. I mean, for God's sake, he really kissed me.

"Everything's going to work out, Fair Hair," he said softly, withdrawing. "We're both too smart to have it any other way. At least I know I am."

As he stalked off toward his own desk, I sat back and took in the soothing frenzy of the newsroom, the various editors racing around assigning excited reporters to every conceivable facet of the biggest murder to happen in this city in years. Normally I'd be all over the room, chatting up my colleagues, working the phones, looking for a news break of my own. But perhaps because they knew of my tight relationship with Paul Ellis, the editors were cutting a wide swath around me.

By the way, it's not a pretty place, the newsroom, not unless your idea of pretty is a collection of cheap, scratched furniture as far as the eye can see, all of it covered—even in the age of the DVD—with old newspapers, reams of documents, yellowed press releases, never-read faxes. The sounds were that of clicking keyboards and conversational rumble, marked by the occasional verbal glare of a television set and Barbara, the receptionist, calling out over the loudspeaker, "Holding a call for . . ."

Pretty? No. Try beautiful. Truth is, newspapers represented the one constant in my life, the place where I had grown up, come of age, then began the brisk, byzantine march through adulthood. Women came and went. Beliefs sometimes changed, goals and ambitions were altered in ways subtle and serious. But always, always, there was the newsroom, where a motley collection of skeptical and, yes, sometimes cynical reporters and editors gathered every day of the week, every week of the year, in a regal pursuit of truth. And the truth is what we needed now.

Too soon, every penny-ante politician in town would be talking to every nickel-and-dime television reporter about their love and respect for Paul Ellis, who, by the way, they barely knew. Too soon, the police commissioner would be issuing statements expressing "confidence" that his department would "administer justice" as his detectives were given time to "pursue strong leads." Meanwhile, for all anyone knew, his investigators lacked even the hint of a valid clue.

But in this room, we looked beyond the words to the reality, beyond the contortions to the truth. Our collective bullshit meter was set on high as we probed and measured, worked the phones, pored over documents, researched history and peered into the fog of the past and shadows of the present, sometimes successfully, other times not, but always in the name of what was new and what was right. Usually, anyway.

But it's different when you're part of the story—woefully different, I was quickly learning. Now I sat at my desk amid the furor wondering if word of the paper's imminent sale would somehow leak out, and what it might have to do with Paul's murder and the attempt on my own life, not to mention John Cutter's death five years ago, though I guess I just did, and for increasingly good reason.

Out of the haze of my mind, I suddenly noticed Brent Cutter standing a few feet away—Brent Cutter of the Cutter-Ellis publishing family, Brent Cutter as in, John Cutter's son. Like many Boston Irish of my generation and the one before, I've been accused from time to time of being something of an Anglophile. But here was Exhibit A in why Irish was best. Brent was more than a few years older than me, a creature solely and completely dedicated to the pursuit of cold, hard cash, an untalented nudge of a self-entitled man who knew the journalism business like I know a woman's needs, which is to say, not at all. He was born on third base and thought he hit a triple, in title the Cutter-Ellis Publishing Company's president, but more like a CFO, and I used to picture him sitting in his cushy office on the executive floor constantly punching the keys to one of those calculators with a roll of printer tape, but barely able to write so much as a memorandum to share his thoughts with his many underlings. I'd be surprised if he read the newspaper every day except to take note of the number of ads.

He was, according to Paul Ellis, always the first to recommend layoffs at any prediction of a recession, only to be overruled, thankfully, by the publisher. He insisted on reviewing every weekly expense voucher turned in by every reporter and editor, and would think nothing of kicking them back with the handwritten scrawl across the top of the page, "Is it really necessary for a reporter to dine at the Four Seasons?"

I thought so, yes, but that's not really the issue right now.

Of course, every other month he'd jet off to the Caribbean or the capitals of Europe for a two-week vacation in another five-star hotel, ostensibly to relax after all the hard work he was doing back in Boston.

Screw him. To be honest, I don't think I'd ever seen the guy in the newsroom before, except for one time two years ago at a going away party for retiring editor Bob Appleton, when he no doubt came down to make sure we didn't spend too much of the company money on free food for reporters and editors.

Still, the hour was a difficult one, so when he showed up at my desk, I stood and greeted him politely. "It's terrible, Brent," I said. "But everything's going to be all right."

He nodded. He was a tall guy with a thick head of jet black hair that he always wore slicked back like a Wall Street financier, a Gordon Gecko type. He wore custom-fitted suits and handmade shirts with expensive cufflinks—an accessory I've always regarded as remarkably inane. To a few narrow-minded women, he was no doubt good-looking and confident. To me and other right-minded individuals, he was a self-involved prick. I hope I didn't just say that out loud.

He nodded in that overly assured way of his but it was so painfully obvious that he was scared out of his wits, way out of his league, and that any reach for calm was a failing act. He said, "I've got the cops coming in to see me, a detective by the name of Travers. Luke Travers. What do you know about him."

Luke Travers and Brent Cutter. Put them together and you've got nearly half a personality. I wish I could watch through a one-way mirrored wall.

"You'll like him," I said.

He gave me a curious look, so I added, "He's fine. By the numbers, reasonably straightforward. He's not going to solve the O-ring problem on the space shuttle, but if the case is obvious, he's the guy to crack it."

"So he's not going to try to pull a fast one on me, right? No need for me to get a lawyer?"

Interesting that the family member feels the need to have counsel in his first meeting with the law. I replied, "If you think you need a lawyer, then by all means, I'd secure one. If you didn't do anything wrong, which I'm sure you didn't, why bother?"

He nodded again, visibly nervous now. Brent's idea of adversity was a long line at the chairlift in Aspen.

"You're right," he said, gravely. "I'll let you know how it goes." And he turned around and walked out, careful not to touch the piles of discarded newspapers that lay all over the room.

I sat at my desk and let my mind wander back to the previous morning, to the look on Paul's face when he told me about the forced sale. Then I thought of the way he looked on the gurney, the holes in his forehead, the vacancy of his eyes.

With that, the memories came flowing back. I remembered the first time I met him. My own father, Arthur Flynn, was, by any estimation, a wonderful man, thirty-two years an overnight worker in the *Record's* pressroom, presiding over the publication of the paper five days a week with more pride than any editor in the newsroom. He'd carry the paper home each morning as if he was holding the Holy Bible, place it carefully on the kitchen table, and slowly, methodically turn each and every page while he ate his English muffins and sipped his black coffee, reading the stories, analyzing the photo reproductions, and gauging the ink counts. Every time I came downstairs, ready to head to school, he'd look up at me amused and say, simply, "The *Record's* here."

My father died before he could see me enter the business. He had fallen ill with cancer my senior year in high school. He was the night pressroom foreman, and Paul Ellis, then the president of the company, came to our house in South Boston one afternoon to visit him. I'll never forget it. He drove himself, in a Ford LTD. He walked across our tiny front yard, knocked on the door, and when I answered it, he said simply, "Hi, I'm Paul Ellis. I work with your dad."

Work with your dad. The guy owned the entire newspaper, and he's telling me he worked with my dad. It was love at first sight.

Then he's sitting next to my father and I'm in the other room and I hear him say, "Art, you've given your life to my family paper. I fully expect you're going to get better and come back to work, but in case you don't, you'll continue to collect your disability pay right until your pension kicks in. I also want you to know, I hear you have a smart boy here. I'm going to pay for him to go to college wherever he wants. I never want that to be a worry for you."

My father was so overcome that he couldn't even offer a reply.

Paul Ellis. Along with his cousin, his predecessor, John Cutter, he took what was a perfectly average newspaper and transformed it into a national force. He hired the best editors, spent lavishly on some of the country's most gifted writers, myself included, and during times when other newspapers were shrinking their news holes to save money, he expanded ours, making it nearly as coveted a workplace and respected an institution as the vaunted *New York Times*.

And he found that good journalism was good business. Five years after he started, his investments began paying off, and his paper quickly became the dominant paper in the Boston market, the publication of choice for those in the city and the growing suburbs. The *Record*, quite simply, fulfilled its name, becoming the newspaper of record in New England. Readership soared, as did advertising. Flush with money, the journalism just kept getting better.

I was twenty-four years old, a young reporter with a suburban Boston paper, when he called me at my desk one day and, in a formal sounding voice, said, "Mr. Flynn, this is Paul Ellis of the *Record*. I want to make you a job offer. I'd like you to come to my newspaper and be a general assignment reporter."

My father had died two months earlier. My mother died just weeks after that—I've always believed of a broken heart. I had few job prospects. My mind was a fog. "If you're half as good a reporter as your father was a pressman," he said on the phone that day, "then we're going to have a long and successful relationship. And since you've been kicking the hell out of my poor reporters virtually every day for the last two years, I have no doubt that this is true." I accepted on the spot.

When John Cutter died five years ago, Paul Ellis ascended from president to publisher and never looked back. It was a devastatingly sad time at the paper, but Paul proved a reassuring presence. He promised that the *Record* would continue in the great Cutter-Ellis tradition. He accepted Brent Cutter as his president. He began expanding the staff at a time when other newspapers were cutting back.

And now, with the nonchalance of someone shutting off their car headlights, he was forever gone.

So the news lead on this day was that two publishers of *The Boston Record*, John Cutter and Paul Ellis, died within five years of each other, one of a heart attack, the other of what appeared to be a random street robbery. The casual observer would say we were cursed, but sitting in the heart of the newsroom, knowing what I knew, feeling what I felt, I couldn't help but believe otherwise.

I looked around me at all the reporters and editors scurrying every which way in pursuit of every possible scrap of information in the murder of Paul Ellis. There were questions they wouldn't think to ask, because they wouldn't know to ask them.

I'm overtired, I thought to myself, and being overly dramatic, even melodramatic. Maybe Paul was wrong about John Cutter. Maybe that assailant in Florida was just another random robber. But I didn't believe that. In this business, we're trained not to believe in coincidence—not unless you wanted to work back on the Style page.

I knew just one thing then, and I knew it clearer than I've ever known anything else: It was time to get to work.

nine

My FIRST CALL WAS from Paul's wife, Polly. Yes, Paul and Polly, a favorite pairing of the gossip columnists at the *Traveler*, the *Traveler* being the local tabloid, or what the know-it-all media analysts invariably call our "feisty competition." She was, understandably, a mess, though I'll admit here that even on her best days, she had more than a touch of Wasp eccentricity—what the less polite might call inbred lunacy. Paul adored her. "She keeps me young," he used to say with a distant smile. Indeed, she'd keep Bob Hope young.

Anyway, she was flying back from California and said she wanted to hold the memorial service on Wednesday morning, two days hence, at the Trinity Church in Copley Square in Boston. She asked if I would be willing to "say a few words." Sure: Somebody, anybody, help us.

Then came the calls from a couple of members of the Cutter-Ellis board of directors, each of whom casually inquired about my own career intentions, given that Paul, they said, had always spoken so highly of me.

My politic answer: "I'm in such a daze now I don't know what I want for dinner." Truth is, I didn't know if I even wanted dinner.

And finally, Detective Tommy O'Brien called.

"We were just up talking with Brent Cutter," he said. "Is he always that much of a nervous Nellie, or is he acting strange?"

"He's not what you'd call Cool Hand Luke," I replied.

Silence, so I added, "He's a bit of a jackass, but I don't know of anyone who could easily handle the fact that their relative, who is also the boss, was shot three times in the head and killed in the parking lot of their office for still unknown reasons. I wouldn't be too concerned by him."

"Good point. Travers wants to come up to talk with you. He seems a little anxious about it. I don't know what the hell happened between the two of you, but are you alright with that?"

"Tell the prick to come up," I replied.

"Jesus Christ. This story I have to hear."

I didn't reply, so he said, "Fifteen minutes okay?"

I thought for a moment, and replied, "No, give me about an hour."

As soon as I hung up, I walked out of the newsroom and up into the paper's executive suite, where my aim was to peruse—alright, rifle—Paul's office looking for his files dealing with the takeover bid as well as any overt clues that might lead to his killer—while at the same time saving the newspaper. Maybe I should have eaten a can of spinach first.

Understand, the executive suite is nothing like the newsroom, in that it's civil, even nice, like the offices of a real company, complete with a paneled boardroom, rich, burgundy rugs and antique lamps with hunter green shades. Paul's office even had a fireplace. The newsroom, in comparison, is like the factory floor.

But as I walked into the reception area, I immediately saw several strips of garish yellow "Crime Scene" tape spread across his open door, and if the tape didn't make the point, then the uniformed cop standing in front of it did. Time to go to Plan B.

The entirety of Plan B involved me walking over to Paul's longtime secretary, Amelia Bradford, as if that was my intention all along. Look, no one ever accused me of being one of life's great strategists. She was sitting at her desk in tears, makeup streaked down her dignified, well-preserved face. She got up and hugged me and we both talked for a while about what a great man he was and what an awful world this has become.

Soon, other secretaries and company officials gathered around, everybody sad and a little bit nervous about what an uncertain future would hold.

I always felt a little awkward in the executive suite, like a young teenager sitting at the adult table at Thanksgiving dinner. In other words, I wanted to get out of there quickly. But before making my way out, I stopped in Brent's' oversized, overstuffed office down the hall. He's one of these guys who has his diplomas on the wall—high school, undergrad, and his MBA from Wharton, alongside a collection of absurdly cheap prints of Boston landmarks, the same kind of things that hang in the family rooms of McMansions in so many treeless, suburban subdivisions. In all, his office was exactly suited to his personality—completely and entirely without imagination.

When I walked in, he looked relieved that his interview with the Boston Police had ended.

"No problems, no sweat," he said, standing up at his desk as I approached. "This Travers seemed to be a cool guy."

I knew they'd get along. I said, "By the way, have you gotten any calls from the board of directors?"

He sat back down. "No," he replied, and looked at me darkly.

"No big deal. I've gotten a call or two. I think they'll want to have some sort of meeting, probably next week. We should have a talk before then, don't you think?"

Walking back, I wished the police guard a "good afternoon" and made my way to the friendlier environs of the newsroom, where I snapped up the telephone and punched out the familiar extension to Robert Fitzgerald, the person whose advice I needed most right now.

"Dear God, Jack," he said in that deep, almost Shakespearean voice of his. "I've been trying to track you down. Tell me how you are."

"I will, I will, but I need to do it in person. Sorry I had to hang up so abruptly this morning, but you caught me at an awkward time. Long story."

He said, "Of course. I've been waiting to hear where you were. I'll jump in a car and be over there in ten minutes."

I quickly interjected, "No, stay right there. It would do me good to get out of here for a while. I'm leaving now. I'll see you in your office."

I called for a taxicab, took a long, panoramic gaze around the newsroom, at all the reporters madly working the telephones, at the editors gathered in a circle of chairs in one of their glass offices brainstorming the day's coverage, at Mongillo sitting with his feet up and a receiver pressed against each ear. He saw me looking and flashed a thumbs-up, then held one finger up to tell me to hold on. A moment later, he came waddling up to my desk, flush in the face, asking where I was going.

"Not that duplicitous prick," he said when I told him. It would be an understatement to say that Mongillo didn't hold Fitzgerald in the same high regard as I did.

"Don't start."

"He's a fraud."

I said, "This isn't the time to resolve or even address it. I'll see you in a while."

Fitzgerald's office, by the way, sat not in the newsroom, but in downtown Boston, on School Street, in a neighborhood of narrow, crooked byways mobbed with shoppers, tourists, and businessmen. One could make the exotic argument that the area looked like ancient Rome. Years ago, the newspaper used to be situated downtown as well, but when the Cutter-Ellis's vacated the central city for the convenience of sitting aside a major highway, Fitzgerald didn't want to leave. So rather than lose him, whoever was publisher at the time leased him his own office on the second floor of a brick townhouse, and he's been there ever since.

On the way downtown, the cab, of course, reeked of one of those tree-shaped air fresheners that can't possibly conceal a smell worse than it exudes. The vinyl covering the backseat was torn, exposing the foam beneath. Every door rattled at the mere anticipation of a bump.

At first, I looked carefully around for a white Cavalier, before realizing how utterly foolish a thought that was. I snickered to myself, then just looked at the cars behind us to see if I recognized anyone driving them. The good news was that I didn't.

So I tuned it all out as I looked at the downtown skyline, reflecting on a city, on a life that seemed to be changing like the numbers on a digital clock. Used to be that Wasps ran the entire show, and I'm not necessarily saying that's a good thing, but at least it was easy to understand. You knew the score. Wasps were in positions of authority and money. The Irish worked as cops and firemen. The Italians ran the mob and the food stores. Everyone else fought for the scraps.

No more. Oh, there are still plenty of Lodges and Cabots and Roosevelts around, but they're mostly in the suburbs now, commuting quietly to work in unheralded positions counting money in investment houses or practicing corporate law in white-shoe firms. The Irish and the Italians took over the State House and City Hall, and have risen to the boardrooms of many of the city's biggest companies. Look at the Flynns as a reasonable example. The old man worked in the pressroom. His kid is in the newsroom, and was even invited to ascend to the front office.

The problem, everyone's problem, is that those companies got bought out by bigger companies, and it increasingly seems that the entire metropolis that is Boston is a wholly owned subsidiary of New York. Bank of Boston is now Fleet. Jordan Marsh is now Macy's. The Red Sox are owned by out-of-towners who made their fortunes on Wall Street and in Hollywood. And even *The Boston Record,* after one hundred and twenty-seven years of local ownership, is at risk of falling into out-of-town hands.

Mind you, it's not all bad. We used to be some sort of puritanical, quirky little backwater where cousins married each other for the money, baked beans were a gastronomical achievement, and Talbots and Brooks Brothers were haute couture. Now the city is more than 50 percent minority, which means that blacks and Hispanics aren't a minority at all, and a simple walk through the shopping districts reveals a booming melting pot of races, ethnicities, styles, and fashions.

Speaking of which, I jumped out at Downtown Crossing, pulled open the heavy, unmarked door to Fitzgerald's simple brick building, and trudged up the wooden stairs.

When I arrived at the landing, he was there to greet me. We embraced silently, his arms engulfing my shoulders.

"Jack, I am so unspeakably sorry," he said, his voice thick and raw with emotion.

He stepped back, and so did I. The scene had a sense of déjà vu to it, for good reason. He led me across the hardwood floors, through a single door and into his office. The furniture was all antique. The sconces on the wall were brass. The floor-to-ceiling bookcases were packed with signed first editions from some of the world's most notable authors. We both sat down, he in a Boston Rocker, me in a facing leather chair.

"Are the cops giving you any information about who did this, or why?" Fitzgerald asked.

I slowly shook my head. "Right now, things point to a robbery, but the detectives outside say they don't have any suspects yet, and I don't think they have any real clues."

Regarding Robert Fitzgerald, he was, to say the least, an institution, and still very much an active one. He was tall and distinguished, nearing sixty-seven years old, with a shock of silver hair that framed a patrician face that is best described as knowing. Indeed, he knew things that most mortal men did not, saw things that few others would ever see. He's sat in the Oval Office with presidents, visited the private Georgetown and Beacon Hill salons of so many senior government advisers, toured far-flung countries with United States ambassadors and foreign heads of state, provided solemn advice in the plush working suites of corporate titans. He is a fixture on the Sunday morning talk shows, his demeanor unfailingly easy and always smart. He is the best representative this newspaper could ever have, and one of the best newsmen I would ever know.

And, if our schedules allowed, every Monday afternoon since I arrived at the paper more than a decade ago, he would share with me his knowledge, his experience, his expectations, and his ambitions. We would gather in this office from noon to one P.M. to talk about the *Record*, about newspapers, about journalism in general, in what often proved to be the kick-start to my week. Early on, he saw in me a talent that I took a while to see myself—no small virtue on his part. Give him credit for a lot of things, but at least grant that he has a great eye. He was my mentor, and he was my friend.

"Well, you know if they've ever taken a case seriously, this will be the one," he said.

We sat in silence for a moment. I gazed out the pair of small-paned windows that overlooked the street below, where throngs of determined people brushed past each other in opposite directions. I wondered if they had already heard of Paul's murder. I wondered if they cared. My gaze drifted momentarily over his massive wooden desk, rumored to have once belonged to Nathaniel Hawthorne.

I turned back to Fitzgerald. He sat in his shirtsleeves with a navy blue bow tie. I said, "It's a mess, Robert. There's something I haven't told the cops yet, and I want you to keep this confidential."

He nodded and pulled his reading glasses off his handsome face. I continued. "Paul and I met yesterday morning in the Public Garden. He told me that the paper is the target of a hostile takeover. He was trying like hell to fight it, and today was the day he was going to get some answers, but he warned me that it looked like he wouldn't be able to ward it off. Campbell Newspapers, if you can believe it."

We looked at each other again. Under his breath, Fitzgerald said, "Good God."

"You realize, Jack, that you have to go to the police."

I hesitated, and he quickly said, "Jack, you're not just a reporter now. You're a potential witness with valuable information. Your friend and boss was murdered. We don't know who killed him. You have to cooperate with the authorities, because you know as well as I do that the takeover of *The Boston Record* is more than likely linked to Paul's death."

I nodded, my eyes on the floor. "I'm meeting with detectives in about twenty minutes."

More silence between us, then I said, "I just needed to tell someone first. I wanted you to know. I need you to keep quiet until I figure out how to handle this internally. Not even Brent Cutter knows."

"You have my silence," Fitzgerald said. In a more paternal tone, he added, "But you know what you must do."

"I know."

I stood to leave. I thought about telling him Paul's suspicions of John Cutter's death, and my subsequent trip to Florida on his behalf.

But as the words formed on my tongue, I held back for reasons unknown.

In the silence, he said, "I was planning to fly to the capital tonight to meet with some friends in the White House and on the Hill on the Randolph nomination. But I'm not going anywhere with this hanging over the paper. I'll be in my office, and I'll keep in touch with Leavitt and Randolph. Let me know whatever you need."

We embraced again, in silence, and I left.

Luke Travers walked up to my desk with barely a sound, the *Record* security guard escort, Edgar, lagging a few paces behind. He was about my age. His suit looked handmade, though I don't think I even know what a handmade suit looks like, except that it probably looked like what he had on. He wore a shirt that required cufflinks, which, as I've said, is something I've never understood. Buttons are so much easier. His facial stubble was even more pronounced than a couple of hours earlier. In total, he looked not so much like a homicide cop as he did a downtown lawyer or Goldman Sachs stockbroker who was trying too hard to look like something he wasn't—meaning young and stylish, worldly, and smart.

I had to quell the urge to punch him in his too-pretty mouth. I looked up and nodded without speaking.

"Thank you for taking the time," he said, formal, flat.

"Come with me," I replied, and I slowly stood up and walked across the newsroom, never giving him the dignity of even a backward glance. As we moved in silent, single file, I could hear the newsroom hush all around us, the reporters staring at us with the kind of curiosity that wouldn't die without an explanation. I led him into a small conference room with a glass wall looking out over the metro department and sat down at a round table just large enough to accommodate six chairs. He sat across from me.

"What can I do for you?" I asked, stone-faced, my elbows on the wood tabletop, my body slouched from the weight of a day that wasn't even half over. I had a view of the entire newsroom past his stupid head. He had the better seat because it had a view just of me. This was our version of a police interrogation room.

There were no niceties in this conversation, no veneer of humanitarianism, no attempt at an emotional connection. We were about nine months and a broken heart away from that, and the year could never be taken back and the heart never repaired.

"My understanding," he said, "is that you were like the son that Paul Ellis never had." He looked me in the eye, and when I met his stare, his look shifted down to a few sheets of paper he held in his hand. What he said was an overstatement, but I had to give him credit for at least immediately discerning that we had had a special relationship.

He continued, "It's early, but right now, we don't have a whole lot. We don't even have much in the way of theory. We've determined that the victim was confronted in the parking lot. He either dropped his briefcase in the roadway area, or he flung it at his assailant. If it was the latter, there's a chance of retrieving DNA evidence from the briefcase, and we're in the process of having that examined now.

"The victim was either led to an area between the trucks, or more likely, fled from the roadway to the trucks, with the killer in pursuit. Based on loose sand and dirt on the victim's clothing, and the imprints left on the ground, it appears he spent some amount of time beneath one of the trucks, presumably in hiding. Ultimately, as you know, he was shot three times at very close range—a few inches—in the forehead. From the blood splatter, it appears he was standing when he was shot. The M.E. is positive he died instantly, and he's believed to have died sometime yesterday morning."

I didn't like Travers calling him "the victim," as if, dead for a day, Paul had already lost his identity in life, and was no longer known for his great accomplishments, but rather for the violent manner in which he left us. But I was too drained to correct him, and too stunned by the realization that I was probably the last human being, his killer aside, to see him alive.

I was picturing the old guy, in extraordinarily good shape, running for his life in the sun-splashed lot where I had parked every day for the last however many years. I imagined the look on his handsome features, the thoughts racing through his agile mind when the killer raised the gun to his forehead. I tried to shake these visions to concentrate on what Travers was telling me.

Travers: "At first blush, the killer doesn't appear to have left a whole lot behind. We've taken some shoe imprints, but they're vague at best. The coroner will go over the victim's body carefully to make sure there's nothing in the fingernails or anywhere else. And there's the briefcase. Other than that, we canvassed every square inch of the area with our very best guys, and have come up dry."

He paused, looked at me carefully, and said, "So the question is, Why?

"Is it a random act of robbery? Maybe that's exactly what it is, but I don't think so, because why here, in the parking lot of a newspaper with one of the most prominent members of our community?"

Travers continued, "Is it an assassination? Possibly, but that gets us back to the why question. Why does someone want to murder the publisher of the town's major newspaper in broad daylight. This isn't the busing era anymore, thank God."

Another long pause, during which his eyes seemed to dissect mine. Then he said, "So I'll ask you, Why?"

I just shook my head and stayed silent. I knew I was supposed to tell him what I knew, but I couldn't bring myself to do it, either physically or emotionally. I couldn't share anything with him, couldn't confide, couldn't crack a window even the slightest bit, not after what we'd been through. He asked, "When's the last time you saw Paul Ellis alive?"

"Yesterday morning, at about seven A.M. on the Public Garden."

He looked surprised. He calmly said, "Go ahead."

"Before I do, I have a recommendation for you."

Travers said, "Yes?"

"Get off the case. You do, and I might suddenly turn into a fount of information. But not until then." I said this in my flattest voice with my most direct tone.

Before I was even done with my helpful suggestion, Travers was shaking his head.

"Not going to happen," he said, locking stares with me. "This is my assignment, my case, and I'm going to solve it, and any history that you think—think—we might have is just that: history. It's not going to get in the way on my end, and I'd suggest you don't allow it to get in the way on yours."

Far easier said than done, as will quickly become obvious. Hatred can be a mountain, with jagged peaks and virtually insurmountable terrain.

I said, "You're making a mistake, and I'm going to make damned sure you pay for it."

He ignored that last remark. "So why did you see Paul Ellis yesterday morning on the Public Garden?"

I paused, began to talk, hesitated some more, and said, "Nothing that I care to share with you here."

Anger flashed through his eyes. "You can either share it with me or with a grand jury. Your choice."

"I'll take the grand jury," I replied. "Smarter people, and better looking." He didn't mention the third option, which was detailing what I knew in the pages of my newspaper. In fact, I was already mapping out my lede and first few paragraphs in my mind, as reporters tend to do.

He stood up abruptly and strode to the conference room door. He turned around and said, "You could help yourself and help the Cutter-Ellis family by helping me." He lingered for a moment, seeing if I had something to say. In the gush of silence, he walked away.

ten

THE NEWS-GATHERING CRAFT is hardest when there isn't actually any news, when over-talented reporters are forced to work the phones and the city to make something out of nothing in order to fill the seemingly endless pages of the next day's issue. It is at its most delightfully stressful best when news is exploding all around us, when there is an unabashed certainty of a public's thirst for information, as there no doubt was in the mysterious death of Paul Ellis. And the *Record,* as so many thousands of times before, would be the paper that all of New England turned to the next day for the best information.

All of which is to say, the newsroom at eight P.M., on an extended deadline, was electric. Teams of reporters worked every conceivable law enforcement source they had, and some they didn't. They shouted, begged, pleaded, and negotiated over the phone, they staked out the crime scene, the police headquarters, the FBI's Boston office. Along with the news, we had a lengthy obituary marked for the front page, an elaborate profile of the Cutter-Ellis family, a who's who among the investigators. What we didn't have was the truth.

So I sat down at my desk and wrote what I had just refused to tell Travers. I detailed the Sunday morning meeting with Paul Ellis, his warnings about the takeover, his hopes that he could somehow find a way to avert it. I was, I'm quite certain, the last person he saw while he was alive, his killer aside. Of course, I left out his suspicions over John Cutter's death, and made no mention of the threat on my life.

As part of the story, I called the headquarters for Campbell Newspapers in Moline, Illinois, to seek official comment about their takeover bid. A young, snitty spokeswoman informed me that the company officials would have no comment, and not to take their lack of comment as any confirmation of their interest in buying the *Record*. Thank you very much.

When I gave the story directly to Justine Steele, the editor-in-chief, she turned white as she read it—a good thing to have happen in a newsroom.

"Do the cops know this?" she asked.

We were sitting in her corner office, she behind her wide desk, me in a settee on the other side. The view was of nothing more glamorous than the cars shooting by on the Southeast Expressway and a scantily clad woman in a seductive pose on a nearby Gap billboard. I shook my head.

"Don't you think they should know this?"

I said, "Well, they'll know it tomorrow." That answer having not quite cut it, I broke an awkward silence by adding, "I also know that Paul loved nothing more in life than when the *Record* broke major news. I think he'd get something of a kick out of this."

Steele raised her eyebrows and smiled as she continued to look at the printout in front of her. "I'm never going to say no to an exclusive," she said.

I said, "If I give this to the police, someone over there leaks it to one of the local TV stations, or more likely, the *Traveler,* and they in turn have a field day with it in tomorrow's paper. I think the *Record* ought to let the public know about what's going on with the *Record,* on our own terms."

She nodded and said, "I think you're right."

That decision behind us, I said, "There's something else."

By the way, time was hardly an ally here. As I said, we were on deadline. The story was somewhere north of enormous. The room was controlled chaos. But typical of Justine, she was an island of calm, and as such, she gave me an expectant nod. I continued.

"Someone took a shot at me this morning."

Her face grew alarmed, but she remained silent.

"Someone I don't know. I was in Florida, just west of West Palm

Beach. The guy was following me in a car. I pulled over into a rest area and he pulled over too. When I approached him, he didn't like that and he chased me around the building, into a swamp, and shot at me."

Now Justine looked bewildered. She shook her head and said, "I don't get it. First, what the hell were you doing in Florida? Second, did this guy shoot at you out of anger, or was he following you with premeditated plans to kill you?"

Ah, a good newspaperwoman, asking the two questions that cut to the heart of this matter.

I replied, "Confidentially, and I mean that, I was in Florida because Paul told me yesterday morning that he feared his cousin, John Cutter, died of suspicious causes five years ago. I tracked down the homicide detective who'd been on the case, retired now, and paid a visit to him.

"On question two, I really don't know. Like I said, the guy appeared to be following me. But I don't want to jump to conclusions. Maybe I just ticked him off in the parking lot. But I don't think so."

She rubbed her hands across the smooth skin of her face. "Jesus Christ. Do you think we should hire you protection?"

Interesting proposition, but I declined it, perhaps foolishly so.

As I got up to leave, I turned around in her doorway and said, "That was a great hit that Fitzgerald had yesterday on Randolph. I think I've got something to add to it. I've been working on a story that says Randolph inflated his prosecution record back when he first ran for governor."

As I spoke, Justine leaned forward and I got a look on her face as if I just put a plate of prime rib in front of her, medium rare, only in this case, it was something better.

I continued, "The best I can tell, I think he just plain exaggerated the numbers to make him look like he had the best record of all the district attorneys in the state."

"How close are you?" she asked.

I knew, on the one hand, that we wanted to get this into print as fast as possible, before any of the national media parachuted into town and discovered the same. On the other hand, the story, once printed, would be scrutinized every which way from a fiery hell—by Randolph's aides, Randolph himself, the White House, and the Senate Judiciary Committee, which had to approve his nomination. It had to be so clean that you could bathe with it.

"I need a couple of days to plug holes and get a few facts straightened out."

She began standing up and said, "Take the time, but if you get a whiff of competition on it, flag me."

As I walked out her office door, Steele said to me in a decidedly more sympathetic tone, "Jack, watch yourself. And let me know whatever I can do to help."

eleven

Tuesday, April 24

WELL, EVERY DAY BRINGS something different. Yesterday, for instance, brought murder and mayhem. Today might bring some answers, but at the very minimum it should bring a new apartment, because murder or no murder, mayhem, or inner serenity, I was off this boat in just a few day's time. Perhaps this is what Fitzgerald—Robert, not F. Scott— meant when he said life is for the living—even the most mundane parts of it.

What F. Scott said was, "So we drove on toward death through the cooling twilight," a gorgeously constructed line that was starting to have special meaning for me.

I woke early, planted myself on a rickety old picnic bench in a grassy park along the edge of the park, and studied the myriad stories in the morning papers about Paul Ellis and his family, all while sipping a fresh-squeezed orange juice under a shower of springtime sun. The *Record* was jarringly complete, including my own front-page story on Paul Ellis's eleventh hour bid to block an ongoing attempt by Campbell Newspapers to buy his family newspaper. It was the biggest news break on the biggest story in town, as well as the first time in my career I'd ever felt anything but elated at giving readers something they couldn't get anywhere else. The *Traveler,* meanwhile, was uncommonly kind, aside from their screaming front-page headline, "Cursed!" They quoted unidentified police officials pointing to the likelihood of a robbery attempt gone awry. In some ways, I hoped they were right.

It was what the paper had inside that was more bothersome.

Anchoring its daily gossip column, "Scene and Heard," was a fat item about the *Record*'s own Robert Fitzgerald, a regular target of snide attacks from sundry second-tier reporters in this town.

The section was headlined, "Untruths and No Consequences." This, I knew, would not be good. It went on to detail how Fitzgerald had written a story the previous month about a pair of twins who had been placed in a foster home as four-year-olds some thirty years ago, were separately adopted, and met by coincidence when they moved to the same neighborhood of an unnamed Boston suburb. They each had children of their own and were talking about their backgrounds at a local park when they came across the stunning truth that they were sisters.

In the original story, Fitzgerald used what he said were the women's real first names, but withheld their last name on their request, as well as the town to which they moved.

But in this gossip item, the *Traveler* said it went through all state adoption records by hand from the year in which the girls would have been pulled from the foster home and found no one with their first names. It also quoted retired state officials from that era as saying it would be highly unlikely, if not downright improbable, that sisters would be split up like that. "Either the world is lying, or once again, Robert Fitzgerald of *The Boston Record* is," the item concluded.

It felt like the roller coaster of life had just jumped off its tracks. I crumpled the pages up and slam-dunked them into a nearby trash can, where, for my money, the thing belonged. This wasn't exactly what my paper needed right about now, which was probably exactly why the *Traveler* was doing it.

I punched out Fitzgerald's home number on my cellular phone.

"Robert, you see the *Traveler* today?" I asked.

He sighed. "I ignore the *Traveler*, even when I read it. And yes, today I read it."

There was a slightly awkward pause between us, and he said, "Jack, the women exist. The story is true. One of them called me up herself to—"

I cut him off. "Robert, there's absolutely no need to explain anything to me. I just called to say that there's no question in any intelligent person's mind that a bunch of jealous twits get their kicks out of attacking someone who has risen to the top of the field. That's just what we do in this business, Robert, at least the worst of us. We just try to bring people down."

"Thank you, Jack. I won't let them, but I am getting tired of it all. Someday soon might be the right day to retire." He paused again, then said, "And you ignored my advice on going to the police with your information about the takeover bid but I must say, that was one hell of a story you had on the front page."

And so forth. I complimented him on his eloquent front-page profile of Paul in that day's paper, and we hung up with plans to talk that afternoon.

First on the day's agenda, a longstanding appointment with a real estate agent in Back Bay, followed by a day of working on the Randolph nomination and Paul Ellis's murder. I made a quick call on my cell phone to the city desk, where I was told that no arrests had occurred and no news was made overnight.

My next call was to Mongillo. It was only seven A.M., a good hour before most reporters would begin the long process of rousing themselves awake. But I knew from experience that Mongillo was slogging away on the treadmill of the Boston Sports Club, a headset over his huge, sweaty crown as he dialed out the first of his many dozens of phone calls for the day.

"What are you hearing?" I asked.

He was breathing hard, wheezing at times. I heard him gulp in air to collect himself.

"Jesus Christ, Fair Hair. The fucking cops are apoplectic over your story today, throwing around words like 'obstruction of justice.'"

"Yeah, well, the hell with them."

"I keep hearing about bad blood between you and Travers. I've got to hear the full story. Anyway, yesterday they had nothing. Starting this morning, they're all over this Campbell connection. They already have two detectives out at Logan catching a flight to Chicago to interview

Terry Campbell. I've got calls out right now, and will hit you on the phone soon as I learn more."

He added, "And by the way, you see Scene and Heard today? I don't like to say I told you so. Actually, fuck that. I do like to say I told you so. And I did."

"Bullshit," I said. "That was weak, and you know it. They're just out to kick us when we're down."

"I don't know," he said, in an almost taunting manner.

I steered the conversation someplace more pleasant and productive. "Hey," I said, "we've got to get together today on the Lance Randolph hit. I'll show you the records I have and we'll divvy up the work. We need to get it in the paper as soon as possible."

"Ready when you are."

"I'll be on the cell this morning. With all this going on around us, I've got to find a place to live. I'll see you in the newsroom late morning."

As we hung up the phone, I swear to God I could hear him lighting up a cigarette.

The cell phone wasn't down on the table more than five seconds when it rang with Travers on the other line.

"Well, I hope you're pleased," he said, without introduction. "You effectively hindered the investigation into your publisher's murder because you thought you could tuck it to me. You're only hurting yourself."

"Can I help you with anything?" Stern, straightforward, aloof.

"I'm only going to ask you this once. Is there any other information you have that might help us catch Paul Ellis's killer?"

I said, "You know everything I know." And I hung up.

Perhaps the most extraordinary accomplishment of modern man is the ability to map the human genome, to be able to scientifically predict the onset of individual disease and then take definitive steps to eradicate it. But hard as that's been, it hasn't posed nearly as difficult a challenge as trying to find a landlord in Boston that will allow a dog. For this reason, I had decided to buy a condominium in Boston of my very own.

Should be a happy occasion, right? Well, not exactly. Life, like journalism, is all about context, and this was in the context of one of the biggest failures I hope to ever see.

It's funny, though not really, how you can never in a million years imagine an end to a relationship that is just beginning, and such was the case with me and Elizabeth, who I sometimes fear is the last woman I will ever love.

We had met a little more than a year before, of all places, on a story. A deranged father from Auburn, Maine, in the midst of a divorce went out and firebombed the day care center that his four-year-old boy attended every day. The guy, it ends up, was about to lose all visitation rights, and decided that if he couldn't see his own and only son, then nobody else would either.

I'm a little beyond covering breaking crime and grime stories, but the paper was short-staffed that day, so I threw my hand up, then just about set a land speed record getting there, just in time to watch three children carried out of the ash and rubble in tiny black body bags that shone in the light of the surging television crews. It was the coldest, bleakest day I've ever felt. The entire city of Auburn seemed to gather at the scene of all the carnage—parents in navy blue factory uniforms and waitress aprons desperately searching the crowd for any sign of their own kids, city officials looking to help rather than mug for the cameras, locals who simply, sincerely wanted to lend some moral support.

As the frigid late afternoon seeped into the unbearable cold of a Maine winter's night, the crowd finally thinned out. The mayor and his crew returned to a situation room in the warmth of City Hall. The victims' families returned to painfully empty houses and lives that would never be the same—an emptiness I knew all too well. My feet were so cold I could barely walk as I hobbled back to my car while trying to compose the story in my head.

It was then that I caught a glimpse of her across the way. She had her laptop computer powered up on the trunk of a State Police cruiser and she stood in the enveloping dusk tapping at her keyboard, occasionally taking long glances over at the fire scene in front of her as if playing out the tragedy in her mind. She had on a ski jacket and a black wool hat pulled low over her head, and her nose was so ruby red it looked like it might just fall off on the icy ground.

But it was her eyes that I remembered best—big, haunting eyes, oval-shaped eyes, eyes such that when she looked up and momentarily met my gaze from about ten yards away, it was as if someone had just flicked on a light, her eyes were that bright. My heart began pulsing. She looked back down at her computer and didn't seem to give me another thought.

That night, after filing my sad story and transmitting it down to Boston, I sat at the bar of the Holiday Inn in Auburn eating an under-cooked hamburger and reading the *New York Times* in a failing bid to forget most of what I had seen. I hope I'm not alone in conceding that all roads eventually lead to myself, so I ended up sitting at the bar reliving that awful morning three-and-a-half years ago when Dr. Joyce led me into a nondescript conference room at Georgetown Hospital to tell me that my wife and newborn daughter had just died at birth. Death was everywhere.

When I got up to head for my room that night, I saw her sitting alone at a table right beside the bar, picking at an unappetizing-looking vegetar-ian dish and sipping a glass of red wine. She had a few sheets of scribbled notes spread across the table, and her long brown hair was mussed, obvi-ously from the wool cap. Her face, strangely familiar, appeared tired.

Unfortunately, I lack the chromosome that allows me to talk easily to women I don't already know. Those rare times when I summon the courage to approach one of them, I end up saying something like, "The thing I like best about spring is that my hair stops being so staticky." I actually said that once, but I'll spare the details for now.

But fortunately for me, as I walked by her table she tossed me a lazy smile and said, "Tough story, huh?" I may not be able to talk to women about anything, but I can talk journalism with anyone.

"They don't get much tougher," I replied. Confident, reserved. I reached my hand out and said, "Jack Flynn. I write for the *Record* down in Boston."

She shook my hand firmly while staying in her seat and said, "I've heard of it." Another lazy smile, her head cocked a bit. "And you. Elizabeth Riggs. I write for the *Traveler.*"

Oh my.

"I've heard of it."

"This one really got to me," she said, her weary face holding not even a hint of the smile of a few seconds before. As she spoke, she rested her chin in one hand and pushed a fork absently around her plate with the other. "Did you see all those parents, the panic and pain all over their faces? I even saw a fireman, some big burly guy with a mustache, sit on the edge of his truck with his helmet still on and sob."

"Imagine," I said, "dropping off your three-year-old, not that I have one, but dropping off your three-year-old at day care at nine in the morning and finding out at two in the afternoon that there's been a fire, then realizing at three that your kid has been burned to death. How are you ever supposed to get over that?"

Likewise, imagine racing with your pregnant wife to the hospital one morning expecting her to give birth, only to return home alone a few hours later without a thing in your life that even remotely matters? I thought this, but didn't say it. Not the right time.

She shook her head. "I don't even know how I'm going to get through the next couple of days. You know my paper. They're going to want every conceivable angle covered, and all I want to do is go home, lock my apartment door, and be alone."

To the uninitiated, that line would only have stated that she was tired of this story and wanted to get off it as soon as possible. But to the more probing, more perceptive male mind, what it really said was that she lived in an apartment rather than a suburban house, and alone rather than with a husband and a couple of kids. What it said more than anything else was that she was available. What it meant to me was that I was breaking out of my self-imposed funk.

I was standing over her table like a lug, typically unsure what the next move was, when she nodded to the empty chair across from her and said, "Do you have a moment to sit?"

I did, silently. And then we talked. We talked about her paper and about my paper, about how and why we got into the business, about the other big stories we'd covered over the years, about the frustrations of deadline reporting, about how editors never know when to let it go. She asked me about my time in Washington, about my relationship with the president. We drank some wine and then some coffee and one hour turned to two and two to three and finally the bartender walked over and said they were shutting down the lounge. She fixed those eyes on me, those mesmerizing blue eyes, and said, "I feel a little bit better. Tired, but better." And she smiled.

We both got up and walked toward the elevator in silence. Once on board, she pressed the button for three, I pressed four. I moved toward her ever so slightly to see if there was the possibility of a parting kiss. God forbid I do anything more overt. She reacted not at all, so I stopped and abandoned the sketchiest of plans before failure reared its ugly, late night head.

When the door opened for her floor, she turned to me and said, "Goodnight. I'm glad you were there." She looked at me for a long, confident, tired moment and walked off. I mustered only a simple "Nice to meet you."

Suddenly very much alone, I stared down at the floor as the doors squeezed shut. I was staring at the floor when I saw her foot jut between the closing doors, causing them to slide back open. She walked back on, staring at me, probing me. "Do I sound too forward," she asked, pausing right there, almost theatrically, "if I ask you for a good-night kiss?"

I shook my head and put my fingers on her perfect cheeks and kissed her right there on the elevator of the Holiday Inn in Auburn, Maine, at first tentatively, then softly, then a little more passionately. As it continued, I heard the doors shut behind her and felt the elevator begin moving up and remember wishing that I was staying on the top floor of a high-rise hotel, and not just for the free breakfast and evening cordials that go with being on the club level that I like so much. I put my hand on her soft neck, then ran my fingers through that hair that I wanted to touch all night—hers, not mine—and we kissed again, all of it in loud silence.

The doors chimed and opened for my floor, and not knowing anything better to do, not knowing what I was supposed to do, I got off, kind of awkwardly walking backward with undoubtedly an absurd look on my unbelievably happy and surprised face. She gave me a cute little wave and a timid smile. And walking down the hallway to my room, I thought it amazing that something so good could come out of something so bad. Never for a second did it occur to me that I would someday have to think of it in reverse.

Two weeks later, in a fit of uncharacteristic emotion, I told her I loved her. I told her that I didn't ever think in a million years that I'd ever feel that emotion again, but here it was, in all its warm and wonderful glory, all because of her. Never, did I tell her, would I feel even a droplet of doubt.

I told her that as we were walking Baker in the Public Garden at about eight o'clock on a wintry Sunday morning with nary another human being around to see the majesty of a freshly fallen coat of perfect white snow. She was wearing my shirt, my sweater, my favorite cap—"Cabot's Ice Cream, every day is sundae"—and my jacket, in that inexplicable way that women just assume a man's wardrobe, whereas, if we did the same, we'd be considered perverts.

"Never?" she asked me. She asked me this as she blocked my way, boring her huge eyes into mine.

"Never," I said, and she kissed me, engulfing my head in her mitten-covered hands mashing her lips hard against mine in sharp contrast to the cold all around us. I knew then—I probably knew it before—that I would marry her.

We walked another dozen or so steps when she hit me in the side with a closed fist and said, "Never means never, right?"

"Never means never," I replied. I had no idea then the number of times I would hear those words over the next many months, though if I thought about it a little at the time, I could have easily imagined that they'd become the most comforting words I would ever know.

• • •

Suffice it to say that my mood was not particularly good when I arrived at the corner of Beacon and Charles streets on prestigious Beacon Hill to meet my real estate broker. But Julie Morris, God love her, was there to make it better.

On the phone, she sounded perfectly pleasant, professional, knowledgeable about the market. In person, when I met her that morning for the first time, I noticed that she was, I don't know, about nine feet tall, six feet of which were legs, covered by approximately two feet of a black skirt. A good choice not going with that guy named Horace over at All-State Realtors.

More to the point, she showed me a couple of places that were remarkable only for their price, which was, in a word, outrageous. I feared she might have some false assumption that because I was well-known around town, that I was also rich, which I'm decidedly not. Anyway, buying property in Boston is like purchasing a diamond—no one knows exactly what they're doing, and there is absolutely no chance of achieving perfection, the only goal being not to get completely screwed.

The third place I liked before we even went inside, first because she let me know the price, which was much more in my range, and second because it was situated in a stunning turn-of-the-century—the last century, by the way—brick townhouse on the flat of Beacon Hill, just a couple of blocks from the Charles River and the Public Garden—two places where I often walked with Baker.

We went inside to an elegant though understated lobby, with mail and assorted catalogs resting on a nice antique buffet. She unlocked the only door on the parlor level and we stepped inside.

Seeing a house or an apartment for the first time is like coming face to face with a blind date. You know immediately, within about three seconds, whether it's wrong. You may not know for another thirty or forty years if it's right.

This place passed the first test, and then some. The living room, with huge bay windows overlooking Brimmer Street, had soaring ceilings and elaborate bright white moldings set off against dramatic bluish-gray walls. Someone obviously still lived here, and the furniture, set around a marble fireplace, was big and soft and comfortable, though easy and clean to the eye. The antique rug was a rich navy blue and burgundy.

"It's only been on the market for a couple of days, and I don't imagine it's going to last," Julie said, locking the door behind her.

She added, reading from a sheet of notes, "It's a short-term, furnished rental right now, and the current tenant is due to be out in a few days, so that's not going to be a problem. It's available to close as soon as anyone wants it."

As she spoke, I was already wandering back to the kitchen, which was in the middle of the apartment, with its own bay window complete with a window seat looking out over a side courtyard filled with red and yellow tulips.

"You can see the modern appliances, all stainless, oversized refrigerator, built-in microwave."

As I walked out of the kitchen, I heard her voice trailing off and saw her out of the corner of my eye approach the refrigerator and look at some photographs stuck on the door with a magnet.

In the back of the apartment, the bedroom was big and bright, its windows rising from floor to ceiling with what agents call a "river glimpse"—a snippet of the Charles in the distance. A pair of women's jeans was tossed on the bed and some running shoes on the floor, and the dresser was filled with black-and-white snapshots set in an eclectic array of frames.

"Jack, um, do you have any questions?"

I turned toward Julie because her voice sounded different, halting. She stood in the bedroom door with her arms folded over her clipboard. She looked at me as if I had just done something wrong, which perhaps in all my self-pity, I had.

"How flexible do you think they are on the asking price?" I asked.

"I don't know," she replied, distant, almost absent. She continued to stand in the door looking at me as I wandered about the bedroom drinking in the mood of the place. There was something familiar about it all, something soothing. Maybe it was the sunlight or the colors on the wall or just the fact that it represented someplace permanent, an antidote to the vagabondish existence I'd had for the past few months.

"Jack," Julie said, "have you seen this place before?"

Her voice was higher now, somewhat nasally. She still stood in the doorway. I still prowled the room.

"I don't think so," I said. "Why do you ask?"

She walked over to the dresser, slowly, and looked at the photographs, picking one up in her hand. I wandered into the bathroom to finish my tour.

When I came out, she said, "You're sure?"

"Positive. Why?"

She had a frame in her hand and held it toward me. "Because your picture is on the bureau." She paused, looking at me. "And on the refrigerator."

I grabbed the photograph out of her hand and sure enough, there I was, posing with Baker on the front steps of my old apartment on Commonwealth Avenue, where I lived when I was married. I had an absolutely ridiculous smile on my face. Baker had a tennis ball in his mouth. I couldn't help but think for a moment that we were a pretty good-looking pair.

I quickly walked out to the kitchen and looked on the refrigerator. There we were, me and Elizabeth, standing outside the Albergo del Sole on the Piazza de Pantheon in Rome, during a quick getaway weekend early last fall. I vividly recalled the scene. An old Italian woman in a black cape was shooting the picture for us. I was whispering in Elizabeth's ear what on film looked to be my deepest, most heart felt emotions. That's partly right. I was telling her I couldn't wait to get her into bed, and she was telling me—smiling for the camera—that I had better hope she was in the mood.

She was, by the way.

No matter. I began to shake and feel nauseous. I flung open the closet doors and rifled through the hanging clothes. There was my favorite black suit of hers, next to my favorite skirt, next to the silk tank top I bought her at a Newbury Street boutique to wear to the theatre one night a year before.

"Shit," I said, not loudly, not even firmly. Just resigned.

All this time, Julie stood there watching me. Eventually, she asked, "Are you alright?"

"It's my ex-girlfriend's apartment." That didn't exactly answer her question, though maybe it did.

She held both her hands to her perfectly formed chest and said, "Oh my God, Jack, I'm so sorry."

"Not an issue," I said, still looking in the closet, not really meaning it. And me being only human, and humans being what they are, I cast a fresh eye around the room looking for anything male, any sign of even occasional cohabitation. I walked into the bathroom again, this time searching for a razor. But nothing. A single toothbrush in the holder, only makeup on the vanity. Elizabeth was a woman living very much alone, which for a variety of reasons, made me feel better.

Julie walked out of the bedroom, I assume to give me a little privacy. I looked at the photographs again, at the happiness spilling across my features, but I didn't think about what a wonderful time that had been in my life, I only thought about how it all ended, how so much seemed to be coming to a premature close these days. My relationship with Elizabeth: over. My wife: dead. My newborn daughter: dead. My parents: dead. And now throw in the publisher of *The Boston Record* who helped make my career. Standing in the bedroom of an ex-girlfriend, to whom I was once on the verge of proposing, my overriding feeling was one of utter loneliness.

The last time I saw Elizabeth was on the Saturday afternoon that I accused her of having an affair. We had been distant the prior few weeks, and my worries had blurred into suspicions, and perhaps my suspicions served as a convenient excuse—an excuse for my newfound guilt, for my sadness over leaving Katherine, my wife, behind, for being more elastic than my conscience was willing to allow. I had gone out a month before and bought a diamond engagement ring, and with that ring safely hidden in a pair of old sweat socks in my top bureau drawer, our entire relationship began to unhinge.

One morning I came home from walking the dog and saw that she had forgotten to log off her computer, and on her email account I saw note after note from Travers@aol.com, so I opened one. It was from Lt. Detective Luke Travers, and it was to finalize plans to meet for a drink.

In the next note he thanked her and wrote about what a great time he had. In the next one he proposed getting together again. After that he mentioned how he could never talk to his own wife the way he could talk to her. And on they went, a bad cliché waiting to ruin a life.

Or perhaps I had ruined it already. I don't know.

Either way, I got dizzy as I was reading them, so dizzy I couldn't see the words on the screen, but I knew what they meant. I loved Elizabeth, even if I sometimes doubted whether I was ready to have her, or maybe I doubted whether I should be ready even if I was. I wanted to have children with her, someday. I wanted to grow old with her and live and joke and laugh as if we owned the entire world. And yet my history nagged and here she was in the present running around with a married cop having a pathetic, seedy affair. She was probably with him that very minute, a thought that caused me to pick up the keyboard and smash it on the desk. And then I sat on the couch, our couch, thought about Katherine and the baby that we never had, and I cried.

When she walked into our apartment, I asked her to sit. I calmly explained that the game was up, that I knew she was having an affair, that our relationship was over and that I wanted her to leave. If she needed money, I'd give her money. If she wanted the furniture, she could have the furniture. I just wanted her out of my life.

"Jack," she said, her face more panicked than angry, "you're wrong. You're absolutely wrong —"

"Are you sleeping with this guy?" I yelled.

"Jack, I'm not having an affair, but we have some real problems."

She made a move to come sit next to me, to touch me. I pulled away and she flinched back in shock.

"Don't fucking lie."

"I'm not, Jack. But we have problems."

No—but. No—but. No—but. The words, the brutal softness of the denial, punctured my already splintered heart.

"You have it wrong," she said, trying to compose herself amid her tears.

But I didn't. I knew I didn't. I knew I didn't because this is what I did for a living. I looked into people's eyes, even big gorgeous ones that I loved more than anything in life, and I saw either truth or I saw lies. And here in my own living room with my own girlfriend on an absurdly hot Saturday afternoon in the middle of an endless July, I saw nothing but lies. My life, as I knew it, as I loved it, was over. Again.

"Get the hell away from me," I seethed. "And get out."

I leaned forward in the chair with my arms on my knees and my hands on the back of my bowed head so she couldn't see me cry. I sat there in utter silence, wondering what was going to happen next.

"You're wrong, Jack."

I ignored her.

"You're wrong." She was crying, almost hysterical. I could barely understand her words, they were so soaked by tears. "Wrong. Wrong."

My head stayed down. I continued to ignore her.

Eventually, I heard her get up and walk back to the bedroom. I heard her fumbling around, crying, wheezing. Then there was a stale, stiff silence, until finally I heard the sound of her overnight bag being zipped, soft, yet it seemed to crash through the still apartment like cannon fire.

She walked back out into the living room. I heard her kneel down and hug the dog, then I heard her quaking in tears as she stood near me.

"I love you, Jack," she said, softly, her nose all stuffed and her voice unsteady. It would have made my heart break if it wasn't broken already.

"Go," I said softly, never looking up.

And she did. I heard her walk to the door and slowly open it. She was convulsing. It sounded like she was leaning against the wall, maybe with her head tucked in her arms, and the door stayed open for several long seconds. Then I heard it softly shut, and the dog came walking back toward me and sprawled out at my feet with a groan, his eyes wide open looking at mine.

Tears were rolling down my face and onto the floor as I wiped my palms across my cheeks, half expecting her to walk back through the door, wondering if she did, what I'd do.

Her fault. My fault. Our fault. Or maybe it was just my life, my destiny, to say goodbye, again and again and again.

I stared back at the dog in the stultifying silence.

"Never means never, right?" I whispered. And then I broke down in another storm of quiet tears.

I carefully placed the vacation photograph I was holding back on the dresser and took a long, deep breath, all those images from all those pictures washing over my mind like foamy waves on the Cape Cod shore where her parents used to have a weekend home. I mumbled, "How did you make such a mess of things?" I think I was talking to Elizabeth, but maybe I was talking to myself, given that I was the only one in the room. I looked at the floor for a moment and halfheartedly corrected myself: "How did we make such a mess of things?" I ran my hands across my stricken face, took one last look around her bedroom, and walked down the hallway to the living room, where Julie was pretending to be reading sheets from her listing book.

"You all set?" she asked me, sympathetically.

"All set," I said with a pathetic attempt at a smile. "I've got to run to the office. I'll give you a call in the next couple of days and see about looking at a few more places."

And with that, it was time to answer a couple of nagging questions from the recent past.

twelve

Six Years Earlier

WHEN THE FIRST OF the network affiliates, WBZ-TV, declared Lance Randolph the winner in his first race for governor, the cheers and chants in the Copley Plaza ballroom were so thunderous that they shook the gold-plated chandeliers above, so infectious that they spread to the fifth floor hotel suite, where Randolph sat glued to the television surrounded by family, aides, and friends.

"Ran-dolph Two! Ran-dolph Two! Ran-dolph Two!"

"Alright already," Randolph said, lifting himself up off a suede-covered wing chair, the smile on his handsome face so broad it could have spread from Boston to the Berkshires.

"Ran-dolph Two! Ran-dolph Two! Ran-dolph Two!"

They were screaming it throughout the cavernous ballroom. They were shouting it in the living room of the presidential suite. His wife was yelling it. His two young ponytailed daughters in their matching velvet dresses were squealing it. Even the kitchen staff in the basement were hollering it, the words echoing off the pots and pans that hung above the industrial stoves.

He stood in the middle of the room trying to quell the small crowd. His wife nuzzled him on the forehead and whispered into his ear, "Congratulations, governor. You're the most decent man I know." His mother pecked him on his cheek and told him in that patently plain way of hers, "You've made me the proudest old lady in the world." Before emotion completely overcame him, he shook a few more hands and shuffled off toward the bathroom to regain his trademark cool.

Randolph Two.

The first Randolph, Governor Bertram J. Randolph, was dead, killed a year before in the most mundane of gubernatorial events—the dedication of a state-funded computer laboratory at an inner-city high school in Roxbury, the most crime-ridden neighborhood of Boston.

At the end of the ceremony, complete with a school marching band, a gang of cheerleaders and a stumbling introduction from an obsessively nervous principal, the governor was led out a side door to meet some of the construction workers who had just finished building the new wing the day before. They stood in a straight line, their hard hats gleaming in the morning sun, like a military unit presenting itself for inspection. The old man, a political institution in Massachusetts, filed down the line, shaking and glad-handing and joking as he so often did. At the end, he turned, gave a long, wide wave, and walked around a construction trailer to his awaiting sedan.

When he got to within about ten yards of his car, a student with stringy, shoulder-length hair and a long white coat—it looked, in some strange way, like he had just strolled over from biology class—walked toward him, earnestly calling out—"Hey, governor."

Randolph smiled, turned, and approached him. The air was filled with dust, the dirt beneath his feet grooved with the tracks of industrial tires. When he was about fifteen feet away, a mere free throw, the kid pulled a semiautomatic machine gun from inside his long coat. He fired not at Randolph, but to his right, at the lone State Police trooper who drove the governor on his official duties. The officer, just forty-four years old, crumbled to the ground, his grayish-blue uniform covered in widening circles of deep red blood.

Then the boy took direct aim at the governor. An airplane flew overhead, but between the student and the politician, there was a long moment of agonizing, excruciating silence. When he pulled the trigger, he didn't just fire once or twice, but what the coroner eventually determined was thirteen times in all, each bullet tearing through Randolph's flesh and exploding into either bone or organ. When the ambulance raced across city streets and over sidewalks a few minutes later heading for the Boston Medical Center, the paramedics inside already knew they were carrying a corpse, not a man.

The kid, a straight-A student named Denny Bogle, placed the long barrel of the gun against the roof of his mouth and pulled the trigger, dead, his own executioner. Another school shooting in a nation decreasingly stunned by them, but this one an assassination as well.

The only man spared in the outburst was the governor's eldest child, Lance Randolph, the Suffolk County district attorney. He was also his father's most trusted adviser, and as such, often accompanied the governor to various speeches and appearances around the Boston area—father and son, a political dynasty in the making.

Lance Randolph, the next day's *Record* reported, stood in the middle of the dirt patch when the first shots were fired. During that long moment of silence when the shooter took aim at his father, Randolph bolted toward the governor, screaming "No! No!" He dove on top of his father, draping his own body over the older man's, but it was too late. One of the paramedics told a television reporter, "We had to pry the younger Mr. Randolph off the governor. He was in some sort of trance or daze, like he was in shock, and wouldn't get up on his own."

Randolph stared hard into the bathroom mirror. His face looked gaunt, the result of a year of hard, nonstop campaigning. But his eyes, his famous blue eyes, still did their youthful dance, and his body, lean from his time on the road, was that of someone two decades younger.

"You deserve this," he whispered into the mirror, the freshly splashed cold water dripping down his face. Louder, he told himself, "You deserve it. You won it. It's yours."

He snuck from the bathroom to the bedroom to towel his face off and change his shirt for his victory speech downstairs. It was there he saw Robert Fitzgerald, the regal columnist for *The Boston Record*, sitting on the edge of his bed staring intently at a television correspondent reporting amid the whoops and screams of the ballroom five flights below.

"Natalie, it is utter pandemonium here," the reporter was saying in an exaggerated scream, a group of Randolph supporters behind him waving signs in no particular rhythm.

"Well, Robert, we did it, me and you," Randolph said, his tone familiar and casual. "We got the governorship back. Your words. My genes. And some great policies, too. Now it's time to see what we do with it."

Randolph buttoned his white, monogrammed shirt and looked at Fitzgerald earnestly, awaiting congratulations or an acknowledgement or any sort of reply. Fitzgerald returned the gaze and said, flat, "You feel good?"

Randolph squinted at him for a moment, perplexed at the point, the underlying meaning of the question. He shook his head and said, "I do feel good. I miss the old man. I wish he were here tonight giving the victory speech, not me. But this is the best thing that a son can do to honor his father's work and memory and love."

He paused, and asked, "You think I'm wrong?"

The sounds of bedlam blared relentlessly from the television set—horns and yells and excited kids in their twenties shouting at reporters that this was the greatest night of their lives. On the other side of the closed bedroom door was a more restrained purr of revelry, but revelry nonetheless.

"No, you're not wrong," Fitzgerald replied, still sitting, his eyes on the television. "You did what anyone would do, and probably should do."

Then he added, "It's just sad for me."

Randolph said, "It's a bittersweet night for you and me both. I keep thinking, what would the old man say in his speech? What would he tell me to say if he ever saw me elected governor. Then I see his blood. I see it spattered on the cuffs of my shirt. I feel it dripping on the backs of my hands."

He stopped, regrouping, collecting his emotions.

Fitzgerald finally stood up from the bed. Randolph tightened his blue-striped tie, working his hand up the silk to secure it at his neck.

The television became quiet, then flipped to a panel of analysts in the studio, one of whom was saying, "It's not quite the Kennedys yet, but the tragedy and the passage of power and the overwhelming popularity sure smacks of a dynastic development tonight, a little bit of history. I'd start watching those young Randolph daughters to see which one has the common touch."

Fitzgerald extended his hand out toward Randolph, who shook it, then moved closer into a soft embrace. They patted each other's backs, and Fitzgerald said, "Congratulations, Lance. Go down there and make your father proud."

"I will," he said. "I will. And I want to make you proud as well."

thirteen

I'VE ALREADY SHOWN THROUGH my journey down to Florida that one of the golden rules of good newspaper reporting is to show up, not call up—a journalistic variation of Woody Allen's 80 percent rule, though I think Woody may have underestimated by a good 10 to 15 percentage points. I can say without a moment's hesitation that Hank Sweeney wouldn't have opened up to me nearly as wide as he did if I had simply called him on the phone and asked him questions from afar.

I bring this up as a proverbial bright idea struck me and I pulled a U-turn in my Alfa Romeo on my way back to the *Record* newsroom from my real estate appointment. Instead, I headed toward the state medical examiner's office, where I suspected there might be some answers to a few questions that hadn't yet been asked, most especially, what did the toxicology test on John Cutter say? If there was ever a time when I could parlay sympathy into pure information, it was now, when my paper and its founding family were in the forefront of the daily news.

I had roughly a million things clawing at my brain and vying for my time right now, to wit, the Randolph story, the future of the newspaper, the empty publisher's suite, the guy who had tried to kill me in Florida and where he went, the murder of Paul Ellis, and the nagging mystery of John Cutter. When there's so much going on that nothing gets done, I find it better to just take them one at a time, and the one I'd take here would be the good Mr. Cutter.

The M.E. resides in an ancient office building in a dreary downtown neighborhood known as Government Center—dreary even by government standards, ancient even by Boston standards, which means pretty damned ancient, hazardously ancient, falling down ancient, corpses rotting in broken refrigerator lockers ancient. But that's an entirely different story, one I already did a while back.

Inside, I asked to speak to the chief spokesman, the unfortunately named—and I'm not making this up—Josh Lyer. I once knew a judge in Connecticut named Aaron Ment—Judge Ment, to those in his courtroom. Baker's groomer is named Cher. My electrician is a guy by the name of Billy Current. I could go on, but I won't.

Regarding Lyer, we had a great deal of contact—he might say excessive contact, dating back a year or so when I reported a three-part series on the unsanitary conditions of the autopsy rooms. I found cockroaches running over the bodies, rats drinking blood spilled from corpses, human tissue discarded in haphazard fashion. We could well be enemies, Josh and I, but I did what no journalism program would think to train a reporter to do: I told him on the eve of the series almost exactly what the first part would say, so he could then use the information to brace his boss. Rather than becoming angry, he appreciated the favor I extended. After the scathing series ran, the state legislature gave the office an additional $7.5 million to clean up the mess and hire additional staff. My pal Josh even called me to say thanks. Some might say he suffered from Stockholm Syndrome. I just said you're welcome.

We settled into his musty old office looking out on, well, absolutely nothing but a brick wall. He had a metal desk with four or five Rolodexes on top, a smattering of reports which I assumed represented the recently deceased, and the standard-issue cup of pens and pencils. Shoot me if I ever have one of those on my desk. Actually, forget the shoot me part. That's not really funny anymore.

"So what in the hell are you doing back here at the state morgue?" he asked me. He had a kind of resigned look in his eyes that people get when they work with the dead rather than the living, as if he had a better understanding of our ultimate destiny than the rest of us.

"Good question," I replied. "The paper's starting to feel like a morgue currently, so I figured I'd cut out the middleman."

He didn't laugh. Hey, no one bats a thousand percent at the comedy game. But I deserve to be cut a little bit of slack these days. You think for a second that Lyer has ever done the underwater breast stroke in a Florida swamp?

I said, "I'm trying to get my hands on some of the reports surrounding John Cutter's death and was hoping you might be able to help me out." Direct, factual, easy.

Lyer cocked his head slightly to the left and asked, "That was about five years ago, right?"

I nodded.

"Might be on the computer," he said as he rolled his chair toward the keyboard and pecked away for a moment.

"John Ellis Cutter?" he asked as he bore in on the screen.

It felt inexplicably strange to hear his full formal name said aloud these many years later. "Yes," I replied.

He pressed some more buttons and watched as some information spilled across his screen.

I regarded his features for a moment—fair-skinned, blond, to the point of appearing washed out, as if he had no discernible features at all. Put it this way, his hair and forehead were the same color. I'd guess he was about forty years old, but could be one of those ageless guys— and I don't mean that in a good way—who was as easily thirty as he was fifty. If boring had a face, it might well be that of Josh Lyer, and if it had a style of dress, it would probably be the thin navy blazer and the tired gray slacks he was wearing that very day.

Lyer said, reading from his computer, "Okay, died on April 24— that's today—at his condominium at the Four Seasons Hotel, sixty-one years old at the time, determined by assistant medical examiner Justin Cobain of this office to be caused by a heart attack."

He looked at me to see if this was everything I needed, and added, "This should have all been on the death certificate, I believe."

"Yeah, it was," I said. "I was wondering if you had any individual test results in there."

He turned his attention back to the computer screen. He was a tidy man, obsessively neat, even, most comfortable dealing with the types of finite numbers—heart weight, blood alcohol content, and the like—upon which doctors of death usually base their findings.

"Like what," he said, matter-of-factly while he scrolled down the computer and brought his face closer to the screen. "You want the kidney sizes, the stomach contents, the eye dilation measurements?"

I hesitated, not wanting to play my trump so soon, but I didn't see much of a choice. I said, "I was wondering what the toxicology tests say."

"Ah, the toxicology tests," he said, giving me a painful W.C. Fields imitation. He seemed to be having a little bit of fun, which struck me as ghoulish. You work in the coroner's office, you take fun wherever you can find it, I guess. "Let's take a look."

He continued to scroll down the screen, peering hard and silently at the words and numbers. You could have heard a liver drop. Luckily we didn't.

After what mystery writers—and bad newspaper reporters—might call a pregnant pause, he kept his eyes fixed on the monitor and said, "I don't see any toxicology test results." He looked across the desk at me and asked, "Do you know for a fact that there were tests done?"

I hesitated again before saying, "Well, I just kind of assumed so."

He looked back at his screen. "No, I don't see it. That doesn't mean for certain that the tests weren't done. They could be in his file and just weren't entered into the computer."

One of the first things any young reporter learns in the newspaper business is that there's always another hoop to jump through before certitude can be reached, always another file someplace else, always another person to call. If you're looking for a John Jones and there are nine of them in the phone book and one has an unlisted number, rest assured that's the one you need.

"Where's the file? Can we get a look at it?" Notice the use of the word *we,* which is by no means an accident. One of the more effective tools of the trade is to subscribe others in your needs, especially others in a position to help, such that they'll see personal benefit in finding information for you.

Lyer grimaced in thought as he stared across the room. "I think they're in the basement. It depends how long we keep them here before we ship them over to the state archive."

He abruptly got up and said, "I might as well go check it out."

"Can I join you?" I asked, standing up.

His albino-like features flashed darker with indecision. He wavered for a fraction of a second. Then he said, "Sure, c'mon."

We both strode out of his office and onto the rickety old elevator at the end of the dank hallway, then down to the musty basement. If the rest of the upstairs was as bad as this, just imagine what the cellar was like. The lighting was poor to the point of being bleak, the walls bare concrete, the floors unadorned by even so much as a braided mat. I kept looking for rats, and because of that, saw little wisps of movement out of the corners of my eyes.

We walked down a warren of hallways and ended up in front of a room blocked off by a floor-to-ceiling chain-link fence. Lyer fingered through his key ring, found the right key and opened the metal door. We both stepped inside. He walked back out and over to a nearby wall, where he flicked on a set of fluorescent lights.

As the lights slowly brightened with a pointed hum, I saw that we were in a sort of cage-like place where manila files lined several rows of shelves all along the periphery and in a couple of rows in the middle. The odor was of mold and old paper, of history. Every file represented another death, and since they were here in the coroner's office, a family tragedy of some sort, with anguish and tears and years of inevitable regret.

None of which seemed to mean a damned thing to Josh Lyer. He had a pen pressed against his lips as he mumbled, "John Ellis Cutter. John Ellis Cutter. I'll bet it's aisle four."

He walked ahead of me into a long, dark, narrow row of files that looked to be arranged by date of death. You go through life marked by a birthday. You go through eternity marked by a death day. Go figure.

He rifled his hand along some files, then pulled one out and opened it up. As he did, I saw the typewritten sticker placed on the cover: John Ellis Cutter. I got a chill on the back of my neck.

He read it in silence in the dim light of aisle four in the cellar of the medical examiner's building while I stood there like a statue, waiting, wondering, hoping. For what, I didn't know, but I didn't know much these days, which was the essential problem, my core dilemma.

Finally, he looked up at me like a doctor holding a lung x-ray. "It doesn't say here that there were any toxicology tests done. That's why there was nothing on the computer."

"If tests were ordered, would that order be listed there?"

I was trying to seek information while not revealing what I already knew.

He flipped through the few sheets of paper that were in the surprisingly thin file and said, "I don't see any orders for tests here, but if there was an order, I can't even guarantee that it would be in here."

"Where else would they be?"

"Tough to say."

A classic, bureaucratic answer, representative of a classic bureaucracy. Even the dead get burdened by the absurdities of government.

"Are the crime scene—I mean, death scene—photographs in there?"

My mind flipped back to Hank Sweeney sitting at that cheap little table in his tidy side yard in the grotesquely hot Florida sun, telling me casually about all the evidence he had collected in his whirlwind tour of John Cutter's apartment.

Lyer looked over at me sharply, his eyes uncharacteristically bright even in the gloom.

He asked, "You know that there were pictures taken?"

"I just assume. Isn't that standard?"

"Sometimes, sometimes not. There is no standard." He looked through the papers again and said, "I don't see any pictures in here. I can't tell if there were any taken."

"You mind if I look at the file?"

He hesitated, looking from me to the folder, and back to me, before he held it reluctantly in front of him. "I guess you're not just press, but almost kin in this case."

I gingerly opened the folder and came across the death certificate, which stated that John Ellis Cutter died of cardiac arrest. I flipped that over and saw another sheet that listed all the autopsy results—weights of vital organs and the like. I skimmed down with my index finger toward the bottom. Where it listed, "Toxicology results," there was only white space. I flipped that sheet and there was only one other page that had Justin Cobain's signature and the time and date of the autopsy.

In the entire file, no mention of suicide, no reference to foul play. Maybe John Cutter's death was as straightforward as it seemed. Still, why weren't the tests done as Hank Sweeney ordered?

I handed it back to him and asked, "Do you guys hold onto the actual evidence anywhere else?"

"It's tough to say whether there'd even be any evidence in this case. It was ruled a heart attack, so anything they had they probably just discarded shortly after the autopsy. But when there is evidence to be stored, we keep it"—at this point, he turned and waved the folder toward the entrance to the cage—"in there, in the archive vault. We'll hold onto some stuff in there for twenty years or more."

He said that last sentence with some pride in his voice, though I'll be damned if I could figure out why.

I asked, "You mind if we check in there to see if there's anything worthwhile?"

He immediately shook his head in a self-satisfied, I'm-a-ninth-grade-girl-and-I-sit-in-the-front-row-and-raise-my-hand-all-the-time-because-I-know-all-the-answers kind of way. Why is it that I'm not a violent person, yet I find myself nearly overcome by a strong desire to punch just about everyone I come in contact with lately?

"Can't. Even I'm prohibited from that room without proper clearance. These files are as far as I can go before I have to get authorization from one of the assistant medical examiners. It would be chaos otherwise."

Chaos. Yeah, right. Like a regular Grand Central Station down here with every Tom, Dick, and Jack Flynn coming and going to find out the hidden truths about their publishers' deaths.

"Can we go get authorization?" Even to me, the *we* was starting to fade in its impact.

He turned around and put the file back up on the shelf. I thought about trying to steal it, because it seems like that's what people do in musty archives that are filled with intrigue and a sense of death. But the file was worthless for what it contained, important only for what it didn't say.

"Look, Jack, there's nothing else. This looks to be a cut-and-dried case of a death by natural causes—a heart attack. I don't think there was any evidence to store, and if there was, we certainly wouldn't have held onto it for this long. This should all be good news for you, no?"

I didn't say anything, pondering, as I was, how to get into that evidence locker.

Lyer said, "I've got to get back to work."

Liar.

We headed out of the cage. He locked it up and flipped the lights out. Then we walked silently back down the concrete hall, to the elevator. We both got out at the lobby level, and I thanked him profusely for his time. I casually asked if there happened to be a side or back exit that I could use. Well, all right, there's really no way to ask that question casually, but he did me the favor of ignoring the obvious and directed me to an employee entrance in the rear. Surrounded by death and nagged by the memory of the mysterious gunman the prior morning, I had a strange feeling about what was to come.

Outside, in a morbid alley where I suspected hearses often called in the middle of the night, I still had the odor of deteriorating documents in my hair and skin. What I didn't have was any better sense of what had happened in John Cutter's apartment at the Four Seasons on this very day five years before.

Or maybe I did and just didn't know it yet.

fourteen

The dining room of the University Club was filled with the clink of fine china and the gentle chatter of the working rich as I glided through the front doors and up to the bar, where Lou, the nation's foremost mixologist, was ready to fulfill my libational desires. This being a lunch, I ordered a Coke.

"Sorry about your publisher," Lou said, sliding me a tumbler filled with ice and soda. "I know you two were tight."

He knows a lot more than that. Lou, all five feet and nine inches of him, knows my likes, my dislikes, my ambitions, my fears, my desires, and my secrets. Not that I've ever told him. Lou, he just knows. It's what he does, which is what makes him as great as he is.

"Thank you," I replied.

"You have a visitor waiting for you," he said, nodding toward the end of the bar. With a bemused look, he added, "I told him cell phones are banned in here, but he ignored me."

I walked down to the far end, and of course, there was Mongillo, his enormous girth squeezed tightly into a booth as he said to someone on the other end of the line, "It's either you or the other guy who's going down. You decide."

He saw me coming and abruptly said into the phone, "Gotta go."

To me, "Hey, Fair Hair. Christ, you smell like shit. You moonlighting at a funeral home?"

Kind of, but I didn't feel like getting into it right now. I sat on the other side of the booth. Lou came out from behind the bar and handed us a couple of lunch menus. I said to Mongillo, "Tell me you have something."

"Issue one, Lance Randolph. I've been on the telephone all morning with every district attorney in Massachusetts. A couple of them tell me they were surprised—meaning, suspicious—when Randolph's gubernatorial campaign put out word that he had the best prosecution record in the state. The truth is, they just didn't think he was all that good. Now they're not saying he was bad—just not the best."

Lou returned and we both ordered burgers, medium. Mongillo asked for a glass of pinot noir. Some things in life you just can't figure.

He continued, "Randolph jumped so far ahead so fast in the polls that these guys felt they couldn't call him into question, because most of them are Democrats, and they didn't want to look like they were challenging their own candidate. And as you've learned, these rates are hard to quantify."

Don't I know it. It took several weeks of sometimes arduous, but usually tedious work, poring over court documents, annual reviews, and state records, trying to put some semblance of a conviction rate together. Bizarrely, there is no clearinghouse for the statistics. What I had might be good enough to put in print, but the numbers still felt soft to me. I wanted anecdotes and quotes to support my cause.

I said, "We need to put something in the newspaper by the end of the week. It's not an option to sit on this."

Mongillo nodded. His cell phone rang, and not just any ring but a Hungarian marching song. Half the dining room looked over at us in disgust, as if I'd just cracked a lewd Pilgrim joke. "Turn that damned thing off," I whispered.

"Sure. And take this knife here and disembowel me."

He punched a button on the phone and it went silent. He said, "We'll be in the paper. Let's start to sketch something out at the computer today and see how fast we can put it together. Randolph have any clue this is coming?"

I shook my head. "I haven't asked him about it yet, or any of his people, but word might have gotten back to him from one of the courthouses where I've been researching."

The burgers arrived with Lou's usual aplomb. Mongillo lovingly spread mustard, mayonaisse, and ketchup on his roll and his fries. I bit into mine plain.

He said before taking his first bite, "Issue two, Terry Campbell. I did a full clip search on him. Serious guy. Rich guy. Conservative guy. Some people say a deadly guy. He plays for keeps, that's for sure. Ask the union out in Columbus. According to the stories, he bought the paper one day, and the head of the pressmen's union was found dead of an alleged suicide the next day. The union guy was a tough son of a bitch who planned to fight Campbell tooth and nail, and then he's gone."

Mongillo started in on his food. It looked like he was holding one of those little White Castle burgers, his hands are so big.

I said, "Did you check his political and 501C contributions?"

"No, bro, I'm so fucking new at this game that unless I have a nationally acclaimed superstar like yourself telling me exactly when I should remove my hands from my sweaty balls and precisely what numbers to dial on the phone, I'm liable to just sit there like a drooling goddamned idiot until dinnertime, at which point I'm more than fully equipped to handle myself."

I mean, is that really necessary?

I chose to ignore the quiet outburst, and asked, "What'd you find?"

He leaned over the table. "I'm not sure yet. He likes contributing money, Terry does, mostly to the typical lineup of right-of-center groups you might expect—the NRA, the Christian Coalition, National Right to Life. He gives big chunks, fifty thousand and one hundred thousand at a time. He contributes to politicians as well, mostly arch-conservative gubernatorial and senatorial candidates around the country—"

I cut him off, asking, "I assume nothing to Randolph, right?"

"Shit no."

"Clay Hutchins?"

"No again. Hutchins is a mainstream Republican. Campbell is somewhere far off to the right."

I asked, "You think there's a story there on Campbell as a fringe figure? That wouldn't play well in Boston, the publisher of the city's most significant newspaper coming from the far right."

Mongillo chewed for a moment, sipped his wine, and replied, "Yeah, but I don't think someone who gives to the NRA and the National Right to Life can be labeled fringe, right? Rational people differ on these issues."

He was right. "Well, who else did he contribute to? Anyone, anything, here in Massachusetts?"

"No political candidates, but records I got from the state attorney general's office show he gave thirty thousand dollars to a small nonprofit group based in the Berkshires called Fight for Life."

I looked at Mongillo and he simply shrugged his enormous shoulders. "I don't know what it is," he said. "I assume it's a pro-life group, but I couldn't find it mentioned in any newspaper clips, and they don't list any disbursements with the A.G.'s office. They've been sanctioned for failing to comply with state reporting laws."

"Fight for Life. Fight for Life. For some reason, it's familiar, but maybe only because it sounds like so many other groups."

We both ate our burgers while the dining room emptied out at the end of another lunch hour, that lunch hour expression not quite covering the duration that most people here took for the elongated meal.

I said, finishing off the last of my hand-cut fries, "Well, we've got to find out about Fight for Life. At the very least, it would be nice to be able to block Campbell from buying the paper. At the very best, it would be nicer to find out if he's connected to Paul's murder."

Mongillo took a last significant gulp of wine as if he was polishing off a cold beer on a hot July afternoon, maybe sitting in box seats at a Sox-Yankees game.

He said, "We will. We will. First let's put Lance Randolph back in our crosshairs."

And with that, we headed back to the *Record* to try to bring order to chaos.

My first call was to Hank Sweeney in the remote outpost of Marshton, Florida. He picked up on about the third ring.

We exchanged niceties, and I told him of my visit to the medical examiner's office, and how there were no toxicology test results, or for that matter, any indication that tests were even ordered or done.

"What?" he hollered, his voice so loud that I had to pull the phone from my ear. His poor wife. She probably just blocked him out at this point in their lives.

"So you're telling me that some little twerp of a deputy coroner disobeyed my direct orders?"

"I'm not sure what I'm telling you. I'm just saying there aren't any results, or none that I could find."

"Let me think about this for a moment. Where you at? I'm going to call you back." With that, he abruptly hung up.

My next call was to an old friend, Adelle Adair, a senior partner with the old-line Boston law firm Horace & Chase. More relevant, Adelle was Governor Randolph's senior prosecutor when he was the Suffolk County district attorney, meaning she was in a position to know things that I wanted to print, specifically about his inflated conviction rate. She'd helped me in the past on various stories, and I went into the conversation with the full expectation that she would help me again. At least that's what I wanted her to think. Journalism, or at least the interviewing part of it, is a mind game.

"Not a chance, Jack. I'm not going there," she replied when I laid out my story. "I can't help."

"Are you telling me I'm wrong?"

"I'm telling you I have a meeting in sixty seconds and have to hang up the phone."

And I'll be damned if that's not exactly what she did. It's becoming an uncivilized world out there in ways too great to fathom and too small to mention.

fifteen

So MAYBE IT BRUSHED up against the pathetic, but as I jumped out of my car in the gravel parking lot at Long Wharf at the end of an extraordinarily long day, I was near frantic to see my dog. Let's face it. I had no wife. I had none of the children that I was expecting to have by now (see above). As of yesterday, I had no publisher. At times like these, you take whatever you can get, and what I could get was Baker. Truth is, I was legitimately thrilled to see him.

I was also thrilled to get out of the musty clothes that I had worn in the coroner's archives—clothes so musty that they caused me to be somewhat an outcast in the newsroom all afternoon as I pounded the telephones with mixed success.

But at Long Wharf the first sign of distress came when there was no sign of distress, meaning my man Baker was neither up on the edge of the boat barking as I came across the lot, nor was he running up the docks to greet me as he usually does when he's been spending the day with Nathan, the old man by the sea who runs the marina.

As I walked down the docks to the boat, the silence was strange and growing stranger with each step. I could hear my own breathing and the creak of the wood beneath me. When I reached the boat, still no Baker. I went downstairs, figuring he might be napping on the bed, but saw nothing. So I walked back down the dock to Nathan's little wharf-side shack and rapped on his door.

Nathan, by the way, is what we New Englanders might call an old salt, a bearded mariner who takes great pains to talk in a Maine accent so thick that it often renders him incomprehensible, which seems just the way he likes it. He's the only guy I know who actually says, "Eyup," which in the Queen's English means, "Yes."

He came to the door in a flannel shirt and a pair of filthy khakis, but more important than that, he came to the door alone. My fear turned to panic.

"Nathan, have you seen Baker around? He's not on the boat."

He studied me for a second as he thought this over. "Well, yeah, I was just with him an hour ago. Last I saw him, he was sleeping on the dock right next to *The Emancipation.*"

"How long ago was that?"

I had heard him say an hour, but wanted him to repeat it, to think about it again to make sure it was right.

He did, and said, "Pretty sure it was an hour, cuz I left him to come inside and watch my National Geographic video here, which is an hour long and is just about ending now."

"Thanks, I'm sure he's around," I said, turning swiftly away and heading back to the boat. I wasn't so sure.

Images—vivid, awful images—filled my mind, images of poor, trusting Baker being shot or stabbed by the intruder who had tried to kill me in the Florida swamp. Or perhaps he was lured into a car or van and driven away, a hostage in some deadly game, the nature or purpose of which I didn't yet understand. Maybe it was innocent. Maybe he was sleeping up in the park or had taken himself for a swim. But I knew that wasn't the case. He never swims without me, and he would never roam away from the boat if he weren't with someone he knew.

I went back to the boat, looked it up and down, inside and out. On deck, I called his name out loudly, the sound of my voice carrying across the black skin of the harbor before disintegrating into the warm hazy night. I called out again, and again, and again, and again, but nothing.

By now, Nathan was walking down the dock with a pair of industrial flashlights in either hand. "The critter's never taken off before," he said as he approached. Then he handed me one of the lights and said, "Here, this'll help."

I took the light and trotted off across the docks to the parking lot. Nathan stayed behind shining a beam into the water beneath the dock. Fact is, I felt far more panicked at that moment than I had ever been in that Florida swamp.

Baker was seven years old—well into middle age, by dog standards, though he acted like anything but, aside from the fact he had injured his back hips in an explosion a couple of years before, which I won't get into now. He ran when he felt like running, walked when he felt like walking, chased squirrels at will, slept often, and he'd look at me like I was an abject idiot if I missed his mealtime by any more than a few minutes.

He was also my very best friend, the only living, breathing creature who had accompanied me through the mourning of my wife, the long, meandering and still ongoing recovery, the joy of meeting Elizabeth, the agony of seeing her go, and always, always, his eyes lit up and his tail wagged at the very sight of me coming through the door. He had one motto in life: Count me in. If I did something, he wanted to do it as well.

By the time I got to the parking lot, I was in a full sprint, though where I was heading, I didn't know. Then suddenly I did. I was heading right toward Baker, who was sprinting across the parking lot toward me. When we met, I leaned down and hugged him hard, too happy to be mad. I saw that he kept looking over his shoulder in that urgent way he sometimes does when he wants me to look as well. So I did.

And in the dusk, walking in our direction at a slow pace, was a strikingly familiar figure—long and lean and confident and elegant and so much more. When she got a few feet closer, she said in her characteristically rhythmic voice, "Hello, Jack. I hope you don't mind."

I straightened up and looked at her square from several feet away, and said in a tone that emanated from that vast emotional acreage somewhere between friendly and aloof, "Hello, Elizabeth." Pause. "You scared me to death. I thought my dog was missing."

"I'm really sorry. The last thing I wanted to do was scare you. When I came down here looking for you, he grabbed his ball and led me toward the park. I just followed. I really am sorry."

I looked down at Baker looking up at me, and I couldn't help but laugh softly to myself. In his dog mind, Elizabeth had probably just come home after an unusually long day at work, and everyone was together again, as they should be.

I leaned down and hugged him one more time, perhaps because I just felt the need to hug someone, and no one else in my present company would do. Elizabeth, still standing just far enough away that I couldn't make out all those features that I knew by heart, said one more time, "Jack, I'm really sorry."

"That's okay."

That was followed by an awkward silence between us. I didn't know what she wanted; she didn't know whether I wanted her here. Finally, she said, "He looks terrific." And then, softly, "And so do you."

"Thanks." I was surprised that my voice suddenly felt weak.

I hadn't seen her since that day I asked her to leave our apartment about nine months ago. We had talked several times by phone after she left, but because we didn't have a lot of things to split up, our contact was almost nil.

More silence hanging in that chasm between us. Then she said, "And I'm really sorry about Paul. I just can't believe it."

I shook my head. She took a step closer, knelt down and scratched the dog's chest. She stood up and said, "And I'm really sorry about the *Record*. That was an incredible story you had today. I can't even imagine the Cutter-Ellis family not owning it. I don't want to imagine the family not owning it. I know how close you were to Paul, how you regarded him, and how he regarded you."

And then, explaining the point of this visit, she added, "I was worried about you, Jack. And yes, despite what you think, I still have a right to worry about you. There's too much going on here for anyone to handle alone. I just wanted to come by and make sure you were okay, and if you're not, to see if I could help. We all need somebody sometimes—even you, even when you refuse to admit it."

Ah, history. It hangs over every thought we think, every word we speak, every action we take. Sometimes, it's good history, compelling us forward with lessons learned. Other times, history sucks. Put me and Elizabeth into the latter category.

To the uninitiated, her visit, her kind words, seemed born of nothing more than loving concern. Think again. In that one little passage, she got in, let me count, one, no two, no three jabs, oblique as they might be. She always accused me of being too independent, of shutting her out, of trying to live my life with an allegiance to someone who had died nearly four years before, mainly, my wife.

I looked down at Baker, not at her, for reasons I can't fully explain. I said, "That's nice of you."

And that line hung out there in the air between us, tinged with both sincerity and sarcasm. Truth is, I'm not sure which way it was meant.

Regarding Elizabeth, she was, in a word, beautiful, and if you'd like more words, try these: gorgeous, elegant, unfailingly sexy, gravity-defying, and in many ways classic. As I've said, she had enormous blue eyes, perfect white teeth, swollen lips, long brown hair that framed a face that could grace the cover of a fashion magazine. She was the type of woman who other women stared at when they passed each other on the street. Men too, most of whom would then shoot me a look of utter, unabashed envy, if not surprise.

Nice perks, all, but no reasons for love. At least that's what I'm supposed to say. What I had loved about the woman was that all her many physical attributes didn't seem to matter to her in the least. She would go days without showering. She would roll in the grass and dirt with the dog. She would bunch her perfect hair in a ponytail or beneath an old baseball cap, preside over a wardrobe made up almost entirely of old (tight) jeans and fraying tee shirts, and barely touch her face with makeup.

She was also one of the smartest, most confident human beings I'd ever met, a straight-ahead writer who could report the living hell out of the news while getting an endless kick out of telling people something they didn't already know, which she did a lot, because people—men and women—liked to tell her things they didn't tell anyone else. She could have easily made a fortune on television, she was that poised, but she recognized the vacuous simplicity of broadcast news and preferred the world of the written word.

That's the good news. On the flip side, she was prone to distended periods of near-maddening aloofness when you—rather, I—couldn't penetrate her exterior with a jackhammer and a team of burly construction workers. Her moods were like the New England weather: if you didn't like it, just wait a minute. And the changes usually came without warning. In some perverse way, it almost added to her allure; there were enough obsequious sycophants out there, male and female, to people an entire life, especially when you've made a national name for yourself by once taking on the president of the United States. She cut a decidedly different figure.

Still, I had learned over the years that aloofness was often about selfishness, and she could be selfish in a world-class kind of way, so I had to ask myself, was she here tonight to selfishly fill some personal void? Or was she genuinely worried about me? More to the point, given her ruthless pursuit of news, was she here to bleed me on Paul's death? Could she be trying to find out what I knew for the benefit of her paper?

That led to another question: Was I happy to see her? Regardless of her motivation, she probably wondered that as much as I did. Actually, the emotions were crashing over me like, well, swamp water. I was physically exhausted from my broken date with death, mentally ravaged by all that was taking place in my life, and here was my ex-girlfriend, walking in from the gloom to check on my emotional sturdiness. I needed someone to tell me what I was supposed to think. So I asked.

"What am I supposed to think?"

She didn't hesitate. She never does. Too confident. "Don't overthink it like you always do, Jack. Just know that someone cares enough about you that she wants to make sure you're not about to lose your mind in all this."

I averted my glance again from her stunning face and stared at my dog, whose face was also stunning but in a different, furrier, more canine kind of way. He kept looking from one of us to the other.

"Look," I said. "I'm exhausted. Somebody tried to shoot me and then drown me about thirty-six hours ago. Tomorrow, I'm going to deliver a eulogy at Paul's funeral. Oh, and this morning, I found myself standing in the middle of your bedroom. So if you'll excuse us, Baker and I will be heading down to the boat to bed."

Let me add here that I wasn't thinking through what I wanted to do, where I wanted this session to go. In fact, my mouth was operating without the typical, often necessary input from my muddled brain. But I did have a vague understanding that by telling her I was in her bedroom that day, when I walked away, I knew I wouldn't be leaving her.

She knew that too. She knows me as well as I know myself. Which is why, as I trudged across the lot toward the docks with an indecisive Baker in hesitant tow, I heard her footsteps fall in behind me. Then I heard her voice ask, "You were in my bedroom?" It wasn't accusatory. It wasn't even incredulous. It was more, almost, amused.

I kept walking; she kept following. Baker now liked this drill.

"I'm looking for a condo. I need to give up the ship, so to speak, next week. The one you're renting is for sale. My realtor took me in there before I realized you were the tenant." Pause, then, "Nice place."

"I don't really like the furniture." Light now, airy, joking. Familiar.

"And you're almost out of toothpaste," I said. Favor returned.

I continued walking toward the boat. She called out, "Do you have any beer?"

"I do," I replied, still without turning around. There's my mouth getting ahead of my mind again.

We both traversed the docks and boarded the boat and Nathan popped up from the other direction and I said, "Nathan, Elizabeth; Elizabeth, Nathan. She thought it would be a good idea to walk the dog without letting anyone know."

"Ah, the ex," he said, shaking her hand. This was getting entirely too bizarre, so I went beneath and pulled out two bottles of Sam Adams Boston Lager. When I came back up and handed her one, Nathan bade us farewell, winked at me on his way out, and left.

We sat across from each other on two teak chairs on the forty-foot boat. She said, crossing her arms close to her body, "Do you have a sweater? It's getting cold out here."

There's that thing with women and men's clothes. So I went back down and retrieved my favorite cotton pullover, navy blue and ribbed. As she put it on, I took a long pull on my beer. I'd be lying if I said she didn't look good in my clothes, and she probably still had half my wardrobe to prove it.

I'd also be lying if I didn't say that I had thought about this moment, this face-to-face encounter, every day for the past few months, hashing and rehashing all the things I wanted her to hear, from my profound disappointment to my so many nights of lonely, relentless hurt to my eventual realization that I just hadn't been ready back then for something as serious as what we had, and that my mind just shut down, maybe defensively, maybe offensively, but I just stopped functioning as part of what we once were.

Instead, I said, "A long day," took another swig of beer, and stared straight up at the star-studded sky. This reticence, this silence, is what it meant to be a man, or at least what it meant to be Jack Flynn. Still, the air felt warmer with her in my presence, like she was some sort of blanket protecting me from the increasingly cold world.

"What do you mean you were shot at?" She sounded concerned.

I told her.

Always the reporter, "What were you doing down in Florida? Don't you have enough going on up here?"

I shook my head. "Long story. Boring story. And a fruitless story." I lied. I think. I hope.

"You called the police, right?" She knows me that well. When I stared out at the black harbor in silence, she looked at me with alarm and said, "C'mon, Jack, someone tried to kill you. Tell me you called the police."

I explained to her that if I took the time to report the incident to the Florida Police, I would have been stuck down in Florida while I had too much work to do back in Boston. It wasn't a viable option at the time.

"So have you reported it to anyone up here."

Yet again, my mouth got away from me. "Well, the guy running the case up here is Travers, and I have no particular desire to go to him with any of my problems and no particular sense that he has the ability to solve them."

That line, and that line of thought, deflated any resuming familiarity between us. She became quiet, looking down at her beer, thinking God knows what. I was thinking of Travers and her, which was like being hit in the face with a cold cloth—wrapped around a brick.

I looked at her carefully and she returned the gaze. Travers. Fucking Travers.

Nothing means forever anymore. Never doesn't mean never.

She was here, but she wasn't mine. She was sitting inches from me, this woman whose body and mind I knew better than any other, but I couldn't have her, mostly because I wouldn't allow myself to have her for reasons that were too complex to fully grasp in my current state. This only fueled my latent anger.

She said to me, obviously trying to change the subject, "You saw the gossip item about Robert this morning, I assume."

"A cheap shot," I quickly replied.

She asked, "You sure?"

I was surprised by the question. She used to agree with me that Fitzgerald was the victim of jealousy. Before I could answer, she said, "I'm the one who researched that story. I was trying to do a follow-up with their real names. Jack, I don't think those people exist."

By now, my skull was pounding, as if somebody—maybe that guy in the Florida swamp—was taking the business end of a crowbar and gradually whacking it against the back of my brain. Images of Travers kept flashing in my mind.

"So you fed that item to the gossip column?"

"It's legit."

I shook my head and laughed a shallow, humorless laugh. My mind was now ahead of my mouth, and I said with great certainty and unmistakable finality, "Thanks for stopping by. Time for you to go."

She's a beauty, this woman, as ambitious as she is gorgeous, which made me wonder anew what the hell was she doing here?

I got up. She did, too. She pursed her lips, and her features seemed to sag as she massaged my face with her eyes. She stared at me for a long moment, silently, such that I could see the little black etchings beneath her stunning eyes, and then she knelt down and gave Baker a big kiss on the bridge of his nose. I seem to remember this happening before.

"Good luck, Jack," she said, straightening up. As she stepped onto the dock and walked away, my eyes were riveted on her. Her walk was my walk. Her face was my face. Her thoughts were my thoughts. There was a time not so long ago when I didn't know where I ended and where she began—which was the way I always thought it would be.

I watched her until she was engulfed by darkness, until the emptiness of this vast space was overwhelming. And then I thought of Katherine, and wondered not for the first time what she would think of Elizabeth. She'd like her, I thought. She'd like her a lot.

And then I realized that she had left with my favorite sweater. It occurred to me that I'd more than likely have the chance to get it back.

sixteen

Wednesday, April 25

THE EAVES WERE FILLED with the haunting strains of "Amazing Grace" as I and five other pallbearers carried Paul's casket slowly down the long center aisle of Trinity Church, through the massive double doors, and into the probing sunlight where, with a quiet heave, we loaded him into the gleaming black hearse that waited on the brick plaza outside.

I know I was supposed to spend the entirety of the hastily arranged service reflecting on all things Paul, what he had done with his life, his family, his city, and most of all, his newspaper. I know I was supposed to be thinking about what a rabbi he had been, a father figure after I had no father, a great newsman and journalistic servant. I was supposed to recall how when other big-city papers around the country slashed staff and shrunk their news holes, Paul would hear nothing of it, and in fact, took advantage of the dour economy to hire more reporters and position the *Record* to be even stronger when better times arrived.

I knew all this. I knew I loved Paul, I knew I admired him. But forgive me for spending most of the hour—my eulogy aside—wondering if I'd soon join two members of the Cutter-Ellis clan lying on my back in an ornate wooden box—pardon my bluntness—dead to the world. And if I was, would it be Brent Cutter, the new publisher, who would insist on standing before a crowded church and deliver a eulogy about a reporter he never understood.

The fact of the matter is, arriving home the prior night to a missing dog served as a bracing slap, a real life's lesson in the reality of my vulnerability. I became increasingly obsessed with the Florida gunman, where did he go, and most momentous of all, where was he now? Lurking on some nearby roof with a laser-scope rifle waiting to cut me down like an animal? I don't think I slept more than five minutes the night before—though admittedly, thoughts of Elizabeth Riggs might have had a thing or two to do with that.

While organ music floated through the soothing darkness of the church, I made a few important decisions about my life, which I hoped would carry on for a while yet—my life, though the decisions as well. First, I'd report the murder attempt, and I'd do it quietly to the Boston Police commissioner, John Leavitt, asking for his discretion and his help with Florida authorities. I didn't want to become the focus of any story. Second, I would reluctantly accept any police protection that he offered, and if he didn't, I would ask Justine Steele to authorize newspaper funds to hire my own guards. Third, and perhaps most importantly, I would use my standing within the newspaper and the Cutter-Ellis families to suggest, urge, recommend, whatever, that Robert Fitzgerald, one of the most respected men in New England, a voice of reason clearer than any other, and my mentor, be the interim publisher of *The Boston Record.* Not bad, ladies and gentlemen, for a guy who still bore a passing resemblance to Swamp Man.

On the issue of Fitzgerald, think about it. He was a fully formed adult with a long, distinguished track record in journalism that included a Pulitzer Prize. He was well known in the industry at large, better known in our community and as faithful as me to the Cutter-Ellis clan.

And to name him meant I didn't have to serve in the post myself, an expectation that became immediately apparent when Vinny Mongillo approached me on the sundrenched bricks and said, "All anyone in the newsroom is wondering, all anyone in town is wondering, is whether Fair Hair has the cajones to try to become the next publisher and save the paper."

His face was close enough to mine that I could smell the pesto sauce on his breath. He was wearing a black undertaker's suit and a car-crash of a purple-and-brown–patterned necktie. Sweat dripped down his forehead and over his eyes.

He added, "I'm telling them all that I know him better than anyone else, and that he does."

"Robert Fitzgerald would make a great publisher," I said.

The sun shone from above, businessmen and tourists passed through the plaza, and students lolled on the immaculate lawn that separates Trinity Church from the Boston Public Library, reading classic books like *The Sun Also Rises*.

"Jack, don't even think about it." Mongillo said.

"I'm going to recommend him."

He gave me a look like I had cuffed his mother upside the head.

"You've got to be shoving a fuzzy donkey dick right up my fucking pie hole."

I unconsciously shot a look toward the hearse to make sure no one heard his rather descriptive proclamation, including Paul.

Mongillo continued, growing even more animated with his big, furry hands, "He's a liar, Jack, a fucking liar. Didn't you read the *Traveler* yesterday? He pipes stuff. I know it. I can prove it. I will show it to you. Do not use your influence to make him the publisher of the newspaper that we both love."

My face flashed red and I said, "We'll talk this afternoon." And I turned and walked back toward the limousine. Mongillo pursued me, putting his hand on my shoulder. I turned and said, "Not here, not now. I need your help, not your petty personal bullshit."

"It ain't petty or personal, and it ain't bullshit. Give me ten minutes this afternoon."

I said, more calmly, "I will, I will. And we also have to talk about the Randolph story. We need it in print before we lose it. Life is getting in the way."

When I broke free and walked toward the crowd of mingling mourners, Cal Zinkle approached me. Cal is one of the city's most prominent lawyers, a longtime friend of the Cutter-Ellis family who was also one of the most vocal members of the *Record*'s board of directors, sometimes with some impact, sometimes not. He grabbed my arm softly and said, "I'm very sorry about Paul," then quietly added, "We have to talk." Apparently, he meant sooner rather than later, sooner as in now, because he guided me back to the perimeter of the masses, not giving me a whole lot of choice to go anywhere but with him. I looked around with a sense of unease. It struck me here and now that I was more than exposed to potential gunfire.

Safely out of earshot of anyone else, though not gunshot, he wrapped his arm around my shoulders in fatherly fashion and said, "Jack, I'll keep this short and sweet."

In another time, in another circumstance, I might have had to quell a laugh at that introduction, mostly because Zinkle is, in fact, short, though I don't know about sweet. Short, as in, very short. He's as polished as a debutante's fingernails, charming, personable. He was dressed in a perfectly pressed navy suit with a matching bright yellow necktie and pocket square—a nod, no doubt, to the season. He had jet black, Reaganesque hair and spoke in fluid sentences as if he was always performing before a jury. If you looked at him without scale, you'd think he stood six foot five, he carries himself that well. But inevitably someone else would come walking into the frame, and you quickly realize that Zinkle stands no more than five foot five, and I'm probably being generous at that.

"Jack, the *Record* needs you," he said. "The community needs you. You have to offer yourself up as the next publisher. Yeah, yeah, I know it might cause some strife, but you know as well as I do that the alternatives are not particularly good."

This intrigued me—not the request, but his early assessment of a field of potential publishers. I looked back at the crowd slowly making their way to their cars for the procession to the cemetery. I looked around at the periphery of Copley Square. I edged closer to him and asked, "What are the alternatives?"

He replied, hushed, "Brent Cutter called me and several other board members last night. He wants the job, and he wants us to meet in emergency session today or tomorrow to approve him. He says he's the heir apparent, the only family member with the executive experience to take over the newspaper at such a troubled time. And in many ways, he's right."

I was afraid of this, and being afraid of this implies that somewhere inside my cranium, I was expecting it. I mean, of course Brent Cutter would try to be the next publisher, for every logical reason. Still, to hear the fear put to words, to hear that he had launched an active campaign to take control of our newspaper, my newspaper, enraged and emboldened me. I didn't want a newly joined feud to be waged in the public eye, nor did I want the paper to be turned over to Brent Cutter for the sole reason that a Cutter or Ellis always served as publisher.

"Is there a board meeting scheduled?" I asked.

"Not a full board meeting, but tomorrow, five P.M., in the newspaper's executive conference room, there's a meeting of the executive committee. Brent was pushing for today, but in deference to Paul, a few of us insisted that we should hold off another day."

I hesitated, and said, "I have another plan." Zinkle looked at me clear-eyed, expectantly. I said, "What about putting Robert Fitzgerald's name before the board, perhaps even on an interim basis until we get under solid footing again."

He nodded as he considered this. I looked behind him again and saw that most of the crowd was now in their cars and the procession was actually waiting for us. If I was destined to be shot at Paul Ellis's funeral, now would be the time.

"Interesting idea," he said. Like so many other power brokers in this town, Zinkle claimed a slot on Fitzgerald's long list of prominent friends. "Have you talked to Fitz yet?"

"Not as yet."

"Jack, you know I love him, and I don't believe any of that bullshit about him fabricating, but he's a throwback. He's old. You were like a son to Paul Ellis. You've made an enormous name for yourself at this paper, and in turn, given the paper a huge credibility boost, national prominence. Maybe it's your responsibility, your destiny, to take charge."

Everybody's engines were running by now, and people were looking our way and murmuring about the delay. I was standing so close to him they might have been wondering some other things as well, but their issues, not mine.

I said, "Maybe, but maybe I'm not the best one for the job right now. Let me talk to Fitzgerald first."

"We need a plan in place by noon tomorrow, because the other option isn't a very appealing one."

With that, I walked hurriedly toward my car, noticeably flinching when a truck backfired on nearby Boylston Street. On my way, Brent Cutter stepped out of the back of his limousine, extended his hand, and said, "Wonderful eulogy, Jack. Thank you. We're all going to get through this together."

Great. He's trying to save his ass while I'm trying to save my life, the newspaper, and while I'm at it, the world. I wondered at that point, though not aloud, whether it would be inappropriate to bloody the company president's nose at a family funeral. Probably, so I didn't.

I pulled open the heavy wood door of St. Sebastian's Church in the Dorchester neighborhood of Boston and paused for a moment while I let my eyes adjust to the dim environs. I'm not sure of the difference, but to me, this was more cathedral than church—with curved, soaring ceilings, massive pillars, and massive stained glass windows that cast an eerie light across the hundred or more rows of empty wooden pews. I was here on a mission of mercy, though it was more secular than sacred.

In the distance, on the altar, I saw a lone figure, and as I walked slowly down the center aisle, I realized he was intently polishing a collection of silver chalices that were spread out across a small table. When I got within a dozen rows of him, he looked up, smiled hard, and said, "Well Jack Flynn. May lightning strike me now." With that, he put a chalice down, climbed down off the altar, and shook my hand.

"Hello, Roger," I said. I pointed at the cleaning rag that he still held in his left hand and said, "You really are a man of the cloth."

He laughed, God bless him, even though it wasn't all that funny.

His name, by the way, was Roger Sullivan. He was my age, a high school classmate of mine, a talented and ferocious hockey player who could outskate and outfight just about anyone he played against, which explains why he made the all-city team twice. I'm not intimate with the church celibacy rules, but I do know that Sullivan, still ruggedly handsome these days, used to get more tail than a zookeeper when I knew him.

Of course, all that changed sometime in his early twenties, when he heard the calling, quit his job as a stock researcher at a downtown mutual fund company, and joined a seminary. Now he had his own parish hard by the old neighborhood where we had grown up so many years ago.

"I'm waiting for the walls to begin shaking and the roof to cave in," he said to me. "I'm wondering what in God's good name brings you here, because knowing you, it's not God's good name."

We stood just below the altar in the otherwise barren church, he in his priest's collar, me in my suit fresh from Paul's burial. I said to him, my tone serious now, "I need some guidance."

"Spiritual?" he asked. He had that familiar mischievous twinkle in his eye as he posed the question.

"Journalistic."

"Big difference."

"Don't I know it."

Then I said, "I'm doing some research on pro life groups and I've run up against a wall. I'm trying to find out about an organization called Fight for Life."

By the way, it's important to note that Roger Sullivan is an active opponent of abortions, but with a twist. Rather than walk picket lines at abortion clinics or preach at Sunday mass, he instead works at teen centers throughout Dorchester, advising sexual abstinence where appropriate. And when he deems that impossible, he guides sexually active kids toward birth control.

For this, the same church that for years tolerated so much pedophilia within its ranks threatened to defrock him. So Father Roger, as the kids call him, took his program underground, secretly providing high school age boys with condoms and steering girls to doctors who might prescribe the Pill. A *Record* reporter uncovered evidence of his network about a year ago and wanted to run a story. Roger pleaded with me to intercede and stop it, and I'm not ashamed to say that I did. And here I was, playing life's perpetual game of payback.

"Bad news," he said. "Very bad news."

My intuition was, as usual, correct. Roger leaned against the banister where people used to kneel for communion. He said, "You're talking about a dangerous, militant group."

"An antiabortion group, I assume?"

"They've gone beyond that these days."

I looked at him expectantly, and he added, "You of course remember that bombing last year at the stem cell research lab over in Cambridge? One of the lead scientists involved in embryo cloning was killed. Nobody's ever been charged, but the word around the pro-life groups is that Fight for Life was behind it. I don't know how you'd prove it now, because I hear they've all but disbanded and moved on to other states. Maybe state and federal investigators will tell you of their suspicions."

Well, so a Hail Mary journalistic maneuver comes true. Any better than this and I'd get down on my knees and say a prayer of thanks— something I hadn't done in far too long. If I could prove in the pages of the *Record* that Terry Campbell funded a fringe group that murdered a prominent MIT scientist, not only would his overtures to the paper be outright rejected, he might well be arrested.

"Any contacts within the group?" I asked.

Roger shook his head. "Not my kind of people."

I turned and quickly made my way down the aisle for the doors.

"Peace be with you," Roger called out to me.

I turned and said, "I think it's too late for that."

Oscar plunked two tumblers filled with gin and tonic on the marble bar of the Somerset Club and said to me in a soothing tone, "You just let me know what else you need, Jack."

Well, let's start with a suit of armor, a bullet-proof car, a greater understanding of women, a takeover specialist to ward off Campbell Newspapers, and in case I get caught in another Florida swamp, a wet suit with a snorkel.

"How about a bowl of pretzels, Oscar?"

"I'll bring them right over."

And with that, Robert Fitzgerald and I made our way through the empty, sunlit bar to a window table overlooking the gorgeous back garden, where the yellow, pink, and red tulips were full and round and open to the shower of light. As we took our seats, Robert said in that deep, sonorous voice of his, "You were beautiful from the altar, Jack. Paul would be so very proud of you. And I am."

I nodded my appreciation and took a long sip from my drink. Normally I don't like to drink during the day. Today I'd make an exception.

Regarding the venue, the Somerset Club is Boston's oldest, and inarguably, most exclusive—read, Waspish—private haunt, which probably explains why it was so empty even during the lunch hour. There aren't many true-blue, old school Wasps left these days, and those who are really don't pay much heed to the old mores like their ancestors did. It also explains why I'm a member. In pursuit of new blood, the club fathers loosened their, ahem, lineage requirements, and with Paul Ellis's help, accepted a young man, last name Flynn, from the hard luck streets of South Boston.

Truth is, I don't use the place very much, mostly because the closest thing they have to a gym is a busboy with the same phonetic name but none of the appeal. The University Club has a gym and several Jims, thus it's where I choose to spend more of my time.

The Somerset Club, though, was also where I came on the day John Cutter was buried five years ago. Paul Ellis invited me there for a drink. We sat and sipped scotch and talked about John, about the changing role of newspapers, about the peculiar difficulties of keeping a family business intact. And at the end, he asked me if I'd ever be interested in coming over to the business side of the paper. I told him no, and Brent Cutter was named president the next day.

It was also the place where Paul, then the company president, took me for lunch on my first day as a *Record* reporter. We dined on turkey clubs as he beamed across the table at me and told of the great relief in having me report at the one newspaper where I belonged.

"You've found your life's calling at this newspaper, just like your father before you," he told me. "And what a great life it's been, and a better life it will be."

Well, times change, even if places like the Somerset try not to change with them. Sometimes that change isn't necessarily for the better, as evidenced by the prospect that the Cutter-Ellis clan may soon relinquish control of the *Record.*

"It's been crazy, Robert," I said, looking down at the table, then up at his face. "Paul's dead. Someone's trying to take our newspaper away from us. And on Monday morning someone took a few shots at me in Florida. I have to start figuring a way out of all this, and I need your help."

He leaned over the table and said, "What the hell do you mean that someone shot at you?"

I told him, and he was surprised I hadn't earlier. Then, just like Elizabeth, he asked if I had reported it to the authorities, knowing full well I hadn't.

"I'm going to tell Leavitt today," I replied. "But look, I have an idea on another front."

He nodded, and I said, "I've thought about this long and hard. I'd like to launch a campaign to have you step in as interim publisher and get us through this mess. The paper needs you more than it ever has before."

I regarded him closely for a reaction. The room was so quiet I could hear Oscar start the dishwasher behind the bar. I could hear the steps of a busboy, I think Jim, walking with a tray of clinking glasses.

Fitzgerald looked me in the eye and said, "My boy, *The Boston Record* has been published by a member of the Cutter-Ellis family for every one of its one hundred and twenty-seven years. Every one." He paused here for effect, squinting at me he was staring so hard. "I'm flattered at the thought, but trust me when I tell you that I'm not the one to break that long and glorious streak."

He paused again, as if the backdrop of silence gave greater definition to his words. I remained quiet as well.

He said, "You are. Paul Ellis looked at you as he would a son, and he wanted you to someday be publisher. I know that for a fact. I want you to be publisher. More important than any of that, you've gone out and learned the business inside and out. You've dedicated yourself to this wonderful paper. You should be publisher." His voice was raised for these last few words.

"Robert," I said, "My name is Flynn, not Cutter or Ellis. My father was a pressman, not a fancy executive. I belong in the newsroom. You know that as well as I do. For chrissakes, I wouldn't know an audit from an Audi."

"You belong," he replied without missing a beat, "where this newspaper needs you most, and right now, that's in the publisher's suite. You know the journalism, the core mission. You hire people who know the rest."

We both sat there in silence, looking around but not at each other, or at least not me at him. What he was looking at, I'm not really sure.

Finally, I asked him, "So you're telling me no?"

"What I'm telling you is that you should seek the job."

More silence, a longer silence. The busboy skirted out of the room carrying an empty tray. Oscar was pulling liquor bottles out of the well and wiping them down with a damp cloth. A young mother with a toddler in a white tennis sweater walked through the garden. I took a big swig of gin and tonic.

"Well then," I said. "How do I go about doing that? At least tell me that."

Fitzgerald reached his hand over the table and held my forearm as he drilled his eyes into mine.

"Son," he said, "I can't tell you how you should be publisher. But I can tell you that you'll make an excellent publisher. You have the foundation. What you don't have in lineage, you make up for in brains. And you have the capacity to grow into the job. And I'll be there to help you anytime you need it, including the day you start."

I looked down at my tumbler, which was either half empty or half full, depending on whether you were in the throes of a bender or in the midst of a twelve-step program. Either way, I pushed it to the side, suddenly figuring I didn't need another drop of alcohol clouding my specious judgment.

"Well," I said, slowly, methodically, almost regretfully, "As always, Robert, I appreciate your counsel." I paused and thought back to all those times that Paul had tried to lure me into a front office job. I thought about Sunday morning, when he let me know that he hadn't even told Brent about the takeover bid, he had that little faith in him.

I continued, "I've got to think this through more. I've got to figure out where the hell my life is going to go from here, and as importantly, where I want it to go from here."

As I said that, I thought back to Elizabeth's visit the night before, her long legs in those faded jeans, the cut of her white tee shirt, the way her brown hair framed her perfect face. Then I thought of the way the moronic Brent Cutter thanked me outside the funeral a couple of hours earlier. Then I thought of the guy wading through the swamp, the look on his face as he took aim at me.

The look on his face.

I had seen him before, or at least someone who looked like him, someone who reminded me of him. I knew when I first saw him sitting in that car that he reminded me of someone.

The look on his face.

The North End. The basketball court.

I slapped my hand on the table, rattling our respective glasses.

"The guy who shot at me," I said, apropos of nothing. "I saw him here in Boston on Sunday night. He was watching me play basketball on Prince Street and he was carrying a gun."

I stood up before Fitzgerald could say anything. I told him, "I'll call you when I know more."

And with that, I went to seek danger, before danger once again sought me.

seventeen

THE PLAINTIVE MOOD OF the newsroom over the past two days had given way to a sense of palpable anxiety that smacked me upside the head the second I hurried into the safety of the building. Reporters were huddled around each other's desks talking in low, dour voices. Sullen editors had lost the spring in their step as they paced the aisles. In a place accustomed to attaining truth and facts, all these good people seemed to have were unanswered questions right in their own midst, and now that Paul Ellis had been buried, their overriding fear was that the *Record* as they knew it would be buried as well. There was not a thing I could do to soothe them.

Ever since I broke into the business as a cops and robbers reporter so many years before, I'd been hearing constantly about how the death knell for the great American newspaper was about to toll.

Back then, we were going to be replaced by network news that brought the daily news into tens of millions of homes in easy sound bites with dramatic video footage. By the late 1980s and early 90s, it was the twenty-four-hour cable stations like CNN and later, CNBC, MSNBC, and Fox 24, outlets that had a sense of immediacy that we, as a once-a-day publication, could never hope to match. Next it would be the freewheeling, lightning-fast Internet.

Well, let me quote Paul Ellis from that talk he gave me in the lunchroom of the Somerset Club the day I pulled back into Boston for good: It's not going to happen, not on our watch anyway.

Here's why: Newspapers in general, and the *Record* in particular, form a bond with the community they cover in a way that any damned Internet site or cable TV news station can only dream about.

It's a crazy world out there. There's information crashing down on people all over the place—from their computer, from their television sets, on their cellular phones, even when they step into a bar for an after work drink and the news is scrolling across one of those electronic signs. We alone, as a newspaper, make sense of it all. We alone, as a newspaper, carefully package it in a familiar but attractive format that people can read at their breakfast table, at their desks in the morning, over lunch, or in their laps as they doze off to the evening television, as Nathan likes to do down at the dock. There are millions of Nathans the nation over.

For anyone who doesn't believe me, come sit some time at the city desk or the newsroom message center and answer the calls and scan the emails that come in by the dozens every hour of every day. People phone with their life's problems looking for answers. They complain about their politicians, about their neighbors, about spelling mistakes on our pages. I once had four retired English teachers write me because of a dangling participle at the end of one of my stories. Damned if I even knew what a participle was, never mind the fact you could leave one of the poor guys dangling.

If there's one thing that Paul Ellis and Robert Fitzgerald have taught me (and there's actually not one, there's many), it's that the trust, the bond with readers, hasn't come easy, and it's the most important thing that we, as a newspaper, have to offer, and one of the key factors that separates us from everyone and everything else in the glibly described Information Age. At the *Record,* under the Cutter-Ellis family stewardship, that trust has been built up over a century-and-a-quarter of work. It's polished every day, nurtured with each issue.

Look, we live in what has become an Internet society with snot-nosed kids in their twenties riding a high-tech rollercoaster by founding high-tech companies that have done nothing but lose money by creating products that you can't even touch or feel. Compare that with what we do here at the *Record.* We produce a daily miracle. Every morning, a motley group of editors and reporters wander into the newsroom at around ten with their cups of coffee and powdered doughnuts. By late in the day, we've written and edited dozens of stories spanning the state, the country, and the world. Then we kick it over to production.

The paper gets printed on machines that hark back to another time. The flyers are added. It gets transported to the loading docks, still warm, piled onto trucks, and, regardless of the weather—whether it be the most glistening June day or the worst snowstorm in the throes of February, it gets delivered out across the New England region, personally to people's front doors by six A.M. or hawked on city street corners.

And notice that now that reality has knocked on the doors of all those dot.com startups operating on nothing more than venture capital whims and quasi-creative dreams, we're still around, publishing every day of the week, every week of the year, making money and making sense.

This is what I found myself thinking as I climbed off my high horse, settled in at my desk and looked around the room at the people who depended on this newspaper and its proper stewardship to make their careers. Vinny Mongillo sat two desks over, a phone tucked under his ear and pounding so hard on a keyboard I thought it might break. Newspaper reporting is the only job he's ever known. He's sent police officers to jail. He got a wrongly convicted murderer released from prison on new DNA evidence. He sends money home to his mother in Revere every week. Gwendolyn Grower sits at the desk between us, the best byline in the business and the best body in the room—a bombshell in every way imaginable. She could pick a politician's back pocket for more information than the guy ever knew he had, without a single regret—until the next day's paper landed on the schmuck's doorstep with that wonderful thud.

How many dreams are being realized in this room every day, how many creative calories burned every hour?

Too many, it appears, for anyone to take a moment to talk to me. I suddenly found myself being treated as a leper, which is to say, I wasn't being treated at all. I was being ignored.

A newsroom, it is important to note, is an incubator of intense gossip. Think about it. The same people who gather facts and write stories for a living are pretty damned good at grinding out information about their own company—information that affects their very lives. I have little doubt that at that exact moment, it was widely known I was up in the air on whether to pursue the publisher's post and lead the charge against Campbell Newspapers. I assumed they'd want me to, but how could I be completely sure? The thought brought to mind former Treasury Secretary Robert Rubin's comment when he was told that the stock markets were going wild on speculation that he was about to tender his resignation. He looked a reporter in the eye and said, "Up or down?"

Enough of this. I got up out of my chair and I could feel a hundred sets of eyes on me. I walked over to Mongillo's desk. He held a fat, greasy finger in the air while he barked into the phone, "I'm not your bitch. You can't keep stringing me along. I need the info—or else." Then he abruptly hung up.

My plan was to be eloquent, even dramatic, to inform my best friend in the room, not to mention the biggest gossip, that I realized that my responsibility was to push to be the next publisher of the *Record,* and no longer could I afford to shirk it.

Instead, I told Mongillo, "Fuck it. I'm going for it."

His face broke out in a broad smile—a warm aberration amid the emotional malaise of the past couple of days. He got up out of his double-wide chair and embraced me, first soft, then harder, patting my back all the while.

"I'll never have to work another weekend again," he whispered into my ear.

"I'll have you back on the overnight shift by next week, asshole," I replied.

"Blow me."

"Bitch."

As I pulled back, he stared me in the eyes and said simply, "Thank you." And that's all I really needed to hear.

I told him, briefly, what I had learned about Fight for Life, and asked him to press his law enforcement confidantes on it.

Back at my desk, I could feel the mood lighten. Or maybe I just felt light-headed at the thought of making more money than your typically paid *Record* reporter. I love money, but more on that some other time. Meantime, Justine Steele, the editor-in-chief, swung by my desk.

"Good job at the service this morning, Jack."

"Oh, you know how it is. You never say everything you want to say, and you always think up the best lines after you're done."

She put a hand on my shoulder and said, "No, I mean it. I wouldn't have changed a word."

Regarding Justine, she took over as editor two years ago. Paul Ellis wisely ousted the former editor in chief, Bob Appleton, after he nearly got in the way of the paper—all right, me—breaking a blockbuster story about the president of the United States in the final days of the last national campaign. Even more wisely, he reached down into our ranks and plucked Steele for the top job.

Boston born and bred, with the thick accent to prove it, she began at the *Record* as an intern; begged, borrowed, and pleaded for a staff job right out of college; covered the far-removed suburbs, the police department; then worked out of our Washington bureau, our Hong Kong bureau; and later became managing editor. Paul wasn't even trying to be politically correct when he appointed her the first woman editor in the paper's history. She was, quite simply, the best person for the job.

Ever since, she's displayed a surprising amount of humility and humanity—unlike the stereotypical woman who gets to where she is by digging her high heels into the necks of so many sisters on her way to the top.

"Jack, I know how close you were to Paul, but we really need you putting your feelings aside and leading the charge on this story," she said. "As it is right now, we have next to nothing new for morning. I need you."

I need you. I never hear those words enough from a woman. No man does. In plain black-and-white, my future had become the proverbial elephant in the room, the unmentionable; I wondered if this was her way of asking what I planned to do next. So I said, "I'm already looking at some angles and shagging down tips. I'm also figuring out what the hell my future is at this place, and whether it's in this room."

She said, "You know as well as I do how big a story the murder of the publisher and the potential sale of the paper is, Jack, and I know as well as you do that you're in an awkward position. I respect the hell out of you for that story you wrote in yesterday's editions. But here's the thing: I really don't want to read anything anywhere else that we don't have first. I need your help on that."

"You have it," I said. She nodded at me, let her eyes linger on mine for an extra second to confirm we had an understanding, and walked back to her office.

I snapped up the telephone and dialed out the number of the police commissioner, John Leavitt.

I got the usual, "Can I ask who's calling," from his secretary, followed by the ever onerous, "Can I ask what this is about?"

"Sure. I just wanted to talk to the commissioner about the pictures we have of him in a crotchless clown suit handing out anatomically correct animal balloons at the Franklin Elementary School."

Just kidding. I said, "I'd like to talk to him about the Ellis killing."

You could win ten Pulitzer Prizes and be not only the toast of the town, but the king of all journalism, and it wouldn't matter a whit to most secretaries, whose sole ambition is to make their bosses seem more important than everyone else.

Case in point: She said in a self-important, high-pitched voice, "We're referring all those calls to Lt. Travers." Before I could say a word, she transferred me. I hung up and called her number back. I explained to her, in as calm and cheerful a way as I could muster, that the commissioner asked me to call him. She had a suspicious tone as she said, "Please hold," then a moment later transferred me without apologies or comment.

"Jack," the commissioner said, picking up the phone, "you're not about to start holding us up for information in this investigation, I hope? I heard about your antics out at the crime scene on Monday."

He had a hint of humor in his voice, which I liked. He was a good, no-nonsense chief who had a strong understanding of criminal justice and a better understanding of people, and, best of all, how the two intertwined.

"No, sir," I said. "I want to report a crime."

And that's exactly what I did as he listened silently on the other end. Finally, he said, "Well, I wish you hadn't waited as long as you did to report it. If I thought we were struggling with this case a few minutes ago, imagine how I feel now?"

Then he went on to say in that efficient clip of his, "First things first. Even though the crime—attempted murder—was committed in Florida, it's obvious that you're being stalked in Massachusetts and you need protection here. I'll assign a detail to you. I'll send them over to the *Record* within the hour. Do not—I repeat, do not—leave the building until and unless you are accompanied by my officers. Insist on seeing everyone's identification cards, not just their badges. No one will be insulted.

"Second, I have to immediately pass this information on to Lt. Luke Travers, who's directing the case—"

"Sir, I have a problem with that. I need discretion here, and Travers and I have some personal issues—"

"He's told me you've had a prior disagreement—"

"Did he tell you what it was about?"

"No, and I'm not interested."

That means he did.

Leavitt said, "I have no choice, for your own safety and for our hopes to solve Paul Ellis's murder, to pass along the information. I also have to make Florida aware of it, and you may be summoned to whatever county this occurred in to file a report."

Things were out of my control. I just had to sit and go with it, and truth is, in some small way, given all the other decisions I had to make, that was okay by me.

Brent Cutter looked up from his desk surprised—or maybe it was annoyed—when I strode through the door of his outsized office.

"Jack," he said in his typically unctuous and condescending tone, "this isn't the newsroom up here. We have structure. We make appointments."

Yeah, and we look out only for ourselves, apparently.

"I just need a minute," I said, clipped, businesslike.

He stood up on his side of the compulsively neat desk. I remained standing on mine. We must have looked pretty odd to the secretaries who sat right outside his door.

I said, "I understand you're making a bid at an executive committee meeting tomorrow to be the next publisher of the *Record.*"

He stood impassively, until he finally moved his head as if to nod. You could have heard a clock ticking, if he had one, which he doesn't, because he gets his time, makes his appointments, functions as a human being, all from the two computers that sit on his desk. I don't know why that bothers me so, but it does. A clock, for God sake. Get a clock.

As I fixed my stare on him, he said with a dismissive smile, "Jack, this is all way above your pay grade. You make sure you cover Paul's murder well. I'll make sure we have the experienced family leadership to lead us through this most difficult time."

Experienced family leadership. This most difficult time. The corporatese was sickening, but I maintained composure.

"Brent, as a courtesy, I want to inform you that I also plan to go to the meeting and, at the request of some current board members, I'm going to ask to be instated as the next publisher."

Information delivered, mission accomplished, I turned to walk out the door. He said, his voice firmer now, "Jack, you try that and you'll get eaten alive. I'll make sure of it. You don't have the skill set to run this paper. You don't have the background. And you don't have the name.

"You might be good at what you do down in the newsroom, but this is a whole different endeavor up here. The next publisher needs experience in financial management. He needs to understand the intricacies of circulation figures and advertising revenues. He needs to be able to multi-task at the same time as he leads."

Skill sets. Endeavors. Multivitamins or whatever it was he said. I kept thinking of those Flintstone tablets I took as a kid. I used to like Barney best, though I guess that's not important now. I wondered what Paul would tell me to do at this very moment.

I turned back around to face him and said, "Brent, the next publisher has to understand the news business, nothing more, nothing less. He has to understand what it is and what it means to put out a great newspaper. On that front, you don't have the first hint of a vague clue."

His face flushed even a deeper shade of red, like that of a Twizzler. "Jack, like I said, you're good at being a reporter. I respect you for that. But you're way over your head up here. These are changing times. Family-run papers like these might not survive much longer without some major changes."

Major changes?

"What the hell are you saying?"

"I'm saying the next publisher has to be a realist, and he has to understand business principles. You're not and you don't."

Touché to Brent for his uncharacteristically rhythmic use of the English language. Maybe he was his father's son after all, though obviously not. Speaking of whom, John Cutter was probably rolling over in his grave these days, for a lot of reasons, not the least of which was the behavior of his son, which ranged somewhere between foolish and blasphemous.

"So you'd sell out to the Campbells?" I asked that flippantly, assuming a steadfast denial on his part. I mean, selling out the Cutter-Ellis–owned *Boston Record* to an utterly mediocre chain—complete lunacy, right? Right?

After a pause that carried on too long, he replied, "I'd listen to what they had to offer. We have no choice anymore. For God's sake, Jack, Cousin Paul understood that."

Paul understood no such thing, but I didn't have the patience or the inclination to explain that to him here and now. So I just shook my head and said, "Brent, I'm sorry it's come down to this, but I'll see you tomorrow afternoon at the board meeting." And I walked out.

When I arrived in the newsroom, Barbara, the chief receptionist and my surrogate mother, told me, "Honey, clear out your voicemails. All your calls are getting bumped to me and I don't know where the hell you are anymore." Apropos of nothing and everything, she added, "I don't even know if we're going to have a job tomorrow."

At my desk, I listened to the thirty or so phone messages and one particularly pointed call from Luke Travers, the lieutenant with the Boston Police Department, telling me in no uncertain terms, "I want to remind you that each time you choose to withhold information, you're hindering our investigation." How nice of him to care.

After him, along came the melodic voice of a young woman who identified herself as Lindsey Nutter. Her name didn't ring a bell, but her tone certainly pressed my buttons—not to carry this telephone analogy out too far. She was confirming our date for nine P.M. of that very night at Café Louis in Boston's Back Bay. I flipped to my datebook and saw her name with the notation, "Harry's friend," and remembered that my college roommate in Washington, trying to get me over my rather pronounced post-Elizabeth funk, was trying his hand as a faraway Cupid. Obviously she didn't read the papers to see the kind of, well, conundrum I was in. I figured, what the hell, I could use some newfound female companionship to give my brain a rest, and I could sure as hell use a drink.

As I was preparing to walk out of the newsroom for the day, my phone rang and I instinctively snatched it up with my trademark, "Flynn."

"Jack Flynn?"

Impatiently: "Yeah, you've got him."

"Mr. Flynn, this is Terry Campbell, chairman of the board at Campbell Newspapers."

Terry, by the way, is a man. I hate when men have women's names like Terry and Carroll and Kim and Pat, though there's something sexually appealing about the converse—women who are named Toni or Sam or Ronnie, but I guess that's not really important now.

"What can I do for you, Mr. Campbell." I refused to allow my voice to betray any emotion. If anything, my tone was entirely uninspired and unimpressed—standard issue reporter, you might say.

"Well sir, I was wondering if you might be so kind as to give me a few minutes of your valuable time for a personal meeting to discuss the futures of our respective companies. It's been made clear to me that you might be playing an important decision-making role at the *Record*. You might find such a meeting"—and here he paused the way some people do when they're trying to make an unsubtle point—"very beneficial."

Yeah, but did my life depend on it?

"To tell you the truth, Terry, I'm rather busy these days. Perhaps you might want to call our human resources director if you want to talk about benefits."

He didn't laugh.

"I can guarantee you that I'll be brief."

Brief, as in, bang, bang, you're dead. I smiled to myself.

I quickly weighed my options. Not to meet means never to know firsthand what he wanted, to lack the essential information he would have provided, good or bad. In my business, information is currency, firsthand information being like gold coins, accepted and understood around the world.

"When?"

"Tomorrow morning, eleven A.M., the Ritz-Carlton."

"See you then."

eighteen

A LOT OF PEOPLE, too many people, regard my quaint hamlet of Boston like it's some sort of backwater populated by vanilla-flavored Wasps who wear brown shoes with navy blue suits and believe fish and chips represent a gourmet meal. They look at us like a New York annex, not so much a younger brother but a distant, poor cousin, unfashionable, unsophisticated, even uncouth.

To them, I would highly recommend a visit to Café Louis, where the grilled margherita pizza, the linguine in a Tuscan meat sauce, and the Baby Baci cake, served warm with homemade cinnamon ice cream are as good as anything that the waiters might serve at the Union Square Café or the Gotham Bar and Grill.

The restaurant is a rather austere room—the interior designer I'm sure would call it "minimalist" and charge $500 an hour for putting nothing in it—in the back of the renowned Louis clothing store, an establishment where neckties fetch upward of $100 and shirts twice that much. Best as I can tell, you need a mortgage to buy one of their suits. If I'm paying that kind of money for anything, I expect it to come with windshield wipers.

Not that I'm claiming poverty here. Paul did offer me a small stake in the company to keep me around a couple of years back after I broke that White House story. But Paul's also a Wasp to the core, and he put the stock in trust, meaning I would barely see a dime until I was likely living in a place called Pleasant Manor and preparing for my eternal home at Shady Acres. But hopefully it would be enough that I wouldn't end up in Marshton.

Back to Café Louis. I arrived a few minutes early, exchanged greetings with Matt, the congenial maitre d' who sported a slightly disheveled look that probably involved clothes that cost more than my car, and took a seat at a corner table with my *New York Times*. I ordered a Sam Adams from a waiter with a goatee and a collarless shirt who called me "dude." Didn't matter. I just wanted twelve ounces of icy, golden lager, every one of which I needed right about now to put the day in perspective and ease my angst over what was about to come.

I don't do blind dates. Why I was doing one now is tribute to the persuasive powers of Harry Putnam, a longtime friend who told me repeatedly and forcefully that I was making a mistake by walking away from my relationship with Elizabeth, and okay, if I insisted on doing it, here's someone who might relieve the pain. Actually, what he said was that I'd be an obtuse idiot for not taking Lindsey Nutter to dinner, if not to bed. That last part was pure Putnam, not me. I've never even seen the woman, thus the descriptive *blind* before the object *date*.

Initially I had recommended lunch at the venerable Locke-Ober Café, a Boston institution that was in existence long before salmon was raised on farms and chickens were given free range. Even with a new celebrity chef, they still have liver and onions on the luncheon menu, and a goodly number of silver-haired men swear it enhances their sex drive, though maybe "sex walk" is a more accurate term.

I also suggested lunch because unlike dinner, which can lollygag for hours, the noon meal has a purpose, a beginning, and a reasonably defined end. As important, it can be cut short if need be with the simple line, "I'm sorry, but I have to get back to work," an excuse not entirely incongruent with my chosen profession.

When I called Putnam to report back on my brilliant plan, his response was as follows: "Being a good reporter doesn't mean you're smart. You really are a dumb fuck, aren't you, Flynn?"

I'm open to suggestions about how I'm supposed to respond to that. With none immediately available, I followed his direct orders to reschedule the meeting from lunch to dinner and to change the venue to a place, in his words, "a little less nineteenth century."

"Not," he added, "that there's anything wrong with that. Next time I'm in town, the chateaubriand at Lockes is on you."

Lindsey arrived. In the split second that she glided to the table in a flash of bare arms and long legs, I realized she was every bit, every inch, what Putnam said she was, which is inexorably, singularly gorgeous, with silken blond hair that flowed just beyond her shoulders, cheekbones so high and firm they looked as if they required a zoning variance, and a body that was at once lean and elegant yet wonderfully curvaceous, a veritable Disney World adventure ride, something called, say, Nirvana.

She was wearing black pants and a white tube top with a black sweater slung over her shoulders, the arms tied in a delicate way across the bronze skin of her upper chest.

Paul who? John died how? Just kidding. A little gallows humor. I was drunk on aesthetic joy.

"Hello."

That last one was me. I acknowledge that it scores low in the creativity department, but it was the best I could do for the moment, feeling as I did.

After concluding proper introductions, she sat down with an enormous smile and said, "So you write about politics, right?"

She had obviously rehearsed her opening line on the way over. Good for Lindsey.

"I do," I said, "sometimes, but that's not all."

That seemed to throw her for a moment. Then the waiter taking her drink order seemed to throw her for a moment as well, but that's okay.

"Well, I have a question for you," Lindsey said when the waiter went off to get her something cool, besides me.

She looked at me for a moment and I looked at her, ever so slightly nervous about what was to come.

She asked, "I've always wondered, do congressmen live inside the House of Representatives?"

Her words quickly brought to mind Putnam's previously opaque warning: "Better to engage her optically and physically than any other way." I was beginning to realize how sage that counsel really was.

"Well, um, no, most of them have apartments where they live. They work out of government offices right near the House of Representatives, in, for example, the Cannon House Office Building, and they go to the floor of the House to debate issues and to cast their votes."

"Then why do they call it a house?" she asked, proud of herself for catching such a historical incongruity. Then she added, "It doesn't really even look like a house."

She had, I'll point out, something of a little-girl's voice to her, not that that's a bad thing or anything like that. I state it in neutral tones, purely for descriptive purposes.

"That's a good catch," I replied.

I wasn't quite sure where to take this. I allowed my eyes to follow the flow of her hair for a moment, just to try to make myself believe that this whole thing might be worthwhile. Even when I got to where her perfect strands fanned out on her bare, bronze shoulders, I wasn't sure if it was.

Here goes. "Let's see, a house isn't just a place where people live. It's also a place where business is done, or where a legislative body meets, like the House of Commons in London." I paused, realizing I didn't want to make her feel bad, and added, "It's one of those funny little words with multiple meanings. Trips up a lot of people."

She seemed perfectly pleased with all this. In point of fact, she was looking down at her nails and abruptly announced to me, "My manicurist went back to Vietnam for an entire month. It doesn't really seem fair."

I'm not very good at this dating thing in general. I'm specifically not good on a date with an intellectually challenged but stunningly beautiful blonde on the night of my publisher's burial, just a little over forty-eight hours after I was shot at myself.

"No, it doesn't." At this point, I was looking around for the waiter, wondering if we might speed up the meal.

"And I've never understood why one of those political parties chose a donkey as its mascot. I mean, a donkey, that's like a jackass, right?"

I looked back at her just in time to catch her twirling a few strands of blonde hair in her fingers. Okay, so I wasn't altogether ready to give up quite yet. Intellectual stimulation can sometimes be so overrated.

"Great point."

She beamed. She was warming up to the conversation, which I can't say was necessarily good.

"Do you get a free prescription to the paper?" That was Lindsey again.

"Um, well, no, but I tend to read the paper in the newsroom every morning, where it's free anyway, and on the weekends, I'm out and about, so I just go and buy it from a guy at the corner."

As I was looking around for our waiter, I started getting agitated that I didn't get free home delivery. For chrissakes, I've worked there umpteen number of years, and I'm still shelling out $2 bucks every Sunday?

I wondered what Elizabeth would think if she happened by this conversation. She'd raise those perfect eyebrows and purse her plump lips into a smile of curious amusement. I could see it now. I mean, I could really see it now, because here's what happened next:

The busboy came over and refilled our water glasses in a gush of liquid and a cascade of ice.

As he walked away, behind him, in the doorway, at the host's station, I saw standing there a tall, elegant woman as familiar to me as my own image in the mirror, only much more appealing, hard as that is to believe.

At first, she was looking around the room, then her eyes fell on mine and she squinted as if to make sure she was seeing what she thought she saw. A smile spread slowly across her beautiful features, beginning at her lips and moving along her cheeks and into those eyes. She gave one of those little waves with her hand in front of her that a Miss America contestant might call "washing the window."

My breath caught. My heart was in my throat. I'm trying to think of some other such clichés, because every one was true, too true.

"That's so incredible that you're a writer because I've always wanted to write a children's book about a poodle from outer space."

I nodded. "Great idea. Does his doghouse fly?"

Elizabeth's eyes slowly shifted away from me and I followed her line of sight—across the host's stand, past a waiter who was hustling through the room, until I saw the man standing near her, also a familiar figure, though not as familiar as Elizabeth.

My first emotion, strangely enough, was relief—relief that she wasn't still with Luke Travers. Don't ask me to explain it. It's just how I felt.

My second emotion was one of embarrassment. I felt silly, superfluous, almost impotent, watching a woman I once—once?—loved standing in this restaurant with yet another man. It seemed to matter not that I was sitting with a drop-dead beautiful woman because I was obviously, increasingly irrelevant in the life of Elizabeth Riggs.

I bore in on him, watching him reach out and touch my ex-girl-friend's wrist. I saw her give him a half-smile, though whether it was sincere or polite, from this distance I didn't know.

But who the hell was he?

I remembered seeing him interviewed on the news in some capacity. He was tall and much as it pains me to say, handsome in a rugged kind of way, tanned, which I thought strange for April—with hair so thick he all but needed a John Deere tractor to brush it.

He wasn't in politics, or I'd more than likely know him. He wasn't a movie star, or he wouldn't likely be in Boston with any regularity.

Then it struck me—an athlete. A baseball player. The veteran second baseman that the Red Sox had acquired before the start of the season in a celebrated trade with the Minnesota Twins. His name, his name, his name—yes, Fielder. Jay Fielder. I made a mental note to put him on that list with Josh Lyer. I knew I was right when I realized that the team, beginning a nine-game homestand, had a night off.

The waiter placed our entrees on the table with his standard, "Enjoy." Lindsey kept talking about a poodle that could communicate with kids through a magical Etch-a-Sketch. The host began walking toward the opposite side of the room. Elizabeth flashed me a quick, emotionless look, then all I saw was her back until they settled at a table that was partly concealed by a wall, which was just as well. From there on, it wasn't that my food didn't taste good, it's just that it had no taste at all.

My ex-girlfriend with a professional athlete, a Major League baseball player. She didn't even like sports, at least not when I knew her, and I knew her for a long, long time. I did a quick inventory of my memory for any knowledge I had of the guy. He had been, best that I knew, a career infielder for the Twins, an occasional all-star who was well past his prime, picked up by the Sox this year because our regular second baseman had hurt himself surfing in the off-season.

A decent guy, I think I'd read, a workhorse who didn't get too caught up in all the press.

Prick.

A while later, when the waiter came back around, Lindsey gladly accepted the proffered dessert menu and ordered a double cappuccino, which only extended my awkward agony. Unfortunately for me, I was losing sight of her physical attributes, which drained the meal of any real purpose. By now, I saw diners stopping by Elizabeth's table and reaching out their hand, I assume to shake Fielder's, though I couldn't see him because the wall blocked my view. I saw a pair of busboys go up with what appeared to be a menu for him to sign, looking like they had just won the lottery as they walked away. I heard an attractive woman at a nearby table say to her friend, "Oh my God, he's even better looking in person. What would you give to get him into bed?"

That just about did it. Lindsey ordered an apple tart and I made my way off to the men's room to throw some cold water on my newly feverish face. Fortunately the restrooms were on my side of the restaurant, meaning I didn't have to pass their table, which by now seemed like some sort of Mecca. As I stood, I saw Fielder smiling warmly at another fan who approached with pen and paper in hand.

In the sanctuary of the men's room, I thought about how I'd pitched a no-hitter in Little League, and how slightly pathetic that seemed now. I wondered why women were so impressed by athletes.

Was it about their celebrity, being with someone who others wanted? Was it about their bodies, meaning sex? Was it about the gargantuan amounts of money that they invariably made? I always thought Elizabeth operated at a higher level. Now I was learning things about her I really didn't need or want to know.

And what's the flip side? That Fielder was a wonderful and smart guy who perfectly well understood that playing second base for a Major League baseball team was nothing so noble as researching a vaccine for AIDS or teaching English at an inner-city high school? Did I really want them over there debating *The New Yorker*'s review of Philip Roth's latest novel?

I dried my face with some of those upscale paper towels that almost feel like they're made out of cloth, and stared at myself in the mirror as if I was some sort of beautiful starlet, minus the beauty and star power. Even in the flattering light of a well-designed restroom, I had black circles etched under my bloodshot eyes. My face looked gaunt. My hair even looked tired, split at the ends. Mind you, I'm not necessarily prone to self-criticism, but a handsome athlete I was not.

I walked out, craving an exit.

"That's one gorgeous woman."

"That's one extraordinarily handsome guy."

That was Elizabeth, followed by me. She was standing on the other side of the bathroom door, smiling such that I saw all those familiar crinkles around her huge blue eyes, half of which I'm quite sure I caused from a pretty long run of pretty good jokes.

She was also wearing black pants, the kind that don't go all the way down—I think they're called capris. Whatever, her body was as beautiful as ever. Her hair flowed every which way and I had a quick and unpleasant mental image of her carefully blow-drying and styling it for the man she was with now. Her skin was stunning, complete with all the little grooves and marks I knew so well—the aforementioned laugh lines, a little mole on the lower side of her left cheek, a small depression beneath her right eye that she loathed but I loved.

"He's killing me," she said, flat, as if she was talking to a girlfriend. We were both standing at the far end of the bar, out of sight of anyone in the dining room. "I'm supposed to be impressed by all this stuff, right?"

My heart immediately lightened some, the knots in my stomach loosening. I think I smiled, but I'm not sure.

"Only if you like that type," I said.

"I mean, he's spent the last thirty minutes telling me about the season he won his first batting championship—" ouch—"and he hasn't asked me a single question about what I do for a living. I'm a writer, a reporter. That's pretty fucking interesting. And he hasn't asked me one single thing."

She was getting more animated as she talked, not to mention louder and, obviously, profane, which is to say, sexy.

I said, "Well, you're the one who went to dinner with him."

An older gentleman squeezed by us to get into the bathroom, forcing Elizabeth to crowd into me for a minute, giving me the opportunity to feel her skin against mine, to smell those wonderful smells I once knew so well.

"I don't know," she replied. She said it in that resigned kind of way. "Kelly begged me to do it. You remember my friend Kelly? The one with the hair? She does press work for the Red Sox now and told me I'd be doing her a big favor." Pause. "She owes me huge."

Silence, but a light silence. My world was coming back together again, even if it wasn't really my world anymore.

"And who's the girl?" she asked. "She's a knockout."

"She's some sort of model." So I lied, but it was well within the realm of the possible. "Harry set us up. I didn't want to do it, but he really pushed me. She's over there complaining about her podiatrist or pedicurist or whatever moving back to Hanoi. I don't think I can take much more of it."

I peered around the corner into the dining room. Lindsey was staring straight ahead, vacant, perfectly content. Farther away, Fielder was talking to three men in suits who were gathered around his table, all of them laughing and talking at once. I saw one rear back and give him a high five.

Elizabeth said, "Come rescue me?" Her eyes bore into mine. The look on her face was sincere and a little playful. Her tone, though not pleading, was certainly suggestive, more real than flirtatious.

I shook my head slightly, began to walk away and said, "Better that you get me some season tickets."

Back at the table, Lindsey said, "I almost forgot to tell you something. I wrote for the newspaper at my community college. I used to do a fashion column."

She beamed.

"Did you really?" I said. A few minutes later, Elizabeth walked by our table on her way back from the bathroom and gave me an exaggerated wink—joking, of course. I wasn't sure how I felt about this renewed sense of familiarity, but I knew I felt better about it than the alternative, which was her gushing all over some baseball player while I taught my date freshman politics—and that's high school freshman, not college.

I asked Lindsey, "Do you like baseball?"

"It's awesome!" she said. "I love putting a hat on and going to the games and eating hot dogs and Cracker Jacks."

No, I couldn't. I thought about it, but I couldn't. She was once my very serious girlfriend, the epicenter of my entire existence for what I assumed would be all of time. But we had given that all away, me and her, willingly, recklessly, defiantly. She was making a play here, yes, but how could I be certain that she was doing it out of any visceral, emotional desire, or only to atone for past sins, to make herself feel better? How was I to know that if we did start a relationship—and I understand I'm getting ahead of myself on this—that every time she said she loved me, every time she nuzzled the back of my neck in that way she used to do, it was only to wash away the past, her time with Travers.

I left her back then because I was furious and because I was betrayed and because I was confused. As important, I left her because of the alternative. Had I stayed, our relationship, and my life, would have become a house of mirrors. I would have forever been asking the question, were things happening for the reasons they should happen, or was everything just a bizarre reflection of the betrayal, and did that betrayal occur because of my own obtuse sense of self, my inability to get over my own tragic past. Well, I knew one thing now: I sure as hell wasn't going over to her table. Unfortunately, I knew another thing as well: I'd spend another lonely night pining for what I once had, or what I thought I had, what I hoped I'd always have. You can't win on this carnival ride of life, at least when the other sex is collecting the tickets and pulling the levers.

I gave the check a quick once-over as Lindsey relayed the last plotting details of the alien poodle with the flying doghouse and the mystical gameboard. When I looked up to hand my American Express card—all right, already, so it was my corporate card, so what—to the waiter, I saw that the figure standing at our table wasn't the waiter at all. It was Elizabeth, who said, "Why hello there, Jack. Long time, no see."

I gave her something of a vacant stare, or as vacant as I can be with her, because good or bad, there's always something going on inside.

"It doesn't seem to have been all that long."

"I want you to meet Jay Fielder. Jay, this is Jack Flynn."

We shook hands as I said, "Very nice to meet you, Mr. Fielder. You have an interesting dinner companion this evening."

He didn't really respond and I quickly realized why. I saw his eyes drifting toward Lindsey's legs, which were crossed in front of her in full view of virtually the entire room—and it's safe to bet that virtually the entire room was taking advantage of the view, or at least the male portion of the room.

"What do you do for a living?" That was me, being an asshole, trying to break Fielder's trance. To say the least, I didn't like the fact that not only was he dining with my ex-girlfriend, but he thought it perfectly acceptable to leer at my date as well.

He looked at me like he had forgotten I was there, then said quickly and without betraying any hurt, "I play second base for the Red Sox."

"Yes, of course," I said. "I thought I'd heard the name."

From the grandstand, Elizabeth asked Lindsey, "What do you do?"

She smiled and twirled her hair and said, "I do a little lingerie modeling."

I did a double take. She hadn't told me this. She told me she was a paralegal for Hale and Dorr. As she made the proclamation, she shot a coy glance at Fielder to see his reaction, though she probably would have been better served to look at his crotch rather than his eyes.

Fielder said, "Wow, I did a little underwear modeling myself." Of course he did.

Lindsey giggled, though I'm not sure why. The waiter came and took my card. Fielder sat down at an empty chair without an invitation. Elizabeth poked me in the shoulder and when I looked at her, she made an exaggerated eye movement toward the door like she had done at so many cocktail and dinner parties before.

"At first I didn't like it because it would get cold in the studio," Lindsey said.

"Oh my God, I can't believe I'm hearing you say that, because I felt the same way," Fielder replied.

Elizabeth hit me again. The waiter brought back the check, as well as two orders of the Tuscan linguine that I had requested to go.

I asked, "Lindsey, did you drive?"

"I took a cab, so I'll just take one home," she said.

Fielder: "Don't be silly, I'll give you a ride home. You don't mind a convertible, do you?"

I rolled my eyes, but the only one to notice was Elizabeth. She laughed softly, then said, "Well, Jay, thanks for dinner." She was showing exceptional tolerance for a woman who was being completely, overtly blown off by a big league ballplayer and big-time asshole.

"It was great." He said this without barely turning around. To Lindsey, he asked, "Did they do mostly front shots, or from behind?"

Much as I wanted to, I didn't hear the answer because Elizabeth leaned into my ear and said, "Get me the fuck out of here and I'll never ask you for anything again." Seemed like a reasonable deal. So I did.

Outside, in the fragrant air of a cool spring night, I said to her, "Well you don't seem too upset about being ditched by one of the city's most famous and eligible men."

She replied, "I'm with another one right now. Life has a funny way of working itself out."

Does it?

As soon as we stepped out of the restaurant, two hulking men in dark clothes began following us, but I should add here that my security detail had begun, and the two men, Gerry and Kevin, were part of it. I turned to them, handed over the containers and said, "Guys, the best pasta in town. As the waiters inside say, enjoy."

As soon as we stepped away from them, Elizabeth whispered into my ear, such that I could feel her breath on my skin, "Jack, who the hell are they?"

"Boston's finest," I said in a normal voice. "Long story." When I turned around, the guys tipped the containers of pasta to me in a show of thanks.

Elizabeth was walking close to me. After a few paces, she put her hand around my wrist like she used to do whenever we walked or sat on the couch together. She tried to be absent about it, nonchalant, but too much time had passed, and her very touch came as such a surprise that I'm pretty sure I flinched and I know she fumbled.

"Do you have your car?" she asked.

We were walking by a Porsche Boxter with the top down. I took a wild stab that it was the ballboy's car. The license plate—FIELDR—kind of aided my guess.

"You don't mind a convertible, do you?"

"Does it have dog fur all over the seats and remnants of Baker vomit on the floor?"

"Yes."

"Good. It's my favorite car in the world."

She kept her hand wrapped around my wrist and walked in step with me, close. I didn't know where this was going and my brain was too tired from the day to try to figure out if it might be someplace good. I was surrendering to emotion, which wasn't necessarily a smart thing, but maybe not foolish either.

As we reached my car and I employed some of my good breeding to open the passenger-side door, a lone figure, a man, came walking out of a little grove of bushes. He was only about ten feet away and I immediately shot a look back at the cops, who were watching us, but they did nothing. I quickly helped Elizabeth into the car—maybe a bit too quickly. Assuming danger, I damn near shoved her inside.

I slammed the door shut and turned to face the figure, who continued walking directly toward me. I was bracing myself for gunfire, the piercing sound and the resultant pain. I had no idea why the officers weren't stepping in. Were they already eating their linguine with the Tuscan meat sauce? Were they traitors, my cops?

He was walking around the front of my car now, looking at me through the dark, this oversized, almost bear-like man, black and full of flesh. He pulled his hand out of his pocket and I flinched, but rather than shoot me dead in the parking lot of Café Louis where I had a heart full of desire and a stomach full of grilled pizza and chocolate cake, he let his fingers fall absently on the metal hood and said, "Damned nice car. Wouldn't I love one of these."

The voice was so familiar, so soothing, and as he emerged from the shadows and into the streetlight, I saw the face of Hank Sweeney.

I smiled and asked, "What the hell are you doing here?"

"What, just because I'm sent out to pasture in Florida, that means I can't come play in the city anymore?" He said this with a whimsical tone and a smile, like he was thrilled to be in his hometown.

I shook his hand. "Welcome back," I said.

"Good to be here."

He leaned on the car and reached into his shirt pocket for his cigarettes. I looked over at the bodyguards, who still hadn't moved. Obviously they knew Sweeney had been waiting. They were probably the ones to tip him off on my whereabouts.

I opened the car door and gave Elizabeth a head nod to step out. As she did, I said, "Hank, Elizabeth, my, well, former friend. Elizabeth, Hank, a retired Boston Police detective."

He looked at her, amused, and shook her hand.

"Exes, step-kids, half-kids, foster kids, rescue dogs. Things aren't so simple these days, are they? I don't know how everybody does it. Christ, I've been married to Mother for fifty years come July. She's all I know, and at this age, she's all I'll ever know."

"Nice to meet you," Elizabeth said, flashing her disarming smile.

Sweeney looked at her, then at me. He seemed to grow aggravated, but I think it was fake. "Why the hell aren't you still, ahem, friends with this young woman anymore? You lose your mind?"

Maybe, but also her fidelity.

Elizabeth said, smiling, "Life's complicated."

"Don't I know it," Sweeney replied, leaning back on the hood and nonchalantly lighting his cigarette.

Interesting as this philosophical exchange appeared to be, I'll confess to being a little more than a little curious as to why he journeyed a thousand miles aboard a jet plane, tracked me down on a date at one of the nicest restaurants in town, and showed up at my car door unannounced. So I asked him, "Lieutenant, I hope you don't mind me asking you this, but what the hell are you doing here?"

He stretched his arms over his head, blew out his first mouthful of smoke, then he yawned.

"Because I like the weather better up here," he replied. "Because I like the Red Sox more than the Marlins. Because it doesn't smell like age and disease. Because people drive at normal speeds. Because there are young people along with the old people."

Elizabeth smiled at him—not one of her fake, polite smiles, but a full-on, crinkle-eyed smile. I didn't.

Instead, I repeated myself. "Lieutenant, what are you doing here?"

He looked me flat in the face with his brown eyes that could have been that of a Boy Scout rather than a seventy-year-old man. Then he looked briefly at Elizabeth, and finally, down at the ground.

"Because there's something I didn't tell you," he said, letting his eyes float back up to mine. "I think we need to talk."

nineteen

THE TWO OF US, myself and Hank Sweeney, strode through the front gates of the Boston Public Garden and past the statue of George Washington on horseback as the night air turned cool and the glow of the lanterns cast eerie shadows around the bushes and tulip beds that lined the concrete paths. The two plainclothes bodyguards stood watch out of earshot, though hopefully not gunshot, while we took a seat on the exact bench where Paul and I had sat just three days before.

Three days. Seemed more like three weeks. Hell, three months, or even three years.

By the way, it will become relevant to note that I had given my former girlfriend my car to take home for the night, or take wherever.

"How will I get it back to you?" she asked as she sat in the driver's seat and I stood at the door in the parking lot of Louis. The words were innocent, the tone wasn't, not when you knew her, which I used to better than anyone else on Earth. I didn't know if that still held true.

"You'll find a way," I replied.

As she started the ignition, I heard her say in a low voice, "Maybe I better just take it to your place now."

Before I could reply, she was off.

"So you held out on me." I said this to Sweeney as I looked him square in the eyes, though I said it with amusement rather than anger or annoyance. Of course he had held out on me. I knew he would before I went down to Florida. I knew it when I was with him. I knew it now. He's a cop, I'm a reporter, and that's just what cops do to reporters. It's one of those unimpeachable facts of life, like dogs licking their privates. They can, thus they do.

He ignored me, which is another one of those things that cops do to reporters. He looked around the dimly lit park, at the black beneath the trees, at the shadows from the lights, and said, "I used to take my lunch breaks down here when I was just starting out over in District 3, and Mother would come over and meet me from her office. All the high-priced lawyers were out here and the pols from the State House and the rich people from Back Bay and students would lie on the grass and read, and we used to walk around the pond, me in my uniform and her all gussied up from work. Sometimes we wouldn't even say any-thing, we'd just walk, and it was the best part of my day. We saw Katherine Hepburn in here once."

He paused before adding, "We didn't have any kids then."

My mind and intent were obviously elsewhere, so I asked halfheart-edly, "Did your wife make the trip with you today?"

"Nah," he answered, softly, but in a tone that said it was a dumb question. "No, she doesn't travel well these days. The years haven't been as good to her as they've been to me, so she mostly stays put. She likes it down there."

"But you don't."

He turned toward me.

"Son, at my age, it doesn't really matter what I like or don't like anymore. I'm just happy to be above ground rather than in it."

He looked straight ahead again, his elbows resting on his knees. I've said it before, but it's worth repeating, Hank Sweeney was a large man—not large as in monstrous or freakish, but just big all over, with big hands that led to wide forearms and broad shoulders that framed a barrel chest. You could tell he was handsome in his younger years when he walked around the park in his patrolman's uniform with his pretty wife clutching his arm. He had probably been a football standout at some local high school.

I nodded. "I'm starting to know what you mean."

There was a long silence between us. He knew I wasn't interested in talking about his family or his history, and I knew that's not what he had flown a thousand miles to Boston to discuss. Finally, he said, "Yes,

I held out on you, but it might just be meaningless. I didn't want to get you all in a knot."

I said nothing. As a reporter, you never get in the way of someone about to tell an important or interesting or just plain old good story. This, I suspected, would be all of that, so I leaned in and looked at him expectantly.

Sweeney looked back at me and said, "You remember I told you how I played your old publisher's case exactly by the book."

I nodded.

"Diagrammed everything, numbered everything. Ordered tests. Christ, you could have taught a class on sudden death procedures just on my reports, they were so perfect.

"But down in Marshton, you asked if anything at the crime scene raised my suspicions, or bothered me, I think you said. I didn't answer you, but yeah, something did. It might be nothing. It's probably nothing, but when you tell me there's no lab report on it, that really burns my ass hairs."

I twitched on the bench. As he talked, his face started to glow, like a little boy who just sprinted toward home plate. I'm not sure if it was from embarrassment or from his self-professed anger. I stayed silent, just watching. He continued.

"There was a tissue on the bathroom floor." He paused for effect.

"It was sitting behind the toilet, as if someone had meant to throw it in and flush it away, but missed." Another pause. He was very comfortable talking business and procedures and seemed to revel in story-telling. In his line of work, he had a lot of them, and it's probably good to get them out, to share the emotions of staring at so much death rather than keep it all inside, as I'm sure too many detectives do too much of the time.

"It caught my eye for a couple of reasons. Most important, the rest of the bathroom floor was so clean you could have eaten a lobster dinner off it.

"I asked a few questions and learned that the maid had cleaned the bathroom late the previous afternoon, so the tissue was definitely new."

I interrupted, asking, "But couldn't he have just missed the toilet himself?"

His expression didn't change. "Of course he could have. He might have just blown his nose and flicked it in the toilet as he turned away and never even known he missed." Yet another pause.

"But I did a quick comparison. The tissue on the floor was baby blue. It was a Kleenex, I believe, something that comes out of one of those boxes. There was a box of tissues in the bathroom, about half empty, but the tissues were white, not blue." He looked at me hard, seeing if I was following. I was, but wasn't yet as excited as him.

"The toilet tissue was white, not blue. There was a box of tissues in each of the other two bathrooms in the condominium, but they were all white, not blue. So the tissue on the floor came into the apartment from the outside. Someone brought it in."

It all seemed very weak to me, so I asked, "Couldn't John Cutter have brought it in himself? Maybe that's the kind of tissue he had at work, or he kept a sleeve in his car, or he stopped and grabbed one at a restaurant that night."

"Of course. All good questions. And the tissue was the same kind they had in the public men's room off the lobby of the Four Seasons Hotel downstairs."

As he said this, I glanced to my right and, through the still-bare trees, saw the lights of the Four Seasons hotel glitter in the near distance. It was a beautiful hotel that suddenly took on the aura of a death trap.

"I asked employees in the hotel restaurant if Mr. Cutter had been in the previous evening for dinner or drinks, and he hadn't."

I said, "But couldn't he have grabbed the tissue at some earlier point? I mean, surely that tissue could have been in his suit or pants pocket for a while, no?"

"Again, of course. But I'm still left with the same question I began with." He paused for a longer break than usual. "I ordered tests to be performed on that tissue, to see what, if anything, was in it or on it. They were fairly routine tests, just to cancel it out for any evidentiary value. But according to your review of the report, that test wasn't done. Why the hell not?"

He looked at me, his dark skin blending into the blackness behind him, and I looked back at him, not sure what to say. I couldn't really feel the cool anymore, though all this talk of tissues was making my nose itchy. I'll point out, probably because my olfactory senses were on high alert, that the park smelled of freshly turned earth.

I mulled his assertions, his concerns, for a minute as we continued to meet each other's gaze. I finally said, "So tell me what you expected to find?"

"What did I expect to find? Nothing, really. Probably just as you said, Mr. Cutter picked the tissue up somewhere else, meant to toss it in the toilet, and missed. That simple. But like I said, show me a dog and I'm assuming it's a cagey wolf waiting for the right moment to disembowel you."

He looked out at the duck pond and the light from the lanterns that danced across the skin of the black, glassy water. Then he set his gaze back on me, somewhat amused now. "You asked me what I expected to find. But you didn't ask me what I feared I'd find."

He was into the theatrics of it, so I played along. I raised my eyebrows and said, "Yes?"

"I don't want to raise any red flags, but whoever the hell didn't do the tests I requested has already done that for me. What I feared I'd find was some sign of poisoning."

He paused, arching his back to stretch. Then he added, "Specifically, when someone ingests arsenic, there's typically a foaming in the nasal passages that manifests itself in the victim's nose, and occasionally, in their mouth. I didn't find any visible sign of that foam in or on or near Mr. Cutter, but I just wanted to make sure that a killer didn't clean him off and mistakenly leave the evidence on the bathroom floor."

I sat there stunned and silent and confused and appreciative. A homeless man came walking toward us and the two bodyguards blocked his way and steered him in the opposite direction. I looked up and saw a nearly full moon perched atop the buildings of the downtown skyline.

Arsenic. The lead police detective on the case had been secretly concerned that someone intentionally poisoned the publisher of *The Boston Record,* so he ordered some toxicology tests. And those tests were never done, or at least recorded, and the apparent evidence is nowhere to be found.

As Sweeney might ask, when is a dog not a dog? When it's a wolf.

"What's your gut tell you?" I asked.

"Well, on one level, it tells me I wish I had eaten dinner with you at that Louis place, because I'm starved."

I didn't laugh, so he added, "On quite another, it's unsettled. There could be an easy explanation for all this. Someone might have been lazy and just didn't bother with the requested reports. Maybe they did the reports and the sheet fell out of the folder. I don't know."

"Or?"

He looked at me square in the face, his features pitched back and his eyes stern, and said, "I really don't know, son, but now a *Record* publisher has been murdered, and I'd like to find out damned quick whether his predecessor was killed as well."

I leaned back on the bench, a little more relaxed now that I sensed most of the news of the moment was already out. "I appreciate that very much," I said, "but I have to ask you, why? Why are you doing this? You don't know me from a hole in the wall."

"Son, don't take this the wrong way, but it's not really about you. Somebody might have disobeyed one of my orders, and I don't like that, especially since it was the last one I ever gave as a Boston cop. Somebody might have been disrespectful toward the dead, and I like that even less."

He took a deep breath and slowly exhaled toward the sky.

"Don't think I'm strange," he said. "But you're a homicide detective, you have a kinship with the dead. They're your clients, and sometimes, they become your friends in some odd, imaginary kind of way. You see them shot up or carved up or unspeakably mangled, and you have to imagine what they were like in life, so you talk to others, you pry into their pasts, you put a personality with the cold flesh that's lying in a refrigerated roll-out locker at the medical examiner's office. And you have to look around the room where they died or on the street or in their car, and imagine what those last moments must have been like, the terror, the pain, the sorrow, and the regret. They're gone, and in many respects, you're their only representative left in life, and it's your job, your one and only job, to achieve justice."

He paused again, staring out across the pond at the empty expanse of blackness.

"That's why I'm here."

I thought of Paul being wheeled down the long aisle of Trinity Church, his casket on the bricks of Copley Square outside, the gun-metal black hearse glinting in the noontime sun, the bagpiper playing "Amazing Grace" as he was slowly lowered into the open earth.

Then I thought of John Cutter drawing his last breaths in his bed at the condominium overlooking this very park that he loved so much. Was he awake when he died? Had someone poisoned him? Did he have a heart attack and pass gently in his sleep?

I turned toward Sweeney, who continued to look straight ahead, and said, "Well, I'm sure John Cutter appreciates it very much, and I know I do. I wish you were on Paul Ellis's murder as well."

He asked, "Any more sightings of the guy in the swamp?"

I shook my head again. He said, "Well, you smell better this time, anyway." Then he laughed.

His laugh was infectious, so I started laughing too, almost despite myself. It's as if, sitting here with a retired detective, being watched by two guards, a pressure valve had been released. I couldn't stop laughing.

I said, "Talk about mucking things up."

"Swamp Man."

We both laughed again—more of a giggle, actually.

When we stopped, he looked at me and asked, "Do you know Robert Fitzgerald?"

I said, "Of course I do. He's one of the best in our business, and a great guy to boot."

He didn't reply, so I asked, "Why?"

"Oh, he's famous. Just wondering what he's like. I used to read him all the time when I was in Boston, and I used to see him around crime scenes now and again. I think he used to be tight with the commish."

"He's tight with a lot of people," I said. "It's amazing how many officials he has feeding him information."

Sweeney looked down at the grass in front of us, then at me again, and asked, "So why do you have an ex-girlfriend that beautiful and friendly." He stressed the prefix *ex* in a demanding kind of way.

"Life's complicated."

I wanted to leave it at that, but he didn't earn his stripes as a homicide detective for being passive.

"Exactly, which is why you don't want ex-girlfriends. You want current ones, good ones, beautiful ones, and then you want to make her into your wife."

"If only it were that easy."

"Well, you're right, it isn't." His voice was lower now, fatherly, confiding. "But good things usually aren't, are they? Me, I've been married so long I can't even remember what it's like not to be married to her, and I'd never have it any other way."

"You're lucky," I said. "Maybe it's generational. My parents had such a great marriage that my mother died of a broken heart right after my father's death. These days, it just doesn't seem as easy, you know? I don't know. I don't know what it takes. I did have a good marriage, but then my wife died, and I don't know what it's going to take for me to get over that."

"Time," he said somberly, staring straight ahead. "It takes time."

The mood had become far too heavy, so I asked, "Where are you staying tonight?"

"Oh, I'll find a place. You're me, all you need is a place to lay down between trips to the bathroom."

I had this awful image of him ambling past the Four Seasons Hotel, where John Cutter lived and died, a solitary silhouette in a dark night, heading for one of the cheap flophouses on the outskirts of the theater district. So I said, "It's not much, but why don't you come crash in my spare bedroom, provided you don't mind sleeping on a boat."

He looked at me amused. "A boat? What do you have, one of those yachts with a foreign-speaking captain who takes you down to the Caribbean every winter?"

"Not exactly."

"Well this is awfully nice of you. Can we get a bite to eat on the way?" And just like that, I had a roommate, and I'd find out very soon, something far more.

twenty

Tired doesn't come near to describing how I felt as we pulled into the gravel lot above Long Wharf, Kevin and Gerry, the two Boston cops, in the front of their unmarked cruiser, and me and Hank Sweeney in the back.

Exhaustion. Complete and total mental and physical incapacitation. I couldn't think. I didn't want to move. The walk from the car down the docks to the *The Emancipation* loomed in my mind like a journey across Death Valley on foot. If my protectors had wanted to carry me like a bride over a threshold, I would have said fine, but no offer was proffered, so I opened the rear passenger door and struggled to my aching feet.

The first thing I saw was my own convertible, sitting in a different spot from where I usually parked it, the sight of it triggering the recollection that my ex-girlfriend had brought it back to my seaworthy abode. She might be waiting for me inside. Elizabeth, hi, you met Hank earlier. Hank, yeah, this is Elizabeth.

Oh boy.

The next thing I saw was another, unfamiliar car, a gold Lexus, parked a few spots away, closer to us. The rectangular lot was usually empty at night, because even in April, I was the only fool desperate enough to be sleeping on a boat. Perhaps someone had come back north for the season. Or perhaps someone was as desperate as me for a place to call home.

As we walked by the Lexus, the quiet creaks and taps of its cooling engine penetrated the haze surrounding my brain with some larger meaning, but what that was, I wasn't quite sure. I only know that I grew agitated, and suddenly more aware. I brushed my hand across the hood of the car, which was warm, which only made me more tense.

"I wouldn't mind catching a Red Sox game while I'm up here," Sweeney was saying, his comments directed as much to Kevin and Gerry, who were walking alongside us. "I saw them in spring training this year, and they looked a little rough up the middle."

I hastened my pace, moving several steps ahead of them. My eyes cut through the dark toward the boat, where a dim light was shining from below deck. As I walked by Nathan's shanty, I noticed another light reflecting from one of his windows. It was about midnight, late for him to be up.

When I hit the long, wooden dock, my legs were moving so fast that I was nearly running, though if anyone asked me why, which I think my police cohorts were about to do, I couldn't have provided a proper explanation. Nervous, easily excitable, suspicious, maybe paranoid. Probably all of that and more. But I couldn't stop. I heard the guys behind me start to move at a similarly fast pace.

When I rounded the last turn and got within about twenty yards of the boat, with the dock creaking and heaving beneath me and the bracing salt air slapping my face, I thought I saw something move on deck, some shadowy object pass briefly in front of a ray of light. Maybe it was an insect or an illusion or simply a shade blowing in the breeze. But now I was in a full-out run.

At ten yards away, my focus grew sharper and I saw the object move again, this time in a darkened crevice of the deck. He or she or it was hunched low to the ground, and moved slowly, deliberately, as if it were trying to hide.

"Freeze," I screamed, my voice thundering through the night air before evaporating over the vast harbor. My legs were hammering toward the boat.

At five yards, my eyes deciphered a human form—a dark jacket, a black ski mask, a stout pair of eyes staring back at me, the eyes darting from me to the three men stampeding from the rear. Then he—or she—turned from me and, in one quick, short motion, jumped overboard and into the sea. I barely saw a splash, and asked myself, is this some sort of exhaustion-induced mirage?

Time to find out. I leaped from the dock onto the boat without ever breaking stride. When I got to the aft side, I stared into the water, saw a murky form briefly surface about ten feet away, and dove in.

It's probably appropriate to note right about now that I don't think Flipper spent as much time performing daredevil water acts as I had in the last few days—no small irony considering that I barely know how to swim. I'll also point out that it was April in Boston, meaning the water wasn't so much cold as frigid, almost frozen, a fact I hadn't considered until my head broke through the surface and I was met with the sudden assumption that I was probably going to die.

Cold? Picture the dead of winter in Glacier National Park in the northernmost point of Montana, with a Dairy Queen Mr. Misty in your hand and your feet in a puddle of slush. Picture being soaking wet and stuck in the freezer case of your local supermarket, your clothes adhered to your purple skin. I wasn't in the water but thirty seconds when my limbs began going numb and my vision blurred because my head hurt so much. Mark Spitz I was not, but screw him because this wasn't any Olympic-style pool.

I treaded water, lifting my head as high as I could in search of the intruder, but saw nothing.

Shouts suddenly filled the air, and I turned toward the boat and saw the massive form of Hank Sweeney at the edge, yelling, "Son, I'm with you." With that, he jumped through the air and cannonballed into the black sea, the resulting waves splashing over my head. Maybe we could get a job as the comic warm-up act at Sea World.

"This way," I cried back, and began thrashing toward shore, figuring that was the direction that the intruder was headed, and also assuming that if we didn't get to shore quickly, we would all suffer from hypothermia.

The moon cast a yellowish glow over the water, and in the dull light, I thought I made out a splashing form about twenty paces ahead. I tried yelling out "In front of me," but the words barely came out, and as they did, they for some reason sounded like "Enema." Go figure.

I swam harder, my arms ripping through the freezing water and my exhausted legs, weighed down by my shoes, thrashing behind me. I was gaining, but not enough, mostly because I paused a couple of times to make sure Sweeney was all right behind me. The cops onboard had thrown him a life preserver and were trying to pull him to safety, which meant they weren't waiting on shore where I really needed them.

I picked up the pace and appeared to be gaining on him. Icy water splashed into my mouth. My private parts felt as if they were eternally numb. I plodded onward, suddenly angry that in my childhood swimming lessons at Carson Beach, the recalcitrant instructors declined to graduate me to anything beyond the level of Minnow. If my Dolphin friends could only see me now.

And then I thought of Elizabeth. Was she on the boat, or had she simply dropped my car off and gone home? If it was the former, did I scare off the intruder before he harmed her, or after? Could he have thought Elizabeth was me and shot her, Elizabeth the innocent victim of a mistaken identity, or was he waiting on deck to ambush me when I came home?

I felt sick over the possibilities. Together, apart, lifelong lovers, mortal enemies—didn't matter. I began pulsing through the water even harder, the intruder still about a dozen paces ahead, but the gap closing.

In Boston Harbor, shore isn't anything so pleasant or easy as a sandy beach, such that I could step from the water and give simple chase to the man or woman who wanted to be my executioner, which is not to be confused with my executor, though maybe I'd soon need one of those as well.

Rather, there are tall, concrete seawalls built to protect the streets and seaside parks from the occasional nor'easter that sends mammoth waves catapulting toward land. I bring this up as I pulled close to shore and saw just such a wall looming over me. I also saw my intruder, up on his feet, lurching across the few feet of litter-strewn, rock-covered dry land between the wall and the water. I stood in the harbor, realized I was only waist deep, and pushed toward land.

When I hit terra firma, my lungs were desperate for air. My extremities were so cold they felt like they might just crack and clunk on the ground (loudly, I might add). I stumbled and fell hard onto the rocks, picked myself up, and staggered toward the wall. That's when a rock, moving at no slow velocity, grazed my head. I never saw it coming, but felt its impact on my temple. I crumbled to the ground yet again, summoned every bit of strength I had, and pulled myself back to my feet.

I gazed upward and saw the intruder scaling the top of the ten-foot wall. He was no longer wearing the mask. He looked down at me as I looked at him, and I was sure, one hundred percent positive, that it was the same guy I had seen in Florida and on the basketball court in the North End. As I made my first move to climb the wall, I looked up and saw him from behind sprinting off into the night.

As I put my hands on the wall, getting ready to climb, the next thing I saw was a floodlight descend from the sky. The pulsing sound of a helicopter filled the air. A man on a megaphone hollered, "State Police. Move away from the wall and lie flat on the beach." So I did, I did, spreading myself out face down on the ground with my arms above my head and my legs a few feet apart, relief overcoming frustration, but fear still coursing through my brain. What I feared was the unknown, and what I didn't know was whether Elizabeth was still alive.

And then it was bedlam. The helicopter landed on the street above the seawall with a blast of noise and a gust of wind. The urgent wail of police sirens filled the air, the lights from the cruisers flashing red and blue in every conceivable direction. As I lay on the ground, soaking wet, quaking uncontrollably from the relentless cold, a floodlight focused on me and a cop yelled from the top of the wall, "Massachusetts State Police. One move and you're dead."

Great. You tell me how to stop shivering. One more minute in this cold and I was dead anyway.

Someone flung a rope ladder down the wall and I watched from the ground as two uniformed troopers quickly descended it. Then I heard another voice from the top of the wall, a familiar voice, that of Gerry, one of my bodyguards, call out, "Hold any fire. That's Jack Flynn. He's okay. He's okay."

Was I?

Was Elizabeth alive?

The troopers, on the rocky ground now, still approached me warily. They had me roll over, felt for a weapon, pulled my newspaper ID from my front pocket, and helped me to my feet. One of them yelled, and I'm not lying about this, "Medics!" It felt like we were on the set of a movie, only I wish my contract provided for a stuntman to play these action scenes.

Within minutes, there was a stretcher, which I refused to lie on. A youngish man in a jumpsuit wrapped me in what looked like an aluminum foil floor-length coat, and, beneath that, helped me pull off my soaking wet clothes. Normally I wouldn't allow a man to disrobe me, but right about now I would have let anyone do anything they wanted, provided it would help me get warm and dry.

A second paramedic, his face just inches from mine, yelled, as if I had suffered ear or brain damage during my nautical exploits, "Can you climb this ladder?"

I replied in a regular tone, at normal volume, "Yes."

As I walked to the wall, a uniformed trooper came alongside me and asked if I saw which way the intruder—killer?—had escaped.

"He went that-a-way," I said, pointing to the peak of the concrete wall. I don't know why I thought that was funny, but I did. The officer didn't.

When I hit the top of the wall I again declined to lie on the rolling gurney—what is it with paramedics and their stretchers?—and searched the crowd for Gerry, the bodyguard. There were a dozen State Police and Boston Police cruisers parked at every possible angle, all their lights flashing and pulsing. Police radios cackled in the night. Floodlights were aimed every which way. Another chopper, I think with a television station, hovered overhead. I saw Gerry about ten yards away gesticulating wildly to an older man in a suit.

As I walked through the crowd toward them, wrapped in my faux spacesuit and flanked by nervous paramedics, I saw exactly what I didn't want to see: The State Medical Examiner's van lumbering around a corner and slowly pulling across the gravel lot of Long Wharf.

Elizabeth.

My head became so light that I thought I might pass out. My stomach began churning so hard that I had to crouch down for a moment, my hands on my knees, thinking I might vomit all over my bare feet.

"Get the gurney," one of the paramedics shouted.

"Fuck the gurney," I said to no one in particular. I straightened up and headed toward Gerry in a jog, pushing my way through various groups of cops.

"You're alright?" he said to me, his look urgent, as I approached.

"Who's dead?"

"Are you feeling okay?"

"Gerry, who the fuck is dead?"

He said, "Come here," and he put his arm on my shoulder and led me away from the group. This scene had a familiarity about it that I didn't like one bit, mostly because I knew only too well where it was leading.

As we walked, my eyes were fixed on the M.E. van in the distance, the two kids in jumpsuits flicking open the rear doors and mindlessly pulling the rolling stretcher out and dropping it on the ground with a little bounce—another night, another victim, life in the big city.

Then I saw what could have been a hypothermia-induced hallucination, or maybe an apparition, something so good I didn't dare believe it to be true. It was Elizabeth, or at least someone who moved in that elegant way that Elizabeth does, someone who looked like Elizabeth, walking across the parking lot toward the bedlam.

Without explanation, I broke away from Gerry and began drifting toward her, bobbing and weaving around clusters of investigators with my two paramedics lagging behind—until I noticed who she was with. She was walking beside Luke Travers. Actually, let me be more specific. She was virtually huddled against Luke Travers, who had his arm draped over her shoulder. She had a nervous look on her face as she scanned the crowd—maybe looking for me, maybe not—and he was playing the opportunistic role of the comforter.

My relief, my joy, flashed into anger, causing too many of those horrible memories to gush into my brain like salt water over cold skin. A moment ago I was euphoric. Now I was furious, not to mention embarrassed. The word schmuck came to mind.

And suddenly I was exhausted, cold, and weak. I turned away before she could see me and walked back toward Gerry, grabbed his shirt and seethed, "Tell me who the fuck is dead."

He looked surprised, but answered. "An old guy who lives in the shack at the top of the dock. His driver's license says Nathan Bowe."

Reflexively, I put my hands up to my eyes and rubbed them until I saw stars and white lines.

Gerry asked, "Did you know him?"

I nodded my head without speaking or moving my hands.

"I'm sorry," he said. He paused and added, "We found him when we were doing a quick search of the area. His light was on in his cottage, so one of the uniforms knocked on his door. When he didn't answer, the uniform pushed it open. It was unlocked. And right inside, on the floor, was Mr. Bowe."

Another pause, then, "He was shot in the forehead, twice." He didn't point it out because he didn't have to point it out, but the modus operandi was nearly the same as in Paul Ellis's death. "It appears that he was shot outside, then dragged inside the shack. It also looks as if he might have skin under his fingernails, meaning he might have been shot after he tried to attack the assailant."

Poor Nathan was trying to protect Elizabeth from an intruder and ended up coming face to face with a guy who would seemingly stop at nothing to kill me.

I watched Elizabeth walking by. Travers wasn't in his usual dark suit, but rather a pair of jeans and a windbreaker with the words "Boston Police" emblazoned across the back. She was also in jeans, meaning she had gone home to change after leaving the restaurant. And she had a matching "Boston Police" windbreaker on that Travers had no doubt given her to help her keep warm. Isn't that cute. Isn't that valiant. Doesn't that make you just want to kill him?

No, I mean it. I really and truly wanted to kill him, but there was too much death going on around me already.

Elizabeth spied me and veered in my direction, breaking free of Travers's grip. At that moment, one of the medics told me in a whiney voice, "We really have to get you to the hospital to perform some tests."

As Elizabeth was coming up on me, calling out my name, the memories, the bad memories, ricocheted around in my mind—the confusion, the loneliness, the indecision, the feelings of complete and total inadequacy that draped me like a hood every day and every night for all those weeks and months afterward.

She came up and hugged me, but I acted frozen—a word I don't use lightly anymore.

"Jack, thank God you're alright," she said, holding me tight.

Of course, she sensed the lack of emotion on my end and immediately pulled back. "What's the matter?" she asked, her expression one of hurt.

"My boys here want to get me to the hospital to run some quick tests."

"I'll go with you."

I said, "No, you stay here. The detectives will need you." And if that wasn't an obvious enough jab, I said, "And I'm sure you're in good hands."

As I turned and walked away, I heard her cry out, "Goddammit, Jack, you're wrong. Don't be an asshole."

Well, maybe she was right, but at that point, I didn't particularly care. Suddenly, I was pulling myself up into the back of the ambulance. Paul's dead. Nathan's dead. I'm apparently next. I couldn't feel my toes, but that's okay, because at that precise moment, I couldn't feel my heart, either.

Schmuck.

twenty-one

THE FIRST SENSATION WAS that of light, then of an unimaginable soft-ness. I opened my eyes to see morning sunshine dappled across a vibrant white comforter in a bed fit for a sultan and his entire harem—a sharp contrast to my tomblike cabin with the worn wool blanket aboard *The Emancipation*. I had just finished what may have been the soundest sleep I've ever had.

Where was I?

I don't know, but it was too nice a place to inspire any worry. This wasn't exactly the kind of environment where hostages were kept. I sat up and looked around at the tall windows and the crystal lamps and the foxhunting prints on the walls trying to answer that question, but my mind began drifting back to the recent past and immediate future.

I thought of Nathan, kindly old Nathan, dead at the hands of someone whose driving goal in life was to kill me. I thought of the meeting I had scheduled for that morning with Terry Campbell, who could well be behind all this. I thought of my appearance that after-noon before the executive committee of the *Record*'s board of directors in an effort to take control of the paper, or at least make sure Brent Cutter didn't have it.

Then I thought of Elizabeth, her almost abnormally large eyes and the look of trauma and worry they carried last night as she walked across the lot, the way she had her hair pulled back in a ponytail as if she was twenty-three, not thirty-five, her tone of voice as she came rushing over to me.

And Travers, all cocky in that way of his, his arm draped over her shoulders as if he alone could make everything alright, as if he was meant to protect her from the dangers of the world that he knew so well.

Did she sleep with him last night? After I left in a pique of aggravation, did he return to her side like the opportunistic asshole I knew he was and remain there until she gradually gave in to the impulse that was so obviously present between them? Had they maintained a relationship for the past many months? Was she so drawn to him that she couldn't help it? Was she with him right now?

I tore the comforter off my body and looked at the digits of an unfamiliar alarm clock sitting on an elegant nightstand that I had never seen before. 6:34, I assumed A.M.

"Rescue me?"

She was so sincere when she asked me this at Café Louis, her eyes at once playful and serious, wanting me to take the bait and lead the night from there.

"It's my favorite car in the world."

She was so familiar when she said this, so normal, so much herself. The oceans that stood between us seemed to drain, the walls began to crumble down, the almost unthinkable agony took a slot in the spectrum of human emotions, ready to give way to something else, like joy, understanding, comprehension, and perhaps even forgiveness.

"Maybe I better just take it to your place now."

And she did. Would she have done that if she were head over heels for Travers? Would she even have been on a blind date with someone so famous as a professional baseball player?

All this is a long way of saying that I'm glad as hell I have a dog. He has more fidelity than Peter Lynch, his affections and loyalties never causing a doubt in the world. Speaking of whom, for safekeeping, he was now staying with friends in the nearby town of Weymouth, swimming at the beach and playing on their sprawling suburban lawn— meaning Baker, not Lynch, though I suspect old Peter's lawn is nothing that Baker would sneeze at.

A firm rap on the door stirred me from my musings and forced me to figure out where the hell I was, which was the Four Seasons Hotel, according to the guide to hotel services on the desk, though don't ask me my room number. Then I remembered. The police wanted to search *The Emancipation* for explosives, so rather than wait up until they were done, I decided to bill the *Record* for a night in a decent hotel where I could catch a few solid hours of sleep and the cops would have an easier time offering protection. And as an added bonus, maybe I would commune with John Cutter.

I got a clean bill from an emergency room doctor, though I didn't discuss with him the most obvious threat to my good health, that being the masked man who seemed hell-bent on my destruction.

By the way, a word about good hotels: love. Two more: unbridled joy. Even inside this place, which I associate with John Cutter's death, I love the soothing, light colors. I love the same-day laundry. I love the elegant moldings and the painted armoire that tactfully hides the twenty-inch television with on-call movies that I had never seen in the theater, because I haven't gone since Elizabeth and I parted ways. I love the free overnight shoeshine. I love the room service waiters who wheel your steak frites and homemade crème brulée into the room and lift the silver dome as if they were introducing the first act of a Broadway play.

Most especially, I loved the fact that I wasn't on that goddamned boat with all the creaky noises and the constant rocking and the smell of mustiness every way you turned your nose.

The knock sounded again.

I threw on a sweatshirt and a pair of jeans from an overnight bag that sat unzipped on the floor and opened the door. An unfamiliar uniformed cop standing with his back to me turned around, startled.

"You knocked?" I asked.

"Not me," he replied, looking at me suspiciously.

"Someone did."

He drew his gun. Now let's everyone just calm down here. For all I knew, it was one of those aforementioned room service waiters who was about to be felled before he could get me a buttermilk waffle with warm maple syrup and a sprinkling of confectioners' sugar—a surprise from the nice management.

As we stood in my doorway, the knocking sounded yet again, from inside, harder and longer.

"Stay here," the patrolman said as he pushed past me into the room. The officer stood in front of the door to the adjoining room, flipped the latch, and opened it.

In walked Hank Sweeney. Oh yeah, I forgot to mention that he came with me last night, another beneficiary of the *Record*'s unknowing and newfound largesse. It was the least I could do for a guy who leaped into a freezing harbor to try to protect me from an unknown killer and well-known sub-zero elements.

Sweeney and the cop exchanged casual greetings like they knew each other, then he turned to me and said, "You get your needed shut-eye?"

I walked back into my room as the patrolman walked out. My hair was matted in some spots and no doubt sticking straight up in others. My eyes felt caked in sleep, and my arms and legs were still heavy from the aqua exploits of the prior night.

I didn't answer, instead asking, "Christ, how early do you get up?"

"For good, or to go to the bathroom, because I do that every hour or so." He laughed, then said, "Oh, I've been up for about an hour now. I went down to the lobby for breakfast. A couple of eggs with some sausage and hash browns and coffee costs thirty-two dollars. It's six dollars for a glass of OJ. Six bucks! The waitress said I could just charge my room. I hope you're not going to get fired."

I said, "I might, but not because you had the lumberjack special."

"Oh, I brought up the papers." He walked into the open door to his adjoining room, then came back and tossed the *Record*, the *Traveler* and the *New York Times* on the bed with a pleasant-sounding thud.

"You mind if I make a long-distance call?"

I shook my head as I glanced at the papers. The *Record* played its story on the cover of the second section, the City page, its headline reading, "Mariner Killed in Harborside Cottage." Many graphs into our account, it noted a chase by sea and helicopter, but it said that details were still sketchy. I purposely played no role reporting or writing the story whatsoever, and felt bad about that, but not so bad that I was ready to correct the record, so to speak—not, at least, until I got a handle on what the hell was going on here. Overall, nothing particularly, or even remotely, revelatory.

The *Traveler* had a front-page headline saying, "Old Salt is peppered." Obnoxious as hell, but you have to give them credit for creativity. A *New York Post* reporter once explained to me that the four best words any tabloid editor can put in their front page headline are cops, dogs, tots, and hero. He said his dream headline would be, "Hero Cop Saves Dog and Tots." Someday.

Scanning down, it was the drop head—the smaller headline right beneath it—that caused me to jump: "Link to *Record* slaying probed."

The second name in the double-truck byline was none other than Elizabeth Riggs, former girlfriend, ace reporter, ruthless bitch. I'm sorry, did I just say that?

The story went on to say that victim Nathan Bowe was murdered just a hundred feet or so from the yacht in which "noted" *Record* reporter Jack Flynn lived. All I've done in this business, and the competition begrudgingly describes me as "noted." Maybe I would have been better off following my father's path into the pressroom. Sure, the hours are awful, but no one's taking potshots at me all over the place.

Anyway, the story also detailed how Flynn—that's me—was currently being protected by two city police officers, who were working as bodyguards, following an attempt on his life earlier in the week, according to police sources familiar with the case. As I was reading the story, I thought that whoever wanted me dead might have it easy, because my head was ready to explode right there and then. Either Elizabeth took what I told her and stuck it in print, or Luke Travers gave her basically the same information, and she assumed carte blanche about using it without violating my trust.

Either way, I had been completely used, and I was made to look like an absolute fool. Close followers of Boston's legendary newspaper competition might note that the *Record* had not yet had word one about the threat on my life, and today's editions carried no reference to any possible link. I know one true thing in life, and that's this: I don't like to lose.

I came to a full boil, then tried to bring myself back to a rapid simmer. On the other side of the room Sweeney talked into the telephone to what sounded like an answering machine, with a slightly softer voice than normal. "Hey there, Mother. I'm in Boston. Weather's great, a lot cooler than what we're used to. Jack and I have already talked quite a bit, and I'm going to hang around here for a day or two and see if I can't help him out. I'll give you another call soon."

By now, Sweeney had hung up the phone and was staring at me staring at nothing.

"You okay?" he asked, concerned. I shook my head.

"What is it?"

I shook my head again. No one who's never worked in a newsroom understands the nature of the competition, the intensity of it all, the humiliation of such public defeat. Everyone just thinks news is news, and if one paper, one network, has something that no one else does, then that's just fine because everyone else is just going to put it into print or on the air the next day, right?

Wrong, but that's another story, and one I didn't feel like telling right there and then to Hank Sweeney, wonderful a guy as he is.

So I pushed it to the back of my mind and considered my new reality, which seemed to be a life on the precipice of death, if one bungling assassin had his way. Physically, I felt a little weak but generally fine, which is to say, I don't think I was ready to take a dip at Carson Beach with the L Street Brownies, but I was certainly ready to do just about anything else, first and foremost being rescue the family-owned newspaper that is *The Boston Record*.

I asked Sweeney, apropos of nothing, "Why'd you jump in the water last night?"

He fidgeted a bit in a boyish kind of way and said, "I don't know. You were wet. I was dry. You were in the harbor. I was on land. Seemed like the right thing to do."

I smiled at him and said, "Well, thank you."

He nodded, modestly. "It's my job."

He's retired, but I didn't have the heart to point that out to him. Instead, I smiled again and said, "You were a big help."

"Screw you."

With that declaration, he stood up straight, slapped his hands on his thighs and said, "Well, I have a Kleenex to find, or at least a report about same."

I gave him my cell phone number and asked him to call me with whatever he found, whenever he found it.

"Guy in my complex had one of those. All I have to do is dial it directly and the call goes right to you, right? It's not like a pager where you call me back and all that?"

"That's right."

"Amazing."

It is. A guy who can put people away for life based on the most advanced, scientific mitochondrial DNA testing is wowed by a cellular telephone.

I looked around the room at all these new creature comforts and the stunning view of the sun-splashed park outside the massive windows, and said to him, "If you don't mind, plan on staying here again tonight. We're a little exposed on that boat." I caught myself and added, "Assuming you're able to stay again tonight."

He nodded. "Mother's going to love it when I show up at home with all these fancy soaps and shampoos."

As soon as he left, I snapped up the bedside phone and called one Vinny Mongillo, who was no doubt sweating buckets on the treadmill at his luxury gymnasium. Not quite seven A.M., and he picked up the phone on the first ring.

"Mongillo here."

"Flynn here."

"Jesus Christ, Jack, I had a cat growing up who didn't have as many lives as you do."

"Yeah, but he was probably better with a litter box."

All right, weak, I know, but note the aforementioned time.

"I got skunked by the *Traveler* today, by Elizabeth. Come hell or high water, we're getting that Randolph story in tomorrow's paper. We're coming back at them with a vengeance."

By the way, this is worth noting. When you lose on a story, the only possible antidote is to kick the living hell out of the competition the very next day, to kick them so hard they lose their ability to even come back at you. It's not often I lose to begin with, but when I do, watch out. Someone pays. In this particular case, it would be Randolph. In war—and that's what newspaper competition often feels like—I believe this is called collateral damage.

"I'm with you."

"I'm going to have to lean hard on you to put it together. I've done a lot of the work over the last couple of weeks, but I'll meet you in the newsroom later today to go over it."

The phone wasn't down but five seconds when it rang and I stared at it for a long moment, wondering who the hell knew I was here. Twenty minutes ago, I didn't even know I was here.

I picked it up. It was 6:55, according to the alarm clock next to the phone.

"Jack, it's Elizabeth. We have to talk."

"Damn right we do. You screwed me, big-time. That why you came over the other night, to pump me for information? That why you wanted to leave the restaurant with me last night? Are you that desperate for a scrap of news that you trade on our former—" emphasis placed here on the word "former"—"relationship?"

"Jack, first off, the other reporter got the bodyguard info independently. Once we had that, the editors were doing a story with me or without me. I added the stuff on the possible link because I couldn't imagine that you wouldn't use it. I wasn't looking to beat you on your own attempted murder. I just couldn't let the *Traveler* fall behind."

The word bullshit comes to mind, but I had to give her one point: I should have used the material myself. I was spread too thin, I was running so hard, that I was losing some of my judgment.

She said, "We need to meet. I want to go over something with you."

"No way, not today. You're the competition, which became painfully obvious in this morning's paper. After this is over."

"Then it may be too late."

She was good at piquing my curiosity. She was also an excellent reporter, among other things. But I resisted.

"Maybe tomorrow," I said. "Today's just not going to work."

She began arguing, but the other line rang, the noise jolting me upward as I sat on the edge of the sun-splashed bed. What, did everyone but Mr. Magoo know exactly where I was supposed to be, quote/unquote, hiding?

"Hold on." I pressed the hold button, then the button for the other phone line, and announced, "Jack Flynn here."

"You fucking prick. Let me tell you something, you fuck. When you least expect it, you're going to turn around and feel the cold barrel of my gun pressed up against your forehead."

The voice, that of a seething, irrationally angry man, was too familiar, as, unfortunately, was his message. "Who is this?" I asked. Dumb question, I know. I wondered if anyone has ever answered it honestly and thoughtfully.

Not yet seven A.M., and I had my ex-girlfriend on Line 1 and my would-be killer on Line 2. I didn't know which one could do me more harm.

"I'm the guy who's going to kill you. I'm the last guy you're ever going to see alive. I'm the guy you're going to beg and plead and cry in front of, and when you're done, I'm going to stick three bullets in your stupid fucking brain and watch you die, just like I did with your publisher. Then I'm going to spit on your bloody fucking face."

He certainly had a way with words, my intended assassin. By now, I recognized his voice as the one I heard a few nights before—"Fucking dog," he said in that same contemptuous way—on the basketball court.

I quickly reached into the top drawer of the nightstand, pulled out the Holy Bible, and flung it across the room at the door, hoping it might deliver yet another miracle. Sure enough, there was a knock, a cop yelling, "You all right," and then a key in the hole.

When the officer walked in the room, I pointed at the phone and mouthed the words, "Killer on Line 2." Hey, it's a life, albeit a threatened one.

I said into the phone, "Why don't we meet someplace and talk this thing through?"

"We'll meet," he said. "We'll fucking meet. We'll meet exactly when I want us to meet, and it will be the last thing you ever do."

Across the room, the cop whispered into his portable radio. In front of me, the light for Line 1 continued to flash.

"Look, let's just talk about this for a damned minute."

He laughed into the phone, a sinister, wheezy laugh, and said, "Fuck yourself."

He hung up just as three plainclothes officers rushed into the room.

I immediately pressed Line 1 and said, "I'm going to have to call you back." And I hung up, Elizabeth's voice leaking from the receiver as I thrust it down.

twenty-two

Terry Campbell was sitting on the corner stool of the Street Bar at the Ritz-Carlton Hotel when I strode in shortly after eleven A.M. I recognized his face from our brief encounter when he tried to hire me away a couple of years before, walked right up to him and introduced myself. He shot me a blank, bloodshot stare, stuck out his hand and said it was nice of me to make the time. I neither shook nor replied. His hand just hung there for a moment until he self-consciously pulled it back to his side. I don't imagine that really pleased him. I don't pretend to particularly care.

Campbell was tieless, which is not to be confused with tireless. He had on a blue button-down shirt open at the neck beneath a navy blue blazer, a pair of gray wool pants, and tasseled loafers. I hate tasseled loafers, but figured that pointing out my distaste for such things might be the wrong way to launch our hopefully brief though possibly deadly relationship.

Beyond the clothing, he had one of those faces that looks like it was mashed against a concrete wall at some early point in his childhood, flat with a forehead so wide and sprawling you could strip a cigarette billboard across it, all accentuated by a line of brown hair receding faster than a Kennebunkport tide. He looked, in short, like a bulldog, or one of the bad guys in a Dick Tracy comic strip, mean, even thuggish, someone accustomed to striking fear in his business adversaries from his appearance as much as his brains.

But brains he apparently had as well, at least when it comes to making money. He had already struck his first few million in an oil field somewhere in the godforsaken center of Texas when someone somewhere told him there was yet another kind of black gold—ink. So he bought a mid-sized newspaper in Mobile, Alabama, then another one in South Dakota, then another in Ohio and Illinois and eventually in sixteen states, twenty-seven newspapers in all, each of them becoming nearly identical in style and tone to the one he bought before.

His modus operandi was well grooved, not subject to even the slightest degree of deviation, according to my research of the past few days. He would install a publisher-editor from his corporate office. That figure, the same man, in many cases, who traveled from one new acquisition to the next, would then cut the editorial staff, sometimes by as much as half, meaning reporters and mid-level editors were simply shown the door with two weeks' severance pay. He would hire fancy graphics specialists and buy souped-up full-color presses, so he could then appear at the monthly luncheons of the Rotarians or the Chamber of Commerce and gleefully report how much more money Campbell Newspapers was spending on the new and improved product.

All the while, the news hole—the part of the paper devoted to actual news, named such because newspaper ads are always laid out first—was dramatically reduced. The paper shrunk in size. Wire reports filled the front pages because they're cheaper to produce than staff-written stories. Local events went uncovered. Campaigns were given nary a nod. Government officials were provided no oversight. And ads were printed in blazing reds and blues and greens. The advertisers, smitten with the appearances, willingly paid more. And when they did, they often got favorable news stories written about them, as part of what Campbell liked to call "knocking down the archaic wall that isolates a newsroom from the rest of the thriving world."

Well, archaic is one way to put it. Sacred is another, and in the parlance of the times, Campbell's philosophy sucked, and for my money, so did he.

But in business parlance, it was revenue positive. See. I could be a publisher. The circulation levels were generally maintained by the jazzy graphics and splashes of color and the AP stories he played on the front page about the three-year-old in Oklahoma having his arm torn off by a white Bengal tiger traveling with a western circus. And the profit margins soared into the stratosphere, at least 30 percent at every one of his papers, according to the reports I was reading, and at some papers, closing in on 40 percent. They were the darling of Wall Street, causing other newspaper chains to ape their every cut and gimmick.

Best as I could tell, though, their strategy rarely involved rampant, violent deaths at the papers they were buying. Note the word rarely, rather than never, because in one case, at some middling paper in Ohio, Mongillo had informed me that the head of the trade union was found dead of a gunshot wound days after Campbell bought the newspaper. The medical examiner determined it was self-inflicted, but news reports at the time cast no small amount of doubt.

Financially speaking, compare his profits to a paper like the *Record* which, while publicly traded, was essentially family-owned. We kept raising the staff levels. We rarely put wire on the front, preferring to cover major stories with our own reporters. We broke stories that other, even larger papers had to follow. We maintained reporters abroad. We had blanket coverage at home. We gave readers a regular diet of in-depth, multi-part investigative projects. And most of the time, our profit margins hung in the 22 percent range, high enough to make plenty of money and maintain the craft at an excellent level, though not so high that Merrill Lynch brokers coveted our stable stock, particularly because in bad times, recessionary times, our margins might dip as low as 16 to 18 percent without anyone in the front office getting panicky.

Paul, and before him, John Cutter, believed that good journalism made for good business, and good business provided for good journalism. What they never did was intertwine the two.

"I understand this isn't an easy time for you," Campbell said. We were both standing awkwardly at the bar, him on one side of his stool, me on the other. He said this without a trace of sympathy in his voice, but rather as if he was repeating a weather forecast he had just heard. *Record deaths behind us, an unsettled system hovering over the area, the threat of more violence on the way.*

I didn't reply. My silent defiance told him to get to the point. At least that's what I meant it to say. He asked, "Do you care to sit at a table?"

"Sure," I replied, and we did.

The Street Bar at the Boston Ritz-Carlton Hotel, for anyone never blessed enough to have been there, is a cloud of tranquil formality in a world of casual chaos. If that sounds a bit too much like a brochure, well, forgive me, because it's the truth. It derives its name because it is situated on the street level, that street being Arlington Street, which overlooks the stunning Public Garden. But it's the view within that is the most noteworthy of all.

The walls are hunter green, the dimly lit sconces pure brass, the gray-haired waiters all in black tie. And the drinks, the drinks. Well, let's not kid ourselves. They're like any other drinks, only twice as expensive. But it's worth every dollar to sit on the soft settees and plush upholstered chairs while tossing down handfuls of complimentary mixed nuts from the ornate silver bowls.

We took our places at a window table overlooking the sidewalk, the street, and beyond, the sun-splashed park where just four days ago Paul had warned me of this guy I was sitting with now. Four long days ago. As I sat, I noticed Gerry Burke, one of my bodyguards, standing on the sidewalk looking in the window at me looking out at him. He gave me a sheepish smile and stepped out of sight. Kevin Hart, his cohort, stood at the doorway to the bar in a tan Secret Service–style vest. There was another undercover cruiser idling at the hotel entrance with two more officers inside. After last night's incident, Commissioner John Leavitt was taking even fewer chances today.

The waiter materialized at our table like an apparition to take our drink order. Campbell asked for a scotch, straight up, I asked for a ginger ale. As I've said, I don't like drinking before five unless there's some good reason for it, and Terry Campbell certainly wasn't reason enough.

"I'm very sorry about your publisher, Jack. I understand from many people that the two of you were quite close," he said, picking through the nuts to find the cashews. I hate when people do that, but again figured now was not the time to point this out to him. He looked at me and I looked at him. He was trying to tell if I'd be malleable in his hands, an instrument or an impediment in his grand business plan to buy one of the most respected papers in America and make it his flagship. I was trying to tell if he was a killer, capable of taking Paul Ellis's life, or more likely, hiring someone to do the same. I couldn't tell yet, and I suspect, neither could he.

"I think you know this already, but I feel the need to restate it because of your hostile attitude here, but I had nothing—nothing—to do with Paul Ellis's death."

He paused to eye me for any reaction. I didn't give him one.

"I'm an honest, hard-working journalism executive," he said.

Seven words, four lies. That's pretty good, maybe even some sort of record. He should consider a career in Massachusetts politics. His use of the word journalism caused my skin to crawl, like an earwig was scurrying across my nerves. Nonetheless, I stayed silent.

The waiter came by and put the drinks on the table, pouring my ginger ale in front of me from a small Canada Dry bottle, and his scotch from a little decanter.

I didn't want to talk about Paul with this creature. I really didn't want to talk about anything with him except for the business at hand, and even that, only because I had no real choice. I said, "We'll find Paul's killer soon enough." I said this as I tossed some nuts into my mouth, casual. "But that's not what you called me here to discuss. You have some business to go over?"

I looked at him expectantly but blandly, dismissively. He seemed about to argue with me, then smartly decided it wouldn't do anyone any good.

Instead, he said, "As you know by now, I want to buy the *Record*, and if you're willing to back my bid, to speak in favor of it, I'm prepared to offer you a financial package so generous that you won't ever have to work another day in your life."

"I like to work."

He gave me an annoyed look and said, "You can work. You can donate the money to charity. You can give it to your kids. You can buy a yacht and sail the Mediterranean. You can do anything you want. What it means is freedom, and freedom is whatever you decide to make of it."

With that, he reached into the breast jacket of his blazer. For a second, I thought he might be pulling out a gun. But instead, he had an envelope. He gently opened it up, unfolded the single sheet of paper inside, and slid it across the table toward me.

"This is what you'd get paid in the event of a sale."

I fixed my gaze on his face. He sipped his scotch and tossed a couple of more nuts into his mouth. I clanked my ice around my tumbler without taking a drink. My elbows were up on the table, my chin resting on my right knuckles. Outside, the sun was pouring down, but on the more civilized side of the tinted windows, the light was discreetly dim.

Finally, I lowered my eyes to look at the numbers, and what I saw I had to assume was a typo, meaning there were two too many zeros. I looked at it again, trying to mask my surprise.

My first impulse, so long as it's never repeated, was to shout to the heavens, "I'm rich, I'm rich." Not only could I finally buy that summer-house I always wanted up in Maine, I could probably buy the entire coastline, maybe even the state.

Instead, I kept my chin in my hand and asked Campbell, "What did Paul say when you made him this offer?"

He hesitated, then said very carefully, "He told me he couldn't at this time support the sale of the *Record*, though he would keep an open mind on the topic."

"Bullshit," I replied. "Paul would only sell to you over his dead body, and I won't even let him do that."

His annoyance now transformed into anger. No doubt he was surprised that I didn't look at the figures he was throwing around and melt in his arms. "You may not have any choice. And this deal won't be sitting on the table for long."

"Oh, I'll always have a choice, and my choice will always be no. Just like Paul, I'll have to be dead before this paper is sold, so you can keep on trying."

He pinched his right index finger and thumb into his tightly shut eyes. The waiter chose that inopportune time to ask if we wanted another drink, and Campbell snapped at him, "Not now." I didn't want him thinking he could answer for me, so just for kicks, I said, "Sure, I'll take one."

He collected himself for a moment, caught my stare and said, "Look, Jack. I'm telling you this as a favor. I'm telling you this as someone who's had a pretty successful run in this business, as someone who tried to hire you before. Your newspaper is a relic. It's a dinosaur. It's gray and it's old and you haven't updated it to fit the times."

The waiter came back with my ginger ale and pointedly ignored Campbell. I shook my head but he kept speaking, growing more animated. "People don't care about politics anymore, and that's what you guys cover. People don't have the time to read the fifteen-hundred word stories you put on the front page about wars in places they'll never go. They don't have any interest in reading your five-part series on mayors taking kickbacks or the FDA approving drugs a year ahead of time"— two projects, I'll point out, for which we won Pulitzer Prizes.

He took another sip of his drink, which was mostly melted ice by now. He continued, "People want quick and easy. They want nice graphics that explain in a few seconds what stories can't relate in ten minutes. They want pretty pictures. They want short, crisp stories that don't jump to other sections of the newspaper. They want the box scores to last night's baseball games and the five-day weather reports for where they live and wherever their vacation houses might be. That's what they want. That's what we give them. And that's why we're better, more successful, and more profitable than you.

"You people keep running the *Record* the way you're running it and you're not going to have a *Record* to run for much longer. You're going to drive the thing right out of business. You sell it to me, you preserve it for another century, the Cutter-Ellises make a nice profit, you make a nice profit, and Boston remains a two-newspaper town, just like it should."

He was done. I had the first inkling of a headache. A cloud must have floated by outside because the street became darker than it had been, making the lounge darker still. Two more shades and it might match my mood.

I looked down at my drink and the table beneath it. I thought about the small army of consultants we'd had through our executive offices and the newsroom, the ones who said too much of what Terry Campbell was saying today—shorter stories, cleaner graphics, more consumer reporting, news you can use. Light, tight, and bright.

Paul didn't like them, but he listened to them. And the paper went out and modernized itself. We were among the first to buy color presses. We started a consumer beat. We created a commuting beat. We hired more lifestyle reporters. And in general, we tried to shorten the length of our stories, usually, but not always. But we didn't stray from our core mission, not then, not now, not ever. When I was going toe to toe with the president of the United States a couple of years ago, nobody said to me, "Hey, Jack, forget about politics. We need you to do something on rising cable rates."

"Let me ask you something," I said, pausing to collect my thoughts. "When the banks in Boston implement a secret policy of not giving mortgages to working black families in urban neighborhoods, who's going to report on that? Who's going to challenge that?"

The *Record,* I left unstated, already had.

"When the president of the United States tells a life-defining lie, who's going to report on that? When building inspectors look the other way from life-threatening code violations, when auto dealerships fuck with odometers, when cops sodomize drunk driving suspects, who's going to let the public know about that?"

I paused to collect myself and catch my breath. I thought of Mongillo working police headquarters every morning, chatting up sources, racing out in the dark of the night to murder scenes, approaching cop cars with flailing lights in dimly lit alleys in the worst neighborhoods of town.

I thought of Paul Ellis, poring over the financials in the teeth of the last recession, watching our stock price plunge, seeing his own net worth cut in half, telling his staff, his paper, to keep our eye on what mattered most, and that was producing the best *Boston Record,* day in, day out, that we possibly could. If we did that, he said, things would be fine. Well, we did, and things were.

I thought of my own father, his ink-stained green apron spread over his lanky frame, proudly working in the *Record* pressroom until his legs gave way from disease and he had to be carried out by two of his best friends—also lifelong pressmen.

Campbell was about to intrude on the silence, on my thoughts, so I cut him off.

"Not you," I said, the volume of my voice, the strain of my tone surprising even me. "Not you. Because you're out there publishing stories about how SUVs are fun and safe and how barbecue cooking is a nice way to spend time with the whole family, all in two hundred and fifty words or less, while splashing polls on people's favorite primetime comedies on the front page."

He shook his head in disgust, muttering, "You'll never get it."

I pounded the table with my right fist, causing some of the nuts to splash out of their bowl. Truth is, I was throwing a full-out nutty, the likes of which I hadn't thrown in a long, long time. Maybe things like death and deception were starting to catch up to me. Maybe it was the sight of Elizabeth with Travers. Or maybe I really cared about my paper.

What's the worst that could happen, that I'm barred for life from the Street Bar at the Ritz? All right, that is pretty bad, but fortunately I didn't consider that possibility as I continued my rant.

"No, you'll never get it," I seethed. "You'll never get why owning a newspaper is different from owning a widget company. You'll never get that we're not given First Amendment rights just so we can print stories about rock stars in drug rehab. You'll never understand that sometimes, the bottom line isn't the bottom line."

He stood up. "You're useless," he told me. Yeah, I'm useless. I'm fucking useless.

He grabbed the sheet of paper back with all that money that I could sure as hell use but didn't particularly need.

"Fuck off," I told him. "Fuck the hell off." All right, it's not eloquent, but it made the point. Just to be sure, I added, "And it's not going to look good when we run a story in the next couple of days saying that you're a major contributor to militant groups pushing fringe causes."

He stood glaring at me, and I was glaring back at him. I caught the waiter out of the corner of my eye looking on in horror. Their idea of conflict in here is people politely fighting over the bar check.

"I'm going to take you down, Jack," he seethed.

"Like you took the MIT researcher down?"

His face quickly changed from fury to curiosity, almost as if I'd flicked a switch. He asked, "What the fuck are you talking about?"

"You know full well what I'm talking about. And so will the rest of the country when we run a story about it."

When he spoke again, even his tone had changed. "Jack, I don't know what you're talking about. What do you mean?"

I shook my head and derisively said, "Fight for Life. It's a Massachusetts group. You gave them money—thirty large. They used it to bomb a stem cell lab in Cambridge. You're screwed."

He grew angry again. "I don't know about any stem cell group and I don't know about any Cambridge professor. I do know this. I'm going to own you. Own you!"

"You don't have it in you. And if I find you trying to put your grubby fucking hands on my newspaper again, I'll break them."

"That's not what the company president says." Then he started across the lounge. Just a few paces away, he whirled around and walked back toward me until we were chest to chest, as if we were a baseball manager and a home plate umpire arguing over a called third strike.

"By the way," he said, his voice tight as a rope but strangely calm, "I eat assholes like you for lunch."

"That would explain your bad breath," I replied. Not bad, considering the circumstances.

He fixed a look of hatred upon me the likes of which I hadn't seen in a long, long time—or maybe I had, on the basketball court the other night and in the Florida swamp soon after.

He said through gritted teeth, his jaw barely moving as he spoke,

"People who fuck with me don't come out of it real well. Let's be real clear on that."

With that, he stalked off without ever saying good-bye, probably because he knew, because I knew, this wasn't the last we'd see of each other. I ended up picking up the check. The man, I tell you, had no class.

twenty-three

WE WERE AT A FAIR one night, Elizabeth and me, at one of those traveling summer carnivals with the Round-Up and the Twister that comes through the town in Maine where we rented a beachside cottage for a couple of weeks in August.

It wasn't late, maybe 8:30 or nine, but the sun had set and the sky was dark and the blinking, flashing fluorescent lights from the rides and the games and the fried dough stands gave me the sense that we had drifted far into the night, deep into another world, one, that I wasn't so sure I liked. I don't like carnivals in much the same way that I don't like clowns, because even as an overly analytical kid, I always suspected that the heavy makeup and the painted smiles and the bulbous noses hid something that was interminably sad, something that needed to be concealed. The reporter in me always wanted to get behind the façade.

Specifically, I didn't like this particular carnival because of the line of smiling, stuffed cats that were mocking my every throw, which didn't come cheap at three for $2. You knock two down, you win a prize. Knock three down, win a massive stuffed animal, the kind your wife or girlfriend carries around in a show of pride for her man, the hunter, if only as a goof. I wanted one, but the unfortunate fact of the matter is that I hadn't hit a single goddamned cat, each of my throws bristling through what seemed like their excessively furry trunks. My pockets were already twenty dollars lighter for my failure.

"I thought you told me you pitched a no hitter in Little League. Isn't that supposed to mean you have good aim." That was Elizabeth, forgetting her role as the fawning girlfriend, at least in public.

I glared at her. She was standing beside me pulling fistfuls of pale blue cotton candy off a long pole. Her face, especially her nose, was tan from the sun. Her hair, air-dried after a day at the beach, was kinky and somewhat disheveled, meaning sexy. She had on my favorite jeans, which I found completely, sometimes embarrassingly irresistible.

"The fucking game is rigged."

The barker heard me and exclaimed in mock shock, "My boy, these carnival games are more tightly regulated than the International Olympics. Have the lady take a throw."

Elizabeth casually picked up a baseball and flung it toward the cats, wildly by my analysis, but not by theirs. She hit one smack in the face, causing it to tumble backward.

"This is hard," she said, looking at me sidelong.

The barker handed her another ball. Another throw, another cat.

"You throw like a girl," I said, even though she didn't.

"You throw like a moron."

Behind me, a kid began wailing, and when I spun around, I saw his taffy apple fall from his small hand and onto the matted grass. He was crying so hard he barely noticed that he wasn't holding it anymore.

Elizabeth took aim and fired. Three throws, three cats. The laughing, the sobbing, the triumph, the despair. I don't know if a man's life could get much worse than that very moment.

She strutted back and forth in front of the stand looking for just the right stuffed animal, her fingers on her beautiful lips and those world famous jeans making her ass look like it sprouted from somewhere up around her shoulders. The kid behind us kept crying, and I began gazing around for his parents or brothers and sisters, but no one came forward.

Finally, I knelt down beside him and said in a voice similar to the way I talk to Baker, "Are you okay."

He was about five, I'll guess, a towhead with a bowl haircut and big brown eyes that were filled with tears. He was crying so frantically that he could barely speak, so he looked at me desperately and said only, "Grampy."

"Grampy. Your grandfather?"

He nodded, his crying slowing down slightly.

"Are you looking for him?"

He nodded again.

"We'll find him," I said. "What's your name."

"Jack," he said.

"No it's not. That's my name."

Out of nowhere, he smiled at me, a shy little smile, but a smile nonetheless. He said, going along with the gag in that way little kids do, "No it's not."

"Honest." I was about to show him my license, but then didn't know if he could read.

Elizabeth returned with an enormous purple dinosaur under her arm, no doubt the most ridiculous animal she could find because she fully expected me to lug it around.

"He's lost," I said, nodding down at him.

She knelt in front of him, brushed the tears off his cheeks, and said, "Everyone who's lost even for a moment gets a free stuffed dinosaur."

He looked at the dinosaur, then at me, rolled his eyes and said, "No sir, but I'll take it." And he did.

I put him up on my shoulders, on Elizabeth's advice, and he scouted around for his grandfather, even calling out, "Grampy, Grampy."

From behind us, someone frantically yelled, "Jack!" Instinctively, I whirled around and found myself staring at an old man in a Red Sox cap, a flannel shirt, and a pair of loose jeans, Wranglers, I think. Never seen him before, but the kid on my shoulders had. He kicked and yelled, "Grampy," and I pried him off and placed him back on the ground.

The embarrassed grandfather mentioned something about a Port-a-Potty and a disobedient kid, thanked us profusely and was on his way, his hand tightly wrapped around young Jack's.

Later, on the way out of the carnival, the noise and the rainbow of lights behind us and the serene dark of the parking lot ahead, Elizabeth locked her arm inside mine and put her head on my shoulder in that way she does when she's descending from a sugar high. The girl eats like your typical adolescent boy and has the body of a supermodel to disprove it. Other women hate her for it. Not me. Anyway, she's leaning on me hard as we walked, looking straight ahead, and she asked, "Hey, Pedro Martinez, do you want to have a kid?"

She knew the answer to that already. She knew about my trip to the hospital, all my expectations, all my dreams, left in the morgue on what will always be the worst day of my life, the shadows of which will linger forever.

I replied, "In time."

"Would now be 'In time?'"

I pulled away, stopped walking, and stared at her front-on. I placed a hand on each of her shoulders and asked, "Is *now* the time?"

She didn't immediately reply.

I felt a lump in my throat. I felt my eyes start to well up. She stared back at me, serious, her hair all wispy and the perfect curves of her face drawn tight around her mouth. She nodded and said, "It might be. I'm late."

"I love you."

"Are you ready? We're not even married yet. We both said we wanted to hold off for another year or two."

I embraced her in the parking lot of the Goose Rocks Civic Association Carnival, the lights and the noise pulsing in the distance, and she folded perfectly into my arms like she had a hundred times before.

Maybe this is exactly what I needed to step out from my own past—a wife, a baby, a family of my own. Never for a single second would Katherine ever leave my mind, but she'd understand, she'd know, that at some point in my life, I had to move on.

Then I picked Elizabeth up for no real reason, calling out, almost singing out, "We're going to have a baby," as I cradled her in my arms. "A baby, right here, ours, always." And I nudged her stomach with my nose.

She smiled, finally, and seconds after, the smile turned into a full throttle laugh, despite the sugar hangover.

I put her down and she embraced me, her long, slender arms folding over my shoulders. She stood on the tips of her toes so she was eye to eye and pressed her mouth hard against mine, passionately, pulled it back a wafer and said, "I love you too."

She pressed her lips against mine yet again and mumbled while we kissed, "Never means never, right?"

Four days later, I sat at work arguing with Vinny Mongillo about whether Geraldo Rivera now counted as a mainstream journalist (Mongillo said yes; I believed no). The phone rang. It was Elizabeth on the other end.

"Well, reprieve," she said, trying to sound upbeat, but her voice tinged with some disappointment.

"Oh," I replied, unable to hide my own regret.

There was silence between us, until I said, "How about we meet at home in an hour to try and make one?"

She laughed, but it was shallow, almost—and I hate to say this—polite. "Now would decidedly not be the time for that," she said.

A month later, our relationship, for all practical and impractical purposes, was over.

I bring all this up because I've spent an inordinate amount of time over the last few months wondering what would have happened if she had been pregnant and not just late, what would have become of us if we had an adorable baby girl some eight months after that carnival, and not just continued in a relationship where the past overwhelmed any prospects for the future.

I honestly don't know, but I do know this. I know that she wouldn't have shot out at me—and I don't throw around that word loosely anymore—as she did that April day, quite literally grabbing my arm as I walked out of the Ritz-Carlton from my meeting with Terry Campbell. She wouldn't have had to.

"Jack," she said, her hands on my wrist and an ambitious spring breeze blowing through her brown hair, "I need you for about five minutes. This is business, and this is something you're going to want to know."

The cops, I noticed, made absolutely no move to help me. They were my bodyguards. For my mental health, I was apparently on my own.

"Five minutes. Go ahead."

We were standing on the sidewalk of Newbury Street, probably not the best place for me to be hanging out these days. For the uninitiated, it's Boston's version of Rodeo Drive or Worth Avenue, with block after upscale block of glitzy boutiques and high-priced chain stores like Armani and Zegna that offer free valet parking. I used to figure, hey, the twelve dollars I save on my car, that's half the cost of a nice necktie. Ends up, it doesn't work like that. Put it this way: If my sniper didn't kill me on this street, the prices eventually would.

The wind blew and the temperature was only what a polar bear would call warm and Kevin and Gerry stood watching from a discreet distance as another unmarked cruiser with two more cops idled at the curb, smoke blowing from the tailpipe into the glassy air.

For the record, Elizabeth was wearing clingy black pants that hugged her thin hips and then fanned out to her ankles, along with a slim matching black jacket. She had on familiar emerald earrings—familiar because I had given them to her after she broke a story that got the Boston school superintendent fired about a year back. She looked, to recycle a word, gorgeous, but it's important not to dwell on such things.

"It's Fitzgerald," she said. "Jack, I know you love him, I know all he's done for you, but there's something funny going on. My editors want a story, something meatier than the Scene and Heard stuff on Tuesday. I'm putting it together now, and just want to make sure I don't cold-cock you with this one, too." She paused and added, "Jack, he's a problem."

I stood there dumbfounded, a compound word I've never quite understood. How do you find being dumb? It's not clear, not simple, not like doghouse or corkscrew.

"It's jealousy, Elizabeth. You're jealous. Your editors are jealous. Your whole pathetic little newspaper is jealous. People read Fitzgerald.

They like him. They trust him. And that pisses you all off to no end."

She shook her head. "I could get fired for telling you this, but I was doing a retrospective on the Codman Square riots, ten years after. You know, the police shooting. Anyway, I was following some leads from some of his stories at the time, and the people he was quoting, the witnesses, don't exist. They never existed."

I said, "People come and go, especially in the inner city. They may have been illegal immigrants or transients or whatever. But they were there. He's the best in the city. Maybe the best in any city."

She gave me a frustrated look. "You're impossible, Jack. I gave you fair warning. I thought I owed you at least that much after today. It's not good for the *Record*. The publisher is dead. There's a bloodbath for control. And one of its star reporters is a liar—in print."

I shrugged. The wintry wind was blowing across the Common, through the Public Garden and up onto Newbury Street, making this conversation even less pleasant than it would have been, which says a lot. "Do what you have to do," I told her. "But Robert Fitzgerald is no fabricator."

"Well," she said defiantly. "I warned you." And with that, she turned and began walking away.

I watched a Mercedes convertible motor past. The college-aged kid driving it had the roof down even though it wasn't even approaching 50 degrees. Then I watched that confident gait of hers, the sway of her shoulders, the swivel of her beautiful hips, the swish of her pant legs. She was trying to help me. The look on her face was a look I knew too well, a caring look, a loving look. I should have called out to her. I should have said thank you. I should have asked if she wanted to get together later to talk about all of life crashing down on me like wreckage from a darkened sky.

Instead, I said nothing. I turned away, walked to the idling car and got inside. There was work to be done, and not much time to do it.

twenty-four

WHEN IT'S A TIP from a source, it's called a lead. When it's a warning from the opposing tabloid newspaper, it's called a disaster. And that's what I had on my hands. True it was only a potential disaster, but life had a way of fulfilling all of its bad potential lately.

I ducked into the backseat of the unmarked gray cruiser idling at the curb in front of the Ritz, snapped open my cell phone and punched out a familiar number. The warm air from the car's purring heater made me realize just how brisk it had been outside.

"Mongillo here." Vinny Mongillo picked up on the first ring, as he always does—not an inconsiderable skill considering that he always has to place another call on hold to get to the new one. He's the Liberace of the telephone keypad.

"We need to talk," I told him.

"Yeah, everyone needs to talk. Who's this?" Not offensive, just Mongillo.

"Flynn, you asshole."

"Jesus Christ. Hold on, Fair Hair."

The line went quiet. I pictured him sitting in the newsroom, his huge frame perched forward in his custom seat, a bucket-sized iced coffee and a box of Dunkin Munchkins on his desk, flipping back to Line 1 to tell a U.S. senator that he no longer had the time to talk but thank you very much for whatever it is that you tried to say.

The line click backed in and Mongillo said, "Where are you? Why aren't you here?"

"Can you meet me downtown, ASAP, at Locke-Ober?"

"No. I hate that place. Like eating in a musty museum. Too nineteenth century."

Everyone's a goddamned restaurant critic these days, especially when it comes to my favorite place in town. So I said, "All right, tell me where."

"Amrhein's. Great steak tips. I'll meet you there in fifteen minutes." Like this is what I had to think about in life right now—the quality of my luncheon steak tips.

As the police driver put the car in gear, Gerry jumped in the back seat on one side, Kevin on the other, so I was sandwiched between two mountainous men in a vehicle with heavily tinted windows. If ever I were to feel completely safe, it would be now, especially knowing, as I did, that this assassin just wasn't all that blessed in the talent department, though I suppose Paul Ellis might disagree with that.

On the drive, I left a voicemail for Cal Zinkle, the downtown lawyer, member of the *Record* board of directors, and most important, friend, seeking some last-minute advice on the presentation I had to make to the committee that afternoon that I had done no preparation for whatsoever, unless you consider living my life as preparation enough, which I'm hoping they do. I also clued him in briefly on Terry Campbell's connection to right-wing groups, most notably the militant Fight for Life. I left a message for John Leavitt, the police commissioner, seeking an update on the investigation into Paul and now Nathan.

Then I called Justine Steele at the *Record*.

"Steele here," she said, snatching up her line. I'll explain that newspaper types aren't particularly well versed in *Emily Post's Guide to Business Etiquette,* or if they are, choose not to adhere to it. The trade-off is, they at least pick up their own phone, which no one else does anymore. Your typical housewife seems to have a spokesman these days to handle all media matters.

We talked about that morning's *Traveler* story about Nathan's slaying, which didn't particularly thrill her. We talked about the need to come back big and cover every possible base. She would assign a reporter to write about the shooting attempts on me. Me and Mongillo would do whatever it took to get the Randolph story in print, just to get revenge on the *Traveler.*

I started to mention the warning I just got from Elizabeth, hesitated, then decided not yet, not until I could speak to who I needed to speak to, meaning Fitzgerald himself. Instead, I said, "Assuming we get it clean, you think the Randolph hit will affect his nomination?"

She said, "Depends on the mood in D.C. These guys all embellish, so the Judiciary Committee members might be afraid of tossing stones, lest their local paper come at them on one resumé point or another. We'll see how it plays out, but it will probably play out quickly. His nomination seems to be on a fast track."

"I'm seeing Mongillo right now on this, and I'm going to ask him to write the bulk of it. This is a crazy, crazy day."

Her tone softened. "Understood. Jack, this story is important, but what you have today is crucial." She paused, then said, "Good luck in front of the board. I'm with you one thousand percent, and so is everyone else in the newsroom. And if any of us can help in any way, just let me know how."

I looked out the window and saw that the glitzy boutiques of Back Bay had given way to the rickety storefronts of South Boston. We had driven less than two miles over the course of just under ten minutes, but had left one world for another.

The Back Bay is old Boston—gaslit lanterns, magnificent nineteenth-century brick townhouses with graceful bow windows, impeccable front gardens, yummy mummies pushing baby strollers with perfect children to the Clarendon Street Park, nannies and cooks gathering at the meat counter at DeLuca's market every day to buy that evening's roast.

Southie is equally white and every bit as historic, but it has long been a refuge for the working Irish rather than the effete Wasps, and a refuge is just how they want to keep it. Visually, the neighborhood isn't much. The houses are wooden, crammed together along narrow streets lined with sidewalks stained with blackened gum. The tiny yards are all impeccably neat. The children wear carefully pressed plaid uniforms as they walk in small groups to their parochial schools. The store windows out along Broadway, the main thoroughfare, are covered with unseemly grates that shopkeepers pull down at closing time with a thunderous clack.

Outsiders? They hate them—the blacks, the young Wasps, the upwardly mobile families who move into the Town, as the locals call it, for its proximity to the water and the financial district. But they don't hate them, as in "they hate them." They hate them for what they represent, and what they represent is an intrusion into a close-knit community that may not have money, may not have lofty goals, but does have an enduring sense of self. They don't, by any measure, want that diluted.

I should know. It's where I grew up. It's where I'll always call home, even if I don't live there anymore. And it's always what I'll regard as the most wonderful place in the world.

The car pulled up in front of Amrhein's, a handsome brick block of a building right on Broadway where the $7.95 chicken piccata was considered outrageously gourmand. Gerry and Kevin jumped out, surveyed the scene, then beckoned for me to follow. We walked into the restaurant single-file, me in the middle. Inexplicably, I had gotten used to this protection surprisingly fast. The specter of violent death has a way of making us embrace any good change.

The painted middle-aged woman flitting about the front of the store looked at my two guards and warily asked, "Table for three, fellas?" Then she spied me, shrieked, and said, "Jack, I thought we'd lost you forever!"

I'll confess that despite my love of all things Southie, I don't come around much anymore—not because I've outgrown it, but because it seems so sad since my parents died. That and the fact that my tastes range more toward chateaubriand than flank steak these days—a fact that doesn't give me much pride, but is a reality just the same.

I stepped forward and hugged Judy McCormick, an old neighbor of mine growing up. We made small talk for a few minutes about who was doing what to who, then I peered around the old-fashioned lounge with the gray-haired bartender and the warren of dining rooms with high-backed booths and red vinyl banquettes and said, "I'm meeting someone. Guy by the name of Vinny Mongillo?"

Her face brightened even more as she reached into a slot on the side of the hostess stand and grabbed a plastic menu. "Oh, cousin Vinny," she said. "Back here. C'mon."

On the way toward the back of the dining room, I asked, "You two are related?" I mean, she had green eyes and auburn hair. Like I said, her last name was McCormick. If she's an Italian, Hank Sweeney's a Swede.

She turned and said, "God no. That's just what we call him, you know, from that movie. All the waitresses love him."

She brought me up to the last booth, where Vinny sat with his back to me reading Page Six of the *New York Post* while sticking half a potato skin in his ample mouth. He turned and said, "Christ, Judy, I thought we had standards in here." She laughed like she really meant it, put her palm on my cheek, and glided away.

I could walk into the downstairs dining room at Locke-Ober, juggle ten rabid foxes while doing my drop-dead imitation of Corporal Agarn on *F-Troop,* and the waiters would inquire—like they had marbles in their mouthes—if I'd like another Coke. Here, you make a lame joke, or just show up, and you get waitresses guffawing and affectionately patting you down. Maybe I ought to find my way home more often.

Vinny, to me, "Whoa there. You, my friend, look like shit."

His cell phone, sitting on the table, rang. He picked it up, looked at the caller ID, and hit a button that stopped the ringing. He put the phone back down.

I said, "Well, let's see. I've been chased through a swamp, shot at, nearly froze to death in Boston Harbor, and hit on the side of the head with a rock. Excuse the fuck out of me if I'm not looking my very best."

"Touchy, touchy." He picked up another potato skin and pushed the platter toward me. I took one as well. Surprising how much a simple wedge of potato can weigh. Not so surprising once I bit into it.

His phone rang again. The ringer, by the way, was still set to the annoying folk tune, or whatever the hell it was. That didn't make it any less annoying. Same routine—he picked it up, looked at the number, pressed a button, and put it back down on the bare Formica tabletop.

"Tell me what's been going on with you," he said. So I did. I filled him in on the chase the night before, on Terry Campbell's denials that morning, on the fact I had a retired police detective up from Marshton, two bodyguards standing in the foyer, a meeting coming up in three hours to try to take over the newspaper.

"By the way," he said, real casually, picking up the last of the potato skins without offering it to me. "Elizabeth felt pretty bad about today's story."

Anyone else hear the sound of screeching brakes?

I said, "What? What the hell are you talking about."

He was quiet for a moment as he tried to get a large piece of potato skin down his gullet. Finally, he replied, "She came by the gym at 7:30 this morning. She was saying she felt really awful that she put the screws to you on the Nathan Bowe killing, and, you know, blah blah blah."

"No. What's blah blah blah?"

"I don't know. I was running on the treadmill. The news was on the TV. Katie Couric was doing this thing on best Vegas restaurants. I was only half listening to her."

Of course. My ex-girlfriend spills her guts to the one guy she knows will have my ear, and that guy is entranced by Katie Couric's analysis of the best steakhouses along the Strip.

A young waitress with a slight Irish brogue came walking up and gushed at Vinny, "I saved you some of yesterday's pot roast. Would you like it in a sandwich?"

"Perfect," he said. "Tell William to cook my fries on the well-done side. And none of that horseradish sauce. Makes my nose itch."

She turned and started walking away without taking my order. Vinny called out to her, "Hey Kelly. I think my friend here wants a bite as well."

Without apologizing, she simply looked at me and put her pencil up to her pad. I ordered a hamburger, plain.

"All right," I said as she left, getting a little aggravated by all this. "Let's air out what we have on Lance Randolph. We've got solid information that shows that he embellished his prosecution record as district attorney during his two campaigns for governor. He inflated his conviction rate on murders, on rapes, on armed robberies and aggravated assaults, and we can attribute that to a *Record* review of all available court data. The real numbers show him to be somewhere in the upper middle of the state's DAs, according to that review, but his numbers show him to be number one in virtually every category."

Mongillo was smiling openly—so openly that I could count about a dozen bacon bits stuck in his teeth. "I love this shit," he said. He made a gripping motion with his enormous left paw and said, "The governor's future, the nominee to be the attorney general of the United States of America, and we have his balls right here. This is why I didn't bother with law school, because of stories like this."

I ignored that and said, "We need to put it together this afternoon. I need you to take over my files and throw in your interviews. I have it half-written already from last week, and I have one more idea I want to explore. But need you to do the rest. Call Randolph's people. Call the district attorney's association in Washington and get a quote putting prosecution rates in perspective."

"Gotcha."

"We need this in tomorrow's paper, come hell or gunshots. The *Traveler* skunked us today. We have to come back at them hard tomorrow."

He nodded.

I said, "Issue number two, Terry Campbell. If we can pin down this Fight for Life group, link them in print to the MIT bombing and show in some way that Campbell knew what he was getting into with his contribution to them, we've killed him—absolutely killed him."

"No easy task," Mongillo said. He was, of course, right.

I said, "And issue three. I need to hear why you don't like Fitzgerald."

With a mouth full of food, he said without hesitation, "Because he's a liar."

I've been hearing that more and more lately. His phone rang again. Same routine. He turned back to me, looked me flush in the face and said with stunning simplicity, "He makes shit up."

I rubbed my cheek with my hand. He folded up his *Post* and pushed it aside. I said, "Like what?"

Vinny deals more in the realm of facts than that hazy world of supposition, so I knew by asking this question, I wasn't going to get rhetoric or hollow accusations in response. And I didn't.

"Do you remember," he began, "that story about five years ago. The narcotics squad raided an apartment over in Roxbury. They burst through the door with a battering ram. There's an old guy, alone, inside. I think he's eight-six. He runs into his bedroom. Four cops knock his bedroom door right off its hinges. Their guns are drawn. They're screaming bloody murder. You know, 'Police with a warrant! Freeze! Get down or we'll shoot!' The guy froze all right. He has a heart attack and dies right there on the floor.

"Ends up, they have the wrong apartment. They're supposed to be in the one across the hall. The guy who died is a retired Baptist minister. The real drug dealer hears the commotion from his apartment, gets nervous, and tries to make a break for it. Problem is, he runs flat into a cop at the back door. People are screaming. There's a guy dead upstairs. Nobody's sure where the drugs are. Somebody takes a shot in the commotion, a cop, and he hits a young detective, shoots him dead, all by mistake. That's two dead. No arrest. No drugs seized."

I nodded. Kelly showed up with our food. In front of Mongillo, she carefully placed an almost comically thick pot roast sandwich on a toasted bulky roll with a heaping order of hand-cut, slightly overcooked French fries, a small ball of coleslaw, and a crisp piece of lettuce nailed by a toothpick to a brilliant red tomato. In front of me, she slapped down a plain hamburger sitting lonely in the middle of an otherwise empty plate.

Mongillo peered curiously at my lunch for a moment, then at his. He cleared his throat and said, "So anyway, Fitzgerald comes in with a column two days after the bungled raid saying that a young narcotics cop who was heading up the investigation mistakenly provided the wrong apartment number in the pre-raid briefing. Ironically, it was that same narc cop who was killed in the friendly fire. Seems to give them a little bit of cover, no? Fitzgerald doesn't attribute it. He doesn't source it in any way. He just states it as fact, Robert Fitzgerald throwing us another little crumb of wisdom from that journalistic mountaintop of his."

Mongillo was becoming more animated now, almost angry. I bit at my burger, which even in its celibate state, I have to confess, tasted pretty damned good. The Bristol Lounge at the Four Seasons Hotel doesn't do it any better at three times the price.

Mongillo continued, "Then it never comes up again. I waited until the search warrants were released. I wanted to review them, check the facts. But you know what? They disappeared. The court documents simply vanished. The magistrate said he didn't know where they were, and the cops said they lost their copy. So they paid a huge sum to the reverend's family and the case was forever closed."

I said, "But that doesn't prove Fitzgerald lied."

Mongillo said, "No, but I heard rumblings on the street. I kept hearing that Fitzgerald's account was flawed, but nothing I could ever nail down."

"Maybe he was given bad information," I replied.

"Bullshit. Then why didn't he attribute it. Then why didn't he revisit it. You know how much I dislike the guy, but I have to say one thing about him: he's not naïve. He wouldn't just take a pile of shit and try to put it into the paper. He wouldn't blindly buy someone's line. He knew what he was doing."

There was silence between us. Well, not quite silence. Mongillo began addressing his heaping pot roast sandwich and making all the commensurate noises that an overly demonstrative Italian would make during the beloved act of eating—sounds considerably louder than a pair of Wasps engaged in an act of sex.

I said, "What else."

He swallowed hard, hesitated, and said, "This is less concrete. But his stories are too neat, his quotes too perfect. He's got simple people talking much too eloquently. Mailmen are talking like great existentialists. He's either making up the quotes, or he's making up the people. Either way, he's a fraud."

I was about half through with my hamburger and losing my appetite fast, not because I was full, but because I felt empty.

I asked, "Which do you think?"

"Most of his stuff is political. He's doing analysis, or he's talking to some government official, and that's all fine. But when he does human interest, too often I can't find the regular Joe or Josephine who he's quoted by name in print. And when he just quotes someone without a name, I know he's piping that."

"What do you mean you haven't been able to find them? You've tried?"

Mongillo took another bite of his sandwich, put it down and lovingly, heavily salted his fries.

Then he looked up at me and nodded, his big eyes meeting mine in some sort of strange look of guilt. I repeated, "You've checked?"

He looked down at his plate. "Look, it's a disease, I admit it. I love the newspaper. I'm allowed, you know, even though I'm not like another son to the owners. It's the greatest place I've ever worked, and it covers the only city I've ever lived in."

He chewed on and swallowed a massive bite of pot roast, then said, "It's always bugged me, or scared me. I always thought he'd end up being an embarrassment to the paper some day.

"So I do a little private fact-checking from time to time. When he quotes someone by name, I look them up in the phonebook, or on the Internet, and if I can't find them, I sometimes swing by where they're supposed to live or work. And you know what, about half the time, these people don't exist."

There was another silence between us. If silence could have weight, this one would resemble an elephant. I knew Mongillo loved the *Record,* but I had no idea how much. I knew he disliked Fitzgerald, but I never realized the extreme depths of his disdain, or its basis.

"Why didn't you ever tell me any of this?" I asked.

He ripped away another piece of his sandwich, chewed, swallowed, and said, "I told you I didn't trust this guy. I told you all the time. You didn't want to hear any of it. The guy's important to you. He's important to the paper. I don't know. I guess I didn't think I could get through to you. Or maybe I like you so much I didn't really want to."

I said softly, "So you didn't do anything about it?"

He stared straight back at me, his big brown eyes set deep in his enormous olive face. He shook his head. "I did."

"What?"

"I told the publisher. I let Paul Ellis know.

"And now," he said softly, slowly, "Paul Ellis is dead."

twenty-five

Seven years earlier

THE LAST LINES OF light were fading from the early autumn sky as Robert Fitzgerald wheeled his Mercedes through the suburban Chestnut Hill neighborhood of stone fences and sprawling estates and slowly came around a gradual bend on Willow Way. And there in the dusky dark he saw a veritable city of satellite trucks parked happenstance on the side of the road, idling police cars, and television news crews doing stand-ups in the pointed glow of powerful lamps.

A State Police trooper standing in the middle of the lane waved a flashlight at Fitzgerald's car and hollered, "Keep it moving."

Fitzgerald pulled up to him, rolled down his window, and said, "I'm trying to get inside."

"No visitors," the trooper replied, barely giving Fitzgerald the dignity of a look. "Get your car out of here before I have it towed."

Fitzgerald put the Mercedes into park, which caused the trooper, a twenty-five-year veteran, to cast him a long glance. "The family requested my company," he said.

It was the governor's house—Governor Bertram J. Randolph. Randolph had been shot and killed that morning in a blaze of gunfire at a Roxbury School in what the television anchormen were saying was the first assassination of an elected official in the state's history. The student who shot him also killed his State Police bodyguard before turning the gun on himself.

"What's your name?"

"Robert Fitzgerald of the *Record.*"

The trooper regarded him for a moment in the dimming light and said simply, "Yes, of course. I read you all the time. Stay here a moment." With that, he walked over to his cruiser, which sat idling at the entrance to the grand, circular drive. A couple of television news producers and reporters inched toward Fitzgerald's car to get a glimpse of who he was, and whether he might be worth corralling for an interview.

The trooper returned a moment later with a clipboard in his hand. He scanned down a list, made a checkmark, and said, "Yes, they're expecting you, Mr. Fitzgerald. I'll move my car and you can proceed right in."

Fitzgerald drove through the opening in the eight-foot-high privet that sheltered the sprawling Bavarian-style house from the usually quiet street. He pulled past a gurgling fountain complete with a statue of Neptune, the god of the sea. The checkerboard-patterned driveway of red-and-white bricks was lined with freshly planted yellow and burgundy chrysanthemums. He had been here dozens of times before, whether to shoot a game of pool with the governor or for grand parties with Hollywood starlets, and still he was stunned at the graceful opulence that defined the lives of the truly, spectacularly rich.

A young butler in a navy blazer and khaki pants, no more than forty years old, greeted him solemnly at the door and beckoned him into the front hallway. "The District Attorney has asked me to show you to the study," he said, clasping his hands together.

Fitzgerald glanced around, surprised at the quiet and the lack of people. Ahead of him flowed a wide marble hallway. A grand, red-carpeted stairway rose to his right. A set of double doors to the left led to the living room, and beyond that, to the dining room, and then the kitchen. A matching set of double doors to his immediate right led to the formal salon, then to the library. All the lights were off in all the rooms, creating an eerie sense of emptiness fitting for the day.

Fitzgerald was about to follow the butler up the staircase when a lonely figure appeared at the other end of the hallway. "Robert?" a woman's voice called out. "Is that you?"

Fitzgerald strode toward the governor's wife, and she to him, and they embraced in the silence of the hall.

"My God, Lillian, I am so incredibly sorry for your loss," he said, his words formal but his tone comforting, familiar.

She began sobbing on his shoulder, convulsing in his arms. "He was my entire life, Robert. He'll always be my entire life." She pulled back and looked at Fitzgerald with her teary eyes and cried out, "What am I supposed to do now?"

He held her tighter. After a moment, she pulled away again, still within his grasp, and said, "And Robert, he loved you. He respected you so."

Fitzgerald wiped a tear of his own from the edge of each of his eyes and regarded the woman before him. Lillian Randolph was small and slender, probably sixty-five years old, with perfectly coifed gray hair, a well-preserved face that exuded wealth, and a surprisingly plainspoken way about her.

She said to him, "My Lance is such a hero. God is this going to affect him."

At her mention of her son, the butler, who was standing inconspicuously a few feet away, stepped forward and said, "Excuse me, Mrs. Randolph, but the district attorney is waiting for Mr. Fitzgerald in the study." Fitzgerald embraced Lillian one more time, and was led up the stairs.

As they walked down the carpeted hallway, Fitzgerald heard the low rumble of muffled conversation in the distance—a sound that became louder with each step. Finally, the young man walking just ahead of him stopped at a closed door, knocked softly, and poked his head inside. A moment later, he moved aside and waved Fitzgerald in.

Fitzgerald walked into the dimly lit study and looked around at the three men in the room. All of them stood up, took a step toward the distinguished reporter, and shook his hand, exchanging niceties and condolences in the process. A cloud of cigar smoke drifted through the air.

Straight ahead, a pair of French doors was pulled open to reveal a small balcony outside. From experience, Fitzgerald knew that the balcony, in turn, overlooked a stone swimming pool, a clay tennis court, and beyond that, a lawn that rolled down a gentle hill toward a stable.

Black- and green-shaded lamps cast hazy light around the room. Two walls were made up of full-length bookcases, complete with rolling ladders that reached the soaring ceilings. The other two walls were paneled by cherry wood.

"Robert, sit down, please," said Jeb Forman, pointing the lit end of his cigar at him. Fitzgerald looked at Forman a moment. He appeared out of place in the room, dressed, as he was, in a pair of faded jeans and an old black tee shirt that said, "Bacardi" across the front. His shaggy hair looked like it hadn't had the benefit of a pair of scissors in what had to have been months. He was young, and his brashness sometimes approached condescension.

Forman was Bertram Randolph's lead political strategist, creator of so many of the successful television advertisements that contributed to the governor's overwhelming popularity.

Fitzgerald sat in one of the matching wing chairs, such that the four men all formed a perfect square, an ottoman in front of each, a side table separating them. Forman was to Fitzgerald's left, Benjamin Bank, Randolph's chief of staff, was to his right, and Lance Randolph sat straight across.

"We're devastated, obviously," Forman said, though he didn't sound it. He took a long puff on his cigar, allowed the smoke to drift aimlessly from his mouth, and leaned toward Fitzgerald. "We've lost a great man. Now it's a question of what else we're about to lose."

As Forman spoke these last words, his eyes flitted to the other two, who sat silently looking back at him.

Fitzgerald, still wearing his gray suit jacket, asked in his deep voice, "Meaning?"

Forman replied, "Meaning politics has become a pretty vicious undertaking in this particular state. Meaning somebody somewhere is going to start spreading sleazy innuendo and false rumors about Lance being the only survivor in today's rampage."

He stopped to take another drag on his fat cigar, blew the smoke into the middle of the square, and added, "You're an old family friend, Robert. You knew the old man before he was the old man. I think it might be in Lance's best interests to describe to you what happened today and you might see fit to make a story of it."

Fitzgerald shot a glance across to Randolph, who stared at the floor in front of his chair. The reporter had to admit to himself that the questions had already entered his mind: How did Lance survive? What did he do to help his old man? Did he flee?

Bank, a nervous little man with a thin voice, cleared his throat and said, "And the bottom line, Robert, is that you're read, and you're believed. If you explain what happened in a bylined story, then it will never be an issue again."

Fitzgerald leaned back in his chair and said, "Well, I'd be interested in hearing what did happen out there today." He looked from one to the other to the other. Only Forman met his gaze.

Forman said, "Lance, go ahead, tell Mr. Fitzgerald." He spoke to him in that kind of weary tone that an impatient older sister might use to her little brother.

Lance Randolph shifted in his chair, stared at his hands clasped on top of his right thigh, and said in a low voice, "It was awful."

He looked up at Fitzgerald with his big, deep-set eyes. He was wearing an open-collared blue shirt, a pair of khakis and loafers without socks. Half his face was side-lit by the dull lamp, the other half lost in the gauzy shadows of the room. He had watched his father die at the hand of a gunman that very morning, and now he sat before the city's preeminent political reporter, hoping to salvage his reputation, to tamp down any questions before they ignited into political flames.

Randolph was thirty-six years old, and to Fitzgerald, he looked every day that young, with his stylish blond hair, the perfect lines just beginning to groove his pleasant face, and the constantly optimistic tone of his voice—tonight aside. Behind him, Fitzgerald saw a nearly full moon suspended in the opening of the French doors.

Fitzgerald reached into the breast pocket of his suit and pulled out a small reporter's notebook, paged it open, and looked back at Randolph.

Randolph said, "He did the school event, no hitches. Just your basic speech, in and out, everyone cheering, music playing, the whole thing. Outside, we met the construction workers. My dad worked the line, shaking everyone's hand, joking. You know his drill."

He stopped for a moment, hung his head, and laughed a shallow laugh. "He said to the last guy, 'I want you to meet my son, the future governor.' He had just started introducing me around that way, even though I warned him to cut the bullshit."

Forman, waving his cigar in the air, impatiently cut in. "The point, Lance. The point."

Randolph shot him a cold look, then returned an easier gaze to Fitzgerald.

"So we come to the end of the line and there's this dirt area between us and the street, marked off by a couple of construction trailers. They just hadn't cleaned it up yet. I said to my dad, 'Let's go back through the building.' But he's still in political mode, and he says to me, 'You afraid of getting your wingtips dirty?'

"So we walked around the trailer and onto the hard-packed dirt. It was maybe twenty yards to the street, probably less. Trooper Gowan, dad's bodyguard, walked ahead of us to open the car door. My father was telling me about a fundraising trip he was planning to California More and more, he was thinking of running for the Senate—"

"The point, Lance," Forman interjected, his words soaked with frustration. "Robert is waiting for the point."

Fitzgerald said coolly, "Take your time, Lance."

Randolph cleared his throat. Someone knocked softly on the door. Before anyone could respond, the young butler came in carrying a tray with a decanter of port and four crystal glasses. He set them quietly down on a sideboard and walked out of the room. Bank immediately lifted himself up, ambled over to the table and began filling the glasses, delivering them in pairs to the rest of the group. By now, Fitzgerald noticed, the moon had risen out of view.

Randolph said, his voice becoming almost trancelike, "And as we're walking I see this kid in a flowing white coat, like a lab coat, come walking around the far corner of the building. He calls out to my father. He says, 'Hey, governor.' And what does my old man do? He's a politician. He loves people. So of course, he starts heading right over to him. I'm standing in the middle of the dirt patch. Gowan's over by the car, the kid is standing near the building, and my old man is approaching him."

Randolph paused, swallowed hard, and continued, his voice so low now that Fitzgerald had to lean forward to hear. "The kid pulls out a gun. He took it right out of the inside of his coat, a stout little semiautomatic. My father stopped in his tracks. I don't know what was going on in his mind. I'm behind him, and I scream, 'Drop it! Drop it.' I look over at Gowan, who's reaching for his sidearm, but it's too late. The kid fires at him and he crumples to the ground."

He stopped and stared at his shoes, at the maroon and navy patterns along the border of the rich Oriental rug. His body began quivering slightly and he brought his hands up to his face.

Forman said, sternly, "Lance, finish the story."

Randolph let his palms drift from his cheeks to the back of his neck. He looked up slightly toward Forman and said, "Go fuck yourself, Jeb." His voice came out like that of a small child.

Forman's face reddened. He slammed his closed fist against the chair's arm. "Lance, we have a state in turmoil. We need you to be clear and cogent and to tell your story."

Bank leaned back in his chair, sipped absently on his port, and gazed out the open doors. Randolph stared again at Fitzgerald who, when he began talking, stared at nothing at all.

"Then he aims at my father. He had the gun down here"—he made a motion with his arms like he was cradling a weapon down around his chest—"and he fires. He kept pulling the trigger. I was about five, maybe eight yards away. I lost my mind. I didn't know what I was doing. I could barely hear the shots. I just raced toward my father.

"The bullets must have still been flying. I didn't hear them. But I saw this kid still holding the gun. When I got to my dad, he was covering his face with his hands, staggering to the side and ready to fall down. I pushed him to the ground and dove on top of him. I could feel his blood oozing out of his chest and onto my clothes. I could hear his last breath leave him. I could see his eyes go vacant.

"I looked up and this kid is still standing over us. He's staring at me, so serene. He presses his finger against the trigger and nothing comes out. So he reaches into his pocket and pulls out another clip. And he says to me, his voice calm as mine is right now, 'This is your lucky day.' And he takes the barrel of the gun and puts it up against the roof of his mouth and blows his head off."

Randolph began quaking more than quivering, staring again at the floor. He looked up at Fitzgerald one more time and said, "I tried to save my dad. I swear to God, I tried to save him." Then he bowed his head and the tears flowed down his young cheeks.

Jeb Forman took a final draw on his cigar, stubbed it out in an ornate jade ashtray, and exhaled hard. He looked at Fitzgerald and said triumphantly, dramatically, "He tried to save his father. I'll repeat that for everyone out there who's trying to figure out how he was the only one who survived." He paused, then presented each word as if they were individually wrapped: "He tried to save his father."

Fitzgerald wrote a couple more sentences in his notebook. Bank drained his second port. Randolph sat convulsing in tears. And Forman slapped his knees against his thighs and said, "Well, I think that's called a wrap."

"Hold on," Fitzgerald replied, his voice low and firm. "Lance, I've got a couple of questions I need you to answer."

Randolph peered up through his hands. Fitzgerald asked, "You were standing right behind your father when the shooting began, right? Wouldn't any errant shots have struck you? Did you feel bullets graze your clothes?"

Randolph shook his head and replied, "No. I guess this kid was accurate."

Fitzgerald nodded and bit his bottom lip. He paged back through his notebook as the room fell dead quiet.

"Here's what bothers me," he finally said, looking across at

Randolph. "The cops told me earlier today that this assassin didn't even empty one full clip. He still had a couple of bullets left in the clip in his gun, and there weren't any empties on the ground. Now you're telling me something completely different, but the physical evidence would say that you're wrong."

Randolph, suddenly wide-eyed, stared searchingly at Forman, who rested his chin on his palm and looked straight ahead, deep in thought.

"Maybe I saw it wrong," Randolph said, visibly frazzled, shaking his head while he spoke. "I thought I saw what I saw, but you have to remember, I'm on the ground. I've got my father gasping beneath me. I'm looking up at an odd angle. Maybe he was doing something else."

"You said you heard your father draw his last breath before the kid changed his clip."

Randolph looked again at Forman, who was now staring at the floor.

Forman broke the silence. "Look, Robert. A state trooper was dead. The guy's father lies dying from thirteen fucking bullets that tore through every conceivable part of his body. He looks up and the kid is still holding a semiautomatic rifle pointed at his fucking face.

"So maybe he didn't perfectly catalogue everything in his brain to relay to *The Boston Record* in hopes that the entire nation has the clearest, most accurate image of what happened on that fucking dirt patch in Roxbury today. Maybe he's just human. Maybe you ought to cut him a little slack."

Fitzgerald glared back at Forman and replied, "I understand, but I'll decide the questions I ask here."

There was a long pause. Forman asked in a condescending tone, "Well then, Robert, do you have any more questions, or are we all done here?"

Fitzgerald sat in his chair, hunched forward, looking down at the words scratched onto the pages of his notebook but really seeing nothing at all. He thought of his best friend in life, his closest confidante, the governor, gunned down in a hail of bullets by some punk kid who confused television drama with daily reality. He thought of the widow downstairs, a beautiful, generous woman whose regal life of privilege was suddenly stripped of its entire purpose. He thought of the young man across from him, thrown into a situation that no normal person could ever comprehend.

What really happened out there today, he wondered.

He slowly folded up his notebook, slipped it into his breast pocket, and shot Forman a cold look. Then he gazed across at Randolph and said, "I'm all set, Lance." With that, he pulled himself up and walked silently out the door.

twenty-six

I PACED BACK AND forth in the hushed, carpeted hallway, wondering what words were being spoken, what direction was being followed on the other side of the oak-paneled double doors that led to the executive boardroom of *The Boston Record*.

Quiet as I was, try as I might, I couldn't hear a damned thing except the sounds of my uneven breathing and the gentle drip of my burgeoning ulcer. I'll confess that I was perspiring under my navy pin-stripe suit jacket, meaning I wouldn't and couldn't take it off. The only rule of business of which I'm even remotely aware goes as follows: Never let them see you sweat.

I knew from Cal Zinkle that Brent Cutter was making his presentation to a sympathetic committee just before mine. I pictured him sitting at the head of the table, his hair slicked perfectly back, his demeanor one of entitled confidence, talking the Harvard Business School talk of skill sets and repurposing and optimum performances and misintermediation. The damned board would probably be splattering drool all over the shiny wood tabletop, forgetting to ask even a single question about his views on community journalism or the future use of the *Record*'s foreign bureaus. "Asshole" is a word that came immediately to mind.

Helpless is another, mostly because that's how I felt. It's a family-owned newspaper, and a member of that ownership family seemed ready to throw it all away. And here I was, at the place I loved more than any other, answering to a group of strangers that I barely knew, trying to salvage a business that wasn't mine.

The door swung slowly open, causing me to freeze in place and lean coolly against the wall as if I was just waiting for the local tavern to open so I could go in and get my first drink of the day, if I drank this early in the day, which I usually don't, though now could be the potential exception.

Out walked Brent Cutter. He wore a fashionable brown suit. He padded toward me, shot a smug look in my direction and said in a whimsical tone, "Good luck."

How do you reply to that? I chose not to, mostly because I couldn't think of anything appropriately witty to say, though I did stare him in the eye as he sauntered past me, staying completely still. Once he was gone, I turned to make my way into the boardroom when the door pitched open again. This time, out walked Terry Campbell, carrying a briefcase in one hand and a legal pad in the other.

He looked at me with that wrinkled, bulldog face of his, surprised but not flustered. "Good afternoon, Jack," he said, as if we just ran into each other in line for an Oreo McFlurry at the neighborhood McDonald's. I quickly recalled my vow to break his grubby hands if he put them on my newspaper again, shot a glance into the boardroom, and decided that this probably wasn't the time or the proper place to fulfill prior promises. Instead I gave him an imperceptible nod and walked into the room.

Cal Zinkle was standing right inside the door. All the other directors were milling about, pouring cups of coffee or assembling cheese and crackers on the side buffet, many of them talking to each other in inaudible tones. Cal put his arm over my shoulder, and before he could say anything, I said in a voice just north of a whisper, "I'd like to kill that son of a prick."

"Easy, tiger," he replied. "We need you on your best behavior right now." He paused and steered me outside the double doors, back into the hallway that was empty again. He let go of my shoulder and said, "He was making his play. Cutter's behind him one hundred percent. They've struck an agreement. Campbell buys the paper and Cutter becomes publisher, with an arrangement to keep the *Record* under local control for the next three years—Brent and this board being in control."

I knew Brent had no small amount of weasel blood coursing through his body, but I must have missed it when he actually grew whiskers and a big, bushy tail. I knew this was coming. I knew the inevitability of it all. But the sight of Campbell, right here in the boardroom of *The Boston Record,* sent tremors of anger through my exhausted body.

Zinkle added, "I know it's infuriating, but right now you don't have the luxury of anger. You have to focus. If you want to make sure that *The Boston Record* remains an independent newspaper with a top-notch publisher, then you have to walk inside that room and give one hell of a presentation."

I'm a natural pessimist, which isn't always a bad thing. It gets your hackles up and your sensors firing and pushes you harder to achieve what you want to attain. With that in mind, I asked, "Are you telling me the committee is inclined to go with Campbell and Cutter?"

"I'm telling you, he has made a formidable and attractive offer."

I shook my head in disgust. I felt the hallway, the world, spinning all around me. Up was down and down was up. There were no touchstones of normalcy any more, none of the serenity of sanity. I asked, "You got my message on Campbell's funding of the militant group, Fight for Life, right? He contributed to the bombing over at MIT."

Zinkle shook his head. "He'll disavow any knowledge of the group. He'll say he had no idea it was a violent organization. And the board here will tell you that's his private business. What the board cares about is the dollars and cents, the stock price."

I stared at him for a long moment, trying to process what I was hearing, though damned if I was able. So I said, "Fuck it. Let's go." And we walked into the room, me ahead of him.

The boardroom of *The Boston Record* is a majestic place, almost antithetical to the pathological disorder of the newsroom downstairs. The table itself is long and wide and glows in the rays of sun that stream through the unadorned floor-to-ceiling windows with the unimpeded view of the downtown skyline. Various directors—there were five of them in the room—came around the table to shake my hand, then guided me to one of the highback leather chairs at the head of the table.

The directors present were Slade Harmon, one of the more

respected black ministers in town; Katrina Pelletier, the editor emeritus at the *Christian Science Monitor*—"emeritus" in this case being the Latin word for "forced out"; Jacob Higham, a successful hotelier, Jewish activist, and, not coincidentally, John Cutter's roommate at Yale; and Barnaby Stone, manager of the world's largest mutual fund. Zinkle made five.

I had no notes with me, and truth is, barely any wits. As I made myself comfortable, Katrina Pelletier, who looks like Janet Reno, only without the good looks and gushing charm, said to me, "As you know, Jack, we are in an emergency session of the executive committee of the board of directors to address the tragic circumstances of Paul Ellis's death. Our first priority is to select a new publisher who can lead the *Record* at this most difficult time. In that regard, I'm glad you are able to join us today. Do you have any sort of statement you'd like to share with the committee?"

All right, I obviously should have been prepared for this question. I sat there looking at her, thinking of Brent Cutter, whose pretty-boy face I'd like to kick in, of Terry Campbell, whose face really can't be kicked in any more so maybe I'd pummel his privates. Then I thought of the men and women downstairs, people like Mongillo and Steele who dedicated their lives to the bread-and-butter work of this newspaper.

"I'll be very brief," I said, folding my hands in front of me and looking down at a distant spot on the table. "I'd like to keep this newspaper under Cutter-Ellis ownership, and under Cutter-Ellis control, even if one of the Cutters doesn't seem to want it anymore. The family has given one hundred and twenty-seven years to this publication. They've taken it through the Great Depression and countless recessions. They've seen it through two world wars, Vietnam, a new war against terrorism. But most of all, the paper has taken its identity from the city, and given the city some of its identity in return. We as a newspaper reported on this city through the violent angst of busing, through boom times, through horrible downturns. And always, always, always, we maintained the highest level of quality, sometimes at considerable cost, because when you're a member of the Cutter-Ellis family, when you run a newspaper this great, when you're in a city as sophisticated as this, that's just what you do. If Brent Cutter can't see himself clear to play a major role, then I offer myself, because at this point, the paper, its quality, is larger than the family itself."

Someone somewhere was playing "America the Beautiful," though I fear I was the only one who could hear it.

I added, "This isn't a chain newspaper with a corporate office in a city where few of us have ever been. It never has been, it was never meant to be. It's owned by Bostonians and run by Bostonians. Paul Ellis sure as hell knew that. He told me as much when I sat with him in the Public Garden four days ago, just an hour before he was killed. He wanted to reject this effort by Terry Campbell, or perhaps more accurately, defeat it. You should all want to do the same."

I concluded, "To that end, I offer myself as a candidate for the next publisher in the rich tradition of the Cutter-Ellis family. I have a vast knowledge of the newsroom. My own father worked for more than three decades in the pressroom. I have an impeccable reputation in this community where I was born and raised. And I will keep this newspaper under Cutter-Ellis control, which is exactly where it belongs." I paused, then added: "I'd be honored to answer any and all of your questions."

I would have liked loud applause and hooting and hollering. What I got was silence and Katrina staring at me like a spectator might look at an animal in a zoo exhibit, something, perhaps, in the Jungle House. Before she could say anything, Barnaby Stone spoke from the other side of the table.

"Mr. Flynn, very nice of you to take the time to come up and visit with us today. I've looked over your career history, which is certainly impressive in its journalistic credentials and background. But I have to ask you, do you have any management or business experience which we arc not currently aware of?"

As he asked the question, he gave me a squinty look, I suspect more for the dramatics than for lack of vision.

I replied, "None whatsoever, but I can tell you that you should never end a sentence with a preposition, as you just did."

Just kidding. I said, "I ran a lemonade stand for three weeks in the summer between third and fourth grades, and our revenues averaged between $3.75 and $4.20 per week."

Kidding again. Now was not the time for humor, at least with these people, and in my current frame of mind, I don't even think I could get a rise out of the people who make the laugh track for *Cheers*.

What I really said was, "My expertise, or rather my strength, is in the newsroom, on the journalistic side of things. I'll admit that up front. But I'll also tell you, in this complicated day and age, with twenty-four-hour cable television and the Internet bombarding every house, that it's not a bad strength to have. On the business side of things, I'll learn it, and in the meantime, and maybe for all time, I'll hire someone who knows that end of things, someone who I can trust."

Stone again: "So you'll concede that you don't know the business end of this company, the circulation reports and the budget figures and the revenue goals and all the complicated equations that lead from one to the other?"

"I know the journalism, which is the point of this company."

Stone replied, his voice growing less polite and more firm, "Part of the point, sir. The thousands of shareholders this paper has would certainly argue that this being a capitalist society and the *Record* being a publicly traded company, its foremost point is to make money."

"And to make money," I replied, trying not to betray the well of exasperation building up within me, "we have to have one hell of a good product to offer, no? So we need someone to massage that product, to oversee it, someone who knows what good journalism is and what it means to the community."

Jacob Higham cut in from the far end of the table. "So if the journalism is so paramount to you, why not become the next editor of the *Record* rather than publisher? As a matter of fact, Mister Campbell and Brent Cutter made that very proposition not twenty minutes ago. They were both in agreement that you would make a stupendous editor-in-chief."

Were they now? Clank. That sound you're hearing is my jaw hitting the floor. Thank the good Lord it's not made of glass or I'd be, as they say, a broken man.

For the record, as we like to say, the newspaper hierarchy goes as follows: Publisher, who is tantamount to the chief executive officer; president, who effectively runs the institution day-to-day; editor-in-chief, who runs the newsroom side of a newspaper; and under the editor, the various lower-level editors, bureau chiefs, reporters, and copy editors.

My first impulse was to get up, storm down to the president's office, and throttle the gaseous snot who sits in there. My second impulse was to stare coldly at Higham and announce, "First off, we currently have an excellent editor of the *Record*. Second, I am not available to be either the editor or the publisher of a *Boston Record* that is no longer owned by the Cutter-Ellis family. I will not—repeat: will not—oversee the dismantling of what is one of the foremost newspapers in the United States and, indeed, the world."

And that's what I said.

Silence. I could hear the heater purr from the corners of the room. Someone clinked a coffee cup against its saucer. Katrina asked in that dullish voice of hers, "Do you understand what minority shareholder rights are?"

No, actually, but I wasn't about to let her know that, and it's tough to tell with this woman whether she's being kind or slicing and dicing you five ways from hell. I replied, "I know that every shareholder of this company has a right to expect that we will produce the very best newspaper possible, and that in the process, we'll also turn a profit. Paul Ellis, and John Cutter before him, liked to say that good journalism made for good business, and vice versa. I'd wholeheartedly agree with that."

Stone didn't seem to be reading from the same business philosophy book. He cut in again and said, "Minority shareholder rights mean that this board you're looking at right here has to do what's in the best interest of the shareholders. If an offer is made for the company which significantly inflates the stock price, we have no real choice but to take it. If we don't, we face the prospect of a long and costly court suit and a deflated stock position. That sets us up as a prime target for a takeover by someone else."

There was a pause. Someone tried to speak, but Stone cut them off. "This compromise, leaving the paper under local control for three years, is about as good a deal as we can cut—certainly better than anything I would have expected."

More silence. I sat there looking at my hands. It didn't seem like there was anything else to say to these clowns. It didn't seem like there was anything left to say to anybody these days.

Katrina spoke up. "Jack, there is, of course, the option of you putting together another purchasing group and taking the newspaper private."

An excellent idea. And I think I'll head home and have sex with each and every one of the Dallas Cowboy cheerleaders tonight. I mulled that a moment—the purchase, not the cheerleaders. Paul had mentioned the same point Monday morning, but if someone of his immense financial abilities thought it impossible to put the funding together, I didn't think there was much of a chance for me, considering I barely have my multiplication tables memorized.

I shook my head and looked down at the table, catching a scant reflection of myself. "We've looked into that already, and it doesn't appear to be plausible," I said.

I looked around the table for a moment, letting my eyes fall, then focus, on Cal Zinkle, who had been uncharacteristically, conspicuously—obnoxiously—silent through the entire session. He averted my gaze. Slade Harmon said, "Jack, none of this is personal, and none of this we take lightly. We'll give your views every possible consideration."

Forgive me, Slade, for being less than enthused by your leadership.

I should have said that, but I didn't. Instead, I did my best Zinkle imitation, meaning I said nothing. Katrina said, "Well, Jack, unless you have anything else you'd like to add, I think the committee has quite a few very important issues and options to talk over."

I looked around the table from one to the next, my lips pursed and my head slowly shaking.

I said, "When you sit in this room mulling the future of this great institution, I just hope you take into consideration the relationship between the Cutter-Ellis family, this newspaper and this city that dates back to the last century. We are all nothing more than stewards of a publication far more important than any one of us. Brent Cutter happens to be a particularly bad steward, which is why so much power is placed in the board. You basically have a choice: You can maintain, and even improve *The Boston Record,* and thus, the city it serves. Or you can destroy it.

"And if you choose the latter, you have to ask, how many residents will be left uninformed. How many politicians will be left unsupervised. How many lies will never be reported. How many bribes will go uncaught. How many campaign promises will be willfully broken. All because this town will no longer have a newspaper with the ability to represent the people and the intelligence to give voice to the voiceless."

With that, I pushed my leather chair back and strode for the door. No one even bothered saying good-bye.

twenty-seven

I USED TO THINK I knew lonely. Lonely was staring down at the angelic face of your wife, sweat still gathered in her hair, minutes after she died in the delivery room of Georgetown Hospital, your infant daughter also dead before she ever drew a breath.

Loneliness is a few years later, the sound of the door languidly clicking shut when your girlfriend walks out of the apartment for the final time, her muffled sobs in the hallway, and then nothing at all.

Lonely was walking through the Public Garden on a drizzling Christmas morning wearing dirty jeans and a frayed shirt in the company of just your dog, watching young families glide by on their way to church, fathers holding the mittened hands of their little girls, peals of laughter, shouts of familial joy.

Lonely was sitting on a wet bench later that afternoon wondering what your life would have been like but for that awful day, thinking how much you miss the woman you married, then wondering if your former girlfriend was decked out in a red velvet dress and flashing that sophisticated crinkle-eyed smile at her new boyfriend's mother.

Now I was learning a new shade of loneliness. Lonely these days was losing your publisher, your newspaper, your livelihood, your pride, your sense of self, your security, finding out your mentor might be a fraud, all in the course of about four days. All of which is exactly how I felt as I staggered from the building into the awaiting unmarked cruiser at the *Record*'s front door.

"Where we heading, Jack?" Gerry Burke, the police driver, asked from the front seat. Good question. Truth is, I had no idea.

I didn't even stop in the newsroom, because everyone would have

241

been asking me how it went, and how it went was absolutely awful. They're looking to me for salvation. Instead, I find out we're about to get bought out by a cheap chain because I found myself incapable of convincing a few board members to stay the course of the last 127 years. The word failure came to mind. So did loser, not to mention jackass.

And at that exact point, I couldn't go home because, well, I didn't have one.

"Holy Name Cemetery," I finally said. Gerry gave me a quick, odd look, as did Kevin, who was also sitting in the front seat.

"Not for eternity. I just want to swing through for a moment and take a look at something."

That something being my father's grave. If you can't function among the living, then pay a call on the dead. At least that's what Dr. Kevorkian used to say. I think.

My cellular phone chimed and I snapped it up. Mine, just to be clear, was set on the ordinary, standard ring—none of this "Hungarian Marching Song" or "Swanee River" for me.

"Flynn."

"Sweeney. Where you at?"

"Physically or mentally?"

"Let's start slow. Physically."

"In the cruiser with your boys. We're heading over to West Roxbury to Holy Name Cemetery."

He said, "Something you want to tell me."

"Yeah, my father's buried there."

"Good for you. We need to talk."

I asked, "You know where Holy Name is?"

He almost sounded angry again in that way he gets. "Know where it is? For chrissakes, it's like old home week when I go over there. I know half the people in the place. I know cemeteries are supposed to depress me, but Jesus, Mary, and Joseph, I walk out of there feeling like a million bucks. I get to sleep in a bed without a top or a velvet lining."

"It's all the way in the back right corner, right under the biggest oak tree in the place," I said.

"Sounds like he's a neighbor of my old friend, Kenny Lonagan. I wonder if they've met."

I had to think about that one for a moment. I said, "I'll see you there."

"Jack?"

"Yeah?"

"What about mentally?"

"Couldn't be worse. But thanks for asking."

"Well, I don't think I'm about to make it any better. I'll be there in ten."

That ancient tree wasn't yet in bloom, and the grass all around the place still looked thin and brown from the harsh winter. But someone had planted two small American flags on either side of my old man's marker, and those flags added a needed dash of color as they fluttered in the chill spring breeze.

I never quite know what I'm supposed to do at a cemetery, which probably explains why I spend so little time there. Do you kneel, do you sit, do you talk, do you read, do you think? I felt like I needed to do all that and more.

The unmarked cruiser idled at a respectable distance, and Gerry and Kevin each stood inconspicuously among graves on opposite sides of me about thirty yards away.

With no one within earshot, no one living, anyway, I said, "Well, Dad, you always wanted me to come work at the paper, so I did. Of course, I think you meant the pressroom, not the newsroom, and right about now, that would probably be one hell of a lot easier, not to mention safer.

"Now Paul Ellis is dead. The paper, your paper, my paper, Paul's paper, is about to be sold, and once that happens, it will never be the same. I don't know as there's anything I can do about it anymore. But Dad, I want you to know, I'm trying. I really am."

I paused, staring at the gray granite stone that said simply, "Arthur

Flynn, 1930–1993." My father was never really the flamboyant type.

"What would you do? The one guy I can ask, Fitzgerald, may be part of the problem." I asked again, louder, "So what am I supposed to do?" Obviously, I was searching for inspiration, and if it was divine rather than pragmatic, so be it.

Silence. The wind rustled through the branches of that nearby oak. The flags fluttered a bit more. A scrap of trash—a discarded Dunkin Donuts cup—tumbled into a bush adorning an adjacent gravestone.

"A lot of people came before me at this paper. A lot of people gave their sweat, their blood, their hearts and their souls to the *Record*, you among them. I'll do what I can to keep it going. I'll do whatever I can to find out how John Cutter died, who killed Paul Ellis, and why."

I grew angrier standing there talking to no one who could overtly hear. I raised my voice and said, "I'm going to get justice if it's the last thing I do. And maybe it will help keep me alive as well."

I heard another car motor up, stop, and a door slam. I saw Sweeney walking across the colorless grass, weaving among the grave markers, heading toward me. He carried some papers under his right arm that looked to be files.

About ten yards away, he paused and read one of the stones, then knocked his hand against the top. "This is Kenny Lonagan, guy I told you about," he called out to me.

Then he looked at the marker and said, "Kenny, this here is Mr. Flynn. Mr. Flynn, this is Kenny Lonagan. You boys are going to be spending a lot of time together so you might as well get to know each other."

He sidled up to me and said, "Hey there, son."

He looked tired, a fact he explained to me by saying, "Jesus Christ, my idea of work down in Florida is watering the yard, and I usually do that with my fat behind planted in a lawn chair. This police stuff is hard work. I don't know how I did it all those years."

That said, he also looked content, even happy, as if he was exactly where he belonged, doing precisely what he was meant to do in life.

I smiled along with him. I couldn't help it. Before I could even get a word out, he handed me a file and said, "Here, take a look-see at this. I don't want you thinking I'm crazy or telling you some tall tales."

I opened up a manila file folder and saw the handwritten words at the top of a standard police form, "John E. Cutter/Sudden death. Four Seasons Condominiums," along with the date. I felt an immediate pit in my stomach. This was the police report, I quickly realized—different than the coroner's report I had perused two mornings before.

"Check out item twenty-nine," Sweeney said to me. He stood a few feet away, looking down at my father's grave.

As I scanned down, he said to me, "I like this color granite. It catches the light nice, but not so much that you can't read it like with a lot of them."

I said, "I can see you in this color."

He snickered, and replied, "Yeah, maybe. Or maybe I should do red so I stand out. Tough to make a name for yourself in this place."

"This where you're going to be buried?" I asked.

He waved his hand at me in that way he does, like I was bothering him, even though I knew I wasn't. "Oh, I don't know. I have to see what Mother wants. Christ, I hope she doesn't want us going down in Florida. We'll be rotted from the damned heat two hours after we die."

I gladly returned to the sheet. Item 29 said, "Discarded blue tissue, located on tile floor behind toilet basin."

"Flip the page," Sweeney instructed me.

I flipped the page and saw another official-looking form that said, "Directive for toxicology test," complete with John Cutter's name, the pertinent death information, and Sweeney's signature and shield number.

He said, "So there was a tissue and there was an order. I'm not some senile old goat, even if I am a senile old goat."

He laughed at this. I continued to eye the file. He asked, "You know where I found that?"

I shook my head.

"First I looked in the police files. Pain in the ass to nail it down. The snots in administration were going to make me wait seven days for this." Louder, angry: "Seven days! Can you believe that shit. So I called the commissioner and he helped me out. I get the file pulled out of the archives, and it's got nothing in it—I mean, nothing. That order was missing, and the list of items in the room was torn out. Someone tore the damn page right in half."

The pale sun was starting to slip out of view and a particularly muscular gust of wind blew in from the west, causing Sweeney to look toward it, then turn to me with a smile. "Weather," he said, the word standing out there on its own like a rock. "I love it. We don't have weather in Florida. You know what? Check that. We have two kinds of weather—hot and muggy, and usually they're on the same day."

"I don't get it, lieutenant," I said. "If someone ripped these out of the file and stole them, then what am I doing with my hands on them now?"

He focused hard on me for a moment, the corners of his lips turning up on his boyishly handsome face.

"Because, son, they stole them from the official file—the file I left in the homicide bureau the day I retired. Whoever stole the records didn't realize that I also kept duplicate files of my own, and when I retired, I had all my duplicates shipped over to the archives. I just had these pulled out today—with no small effort, I might add."

He smiled at me and I held his eye for a moment, approvingly. He said, "What are you doing tonight?"

"Putting my resumé together and checking property values in suburban Kansas City." He gave me a quizzical look. I said, "Long story. But I'll find some time. What are you proposing."

"Well," he said, "The missing files hint at foul play. I'm hoping against hope that somewhere in an evidence locker in the bowels of the coroner's building we'll find an explanation of what happened with John Cutter." He reached into the pocket of his navy blue windbreaker and pulled out a pair of keys strung on a paper clip. "And these will help us get there."

I furrowed my brow. He added, "The coroner's office, the evidence locker, care of some good old friends, or old good friends, however you wordsmiths would say it."

I was struck immediately by what was at stake, not for me, but for him. I said, "You're not going down there. You get caught breaking and entering, you get arrested, you lose your pension—everything you busted your ass for all those years on the force."

Rather than argue the point, he asked, "Jack, tell me the alternative?"

"I go in alone. I've got nothing to lose at this point. Christ, I've already lost most of what I had. There's nothing left."

He regarded me for a moment as I regarded him, then he said, "We go in together. Yeah, I know it's your friend involved, and your newspaper, but somebody messed with old Hank Sweeney, and that was a big, big mistake."

twenty-eight

SITTING IN THE CAR with my police escorts, I still had no idea where I was going, today or in life, so I did what any red-blooded American would do in this age of endless technology: I sat back and listened to my cellular telephone messages.

First up was Cal Zinkle, saying, quite simply, "Zinkle here. Call me." That's four more words than he spoke on my behalf at the board meeting. Next was Luke Travers, followed by Brent Cutter, then Robert Fitzgerald, and my ex-girlfriend. A veritable all-star lineup. I rubbed my free hand across my face, wondering what had happened to this once promising life of mine. Next was Benjamin Bank, the chief political adviser to Governor Lance Randolph, leaving an oblique message asking me to call him. Lastly, Vinny Mongillo's voice came on the phone informing me to call him within the next five minutes or he'd squeeze my testicles until they popped like gas bubbles.

That represented a negotiation I didn't want to lose, so I called him first. He snapped up the phone in typical fashion.

"I'm hearing all bad things," he said.

Leave it to Vinny to have sources within the *Boston Record*'s board of director's executive committee.

"Then you're hearing right."

"Brent Cutter wants to sell us all out? A member of the founding family? You know what we do to those people where I come from? We slap 'em around, then we execute them, then we bury their useless fucking bodies in a shallow roadside grave."

"You know what we do in my culture? We give them the silent treatment, then refuse to buy them a round next time we see them in the neighborhood bar. To each his own." I think I liked his way better.

Mongillo said, "I've been thinking more about our conversation about Fitzgerald. I want to put some stuff in writing. You coming in here?"

Am I going in there? Suddenly, it seemed like the exact right place to go for reasons I couldn't quite explain.

"Yeah, I'll be there shortly. How's the Randolph story going?"

"I'm writing it right now."

From a rapid-fire series of calls, I learned that Fitzgerald, too, knew the committee meeting was an unmitigated disaster, and wanted to get together for a drink to discuss it. Our executive committee, a sieve. I put him off for a day. Travers pressed me for information and wanted to make sure I wasn't planning any other published revelations. He sounded earnest and a little uncertain. When I asked if he had any leads yet, there was a long pause, followed by the wishful words, "Soon, soon."

My former girlfriend informed me that the *Traveler* didn't have the Fitzgerald story solid enough to go with the following morning. I cavalierly told her they never would, but I think she detected the change in my tone, the lack of sure-fire confidence. I hung up before the conversation could stray from official business.

Benjamin Bank, interestingly, told me that the governor would like to meet with me tomorrow. I asked him if he could do it right away because we were preparing a story for the next day's paper. Also, I had a spare hour to kill ahead of the larceny that Sweeney and I had on our dance card for that night.

Bank said it would have to be in the morning, early, before he and the governor left for Washington for a round of courtesy calls on Capitol Hill.

"You should hold your story until the two of you talk," he said.

Another typical politician, firmly believing that the entire world revolves around their tiny little concerns, that oceans will part for their boss and that reporters will hold their stories until blessed with a private audience.

I said, "That's not going to happen. We're in print tomorrow. If you want to be a part of it, if you want to have your say, have the governor call me or Mongillo. You have our numbers."

"You publish, and you're screwed." A different sort of take on that whole publish or perish standard.

"I assume Mongillo has told you what this is about. He's detailed the allegations, right?"

"He has, and you can't cold-cock us with this bullshit at three in the afternoon and expect answers within twenty minutes. You owe us a day."

"I owe you nothing. If your guy wants to talk, and he should, have him call."

He spoke with a tone less confident and more desperate. "Hold your apples and we'll give you something that you're going to find very, very interesting."

Hold your apples? Who uses that phrase anymore? I said, "Terrific. So give it to me today, and we'll be all set. Everyone benefits."

"Tomorrow."

"Then make sure you read the *Record.*"

He began speaking again. I said, "Benjamin, I love this kind of intellectual stimulation, but I have to call my urologist."

We hung up, which left Zinkle and Brent Cutter.

"Thanks for your warm endorsement at the meeting today," I told the former. "Christ, you had me blushing so bad I almost had to excuse myself from the room."

He replied, "Jack, it was over before it ever began, and I'm not going to squander myself on a lost cause. That's not a bad deal you were offered, becoming editor for the next three years. You ought to think hard about it. We're not going to cut anything any better."

I asked, "Did the committee vote yet?"

"We discussed it in detail, but delayed a vote for a few days. But it's foregone, Jack. You're a reporter, not a publisher. We can't run the enormous risk of a shareholder suit. The paper's going to get sold."

"Hey Cal," I said.

"Yeah?"

"Fuck yourself." And I hung up.

And then there was Brent Cutter. I put the phone back in my suit pocket. Fuck him too.

The sedan pulled up in front of 60 State Street in downtown Boston. Gerry and Kevin got out ahead of me and escorted me through the lobby and onto the elevator. I pressed the button for the thirty-fourth floor.

I was paying a surprise call on the rhythmically named Adelle Adair, the senior partner at the Boston law firm Horace & Chase who had hung up on me two afternoons before. Adelle had been Randolph's senior prosecutor when he was the Suffolk County district attorney. I figured it couldn't hurt to give her a heads up on the story of the inflated conviction rate, and she had helped me on a story or two from years gone by.

I convinced the receptionist to give her a call—no small feat in itself. Once the call was made, I was summoned to her office.

"What could I possibly have done to be honored by such a visit?" she asked with a smile as I came through the door, forgetting our conversation earlier in the week. Her office was typically magnificent, with impeccable views of Boston Harbor. She invited me to sit down opposite her desk, and she sat down in her regular chair.

I cut right to the chase. "I have a proposition. You wink and nod at me, and I leave you completely out of a story we're about to pop."

"I like propositions," she said coyly. She could get away with this because Adelle was something of a looker, even in her late forties. "Go ahead."

I said, "We're going with a story tomorrow saying that Lance Randolph inflated his conviction record when he was district attorney. You were his first assistant. Did he?"

She looked at me and said nothing.

I said, "A wink or a nod."

She didn't make a move. Finally, she said, "We're strictly off the record?"

I nodded. She said, "He did, though not anything outrageous. I didn't find out about it until after the fact, when the figures were in the paper. The numbers were tightly held in our office."

"Did you question him? Confront him?"

She shook her head.

"Why not?"

She looked around her office again in an exaggerated fashion and flashed me another smile. "Because a few months after the figures were in the paper, I got a call from some law firms, including this one, asking me to come head up their criminal departments. Suddenly I was hot property. And the lie was on Randolph, not me. I just went with the flow."

I nodded and got up. She stayed seated and said, "So I'm right to understand that a deal's a deal, and I won't see my name in print."

She was right. A deal is a deal.

I strode through the newsroom feeling a pathetic kind of silence in my wake—a little bit of pity mixed with a lot of morbidity. It was deadline in the middle of a huge news week, meaning the place should have been rocking and rolling. Try the blues instead. I walked past my own desk and straight into Justine Steele's corner office and asked what we had for morning.

She gave me the rundown—an update on the Paul Ellis murder investigation, a feature on family-owned papers that have been bought out by large chains, etc. I was to sit with a reporter, who was going to play catch-up with the *Traveler* on Nathan's murder and the tie-in to Paul Ellis and me. The cops were playing ball on it, and I had to as well. She said Mongillo was finishing up the Randolph story, though the governor himself was declining to address the specifics. His only quote, she said, was a warning that, "Statistics can be contorted." No shit, governor.

"Hopefully you'll get something better than we already have. Can you get him tonight?"

"I asked, and they said no. If that changes, I'll flag you. I did, though, speak to one of his former aides, who off-the-record tells me that our reporting is correct."

Back at my desk, Mongillo was the lone reporter courageous enough to approach me—too courageous, perhaps. "I thought I read somewhere that you were dead," he said, that dumb grin spilling over his ample face.

"News of my death has been greatly exaggerated," I replied. "What I'm going through might be worse than death. It's torture."

He handed me a printout of our co-bylined story, with a lede that said, "Governor Lance Randolph, in his two campaigns for statewide office, exaggerated his success in prosecuting criminal suspects when he served as the Suffolk County district attorney, according to a *Boston Record* study of available criminal justice statistics."

Second paragraph: "During gubernatorial campaign debates, and on his campaign literature, Randolph repeatedly presented voters with a much higher conviction rate of murderers, rapists, and armed robbers than he had, according to the statistics. Time and again, he campaigned on the foundation that he was the most successful prosecutor in Massachusetts at putting criminals behind bars, though the hard numbers show that he was, in reality, somewhere in the middle of the pack."

And on it went from there, for about a thousand glorious words, providing an explicit contrast between the numbers Randolph presented during his campaigns and his actual conviction rates. Granted, this wasn't a stain on a blue dress or an undercover FBI agent bearing bribes as an Arab sheik, but it could well be enough to cost him the nomination to be attorney general. The public doesn't like a liar, especially a liar in law enforcement who's piping numbers about crime.

The story said Randolph's spokesman declined to respond to questions. I think Randolph and Bank truly believed we were going to give it the proverbial first blink and hold the story for a day. No way. I read it straight through, nodded at Mongillo and said, "Great job bringing it together. I talked to a lawyer downtown today who used to work for him. That lawyer tells me we're on the mark. This guy could be screwed."

We both walked over to his computer and I watched him hit the "Send" button. The story was on its way toward tomorrow's front page.

With that, he reached into his drawer and pulled out a crisp *Record* envelope, unsealed, and said, "Glad you like. Problem is, Randolph's not the only liar in town. Here's a half dozen examples of Fitzgerald's fabrications. It will stay between me and you until you decide whether you want to bring it up the ladder."

I didn't want to tell him then that I absolutely abhor heights.

I was walking down Charles Street in the heart of what realtors call historic Beacon Hill, having just given Kevin and Gerry the slip and suddenly wishing I hadn't. A few minutes earlier, I had left my newspaper through the loading docks, ducked into a company car, and drove downtown. Knowing there was someone who was actively wishing, and in fact, willing me, dead, I didn't necessarily like being without bodyguards, but I've learned that if you want to commit a breaking and entering, it's usually—though not always—best not to bring the police along.

So there I was walking along a brick sidewalk heading for my rendezvous with Sweeney when a Mercedes Benz pulled to the side of the road and out stepped a pair of goons who looked like a couple of researchers for *Steroid Quarterly.* I kept walking, and they fell in behind me.

I quickened the pace. So did they. Too soon, they flanked me on either side, a fact which should have worried me but really didn't because of all my fellow strollers heading to their opulent condominiums and townhouses after another hard day at work. Witnesses, as I've said, diminish the prospects of crime, though Kitty Genovese might argue otherwise.

The guy on my left cut me off, and the one on the right not so gently guided me up Myrtle Street, a residential side street.

"You boys looking for the Diet Workshop?" I asked as they prodded me up the street between them. I don't know why I said this. Sometimes these things just come out of my big mouth.

Again, the guy on the left, the real creative one, stepped in front of me and blocked my path. The guy on my right dug his fingers into my side, such that I thought he might rip out my kidney and liver and eat them right in front of me.

I stood almost paralyzed by pain, but hell-bent on not letting them see it. As one guy squeezed my internal organs, the other whispered into my ear, "If you don't drop the Campbell story, we won't be nearly so nice next time." I nodded. I think. I was on the verge of losing all bodily control.

And then he let go. Just as quickly as they arrived, they were gone. I leaned against a gaslit street lamp and gave the pain a long minute to ebb away. I just learned one thing in that last violent episode. Terry Campbell might have been an asshole, even a criminal, but he wasn't a killer, because if he was a killer, I would now be dead.

When I walked into Joe & Nemo's on Cambridge Street on the backside of Beacon Hill, our designated rendezvous spot, Hank Sweeney was sitting at one of the cramped tables wearing a black turtleneck and a pair of dark gray slacks, looking like a male model in the April AARP newsletter. His legs were tucked under the chair and he stared intently at an Italian sausage lathered in peppers and onions. He took a ravenous bite and, while chewing, noticed me for the first time.

"My favorite food in the world," he said, his mouth still full. "I'd have this every night, but Mother doesn't let me go near the stuff. Says it'll clog my arteries and cause an early death. I tell her, it's too late for me to die young."

He laughed and took another bite.

"Go order one," he said, looking toward the counter. "It's on me. You can't commit a felony on an empty stomach."

"I'm all set," I replied, feeling my tender side.

He looked disappointed, enough so that I said, "Ah, maybe you're right." I went up and got one, and, on his orders, brought him another.

As we both ate our sausages across the Formica table, he went over the plans with me—entry through the rear door that I had exited two days before, use a pair of penlights he had to make our way through the lobby, access the stairs to the basement, and then use a more powerful flashlight that he also had to find the evidence room.

"There's one nighttime security guard in the building," he said. "Imagine being the night guard at a morgue? I'd rather flip burgers at McDonald's, and the pay's probably better. Anyway, I'm reliably told that he spends ninety-nine percent of his shift in a third-floor office watching television. I would too if I were him. My understanding is that he never goes down to the basement, so I don't get the sense we're under any sort of time constraint."

"Who are you, Clyde Barrow? You ever think you wasted a lot of time on the right side of the law?"

"Quite the opposite, my boy. Carrying a shield helped me get inside the mind of the criminal and understand the mechanics of the crimes they commit." He paused and looked at his half-eaten sausage submarine, then back at me and said, "That's why so many of my brothers go bad. They think they have it all figured out, and they know the other side pays better."

He chewed, I chewed, a lot of pretty young blondes walked past the storefront windows on their way home to their cozy Beacon Hill apartments, looking in at what must have appeared to be a pretty unique pair, this older black man decked out in what could have been a catsuit, and his scared-looking younger friend. It was 8:30, pitch dark.

I took the last bite of my sausage and said, "I still wish you'd let me do this alone. You've got a lot more on the line than I do, and you know how other prisoners are when they have a cop in their midst. You'll be the most popular bitch in the pen."

He looked me up and down. "Ah, it'd feel nice to be desired again." He finished his sausage, swallowed, and said, "And you really expect me to let you go it alone. Christ"—he started pulling this pseudo-mad thing again—"look at you. You dressed for a B&E like a college sopho-more going home to meet his girlfriend's mother. The Good Humor Man doesn't dress in lighter clothes than you."

I looked down at my Banana Republic khakis, then back at him and said, "These are my lucky pants."

"Yeah, great. We'll be lucky to get out of there alive."

"Seriously," I said, "you'll lose your pension. You depend on that. Your wife depends on it. You have kids? They're probably trying to ratchet up their inheritance."

He looked down at the table and his tone became softer, crumbled. "Somebody disobeyed me." He looked me in the eye now. "And that might mean somebody got away with murder on my watch, and they ain't going to get away with it."

We both fell quiet. We watched as a pair of uniformed cops came through the door, ordered hot dogs, and walked out without paying a dime. They never even offered money. Sweeney's face became as dark as his turtleneck shirt and he started to get up to go after them, but then sat back down.

"Not worth the risk right now," he said. "I hate that, though. Hate that. A good cop doesn't take free things—not even so much as a damned hot dog."

I regarded him for a moment as he calmed himself down. "You didn't answer my question. Do you and your wife—what's her name, by the way; I can't call her Mother—have any kids?"

"Mary Mae." He smiled, then said in something of a pitched whisper, "Mary Mae. Don't you love the name? I like the old classics. That's why I love your Elizabeth's name so much."

She's decidedly not mine anymore, though I didn't feel like pointing that out to him at the moment. "It is pretty," speaking vaguely to both names. "Kids?"

He looked down at the scrunched napkin on the table, then at his hands. Without looking up, he said, "Once. A son. Michael."

I knew something was wrong. I knew it because he continued to stare down at the table. So I asked, "What does he do?"

"A cop. Like his old man."

"Around here?"

"Used to be. Boston PD. Drug squad."

"The two of you close?"

"Couldn't have been any closer." Past tense. His eyes passed over mine for a split second, then he turned his head and looked out the window onto the dark street, suddenly morose.

He said, "He was shot on the job five years ago, right as I was getting ready to retire. He died that night in Mass General." His voice trailed off to a glimmer. "They made a scapegoat of him. I live with that every day. Every damned day."

I cleared my throat and stared at Sweeney in profile staring at nothing at all. "I'm really, really sorry. I had no idea."

Almost as if he didn't hear me, he said, "Mother was never the same after that."

"How'd he get shot, if you don't mind me asking? A drug dealer?"

Sweeney turned his head toward me, slowly. He focused his eyes on mine, but there was none of the boyish sharpness I usually saw in them. Instead, he looked vacant, faraway.

He said, "Friendly fire." He left it sitting out there just like that. Two words that took one life and forever changed two others.

I leaned close, my head low to the table as if we were whispering to each other during junior high study hall. I tried to contain my confusion, my shock. "Friendly fire? You're saying he got shot by another cop?"

Sweeney just looked at me, his face suddenly appearing somewhere beyond his seventy years. He nodded in a labored kind of way, then dropped his hand hard on the table and said, "Come on. We have a different case to solve."

And we were off to probe the past, which might well portend the future, my future, my paper's future.

twenty-nine

THIS WASN'T ANY BROKEN down retiree I was with, or the despondent father recalling the death of his cherished son. No, this was a spring deer, loping across the dewy meadow of life, or more specifically, prancing down the darkened alley behind the State Medical Examiner's building. He was silent, but he had a look on his face that spoke volumes, and what it said was that crossing the thin blue line was the most invigorating thing he'd ever done.

"Hold this," he said, passing me a black satchel containing the flashlights and some lock-picking tools that would, if all things went according to plan, not be needed. We were at the unmarked back door. He looked up and down the alley, whisked the keys out of his pocket and carefully and quickly fitted the larger of the two into the keyhole on the steel door. He hesitated for a moment, leaned his body against the building, and turned the key with a surgeon's precision and a Latin lover's steady pace.

I heard it click open, the first small victory of the night. Sweeney turned back and looked me up and down. He whispered, "Next time you break into any other building but a shag carpeting warehouse, I'd advise that you not wear loafers with hard leather soles." He nodded at me, staring me flush in the face. I stole a glance at his footwear and saw he was wearing black sneakers. Then he said, "Get those things off and leave them by the barrel."

I did, but with a disturbing image of a homeless guy wearing a pair of $230 Cole-Haan shoes to dinner at the Pine Street Inn the following night. Sweeney kept his hand firmly on the door and pushed it open one arduous inch at a time. We both slipped inside, and he closed it even more slowly.

That put us in a short, dark hallway that led to another steel door, and on the other side of the door, the cavernous main lobby. He pulled the satchel back and groped ahead of me, the only sounds being the quiet, rhythmic pace of his breathing. I slid along behind him in my stocking feet, keeping one hand on his belt for direction.

In the dark, we reached a door with one of those emergency bars. He slowly pressed against it, and the door quietly pushed forward, exposing a faint crack of light from the lobby. He kept pressing until there was just enough room for us to squeeze through, one at a time. He went first, scanned the lobby and waved me in.

When I pinched through the door, my eyes fluttered reflexively in the hazy light of the musty lobby. As I focused, there looked to be an acre of black-and-white checked tiles between us and the heavy, gray, unmarked door that led to the basement stairs. The ceilings were a good twenty feet high, meaning noises carried off the hard floor and echoed through the vast expanse. Now I understood why loafers may not have been just the right call.

The newspaper stand was boarded up, the front door was chained, the elevator sat open and empty. The mouths of the hallways that led in and out of the lobby were enveloped in gloomy shadows that led only to black. You'll forgive me for thinking there was a haunted look to the whole place, this, after all, being the state morgue. I mean, there were dead people in refrigerated lockers just down a short hallway. If there's a more ghoulish place to find yourself alone at night, someone's going to have to draw a picture of it for me.

This being the morgue, by the way, meant that it would not be extraordinary or even unusual for cops or coroners to be coming in and out of the building overnight, which partially explains why we chose nine P.M. as our target time. Murders are less likely to occur in the early evening than the early morning hours after midnight—at least that's what Sweeney says, and he should know. So we were more likely to have the place to ourselves.

Sweeney started across the floor, hunched low, his short strides smooth, stealthy and silent, like those of an Indian, though maybe that's politically incorrect to say these days. He pulled on my sleeve and I followed close behind, the hard floor cool to my stocking feet. There were about thirty yards between us and the door that led to the stairs that brought us to the cellar. Probably about fifteen yards across, we both heard a loud smashing sound to our right. The hair on my neck bolted up like it was giving me a standing ovation. In unison, we whirled in that direction and squinted through the empty haze. But there was no one there, nothing unusual to see.

"The radiator," Sweeney whispered. Sounded good enough for me, and certainly better than any of the alternatives. He set out again, faster, and I stayed close to his heels.

At the door, he pulled it inchmeal, but it began creaking like a shutter on a haunted house, so he paused, then moved it so slow that mold could have formed on his hand. Same drill—when it was finally opened a crack, he slid through, then I did as well. The staircase was black as a moonless night in a Montana barn.

When the door kissed shut behind us, he whispered to me, "Slow and easy, both feet on each step, hands on the wall. No accidents, no noise." If all of life could be so easy.

At the bottom, he grabbed my shoulder and said under his breath, "Don't move." We stood there for what felt like half of eternity, though I suspect it was really only about ninety seconds. I heard a rustling noise, then he flicked on one of the penlights.

"It's down here," he said. I knew that already, but didn't feel any need to point that out.

If the cellar of the state morgue looked morosely grim in the middle of the day when all the lights were on and there were helpful doctors and happy bureaucrats and curious members of the public milling about one floor above, you can imagine how it looked in the dark of the night in an otherwise empty building with the only illumination being the slightest rays from this tiny handheld lamp. If my heart beat any harder I'd sound like the lead drummer in the Dr. Pepper Marching Band.

Sweeney handed me a penlight of my own and started down the hallway, which zigzagged between cold stone walls and storage closets that held God only knows what—and I certainly didn't want to know right now. We moved slowly, precisely, the narrow bands of weak light from our little lamps poking into the dark like a trawler in a stormy ocean. Sweeney stayed in the lead; I followed close behind. Every dozen or so steps he stopped, held his breath, and listened. Thankfully there was nothing to hear.

Two rights, three lefts and a quart of sweat later, we arrived in the morose gloom between the file cage with the chain-link fence and the evidence locker with what looked like a five-foot-thick titanium door.

Sweeney waved his little penlight through the links, the rays dispersing over the old manila folders. "Every file, a tragic death," he said, speaking as much to himself as to me. "Blessed are the people who leave this Earth on peaceful terms."

He handed me the satchel and dug into his pocket again, bringing out the keys. He shone his light on the locker door, fussed with the key for a moment and, with some effort, shoved it into a padlock. With a swift, steady motion, he turned the key and the lock came undone. The door immediately lurched ajar with a loud shudder.

"Kill your light," Sweeney urgently whispered, his voice sounding more like a hiss.

I did, and so did he, and we both stood in the silent dark as the acrid smell of age and death spilled from the crack in the evidence locker door. The odor was so bad that I reflexively drew my hand up to my nose just to give myself a break.

About two minutes later, all quiet on the coroner's front, Sweeney whispered, "Flick on your lamp." When I did, he put both hands on the sturdy door and pulled it steadily toward him. The hinges groaned in the dark, Sweeney stopped, then did it all over again. When it was open just wide enough, we both slipped inside, and Sweeney pulled the door tight behind us.

He took the satchel, fumbled with it, and pulled out a high-powered flashlight. When he pushed the switch, the wide, firm beam of light seemed warm and friendly, bright like the lamps I used to have in my room as a kid when my parents would read me books like *Harry the Dirty Dog* and *Make Way for Ducklings.* Not that I'm regressing.

He shone it toward the far wall, and we saw that the room—a chamber, really—was about twenty feet deep and another twenty feet wide, all containing a motley collection of cabinets and cases and what looked to be the kind of ancient storage refrigerators and freezers that you would find in a suburban basement. The smell was sharp in the nostrils and hard to the eyes, so bad it made the air feel thick with the sense of death and rot.

"Stand still another moment," Sweeney whispered to me.

I continued to look around the room, aided by him sweeping the area with his flashlight. The ceilings had exposed pipes and wood beams thick with cobwebs. An occasional exposed bulb hung down. The floors were concrete, but covered with an unhealthy layer of dust so thick that it had morphed into dirt. The walls on the far end were jagged rock.

"This is the city's room of forgotten memories," Sweeney said. I looked at him, the eerie shadows flickering on his wide face, and saw how much in his element he seemed. I knocked on his screen door but three days before in that godforsaken swamptown hard by a Florida inland highway, and he seemed amused, smart, somewhat curious. But here he stood surrounded by the relics of death and he appeared fully in control, endlessly confident, almost happy.

I also saw that he was right. Indeed, this was the room where shouted questions were diminished by time to a barely audible whisper, where once crucial clues in life's vilest crimes were boxed and shelved where no one would ever likely see them again, afterthoughts, really.

"I think we're set," Sweeney said.

"Tell me what we're looking for," I told him.

"Anything that says John Ellis Cutter on it would be a good place to start," he replied, his tone lighter than the look on his face. Then he added, "Follow me. I have a hunch."

We walked toward a collection of about a dozen refrigerators on the back wall, some of which you had to pull upward to open, others you just pulled out like normal kitchen appliances.

"Start looking," he said. "When you see something that might be something, just tell me."

We both went to opposite ends, about a free throw apart, and started working our way in. I pulled opened the first refrigerator and saw hundreds of small vials of what appeared to be blood, all of which were tagged with a small piece of adhesive paper, some with a name, more with just a case file number. I shut the refrigerator and walked down to Sweeney and asked, "Does this have a number?"

"5372-97," he said, reeling it off the top of his head. John Cutter's death, reduced to six digits and one dash.

"Shit, that's my lucky number," I replied.

"It will be tonight."

I went through each bottle in the first refrigerator, picking every one up, reading the label, carefully placing it back in its spot. There seemed to be no rhyme or reason for the specimens to be where they were—nothing so obvious or simple as dates of death or the alphabetization of the dead. I think it was a space-available filing system.

I did this in the second refrigerator, then the third, which was a pull-up, meaning I was crouched down. My arms were getting sore from the precise handling and my back weak from bending. It made me think how I hadn't had a decent workout since I shot baskets in the North End four nights before. I'd probably never have a workout so easy and simpleminded again.

I was just opening the fourth refrigerator, noticing that Sweeney was two ahead of me, when a sudden groan erupted from the hinges of the thick door behind us. Sweeney immediately extinguished his light. We both shut our refrigerators, and I heard him fall gently to the floor. A few seconds later, his hand was around my ankle and he whispered, "Down boy." I quelled my sudden impulse to shag down a tennis ball, knowing if I did, it would probably be the last thing I'd ever do.

We lay there on the ground like that for several fat minutes, stone silent and dead still, not to overuse that last analogy at a time like this. Finally, Sweeney put his mouth right up to my ear in a way that I'd really only want a woman to do, and said, "Stay here. I'll be back."

I hope.

He began slithering away, though because of the dark I could only hear him, not see him. I lay in wait, futilely probing the overwhelming blackness of the basement room with my eyes, seeing nothing, hearing nothing—until I heard the door creak some more. Then nothing again.

I grew restless. I felt helpless—not a feeling I'm accustomed to with the full weight of the largest newspaper in town behind me. I considered getting up and roaming through the room, or turning on my light in search of Sweeney, but knew it wasn't the right thing to do, not yet, anyway.

Then, without even a hint of a warning, I felt a stream of hot breath in my right ear.

"Hold this," Sweeney said in a hoarse whisper, handing me the strong flashlight. "Turn it on when I hit your arm and scan the room with it."

I groped for the switch, and he rapped my shoulder softly. I flicked the light on and washed the beam across the room. My eyes hurt, I was staring so hard for any sign of life, which would probably signal imminent death. I poked the light in the various crevices between cabinets and old steel tables.

I looked over at Sweeney and he was in a crouched position with a cocked revolver in his hands moving it along with the beam. So it was more than flashlights and implements in that bag.

We did this for about sixty seconds until Sweeney tossed what sounded like a coin against a metal cabinet on the other side of the room, then called out in a tight voice, "We have the locker surrounded. We see you. Put your hands up, drop your weapon, and step into the middle of the room."

Silence. He reached over and held my arm still so I wasn't waving the light anymore. "Last chance," he said, his voice strained but confident.

Still silent.

Sweeney whispered to me, "Walk in opposite directions."

He went right, I went left. Nothing happened. We reconnoitered at the door. I slipped through the new crack before he could stop me and poked the inky dark of the hallway with the beam of light. Again, I saw nothing.

Back inside, I said to him in something just north of a whisper, "The door must have just slipped open."

He nodded, his eyes still scanning the room and the gun still in front of him, and said absently, "Old building."

He pulled the flashlight from me and walked around the room. I took out my penlight and did the same. We saw nothing, though I'd be lying if I said the shadowy crevices weren't unsettling. He drew the door shut again, and we returned to the business at hand—the search for evidence.

As we meticulously scanned each and every vial looking for the name "Cutter" or the right file number, it occurred to me that here we were in the dark of night up to our elbows in dead people's blood on a blind mission for the truth.

Then, bingo, or as I said to Sweeney—"Bing-fucking-o." There was the name we were looking for, scrawled across a tiny white sheet stuck to a thin vial of blood: John E. Cutter.

I rather ghoulishly held it up to my penlight for a moment, mesmerized by the color. This, physically, is what remained of the late publisher.

Sweeney appeared at my side and gazed at the bottle like an acolyte might look at the Shroud of Turin. He said, as if to himself, "Those bastards did draw blood for the toxicology test." He shook his head and mumbled, "So why not put it in the report."

He pulled a padded enclosure from the satchel—making me wonder what the hell else he had in that bag of tricks—and wrapped the vial tightly before placing it in his own pocket.

"Now the files," he said, his voice soaked in determination. "Someone's obviously gone to pains to hide something, and we're going to stick it in their ear."

There's another one of those phrases that you don't hear all that often anymore. I let it pass and looked around the dusty, dusky room at all the dirt, at the ragtag collection of steel and wood filing cabinets sitting happenstance along the perimeter with a few of them absently, pointlessly in the middle.

Sweeney said, his voice just above a whisper, "We'll split up again. Just take note of the cabinets you've already searched so we don't duplicate. You're looking for boxes, for envelopes, for files, for whatever, that have Mr. Cutter's name on them, or the case number."

We split up and went to far corners of the room. I opened a stout metal file cabinet, and the pungent odor that rose up from the empty drawer cuffed me across the face. My eyes started watering. I turned my head in search of relief and saw Sweeney standing there beside me, his mouth formed to a faint smile.

"Forgot to tell you, use this," he said. He handed me a cloth mouth and nose mask with two rubber bands to wrap around my head. I put mine on, and he did the same.

Holding the penlight with one hand, I riffled through the files with the other—John Algers, Gregory Blinitch, Helen Duncan, Foster Grant, Luther Raymond, and on and on—but found nothing of interest, a fact that relatives of the dead might find offensive, but that's okay. They weren't the ones trundling through here in the dark of the night risking arrest and a whole lot worse.

Second cabinet, same. Third, same again. To add a sense of variety, I turned from the file drawers to a tall wooden cabinet behind me and pulled it open. And there, on the top shelf, eye level, sat a standard corrugated box, two feet wide by two feet tall, and on that box, written in a red marker, were the words "John Ellis Cutter."

In my business, in any business, this is what's known as pay dirt.

thirty

I SUCKED IN AIR so hard I almost swallowed my mask. I looked across the bleak expanse of black at Sweeney, whose shadowy face I could see in the dim spread of his penlight as he poked through a file cabinet of his own. Rather than summon him, I lifted the box down from the cabinet and placed it on the floor. I crouched and gently pulled the masking tape that held it shut, opened it up, and peered inside.

In the narrow rays of my penlight, I saw a mishmash collection of materials. What first caught my eye were some articles of clothing—most notably an old tee shirt and a pair of boxer shorts that he must have been wearing at the time of his death. They were preserved in separate, clear, Ziploc plastic bags. I put those aside and pulled out a file folder, opened it, and shone my tiny light on the words.

First thing I saw was the title, "Toxicology Report," written above an official-looking form. Under it, in the messy scrawl of what was probably a doctor's writing, I focused on the line: "$As2O3$—arsenic trioxide. Positive."

My hands began trembling so much that the light flickered all over the moving sheet of paper. I pulled the mask up onto my forehead and gulped deep breaths of corroded air, without even noticing the taste or the smell. I closed my eyes for a long moment, thought about happy thoughts like Baker romping after a brand new tennis ball on a freshly mown field. And then I returned my attention to the box.

Clipped to the back of the folder was another glassine bag, smaller and zipped shut, and as I shone the light against the plastic, I saw inside a blue tissue, crumpled and old. I flipped back to the toxicology report, scanned down past a lot of chemical mumbo jumbo—at least it was to me—and saw the words: "Evidence (blue facial tissue) As2O3—arsenic trioxide. Positive."

I shone the light into the dark confines of the box again and came out with another sheet of paper titled, "Evidence map," which included a sketch of John Cutter's apartment and a lengthy list of everything that had been marked five years before by the guy who was on the other side of this room right now.

I began scanning down the list when I heard another loud creak, just like the one we heard before. I whirled around and saw Sweeney extinguish his light, so I did the same. In the pitch black, I put the folders and bags back in the box, and pushed the box slowly against the cabinet, getting it out of the way, just in case.

I'll confess, I wasn't nervous like I was when we had heard the noise fifteen minutes or so before, but I did want to take precautions.

I crouched on the ground waiting to feel Sweeney's presence nearby, assuming he'd be crawling over, and in fact, a moment later I felt his hand on my knee and his breath in my ear whispering, "Say nothing." A couple of minutes turned into five minutes, all of them silent. The only thing I could hear was my own wish to be someplace else—like the newsroom, with the contents of this box spread out on my desk.

Sweeney finally whispered, "I'm going to check the door. You wait here."

I said, "I found the box."

He didn't reply, and I don't know if he even heard me. Next thing I knew, he brushed against me as he slithered off across the filthy floor.

I waited, crouched in front of the box, in my mind anyway, protecting it, but from what, if anything, I wasn't exactly sure.

That's what I was doing—crouching, waiting, hoping—when I heard the first crash. It came from an area closer to the door. It sounded like a file cabinet being overturned, and my first optimistic thoughts were that Sweeney had simply bumped into a fragile piece of furniture and toppled it over, and that no one would hear this but him and me.

That crash was followed by an eerie silence. Neither of us wanted to call out to the other for fear of exposing our cover. But I had a worse fear that Sweeney had somehow hurt himself in the crash, even if he was the sole cause. So I set out across the floor in a blind search.

As I crawled through the dusty dirt, I heard only the sound of my own legs and body against the floor. I stopped to get my bearings, probing the blackness so hard with my eyes that my vision blurred, even as there was nothing to see.

And then another crash, this one coming from the far side of the room.

What, I wondered, was Sweeney now doing over there. I stopped in my tracks—literally—trying to penetrate the dark with my eyes, but to no avail. I listened intently, even holding my breath to hear better, though when I did that, my ears pounded and I heard nothing at all.

So I stayed still, waiting, wondering, wishing. And then a third crash, this one right behind me—the distinct sound of a tall cabinet slamming against the ground, the noise echoing off the steel and wood of the other pieces of ragtag furniture all around it. The crash was so close that I felt dust flit through the air and settle in the upstanding hairs on my arms.

What happened next unfolded in a rapid-fire series of lights and noise, like color slides flashing on a dark wall and vanishing to nothing before an image could even be discerned.

First, a flashlight flicked on near the door—the area where I knew Sweeney was initially destined. No warning, no nothing. Suddenly, there was light, a strong, harsh beam. I whirled reflexively toward the source, though I couldn't see in the glare who held it.

Not two seconds later an explosion emanated from my left, the blast echoing off all the steel cabinets and concrete floors and rock walls of the room, and I swirled around to see a red flash in the blackness, then nothing at all. Immediately, the flashlight fell to the floor with a desolate clang. Whoever was holding it—Sweeney, I feared—had been hit.

I remained in my crouch, as silent as I think a human being could be under these circumstances, squinting through the darkness to see who that was by the door. The flashlight remained illuminated, but its beam short and forlorn, directed straight into what looked like a mop of grayish-black hair, which was likely Sweeney's head.

I waited and listened and watched, but there was no movement to see, and the only thing I could hear was the pulsing of my own ears and the beating of my own heart. My eyes were drawn to that beam of light like glue, staring at the hair, hoping against hope for any movement. But nothing.

Then I detected the slightest shuffling, the sound of feet slowly pushing along the dirty floor. I felt dust floating up in the stale, heavy air, landing on my face. I could see nothing, but I detected a presence within feet of me. I could hear someone breathing, the gentle sound of air pushing through nostrils. But it was maddening because the only visible sign of life was that one stout beam shining on what might have been the face of death.

Whatever had passed me was now gone, meaning they didn't sense me as I sensed them. I made a few bold assumptions here. If that was some sort of lawman in the room, he would have announced himself. We wouldn't be standing here in the dark. He wouldn't have fired his weapon and be skulking around in the pitch black. This was probably the same nitwit who had called me in the Four Seasons Hotel that morning—a rather angry gentleman, I must say.

I was busy being a genius when I saw some movement near that beam of light. I focused so hard I thought my eyes might fall out of my head. What I saw was the sickening glint of a gun barrel shining in the light, that barrel being pressed against the salt and pepper hair. I could see nothing else, as if the hand and the body that it belonged to were standing outside of the stagelights.

Then I heard that voice I had heard too many times before over these last few days, a voice like sandpaper rubbing against the civility and sanity of life, the voice of the man on the North End basketball court and in the Florida swamp.

"You've bought the farm, old man," he said, not at full volume, but not at a whisper either. I was standing about ten feet away. All I could see was a small patch of hair and the insidious shine of the gun.

The voice said, "Tell me if you're alone."

I strained to hear, but there was no reply.

I heard a click, like he was cocking the revolver. At that point, there were no other options and no more time. So I burst through the dark, hoping against hope that there was no short cabinet between Sweeney and me, nothing that would toss me recklessly, randomly, into the black room. There wasn't, and a second after I began, I felt my body collide with another, felt the thud of flesh against flesh, and then I started to throttle what I believe was another man's face, my fists slamming into muscle and bone.

I felt a warm substance on my hand, which I assumed was blood. I heard the gun clank to the floor, that sound being one of victory. I felt the rather punishing sensation of a fist slamming into my left eye, but what's the worst that could happen from that, that I'd lose my vision in this fight and wouldn't be able to see?

I kept flailing. I had no real choice. I had a friend on the ground who was either dead or dying. I had crucial records and evidence about my publisher's death stashed in a box in full view of whoever would ultimately turn on the light. It did me no good to duck because I couldn't see anything coming.

I was hit in the chest, elbowed in the face, clawed on my neck. At one point, I was knocked hard to the floor, landing on my back in a cloud of dust that penetrated my mouth and nose. As I lay on the floor, I took a hard look at the light on Sweeney's hair and thought I saw him move, but I wasn't in the best position to tell.

I forced myself up and swung hard at the dark, missing once and then again. I didn't sense anyone nearby anymore, so I stopped and listened, though hearing wasn't easy over the labored sound of my own breathing.

I sensed it before I felt it, a blur of motion coming in my direction like a train emerging from a dark tunnel. And then it struck, a vicious roundhouse punch that caught me fully on the jaw, sending a crackling ache through the entirety of my face and lifting me up off my feet and down onto the ground.

I felt myself start to pass out, but knew in some small space deep in the back of my brain that I couldn't, that if I did, Sweeney would probably die. So I fought, not this killer, but nature. I tried to mumble. I moved my arms, then my feet. I rubbed my face, blinked rapidly, did anything I could to stay cognizant of the world around me.

Then I felt a thunderous blow to my gut, which I knew immediately came from a foot, or as the police call it in their reports, a shod foot. I winced and gasped and balled up into the fetal position. He kicked me again, this time in the arm and chest. I crawled through the dark, trying to get away, but he caught me again.

As I lay sprawled on the floor, I felt something cold on my arm, put my hand on it, and realized it was the barrel of the gun he dropped when I first hit him. I gripped it, repositioned it in my hand, withstood another blow to my lower thigh, and announced in a somewhat garbled voice, "I have a gun. Back off or I shoot."

He slammed his foot into me again, close to my groin. I had the terrifying thought that if he struck any closer, Baker would be the closest thing I'd ever have to a son.

So for that and many other reasons, I aimed at nothing more than blackness and fired. The sound exploded off the walls and echoed again through the dark space, then was followed by an eerie silence. So I fired again, just to the left of where I had before. I kept the gun trained in that spot, then moved it slightly more to the left and down, and fired a third time. It was at this point that I heard a clunk, the sound of a man falling hard to the ground.

I struggled to my feet, my mind still in something of a haze and my body feeling like I was just tossed from a helicopter into a cactus field. I staggered to the door and groped along the wall for several agonizing moments before I found a light switch.

When I flicked it on, several exposed bulbs hanging from the ceiling sprang to life, and there on the floor was Hank Sweeney, blood oozing from his lower stomach. He had somehow rolled over, so he was on his back rather than his side, probably to stanch the flow of blood. His eyes were wide open, making me think for a moment that he was dead. Then he said, "Hey, quick draw, call 911. Tell them there's a cop down."

Oh, yes, there was also a man about ten feet away from him with half his brains blown out of his head. More on that in a moment.

I raced toward the door and into the hallway, flicked another switch and several other exposed bulbs clicked to life. I ran down the zigzag corridor in my stocking feet, up the stairs and into the lobby, where an old black phone sat on a table by the front door. I punched out 9-1-1. When a woman picked up on the other end, I all but screamed out, "Officer down in the basement of the State County Medical Examiner's building on Cambridge Street. We need an ambulance, fast!"

I bolted back downstairs and into the evidence locker.

"Cops and an ambulance are on their way," I told Sweeney, kneeling beside him.

He had his hands down around his lower gut, where his black shirt was stained in a formless circle.

"How bad?" I asked, putting my hand on his forehead for no other reason than that's what my mother used to do to me when I didn't feel well.

He shook his head. He suddenly looked weaker than even a second before. "Don't know," he replied in a strained voice. "I must have passed out when I first got hit. I think I've lost some blood."

"Hang in there for me," I said, my voice growing more urgent. "Mary Mae needs you. She's down in Florida waiting for you to come home, missing you like crazy. Don't give up on that. And I need you. I found a box of evidence."

His eyes were closed as I spoke to him, but opened wide again when I mentioned the discovery.

"What's in the box?" he asked.

"The toxicology tests," I replied. I waited a beat, making sure he was cognizant.

I said, "Positive on arsenic trioxide."

"Those bastards. I knew it." His eyes were hard on mine, painfully, wonderfully aware.

I added, "And a blue tissue. It tested positive as well."

He swallowed hard, gulped at some air, shut his eyes for a moment, and said, "Get the tests. Take the vial of blood out of my pocket. And get the hell out of here before the cops come."

I didn't budge. "Not a goddamned chance," I said. "I'm not leaving you."

I nodded my head to his right and added, "There's also the small matter of a dead man about ten feet away from us." I looked over at the said dead man, lying in a pool of blood and mush that had gathered around the gaping hole in his head.

I just killed a man. The thought, the realization, came over me like a wave. But then I quickly told myself, it was either kill or be killed, and as a human being, my instinct is one of self-preservation. That's why they have something in court called self-defense. And in this case, I was trying to defend Sweeney as well.

He grimaced and said, "Yeah, the dead man. Go get the gun you shot him with and put it in my right hand."

I shook my head. "I'm not going to do that," I said. "No god-damned way."

"Son, do it. If we both get caught here, we lose all this evidence. You'll get detained. I'm in the hospital. We're completely screwed. Get the vial of blood out of my pocket and the test results and get out of here. Now. My brother cops will protect me."

For emphasis, he gulped hard and added, "If you don't go, I get charged with a crime. I can explain me being here. I can't get away with bringing a reporter down here with me."

There was an odd kind of logic to that, cops taking care of cops, the blue wall and all. You invite a newspaper guy into the mix and all that comes crumbling down. Charges get filed. Pensions are lost. Serial mur-ders of *Boston Record* publishers remain forever unsolved.

I put the gun in his hand. "Stand back," he said. And, still lying down, he fired it against a far wall. In the light, the sound seemed even louder.

He said, "Don't lose the tests. I'm going to want to go over them the next time we see each other."

I regarded him for a moment, this big lump of a man with the barrel chest and the black, baby face. How many murders had he solved in his life, how many killers were sitting in some dank cell on this very night because of his dogged work, how many families felt at least a glimmer of justice with all their sorrow—dozens? Hundreds? More?

And now, here he was a victim. John Cutter was a victim. Paul Ellis was a victim. I'm an intended victim. The question, the maddening question, was, why? Who was this dead man just a few feet away?

He looked at me looking at him and said in a voice louder than before, "Get out. For me, for you, for your newspaper, get out."

I stood up hesitantly, my legs stiff from all the crouching of the last couple of hours, my fists aching from whatever it was that I struck. I raced over to the box, grabbed the report and the bag with the tissue and shoved them down the back of my pants. I placed the box back carefully in the cabinet from whence it came and shut the doors.

Back at Sweeney, I crouched down. His eyes were closed again. "Wake up," I said. "They're here in a moment."

He opened his eyes at half-mast. One hand was still draped over his open wound. The other was sprawled at his side with the gun.

"Go," he whispered.

"You're a great cop," I said. "And a better man." I kissed his cheek as his eyes fluttered shut. I took one final look at my victim then ran for the door.

I was halfway down the hallway when I heard what sounded like a battalion of cops and EMTs bounding down the stairs. I yanked open a nearby closet door and stepped inside. A rat skittered across my exposed feet. My face was surrounded by heavy spiderwebs housing God knows what kind of animals—though I presume spiders. I stood frozen until the rush of footsteps gave way to silence, opened the door, and briskly walked toward the stairs.

In the lobby, as I emerged from the doorway, probably with cobwebs on my face and spiders crawling through my hair, a uniformed officer gave me a suspicious look.

"Grimmer than I ever could have imagined down there," I said to him. "I think they're going to need your help."

He gave me the once over and headed for the stairs. And with that, I raced for the alley, wiser, older, weaker, and more desperate than I had ever been before.

thirty-one

I STOLE A SIDELONG glance at Vinny Mongillo standing innocently beside me at the rental car counter at West Palm Beach International Airport, a rotund presence gabbing away on his cell phone with another faceless official back on Beacon Hill, and turned my attention to the pretty young thing with the lazy accent in the unfortunately unflattering brown Hertz jersey.

"Good idea," I said. "I'll go ahead and get the full-sized."

As we made our way from the airport, which, by the way, was crowded with happy tourists arriving from points north for a spring weekend in the sun, Mongillo cupped his hand over the phone and said to me, "If you see a Perkins, stop. Best waffles in America." Next thing I heard, he was saying into the phone, "Fuck him and the patronage cart he rolled in on."

My patience for these theatrics was running thin, mostly due to the exhaustion brought on by the fistfights, the gunfights, the garish discoveries. Just another day in the life of Jack Flynn, intrepid reporter. Right? Well, I hoped not.

Anyway, here I was, destined for Marshton just four days after the last such sojourn almost got me killed, and the man I had initially come to visit was now lying near death—because of me.

Why had I returned? Logical question. The best way to answer that is to explain what happened after I left Sweeney the night before:

First, I paid on a Northeastern University criminology professor by the name of Avi Dents. Get it? Evidence. Just kidding. I'm punchy. His

278

real name is Sam Brookstone, a longtime source of mine. Still in my stocking feet, I brought John Cutter's folder to his house, pleaded with him for confidence, and asked him to tell me what it meant.

He's a rather owlish guy, almost trying to look the role of the academician, with tufts of hair that rise far off a mostly bald scalp, and large, thick glasses. He was wearing a cardigan sweater. Alan Dershowitz looks outright suave in comparison. I mean, who wears a cardigan anymore? Even Mr. Rogers went off and retired. He invited me into his library as he scanned the report, took a long puff on an overly fragrant pipe, and said to me, "The victim in this report was poisoned to death, I dare say murdered."

That confirmed what I pretty much already knew. Two Cutter-Ellis's down, one Flynn to go.

All of which still left something of an accommodation problem. To be more specific, I had abandoned my nice police guard, and I imagined that Gerry and Kevin weren't terribly pleased about that. They also realized, no doubt, that wherever Sweeney was, I had been as well—a fact that could land me under arrest. Keep in mind, I had just stolen state property, to wit, John Cutter's toxicology test results. I had shot a man in the face. I fled the scene. So I called Gerry from my cell phone and left him a voicemail saying I was fine and would be in touch in the next day or two. I called the hospital and was told that Sweeney was in intensive care and had slipped into a coma.

What I needed was a pair of shoes and a place to sleep, if only for an hour or two. So of all places, I returned to Long Wharf, to *The Emancipation,* God bless her. It had been two days since I'd been there; long time no sea. Sorry. Nathan was gone, dead; Baker was still staying with friends in the nearby town of Weymouth; Kevin and Gerry knew how much I hated the place, so I didn't think they'd look for me there. I didn't sleep a wink, less from fear than the incessant rocking.

Around three A.M., I heard footsteps along the dock. Someone rapped on my window. I should have been frightened. I should have been reaching for some form of a weapon. Instead, I yelled, "Who's there?"

"It's Mongillo." I knew it was really him because it sounded like he was chewing on something.

I was wide awake, walked out on deck, and asked, "How the hell did you know I was here? I thought I was hiding."

He put the better half of a Slim Jim in his pocket, if there is such a thing, and said, "A good guess. People are worried about you."

"Who?" I asked. Serious question. Who was left to worry?

"Well, the cops who were supposed to be watching you, for starters, but I guess they're more worried about their jobs."

Sitting under a moonless sky in the throat of a deadly night, we hatched our plan to travel to Florida together. If Mary Mae was as fragile as Sweeney says, I didn't want to give her the news of her husband on the telephone, because it could well kill her. The trip would devour precious time, but I felt the need to go see her in person.

Then I told Mongillo about my encounter with the goons on Charles Street, and my belief that Campbell might be a ruthless businessman, but wasn't a brutal killer.

By seven A.M., before I even got a chance to see our page-one story in the *Record* that morning, my cell phone rang with a rather agitated Benjamin Bank on the other end and a conversation that went like this:

Bank: "I can't believe you ran that story before you talked to us."

Flynn: "Why wouldn't you believe it? I told you that's exactly what we were going to do."

That was followed by silence, which was followed by his exhortation that the governor, traveling to Washington for a round of courtesy calls on Capitol Hill, had to see me that afternoon, and couldn't do it in Boston, as previously planned.

"It has to be done in person," he said.

So we added Washington to our travel agenda. Vinny insisted on coming along for the entire ride to help protect me, though what he'd do in the face of danger, I wasn't exactly sure. Vinny, like any good reporter, also wanted to be where the story was, which was Washington. And like any good reporter, he likes an expense account meal at a good restaurant, and they had plenty of those in Washington as well.

All of which brings us to Marshton. I pulled in front of Sweeney's mint-colored house with the spotless little yard. Mongillo hung up his phone with a look of horror on his face and said, "This is where people go to retire? Mother of God, I'm upping my 401K contribution to the full ten percent on Monday."

I ignored that and said, "Wait here. I want to chat with Mrs. Sweeney alone."

"Leave the car running and the AC on or I'm going to melt away to nothing in this fucking heat."

Not likely, but he knew that already. It was a little after eleven A.M. and as Mongillo already pointed out, the sun was like a tortuous act of an unmerciful hell probing the very depths of our collective soul. I ambled down the driveway, past the Buick Park Avenue that was parked exactly as it had been a few days before, and up to the side door.

I pulled open the aluminum screen door, and unlike last time, the main door was shut tight and, as I found out when I gently tested the knob, locked. I rang the doorbell and heard it chime on the other side of the thin glass window. I waited and listened, but saw and heard nothing move inside.

So I repeated the act—doorbell, wait, listen. Nothing. She might be an invalid, I thought, so I should take my time, keep my powder dry, which in this weather, was impossible. I stood in the raging heat for a few minutes, moving around a bit on the stoop just to create some semblance of a breeze, then I rang one more time. After that, I rapped on the glass window of the door, increasingly harder after I continued to get no response. Obviously, she hadn't driven anyplace, because their car was still here. Maybe she was in the backyard hanging laundry or cooling off a blueberry pie. The problem with that theory is that molten lava wouldn't cool in this climate.

Still, I walked to the back of the house, where there was, indeed, a short clothesline, though nothing hanging on it, and a small patch of grass that looked like it hadn't been mowed in a couple of weeks. I walked up to one of the windows of the house and looked inside. It was their bedroom. The double bed was perfectly made up, some of his clothes were folded on a nearby chair, and a plaque with Sweeney's badge and a letter of commendation hung on the far wall, next to a small mirror. This room essentially told me nothing, though the portable air conditioner in the adjacent window did. It was off, pretty much assuring that no one was inside.

I walked around to the far side of the house, within easy sight of the neighboring house. I glanced quickly in at what appeared to be the living room. There was a television, about a nineteen-incher. Across from it sat a Lazy-Boy recliner, next to a side table holding a large-sized Mr. Goodbar, opened. The carpeting was standard issue Berber. The assorted prints and paintings on the wall were of the type you'd buy in a suburban shopping mall.

"Can I help you with something?"

It was the frail voice of an elderly woman, and I turned slowly around to see exactly that—a lady of maybe eighty-five years, maybe five feet tall in a loose-fitting housedress, standing on the edge of her driveway with, okay, a gun. She had it pointed at roughly my left testicle. I don't think she could see all that well, and her hand appeared unsteady—two facts that I wasn't sure improved my current plight.

I mean, as a kid, my mother didn't even let me play guns or war or cops and robbers or anything else with perceived violence and easy, simulated deaths. Now, in the last five days, everyone I meet seems to be packing heat and are all too willing to use it.

"Hi there," I said, almost too happy. I clasped my hands in front of me, not wanting the woman to get an itchy trigger finger because she thought I was reaching into my pocket. At the same time, I was protecting, nominally, the family jewels.

"My name is Jack Flynn. My identification is right out there in my car—" I made an exaggerated pointing motion toward the Buick LeSabre—"and I'd be thrilled to go get it and show you if you'd like. I'm from Boston, and I'm looking for Mrs. Sweeney."

"You some salesman?" she asked. She talked out of the side of her mouth in a tone that showed she was remarkably unimpressed. Her skin was tanned as leather, but looked even darker, framed, as it was, by her white hair. I noticed that the quaint housedress had a repetitive print of buff surfers on their boards with the phrase, "Hang Ten." Hadn't heard that one in a while.

"I'm not. I'm a family friend. I'm here to see Mary Mae." I thought that by using her first name, that might seal the deal.

The woman said, "You're no family friend. Go the hell back from whatever slime pit you came." With that, she cocked the revolver and held the gun out further from her face.

I shook my head and said, "Whatever you say," and began walking slowly around the front of the house. What an assassin in Boston couldn't accomplish, a woman octogenarian in Florida might.

I'll confess more than a small amount of relief when I arrived at the car unharmed and snapped open the door. Mongillo was yakking on the phone and barely gave me a look. I started the car up and sped around the block, prepared to hear the sound of a tire exploding or the back windshield shattering at any given moment.

When I was young, there was an old lady down the street, Mrs. Irving, who used to hand out Hershey Kisses to the neighborhood kids and we'd gather round and listen to her stories about the days of milkmen and tabletop radios. Nowadays, they threaten you with Smith & Wesson revolvers. Times change, not always for the better.

None of which I explained to Mongillo, because he never hung up. I pulled around the corner, jammed the car in park, hustled out the door, and cut through a neighbor's yard to arrive back at the Sweeneys' side door, safely out of sight of Granny Clampett.

I felt around the top rim of the door molding for a hidden key. Nothing. I checked in and around a nearby bush. Nada. I felt beneath the front bumper of the car for one of those magnetized compartments that holds keys. Again, nonexistent. I came up with the absurd idea of checking under the doormat, a straw rectangle that said "Welcome" on it. And there it was, the house key. What kind of cop hides a key under a mat? Probably a retired and overly trusting one.

When I opened the door and walked inside, I nearly staggered back from the heat. All the windows were sealed shut, and the place had that medicinal kind of Ben-Gay odor to it that causes a reflexive limp and a sore rotator cuff.

"Mary Mae?" I called out, still standing in the doorway, my voice somewhere between conversational and a soft holler. No response. I remained just inside the front door in case she was also a Smith & Wesson groupie. Everybody else these days was carrying; no reason to expect she wouldn't be. These retirees probably had a shooting range next to their shuffleboard court. I called her name again, only louder. The words, though, seemed to get caught in the thick air and fall to the linoleum kitchen floor like a wet rag. In the oppressive heat and the stultifying silence, I was pretty much convinced there was nobody home.

I walked through the neat little kitchen with the plain countertops, tin spice canisters, and GE appliances, into a small front dining room with a formal but inexpensive looking table that had the appearance of never being used.

I felt a set of eyes on me, causing me to peer cautiously around the room, expecting to find Ma Barker or whatever her name is from next door. Then I realized the eyes were part of a collection of photographs on the internal wall. I'll admit, this burglary thing is relatively new to me, even as it's getting old.

The pictures, in fact, were the only sign of life in an otherwise anti-septic room, so I stopped for a long moment to gaze at them, unsure what my next move would be. On top, there was Sweeney's son, I think he said his name was Michael, standing in the driveway of a two-decker house in what was probably the middle-class Hyde Park or West Roxbury neighborhood of Boston, his hair buzzed short, a big smile on his handsome face, a cadet's uniform on his muscular body. My bet is that he was on his way to his first day at the police academy.

The next photograph down showed him in his dress blues against a ruffled velvet curtain in a dimly lit auditorium on what must have been graduation day, serious and proud beneath the stiff brim on his new police cap, his body rigid in pose. The shot below was that of father and son, the younger in his patrolman's garb, the elder in a long drab-tan raincoat that a detective might wear on television, leaning on a desk and laughing at the camera in the confines of a police station somewhere in Boston.

And beside the pictures, this poem, placed in a simple black frame:

A Parent's Regret

Someday, joy will replace the greatest pain
That anyone should ever have to endure.
Until then, until you meet your child in heaven,
A life of tear-stained somedays.

—Anonymous

Don't I know it. I swallowed hard and walked from the dining room, past a front door that looked like it was never used, into the living room that I had seen from outside the house when I ran into the pit bull of a woman from next door. This room had more of a lived-in feel, beginning with the reclining chair that had deep grooves in the cloth cushions. The candy bar I had noticed from the window was melted and goopy from the heat. A pair of remote controls sat on the side table along with an old *TV Guide*. I didn't know people still read *TV Guide*, but I didn't know people still ate Mr. Goodbars, either. Maybe it's a Florida thing, or a retiree thing, which I guess is the same thing.

Anyway, on the carpet next to the chair sat an uncovered shoebox containing various scraps of paper and clipped newspaper stories, so of course, I reached inside and pulled some out. The first one was a three-paragraph announcement in the *Parkway Daily Transcript*, a little neighborhood newspaper, saying that Michael A. Sweeney had graduated from the Boston Police Academy and been stationed to Precinct 4 in the South End. I don't know why that gave me a pang of pride, but it did. I sifted through a program for the academy commencement exercises and a letter from the commissioner assigning Sweeney to the street narcotics unit.

Then I saw a yellowing clip from the *Record* that was dated from five-and-a-half years before, a front-page story with the headline, "Officer, Minister Killed in Botched Mattapan Drug Raid." The lede of the story went on to explain how a young narcotics officer was shot and killed and a city reverend died of an apparent heart attack during a drug raid on the wrong apartment in a Mattapan tenement house. The reporter, Jacob Stein, went on to identify Sweeney by name in the third paragraph. John Leavitt, who was then the police superintendent in charge of detectives and the narcotics squad, expressed regret for the two deaths and said, "This tragic incident is under thorough and intensive investigation. We will find out what went wrong, and we will take all proper punitive and corrective measures."

As I went to place the papers and clips carefully back in the shoebox, I thought of what was missing from this collection, which was the same thing missing from the wall in the dining room—no letters of commendation for Officer Sweeney, no flowery tributes to a fallen brother, no photographs of the mayor presenting the heartbroken parents with an American flag after a funeral fit for a hero. All they had was a generic poem, written anonymously. Then I saw why.

There on the floor beside the cardboard box was another old clip, this one more fragile, the ink worn from constant handling and smudged in one place, as if from a single drop of water. I picked it up. It was a *Boston Record* story, and I was startled to see the familiar byline of Robert Fitzgerald.

The story carried the intriguing headline, "Deadly Mistake," and appeared in the paper the day after the news story of Michael Sweeney's death. The lede was classic Fitzgerald prose: "He was the meticulous architect of what was to be a valiant strike at one of the most notorious and nefarious drug dens in the city of Boston. He met with informants. He conducted surveillance. He filed for search warrants.

"But when the hour came, Michael Sweeney, a young detective, the son of a veteran Boston cop, made one mistake: He led his brethren to the wrong apartment. And that one mistake cost him his life and likely led to the death of an elderly man of the cloth."

The story went on for seventy or so more lines, quoting police officials anonymously saying that Sweeney was an ambitious young officer who made the rookie mistake of relaying the wrong address in the briefing report given to all officers taking part in the raid. Those police officials say Sweeney had a history of being careless in his details. They said the department would likely admit fault in the reverend's death and offer his estate somewhere along the lines of two million dollars. Of Sweeney's death, they said he was mistakenly shot by another cop and implied he had brought it on himself.

I was so engrossed in the story that when I got to the end, I found myself sitting in Hank Sweeney's easy chair, and jumped up with a start.

They made a scapegoat of him.

Obviously something wasn't right here, or someone. I rested the frail newspaper clip on top of the others in the shoebox and began looking around the rest of the living room—the name seeming to belie the present feeling and the mood. Sweat formed on my forehead, along my lower back and under my arms. The smell of the house began making me nauseous. But I forged on, in search of Mary Mae, knowing full well I wasn't going to find her. In that case, what I was looking for, I didn't really know.

I do know there were various knickknacks on the shelves of a bookcase wedged into a corner—some Hummels and several pictures of a dignified, well preserved older woman who I assumed was Mary Mae herself—in one with Sweeney, in another smiling behind the wheel of a new car with the sticker still on the back window. Strange as it sounds, her smile made me smile too. She was like that.

I walked into the bedroom, where there was another photo on the bedside table of the ever-photogenic Mary Mae standing on the balcony of a resort hotel room at sunset. I pulled open the lone door inside the room and saw a closet filled with both of their clothes—hers on the left, his on the right. Most of hers were wrapped in plastic, as if they had just come back from the dry cleaner.

I was thinking that my voyeuristic tendencies were starting to get the better of me and that it was time to take leave when the sound of the telephone crashed through the heavy, hot air. I actually jumped. I regrouped and was, for some strange reason, drawn to the ringing phone, and walked out from the bedroom back into the living room to watch it. The phone, a Princess touch-tone, sat on the bookshelf between a framed picture of the couple and a small silver urn. Mid-ring, it kicked over to an answering machine, and I suddenly heard Sweeney's distant voice saying, "We're not here right now to take your call, but you know what to do at the beep."

It beeped, then came Sweeney's voice all over again, sounding tired, his words slurring into each other. He was out of his coma, obviously, but barely.

"Mary Mae," he said, and then paused. The tape quietly rolled and I moved closer—so close, in fact, that I was standing right over the machine, hunched down trying to hear not just each word, but every inflection. I found myself staring at the turning cassette as if I might be able to see Sweeney's face in it, and maybe that of Mary Mae.

"My Mary Mae, remember how you'd get up on your toes and kiss me when I went off to work and tell me to watch myself because I was the only husband you'd ever have?" He paused as if composing himself, drawing in breaths. It sounded as if it hurt him just to talk.

He continued, "Well, I didn't do so good last night. I took a risk and I got shot right in the gut." I could hear him moan as he moved in his hospital bed. "I know, I know. I'm a horse's arse. I'm too old to be doing this, running around like a kid. You used to tell me that all the time.

"But I'm helping this guy, this reporter, to figure out whether the publisher of the *Record* was murdered, and I think he was. This guy's good. Been with the *Record* for a while. Used to work in Washington. I know you didn't have any use for the paper, but I stayed with it, even after what they did. Anyway, I figure if I help this kid out, maybe he'll help us get some justice. Just a thought."

Another long pause. I stood directly over the tape, still straining to listen, and think I heard him choking back tears on the other end.

"I don't know, Mary Mae. It's an idea. It's tough for me to figure these things out by myself."

Another pause, I thought I heard him convulsing, though I didn't know whether it was in pain or sadness. My hands, helpless, began moving just to give me a sense of action, mobility. At one point, I put my right hand on the receiver and almost jerked it up to talk to him, but just as quickly I pulled it away.

"I'm so sorry that I've been gone so long. I don't like to be without you and I know you don't like to be without me."

I heard a door open, whirled around, and stared into the kitchen, bracing myself for what was to come. Granny Clampett? Mary Mae? Then I realized the sound came from the phone, in the hospital room, not here in the house.

Sweeney said, his tone more upbeat and firm, "Okay, honey, I love you too. I'm going to get myself patched up and get out of here soon." And with that, the line went dead.

My eyes settled on the photograph of the woman, smiling next to her husband, her arm around his waist and his around her shoulder. Then I scanned the rest of the shelf, fixing on the small, silver urn. I picked it up and turned it around and saw the engraved words that I expected to see: Mary Davis Sweeney, 1930–1997.

One of the two cassettes in the machine rewound. The rest of the house was filled with the dull ring of dead air. I stood alone and quiet, staring at the urn, thinking of Sweeney in the Public Garden two nights before.

I can't even remember what it's like not to be married to her, and I'd never have it any other way.

I placed the urn carefully back on the shelf and said, "Mary Mae, old Hank is one hell of a guy."

Then I strode from the living room, through the dining room and the kitchen. I walked out the door, locked it, slipped the key back under the mat, and jogged through the neighbor's yard. The sun was so hot by then I thought I might self-immolate. Sheer desire for the car air-conditioning spurred me on.

I snapped open the driver's side door. Mongillo now had his laptop fired up and his phone hooked up to a headset with a microphone, and continued gabbing and typing at the same time. The air in the car felt so cool it almost felt cold. He cast a quick glance my way when I got in, and returned to his call.

I pulled out my own phone and called directory assistance. I asked for the Marshton Town Hall, was connected, and requested to speak to someone who handles vital statistics. The phone rang again and a frail-sounding woman answered, "Bella here."

I put on my best, friendliest, I-could-be-your-hard-working-son voice, and said, "Bella, hi, my name is Jack Flynn. I'm a reporter for *The Boston Record*. I'm working on a story and need one very quick piece of information that I'm hoping you can help me with."

"Hi, Jack," she said. "I moved down from Boston last year. I get the *Record* sent down in the mail."

I was about to point out that she could read it on-line, same day, free of charge, but decided this probably wasn't the right time. Nor was it the right time to say that quick prayer of thanks to the gods of journalism who seemed to be smiling down on me that very minute. Instead, I said, "That's terrific. This looks like a great town to move to."

"Oh it is," she replied. "We have so many things to do here."

"I can't even imagine. Unfortunately, I'm in kind of a rush right now. What I'm looking for is a death certificate on a Mary Davis Sweeney, who died in 1997. Is it possible to get the cause of death on her?"

"Well, we're not supposed to do this by phone. Normally you're required to come in and fill out an official request, then pay a five dollar administrative fee for the certificate, unless you want a raised seal, then it's twenty dollars."

I knew, though, with the word "normally" that I had her, provided I didn't screw up. I said, "I know this is a hassle, but is there any possible way that you might help a fellow Bostonian out on the phone, and I'll send the money to town hall?"

She paused and said, "Hold on." For the next two minutes, I listened to the Rolling Stones' "Satisfaction" played by Muzak. Who knew?

She picked up the phone again. Her tone was markedly different, less friendly. She said, "Mary Davis Sweeney. Says here she died of a gunshot wound."

"Anything else?" I asked.

She paused, then said, "Self-inflicted."

I thanked her, quickly hung up, and made a circular motion with the index finger of my right hand, signaling Mongillo in no uncertain terms to hang up the goddamned telephone and talk to me. He did, proving once again how much smarter he is than he looks.

I said, "Tell me everything you know about that botched drug raid where the minister died, and tell me what you think Fitzgerald did wrong."

Just one more mystery in the increasingly complex mix.

thirty-two

WE TOUCHED DOWN AT 4:30 P.M. at National Airport, renamed Reagan National Airport, though I refuse to call it that, not because I don't like Reagan, but only because I don't like change. We emerged from the terminal to a stream of warm sunshine and a late afternoon breeze both inviting and fragrant—all of it in direct contrast to Marshton, my dark mood, and hell, my entire life.

This was a town I knew better than most. I settled into marriage here. I was widowed here. I broke the biggest story of my life here, watched my Georgetown house torn asunder, saw too much death and heard far too many lies, and finally, I left myself with no choice: I had to go. Yet, I'll confess, it always feels good to drop in for a visit, if only to catch a burger and a cold Sam Adams over at the University Club grille room, where I remain a member in reasonably good standing.

Vinny Mongillo, by the way, spent the entire flight from West Palm on the AirPhone running up, I don't know, fifteen, maybe twenty thousand dollars in charges. At one point he took my peanuts and drank most of my Coke when he thought I was dozing, and as we disembarked, every one of the flight attendants said goodbye to him by name. I don't think they even gave me the standard, "Have a nice visit." I obviously wasn't on my best game.

Vinny took a cab downtown, to the paper's Washington bureau to work the phones and see if he could develop a follow-up story to our front-page hit of that day on the governor and his suspect record. I hopped in another cab for my planned meeting with the aforementioned governor on Capitol Hill. What he wanted, I had no idea, but to say my interest wasn't piqued would be like Vinny saying, "I'll have the salad." It's neither real nor right.

I didn't know Lance Randolph particularly well, and I liked him even less than I knew him, though it's not lost on me that there should have been a bit of a bond between us. He followed his father into the family business of politics. I followed my father into the family business of newspapers—granted, not at as high or glamorous a level. He took over before he was fully ready. I might take over before I'm fully ready. He's young and good looking. I'm young and good looking. Did I just say that out loud?

Give me just a little something, would you? Maybe no one's noticed, but it's been a trying few days.

So why wasn't I a Randolph fan? Because I thought he had it too easy. I never believed he was forced to pay his dues. I thought he was born on third base and kept telling people he hit a triple. All of which is why I love being a reporter. You get to write what Mongillo and me wrote that morning and take the guy down a peg at one of the most critical points of his gilded life. All this and no license required.

Speaking of which, as I got out of the cab behind the Capitol, I watched a petite young television reporter, bright lights shining on her heavily made-up face, perform a stand-up for the nightly news. "Peter, Governor Randolph spent most of the day shuttling between senators' offices, trying to mitigate further damage from today's *Boston Record* report. He remained unavailable for comment, but in a White House photo opportunity with the British prime minister, President Clayton Hutchins says he sees no, and I'm quoting here, damned reason in the world—end of quote—to withdraw the nomination. As you know, Peter, the president's relationship with the *Record* has been an especially trying one. Back to you."

As the lights went down, I felt a fleeting temptation to tap the woman on the shoulder and explain that I'm the guy who wrote that story for the *Record,* and hey everyone, look at me, look at me. But not my style.

It did, however, give me a quick dose of satisfaction at having broken what was obviously deemed a national story about the president's nominee to serve as attorney general. Having been trotting around the bowels of Florida all morning, I had been detached from the rest of the world and hadn't realized the full impact of our work.

I met Randolph's aide, Benjamin Bank, a nervous little chipmunk of a man in a cheap blue suit, at the southwest entrance to the Russell Building on the Senate side of the Hill. We shook hands, though I didn't exactly pull a muscle trying to make small talk. As much as I was curious, I was also more than a little irritated by the cryptic lead-up to this meeting, and didn't fully understand why we couldn't have used that perfectly acceptable means of communication known as the telephone. It's the classic act of a politician and his self-important aides, thinking that everyone will drop everything on their vaguest whim.

Still, I got bored with the silence, and blurted out, "So, Benjamin, a good day on the Hill?" I asked this suddenly as we walked together toward the Capitol. I might have sounded a little too upbeat because poor Benjamin inched toward the curb and gave me a sidelong look.

He replied, "I think the governor accomplished much of what he set out to do today, which was to make the acquaintance of a few key senators on both sides of the aisle and solidify his personal relationships here in Washington."

Allow me to interpret that for you folks without a Master's degree in Bullshit from the University of Buttsuck, or without a few years under your belt in DC. What Benjamin really said was, "We led the governor around by the nose and he didn't drool on his own shirt or have a visible erection around any women under the age of twenty. We'll call it a win and head back to Boston." What a business.

Forgive me for revealing my mood, which grew more foul every minute that I was forced to be with someone like Benjamin Bank, who lives to lie, at least in public. And for anyone keeping score at home, I am the public, or at least its representative.

My meeting with Randolph was to take place in the Capitol hideaway office of Bill Gillis, the senior senator from Massachusetts. Ranking senators generally get two offices—their regular suite over in one of the Senate buildings and their private getaway right in the Capitol building where they might keep a couch and a soft chair for whatever occasions arise, including, well, nevermind. They often set up a little bar inside, and they hold the only key. As a fellow Democrat from his home state, Gillis played the role of Capitol Hill big brother to Lance Randolph, and as such, provided him some office space and gave him a little tour, which, knowing Gillis, probably included the Monocle for a four-martini lunch. But that's another issue.

We climbed a wide marble stairway and clicked along an ornate hallway with washed marble floors and walls until we climbed another, steeper stairway. We zigzagged down a confusing mishmash of identical corridors, seeming, at one point, to completely double back. Finally, Bank cut in front and motioned with his hand for me to stop at a nondescript office door on our left. He knocked once, opened it a crack, stuck his face inside, and said, "Jack Flynn is here, Governor." He stepped aside to allow me to walk through.

"Hello there, Jack," Randolph said as I stood within the narrow confines of the tiny office. He was sitting on a hunter green leather couch with his feet up on a coffee table, reading through a sheaf of typewritten papers. He stood up slowly, shook my hand and added, "Take a seat." I did, in an adjacent easy chair. Bank closed the door on his way back out.

"Cozy place, isn't it," he said, making a motion around the room with his left hand. "Christ, the Capitol dome is right over there. Had I known you got these kinds of perks, I would have run for Senate instead of governor."

I said, "Well then, it would have helped if your father was a senator rather than a governor when he died or else you stood precisely zero chance of getting elected."

Okay, I didn't say exactly that, maybe because it was slightly too obvious, or perhaps just baldly impolite. But give me a break. There's that born on third base syndrome manifest for all to see, or at least me to confirm.

The office, as I said, was small, but extraordinarily regal, very, for lack of a better word, senatorial. There was no desk, just the couch and the chair upon which I sat and a small refrigerator with some glassware on top of it shoved off into a corner. The floors were dark marble with a mosaic inside the stones, covered in part by a vibrant cranberry-colored rug. The photographs on the walls chronicled Senator Gillis's high-points in Washington—meetings with presidents Johnson, Nixon, Ford, Carter, Reagan, Bush, Clinton, and Hutchins. The one small-paned window looked north with a crystalline view of the Washington Monument and the Lincoln Memorial beyond it.

"How are you, Governor?" I asked.

"I think I'm better at Beacon Hill than Capitol Hill, but give it some time," he said, sitting back down. "Give it some time. You certainly made my life a little more complicated today." He took his stack of papers and turned them upside-down on the coffee table, then met my gaze flush. "I've got the *Washington Post* and the *New York Times* crawling up my ass. All three nets have asked for live interviews. Reporters from around the country are swarming all over the State House looking under every rock in my past, all courtesy of you."

He said this not in any vindictive or caustic way, but almost as a detached observation, and with a shallow smile. Then he added, "Jesus, look at you. You look exhausted."

You might logically wonder how he knew, since we've only met two, maybe three times before. Maybe this was my everyday look. Maybe I was anemic, or had an infant at home, or was perpetually sleep-deprived. But understand that with almost every politician I've ever met, there's this sense of faux familiarity to the proceedings. At one level, I think they try to trick you into believing there's a bond, because with a bond comes an investment, and with investment comes support, whether it be political, financial, or in my case, journalistic. At another level, they spend their days around people who are constantly nodding their heads and telling them, "Yes, sir" or "ma'am" and their nights meeting the general public at community events and chicken dinners. They live life on the surface, putting up fronts, smiling when they want to scowl, bouncing from one crowd to the next, one issue to another.

For all I know, this little meeting with him qualified us as longtime friends.

"I've had a few things going on as well," I said, smiling wanly.

He kept a serious gaze fixed on me. "Well," he said, leaning back, "Unfortunately, I think I'm about to add one more."

He paused, as if to also add drama. I regarded him for a moment. He looked younger than his forty-three years, his smooth skin void of blemishes, his dirty blond hair full and casually combed. His coat hung on the back of the door. He was in his shirtsleeves—those sleeves being unfastened and rolled up to the middle of his forearms. His top button was undone and his blue-and-green rep tie slightly loosened at his neck. He had a look, in total, as if he should be the model on a brochure for a stately Nantucket resort, pictured at an al fresco table, his face kissed by the sun, a sweater tied over his shoulders, laughing at a preposterously funny line uttered by a similarly beautiful woman in his small group— maybe something like, "Imagine if we didn't have turndown service at the inn?"

He looked down, as if trying to figure out how to launch this part of the conversation, though I had a pretty good idea that he already knew. Just as litigators don't ask questions without already knowing the answers, politicians rarely stray far from a practiced script. It's just a fact of modern life.

He looked up at me with his soft blue eyes and said, "You guys were right in today's story. You had it."

Well, if nothing else, I certainly liked that quote. I could form an entire follow-up story off that one quote, under the headline, "Governor Admits to Embellishing Record." I was half tempted to pull out my cell phone and call Mongillo right then and there with the glorious news of a confession.

Then he said, "I need to talk to you off the record, this whole conversation." He looked at me expectantly and asked, "That a deal?"

"I don't know what you want to talk about yet." I said that with the quasi-intention of being an obstinate prick—partly because of my aforementioned mood, but partly because I wanted him more on edge than comforted by this meeting. I didn't want him to have the impression that he was setting the terms.

"I'll tell you, but only off the record. Trust me, once we get going, you're not going to want to be sticking this stuff in your newspaper." He said this almost dismissively.

Well, okay, he had me hooked. How do you say no to this? I said, "All right, off the record."

He leaned forward, his elbows on his knees and his hands clasped together as if in prayer.

"Look, my conviction record got inflated. I don't deny it. I did a pretty damned good job as the Suffolk County DA. I didn't have to exaggerate my rate. It was higher than my three immediate predecessors. It was higher than nine of the fourteen other DAs in Massachusetts. It was higher than the national average."

He stopped and looked hard at me. He remained silent, as if waiting for something, so I gave it to him. I asked, "Then why did you inflate it?"

"I didn't," he replied. "Robert Fitzgerald did. Your star political reporter put the figures into the paper without ever getting authority from me, anyone in my campaign, or on my staff."

My head began to hurt, just a gentle cracking on either side of my scalp as if a pair of holes was erupting in my two temples. Robert Fitzgerald, one of the biggest, most important names at the *Record,* was by everyone else's account, an inveterate liar.

I said, "I'm confused."

Granted, there were probably better comebacks for me to make, but any that were grander, more sweeping, or contained greater depth, eluded me at that particular moment. I added, "Help me out, Governor." I emphasized the word "Governor" as if I was getting in some sort of dig, but what kind, I don't know.

He sighed and leaned back, then forward again. Outside the window, the light in the Washington sky was beginning to fade, leaving us in the descending dark of the office. The two lamps in the room remained off.

"You know, I'm sure, that Robert has some issues regarding the truth."

I didn't, but I was beginning to learn. So I said, "Why don't you explain to me what you mean."

I found myself talking to him not in the tone of respect that I normally extend to someone in a position of authority, even if I was about to put the screws to him in print, but more as an equal, and as I've said, an equal that I didn't particularly like. I mean, give me a break. I've sat with the president of the United States. Some Chipster in an Izod shirt who got his job because of his old man hardly warrants too much of my respect.

He hesitated, looking at the floor, bridging his fingers together, then placing them on the back of his neck as if to relieve stress. Don't for a second think I didn't regard all of this as an exquisite act. Politicians, by virtue of the television age, are actors to their core. If they're not, they don't survive as politicians very long. At least with Ronald Reagan we knew what we were getting, and we got a great one at that—an actor, I mean, if not a leader, but perhaps that as well.

He looked at me again and said, "As I'm sure you know, Robert and my father were very close—a relationship that transcended the politician/journalist thing and extended deep into their private lives. They golfed together. They hunted together. My mother and father got together regularly with Robert and his wife, Eleanor.

"And as you certainly remember, Robert was uncommonly kind to my father in print."

He paused again and averted my gaze, staring at some point on the wall over my right shoulder. By now, his face was mostly in shadow. The sun had faded from the window and the patch of sky that I could see was a vibrant red, almost the color of cherry licorice.

"Something happened to Robert after my old man was shot," Randolph said, fixing on me again. "He lost not only his most reliable source in government, but his best friend in the world. He got lazy, I think, sloppy, desperate to make new friends in power."

A pause again, mostly for dramatic effect, because by the look on his face, I knew that he already knew what he wanted to say.

"And he began to lie. In print. In the *Record.*"

He let that hang out there for a long moment, like an ominous thundercloud having just rolled in across a distant plain.

He added, his voice softer and his tone tempered with apology. "And he lied about me. Good lies. Helpful lies. And I accepted them."

He sat back and gazed through the silence and the shadows at me sitting upright in that chair.

"Lied about what?" I asked, my voice flat, simply inquiring.

"About my record. A couple of months after my old man died, Robert came to my house one night. I had just announced my campaign to succeed my father as governor. I was figuring out my issue stands, getting an organization together, starting in on a message. And he showed up at my door and said he wanted to talk.

"So we drank some port and he asked about my performance as district attorney, and I told him where I stood. He said, 'You're going into this campaign with a lot of advantages, Lance. You'll have a lot of your father's tried and true supporters behind you. You'll get a sympathy vote for what happened at the school that day. You're a handsome young man, so you'll get some votes from women.'

"But then he said, 'You have some baggage, too. There will be a lot of people who think you're trying to take advantage of your father's death for your own political gain. There will be people who will say that you've been riding an elevator, not climbing stairs, your entire career. There will be people who will say you don't even deserve the Democratic nomination, never mind actually being governor.'"

Another dramatic pause. He picked up a can of Coke on the coffee table and took a long swig. "So he told me that I have to show the public that when I did a job, when I served as district attorney, that I was the very best in the state—not second best, not third best, but the very best. I had to have the highest conviction rate. I had to have the toughest reputation. I had to show the public that when I got the opportunity to serve them, I was my own man, with my own exemplary record. I had to show the public that I had earned the governorship, not inherited it. Earned, not inherited. Those, I recall, were his exact words."

He looked at me and I kept my gaze steady on his.

He continued, "So a week later, he runs a story citing these fabulous conviction rates that I had in Suffolk County. Look, I was already pretty proud of my real rates. This ain't Norfolk or Barnstable Counties, with a bunch of shopliftings in the local mall and the occasional wife-beater who pleads out. We have tough crimes, murders and rapes and robberies, and some top-notch criminal defense lawyers in Boston. This ain't Charlotte, North Carolina."

Charlotte, by the way, has an extraordinarily high violent crime rate, but I didn't see the need to point that out to him just then, only not to break his train of words.

He continued, "But he goes and makes them better in print. He said my unpublished conviction rates for the year were likely to be the best in the state. It wasn't as if he had to double them or anything. All he did was embellish them —make them maybe six percent, maybe eight percent better. That day the story came out, the numbers just kind of sat out there. No one complained.

"So I had a choice. Do I publicly accuse my father's best friend, a revered political reporter and analyst for the most powerful newspaper in Massachusetts, of lying, even as he thought he was doing me a favor? Or do I sit there and live a lie that might well help me win the gubernatorial election?"

He looked at me, then down, then at me again. He said, "Well, it's obvious what I did. And now the same newspaper that set me up is in the process of taking me down."

I sat there silent, stunned, exhausted, just to list a few things. Here are a few others: dirty from all the sweating I did that morning in the Florida sun, aching because I hadn't had the chance to exercise in what felt like the longer part of forever, hungry because Mongillo had grabbed my peanuts on the flight. My mind flickered over to the University Club on Sixteenth Street, specifically to the Grille Room on the second floor, where perhaps Lyle might be willing to pour me the coldest beer in Washington—just like the old days.

Back to Capitol Hill. I was thinking of what I could possibly say, when Randolph added, his tone far sharper than before, "But don't think for a second that I'm falling alone. I go down, the *Record* comes down with me. Your reporters, your editors, and especially your publishers, have been hiding Fitzgerald's lies for years. All you people want to do is sell newspapers—first on my successes, and now on my failures. I'll destroy your credibility, Jack. I'll destroy your whole paper. Believe it."

I'm not precisely sure what it feels like to have an elephant walk across your chest, but I suspected this moment might be the closest I'd ever come to knowing. So basically, let's do a quick census of my problems: A second-rate chain is on the brink of buying my newspaper, the governor of my state is intent on destroying it, my publisher and friend is dead, his predecessor was murdered, the company president's a traitor, the star reporter (me aside) is a recidivist liar, I've killed a man, and I'm hiding from the police. Oh, and my ex-girlfriend seems interested in getting back together and I can't get my mind around it.

I asked, "Is that a threat?"

Well, dumb question, I know. Of course it was a threat. It contained threatening words like *destroy*, it was spoken in a threatening tone. But I think I was just trying to buy time.

"Jack, the *Record* has threatened my career during the most important week of it, when I'm about to become attorney general of the United States. I'm only telling you—promising you—that I will not fall alone."

I asked, "What do you want?" I asked this knowing that Mongillo was back at the bureau furiously dialing for news, and all I wanted to do was call him with the word that we were dead-on right. The Fitzgerald part, I'd vastly prefer to leave out for now.

"I want you to drop the story. Obviously I know enough to realize that a retraction is out of the question. But if you don't keep pushing it, the national press may realize it was just a one-day wonder, as Benjamin likes to call these things, and move on before any real damage is done. If you back away, I'll put out a statement tomorrow—I'll even give it to your paper first—acknowledging an accounting error and blaming an aide who tallied the numbers."

I mulled this. How was I supposed to tell Mongillo and Justine Steele that a follow-up wasn't necessary on a raging national story involving the president's nominee to be the attorney general of the United States? Did I even have the ability to persuade them to drop it? If I did, how was I then supposed to have the paper accept and publish a statement that I knew on its face to be an utter and absolute lie?

"How do you know the publisher knew about the problem?" I asked.

He remained silent for a moment. The shadows had now given way to darkness, such that I could barely make out his features. He leaned over and switched on a lamp and we both blinked in the dim glow.

"I just know."

"Bullshit." You don't often say this to the governor, never mind the nominee to the highest law enforcement office in the land. It felt neither good nor bad, because he wasn't at that moment a politician as much as he was a raw adversary gunning for my throat, just as I was gunning for his. When they talk about politics being hardball, the ball doesn't get much harder than this. Remind me to go to some sort of yoga class when this is all over where I can sit in a circle with mostly women, hold hands, and chant.

We were both leaning forward now, aggressive, eyeing each other in a newfound light, as well as newfound light, if you know what I mean, which I think you do.

"I have notes, or I should say, letters. I wrote to John Cutter complaining. He wrote me back saying the problem would be addressed. Obviously, it never was."

I sucked in air, trying to prevent the appearance of gasping. He kept his eyes fixed hard on my face.

He said, more slowly now, his tone casually ominous, "If you don't drop the story, if you insist on pushing a problem that your paper created for me, then I'll give full disclosure to the *New York Times* tomorrow, so it hits their Sunday paper." A pause, followed by: "Think hard about that, Jack. That's your paper, already on the block, with negative front-page exposure in the *New York Times*. What's that going to do to your reputation and future, and what's that going to do to your newspaper?"

Good questions, though I'd prefer to be the one posing any interrogatories. To his, I didn't know the specific answers, though I knew generally that it wasn't good—at all.

I swallowed hard and said, "We need to have a follow-up story of some sort tomorrow. We can't just drop it. That alone will be too suspicious."

Already, I was talking like this was a conspiracy and I was a principal in it. I didn't like the feeling.

He shook his head. "If you have a story, you better go out and buy the Sunday *Times.*"

I subscribe, but didn't see any need to inform him of that right now.

I replied, "Let me find out what we have in the works."

I picked up the telephone on the coffee table and dialed the number to the Washington Bureau. When Rose, the kindly receptionist, answered the phone, I asked to be connected to Mongillo, trying, I fear in vain, to keep my voice as steady and casual as can be.

"Mongillo here."

"Flynn."

"Where the hell are you? Peter Martin—" the bureau chief—"says you're going to want to buy us dinner at the University Club."

Journalists. Always angling for a free meal. "Still on the Hill," I said. "What do you have for tomorrow."

As I spoke, I looked up at Randolph, who was staring rigid back at me.

"Not good, my man. I have a couple of nice leads on some other possible Randolph lies, but nothing I can turn over for morning. Pretty much all we have is a story quoting other officials in Boston and DC saying they don't think this revelation alone will derail the nomination. I was hoping you'd give me the lead from your face-to-face."

Ordinarily I'd be furious that such a story didn't go far enough. At this exact moment, I was elated. It would buy me another day—or more—to figure out how the hell I was going to address this hall of fame problem.

I said, "I've got nothing. He wanted to talk about family and clammed up when it came to him. If we get any more, hit me on the cell immediately. Otherwise I'll be in the bureau shortly."

I hung up, paused to collect my thoughts, and said to Randolph, "We're running a story saying the existing revelations probably won't hurt your chances for Senate confirmation—that according to various current and former officials. If you don't like that, then go to hell. I'm not going to block it."

He seemed taken aback at my wording, but quickly composed himself and said, "That's fine. But I hope we're clear. If you follow it in any possible way, I'm going straight to the *Times*. If you don't, things will work out fine. It's not an offer. It's a demand."

As if on cue, someone rapped on the door, and Benjamin Bank poked his head inside. I swear to God, the guy was such a little rodent that if he grew whiskers, he could be a new Disney character. For all I knew, this whole grand plan, this intellectual extortion, was his idea.

"Governor, your dinner with Senator Gillis is in ten minutes. It's important we leave now if you're going to make it in time."

Randolph nodded at Bank and replied, "We were just finishing up." To me, he said, "It's all up to you how this gets handled. We'll give you Benjamin's cell phone number if you have any further questions."

Just one: What the hell am I supposed to do now? And with that ringing in my ears, I staggered alone through the halls of Congress and gulped at the fresh night air outside.

thirty-three

AT TIMES LIKE THIS, you have to ask yourself why you got into the business of journalism in the first place, why you've spent a career, a life, in pursuit of truth and public enlightenment.

Okay, I got into it because my father happened to work for a newspaper and the owner paid my way through school. So maybe I'm the wrong person to ask.

But as I've said of Paul Ellis, and of John Cutter before him, they looked at *The Boston Record* as their own form of public service, no less noble than a stint served in elective office, and I have to say, I more than agree, especially after my up close and personal with Governor Lance Randolph. And I don't give a rat's furry ass that Randolph accused John Cutter of covering up Fitzgerald's fabrications. I know it couldn't be true.

I had some awful choices to make. I could well go public with suspicions that Robert Fitzgerald had been a recidivist fabricator for any number of years, and had knowingly written a false story about Lance Randolph's record during the district attorney's first gubernatorial campaign. But if I did, Randolph would levy his own accusations of a long-time, internal cover-up, and the paper would become the proverbial laughing stock in the city and in the industry. Even if we were right, it wouldn't matter, because as we defended ourselves, the board of directors couldn't meet fast enough to approve the sale and get the paper in the hands of Terry Campbell. They're thinking of the stock price, not the reputation.

Times like these, I had to prioritize: (1) Save the paper; (2) Save my life; (3) Find out who killed John Cutter and Paul Ellis, and why. I had a vague understanding that these things were in some way linked, but couldn't yet figure out how.

So would it serve the *Record*'s higher purpose, and in turn, that of the public, to drop the story of Governor Lance Randolph and his crime-fighting record? Would it be okay, in this most unusual circumstance, to look the other way when an ugly truth comes knocking on our newsroom door? Would it mitigate the unseen damage if the paper, in turn, quietly and quickly got rid of its star reporter, Robert Fitzgerald, without a public word? And is that even possible, or would too big a fuss be kicked up and the truth come pouring forth?

These were the nagging—no, plaguing—questions I had as I took my first pleasant swig of an exquisitely icy Sam Adams in a little jazz bar just outside of Georgetown called One Step Down. I sat across a rickety table from Vinny Mongillo, who happened to be strumming an air guitar in sync with the band's rendition of Ray Charles's "What'd I Say?"

Earlier that evening, Mongillo and I worked side by side in the bureau for about an hour, retracing Fitzgerald's steps across a random sampling of his stories. Some of the people he quoted by name, we located. Most others we didn't. I had little doubt that these stories contained egregious lies, made-up people, false premises. But the operative words there are *little doubt*. I still had some, and I needed to erase it.

After that, the two of us bolted for the National Airport. Deadlines loomed over the landscape of my life like mines. Monday afternoon, the *Record* board of directors had scheduled its full meeting to determine the newspaper's fate. Tuesday, the Senate Judiciary Committee would begin its expedited hearings into the nomination of Lance Randolph as U.S. attorney general. Before then, I would have to decide if my paper wanted to pursue the truth, or in the name of a higher purpose, avoid it.

Meantime, I had to get back to Boston to meet with the ailing Hank Sweeney, to figure out how to push John Cutter's death into the realm of a homicide investigation, and to confront Fitzgerald. I also wanted to make sure that Sweeney wasn't taking any sort of legal fall for the gunman's death. Unpleasant duties, all, but entirely necessary.

Finally, I was waiting for a break in the murder of Paul Ellis, and wondering every moment if Ellis's death was linked to Cutter's, which is what I strongly suspected. Oh, and one other question: Was I slated to die sometime soon? Jack Flynn, this is your life. Let's just make sure that it continues on for a while.

At National, the last of the USAirways shuttles to Boston were cancelled because of rain somewhere along the route. It used to be, jets would land on snow-covered runways in all but blizzard conditions piloted by men who read *Soldier of Fortune* rather than *Andrew Harper's Hideaway Report*. Now, there's mist over O'Hare and the entire national aviation system goes into three days of impenetrable gridlock. I was stuck in Washington overnight with nothing to do but have a beer.

There were basically just two people in the world whose counsel I wanted (Paul Ellis, my father, and Katherine Flynn not being of this world anymore)—Robert Fitzgerald and Elizabeth Riggs. Fitzgerald, of course, was not exactly the best person to approach anymore, and Elizabeth, the last few crazy days aside, was no longer part of my life. I don't think.

I called Sweeney from the cab back into DC. He picked up his room phone, which was a great sign, and said he was feeling better, that Mary Mae was mad as hell at him for loping around like a rookie cop, and that we'd get some privacy in the hospital room the next day to go over what we had. He said he believed the cops bought his story about shooting the gunman, who was identified as Kevin Clancy, a.k.a. Mike Andrews, an ex-convict who got popped on parole a short time ago.

The police, Sweeney said, couldn't connect him in any way to the Cutter-Ellis family, leaving them to believe he was a hired hitman. Great. Basically the cops were no closer to an answer than before Paul's murder was committed. Among other things, Luke Travers was an incompetent.

Speaking of whom, when we got to the jazz bar, I had an idea and I called him from the street outside. I couldn't shake the thought of this inordinately decent man, Hank Sweeney, sitting alone in his tiny, mint-colored house hard by a Florida swamp, missing his life in Boston, furious at what the police and my newspaper did to his son, talking to a silver urn that held the remains of his beloved wife, a lone tear falling from his cheek onto the clip of a Fitzgerald story that lay on his lap.

Travers picked up his cell phone on the first ring.

I said, "I have proof that John Cutter was murdered five years ago and the police department has been covering it up."

"Where are you?"

An ambulance roared by, its siren in full blare, heading, I'm sure, to the emergency room at the George Washington Hospital just down the street.

I told him, "Don't embarrass yourself. Just listen. A police toxicology test showed that someone poisoned Cutter with arsenic. His death certificate says he died of a heart attack. I have the toxicology test, a vial of Cutter's blood, and a contaminated tissue taken from the crime scene, all in my immediate possession."

"So you have stolen police evidence?"

"It would be police evidence if the police actually used it as evidence. Instead, you hid it away in a basement locker. It's not so much stolen as rescued." Touché.

"How did you get it?"

"I'm a reporter. Someone gave it to me."

"Sweeney?"

"Again, don't embarrass yourself. I've got a proposal for you." Everyone seemed to be making proposals—or rather, demands—so I figured I'd get into the act. I needed to accomplish two things. First, I needed positive, definitive proof of Fitzgerald's fabrications on a large story, not just Lance Randolph's bony word. Second, I wanted to help Sweeney. This was what's known as a double-bank shot. I said, "Give me the name of the informant in the botched drug raid five years ago that killed that minister over in Mattapan. I will personally guarantee you that this has nothing to do with Paul's death, nothing to do with this case. And in return, I'll give you these toxicology tests and tell you everything else that I know."

"You'll tell me everything you know either way, in front of a grand jury," he replied, tersely.

I rolled my eyes and let it show in my tone. I asked, "Are you about to make an arrest in Paul's murder?"

The question was met with a long silence. I thought I could hear him exhaling in frustration on the other end of the line. "We're not as close as we'd like to be," he said. "We've gotten some breaks. The suspected gunman, I believe, is now dead. But I think he was for hire. Who hired him, I don't know."

I said, "If you want to play tough guy, then go through all the formalities. Convene a grand jury. Send me a subpoena. I'll file a petition to have it quashed. We'll go to court. It'll take forever. Meantime, you can read everything that I know every single morning on the front page of the *Record*. Best half a dollar you'll spend. By the middle of next week, you'll be lucky if your bosses even let you answer phones for the Police Athletic League."

More silence—a blessed sound right now. Finally, he asked, "What do you need the name for?"

"Lieutenant, if you don't stop with the asinine questions, you're going to be reading all the answers in tomorrow's *Record,* and you'll also read about how the former publisher was poisoned to death, and how the police department has covered that fact up for five years. What's it going to be?"

More silence. He eventually said, "Give me your number and I'll call you back in an hour."

An hour's just long enough for a homicide detective to dig through old files to find the name of a secret street informant. I gave him my number and hung up the phone without so much as a good-bye.

Inside the bar, Mongillo had taken the liberty of ordering himself a Grey Goose and tonic—whatever the hell that is—and me a Sam. The waitress brought them back and said, "You need anything else, Vinny, my name's Ginny. We rhyme. Just let me know."

"You know her?" I asked, surprised, as she walked away.

"I do now."

I knew I should have brought him to the University Club, where it would be me who knows people.

The liquor flowed, the music played, Mongillo held an imaginary saxophone up to his face, contorting his body and puffing his cheeks. This was no time to get drunk, which probably meant it was every time to get drunk.

"Do you play?" I asked, realizing how little I knew about a man who I counted as a pretty good friend.

"Every once in a while," he replied with a smile. He added, "By the way, I asked Peter Martin to join us. He said to give him a call if we go and get something to eat."

When the band went on break, the lead singer, a slinky brunette with a sonorous voice, stopped by our table and said to Mongillo, "You look like you know what you're doing. Why don't you join us for part of the next set."

Mongillo hit his right hand to his chest, flicked it out and said, "Word." Okay, he didn't do that, but I saw someone do it once on *The Simpsons*. What Mongillo said was, "I'd be digging that." He said it with the biggest, happiest, sloppiest smile I've ever seen. The singer gave me a coy look and left.

Feeling the mild glow of a single beer in the boozy din of the narrow bar, I leaned across the table and told Mongillo, "I'm completely, inextricably screwed."

"We all are, babe, every one of us in our own unique way."

"No," I said. "I'm really screwed."

He polished off the last gulp of his Grey Goose, sucked on an ice cube, and waved a hand at Ginny, who set off in pursuit of another.

Mongillo looked at me and said, "Jack, you have it made. You've made a national name for yourself at a major metropolitan newspaper. You're close friends with the ownership family, though ignore the fact that most of them are now dead and the remaining one in power hates your guts. All right, forget that whole point. Most important, you have a wonderful woman who'll love you to the end of time."

A wonderful woman who'll love me to the end of time? Yeah, me and who else? And why can't I just love her back?

I asked, "What the hell are you talking about?"

"I'm talking about what matters."

"You don't think the paper matters? You don't think losing the paper matters?"

"Oh, I do. I do. To me, it probably matters more than anything else, and that's part of my problem."

I took a long pull from my bottle. He dipped deep into his fresh highball glass of vodka and tonic, gazing down at the table as he did. I looked at him silently, and he continued, "Jack, Fair Hair, look at me. I don't have anyone like Elizabeth Riggs sitting at home, staring at a wall or a dark TV or the pages of a book that she's not really reading, hoping against hope that she might have a slight chance of spending another night with me.

"Jack, you have something I can only dream about—normalcy, a regular boy-girl relationship—"

"It's not that easy," I interjected. "And I don't have it."

He held out his palm to shut me up. "Here's what I have. I have work. I have the ability to pull an on-the-record quote out of a fresh corpse, to spin a New England News Brief into a front-page story. That's all. That's it. Believe me, when I'm sitting at home all alone every night with a frozen pizza watching another inane sitcom, I don't dream about writing more front-page stories. That's not how it works."

I began to say something when the band suddenly began belting out a bluesy song from the small stage. We sat in mutual silence for the moment, both of us watching the singularly stunning lead singer with the flowing hair and the leather pants do her thing. And at the end of the first song, said singer beckoned Mongillo with an exquisitely alluring finger motion. He rose slowly out of his chair, as if attached to a string, drained his glass while standing, and ambled toward the stage.

The saxophonist handed Mongillo his instrument and he wrapped the strap over his back. The band struck into "Stormy Monday," and Mongillo began to play along.

He played what is inarguably the most beautiful saxophone I have ever heard. He played "Early in the Morning." He played "Hootchy Kootchy Man." He played after the band stopped and the crowd was on its feet in spontaneous applause and he walked about the room with his cheeks blown up like balloons and his eyes watering and music coming from his instrument that was like something created by a higher being. And when he put the sax down, he sat at the piano and began to play all over again.

I was on my feet clapping my hands together until they hurt, the self-pity, the worry, the angst, gone for just a moment, courtesy of the amazingly multitalented Vinny Mongillo. I clapped so hard that I shoved my elbow into someone standing close behind me. I turned to apologize and saw something, in retrospect, that may well have changed the rest of my adult life.

She was wearing an old pair of perfectly fitting jeans, a tight white tank top, some dangly earrings. She wore makeup, but not a lot, just right, and her hair flowed down beyond her bare shoulders. She looked at me without saying anything, and virtually without expression, close, her eyes set like headlights on mine, unmoving, just a pool of familiar blue. It's the look she used to give me when I would lie on top of her first thing on a Sunday morning and we would begin yet another fit of slow and wonderful sex.

Beyond us, Mongillo stopped playing. The room echoed with cheers and applause, then the noise finally died down. The band took another break and Vinny, glowing, walked to the bar with them.

I said, "Hello, Elizabeth."

She didn't move away, didn't move any closer, didn't move her eyes even a fraction away from mine. "Hello, Jack," she replied.

I was about to ask her how she knew I was here, but I flashed back to my conversation with Mongillo minutes earlier and realized I knew the answer to that already.

"You haven't run your Fitzgerald story yet," I told her. It was an obvious point. If she had run a Fitzgerald story, it would have been in her paper already.

"It's ready. I have it. But I didn't want to do that to you right now. So I quit."

She didn't want to do that to me, so she quit. Forgive me for repeating, but it took a moment to sink in, the enormity of what she just said.

Around us, everyone returned to their tables and seats after the chaos surrounding Mongillo's stint—well, everyone but Mongillo, who I saw out of the corner of my eye standing at the bar with the band's drummer and lead singer, laughing and carrying on in that way he always does.

"You shouldn't have quit," I said.

"We do a lot of things in life we shouldn't do." She spoke, again, without moving back, hardly moving at all. "We shouldn't shut people out of the present because of something that happened in the past." She said this casually, just presenting the words to me, unconcerned with how I might feel.

I asked, "What else?"

"I shouldn't have left that day. I shouldn't have agreed so readily to part ways with you. I should have fought you every step, refused to vacate our apartment, refused to get out of your life. Because your life is my life. Because my life is your life. I haven't stopped believing that, feeling that, not even for half a second. You might be a jackass, but you're my jackass, and you're always supposed to be my jackass. Always."

My mind, for whatever bizarre reason, flicked to her apartment, to the fact it was void of even the hint of a man except for the pictures of me. I thought about those last awful moments together, the zip of her luggage in the bedroom, the slow sound of her footsteps, the muddled sobs as she buried her face in Baker's muzzle, then the melancholy click of our front door. What was she thinking as she stood in the hallway, tears streaming down her face, a future so markedly different from the expectations of her past?

I asked, "Then why did you cheat on me?"

Still, she didn't move. Our faces were no more than a foot apart.

"I didn't," she replied. "And you know I didn't. You wanted to believe I did, for whatever contorted reasons. You couldn't function with me, Jack. The past got in the way. Your feelings for Katherine wouldn't allow you to completely give yourself to me, and that's understandable. That's something we could have worked on. But then you fabricated this relationship in your mind, made yourself believe I was unfaithful, because that made your decision to split more definitive in your mind, more rational."

Great, I was getting intense psychotherapy, entirely free of charge, right here for the whole world to watch and hear in the environs of a Washington jazz bar.

She added, "And part of it was my fault. He's a cop, a detective. I was stringing him along, using him. I needed information on Fitzgerald, about how he lied in print on a famous, failed drug raid a few years ago. I thought Travers could help me. I couldn't let you know. So I panicked that day. I was ashamed. And I walked out when I shouldn't have. Given the situation, I just didn't know what else to do."

Anyone else have any surprises they'd like to spring on yours truly today?

Working a story on Fitzgerald and stringing Travers along. Made sense, if only to another reporter, of which I was one. I stared down at the floor for a long moment, trying to scrutinize the seemingly inscrutable. Then I looked around the crowd for a moment just to buy a little bit of time.

What must the people around us have thought, the occasional guy, just out of college, squeezing past us with two Budweisers and a pair of kamikaze shots for himself and his best pal, the two of them doing nothing more that night than bouncing from one bar to the next, not a worry in their simple little world.

In the silence, she said, "Jack, I'm incapable, constitutionally incapable of cheating on you. I thought about it. I had, for lack of a better word, an emotional connection to this guy. I severed that connection the day you kicked me out. I put the Fitzgerald story aside, and now that I'm back on it, now that I have it, I don't want it at all. Travers, he means nothing to me, just some guy trying to get more from me than I ever wanted from him, which pretty much defines any guy but you.

"But Jack, you have to look within. You have to figure out how to get over what happened to you in that hospital nearly four years ago, because it's consuming you. I can only imagine how devastating that must be to lose the one you love, to have her die on what is supposed to be the greatest day of your life. And believe me, Jack. I never intended to replace Katherine. But sooner or later, you have to move on. You have to ease up on yourself. You have to allow yourself to understand that you can't spend the rest of your life consumed by grief. You have to let someone else in, and I was hoping to be that someone, now and always."

"Why'd you quit the *Traveler*?"

"I had a choice: put the story about Fitzgerald in the paper, knowing it would hurt you and the *Record* to no end, or walk away from it, knowing that in some small way, I might be helping you."

"What does the story say?"

She shook her head. "I can't tell you that, Jack. I can quit the *Traveler*, but I can't be completely unfaithful to it. I got the story on their dime. I'm not going to hand it to the competition. It deals with an old drug raid. I don't yet have all the specifics. The paper doesn't either. You need to find it out on your own."

My cell phone rang on the table. I stepped over and picked it up and saw from the caller identification that it was a Boston Police number. I said, "Yeah." It was Luke Travers on the other end.

This is one of life's little ironies. I don't know why that lightened my mood, but it did. Okay, so I do know why that lightened my mood.

"The name you're looking for is Eric Glass. On the street, he just goes by 'Glass.'"

"What street might that be, because I need to find him?"

Travers hesitated on the other end. He replied, "I just helped you all I can."

"Good for you. I'll say the same thing when I try to fit your name and the word 'moron' into our lead headline tomorrow. And you know what? When I do, I'll be doing the entire city a favor."

"He usually hangs on the corner of Boylston and Harrison downtown. It's his territory, for crack and girls."

I hung up before my naturally sunny disposition overcame me and

I thanked him. I turned back to Elizabeth. It ends up I didn't have very far to turn. She had followed me the few paces over to the table and positioned herself right against me, her face again about a foot from mine. Her eyes searched my eyes. Her mouth seemed to be drawn to my mouth.

I said, "You shouldn't have quit. I really didn't need you to do that."

She said, "I did it for you, Jack."

God, how I wanted to tell her how I felt. I wanted to move my head the six inches it would take to meet her in the middle of this dwindling divide. I wanted to hold her, then tell her everything that was going wrong and ask her to help me figure out a way to make all of this right.

But here's what I said instead: "I can't deal with us, Elizabeth. I can't get the present straight, never mind the past. I've already lost enough to last a million lifetimes, and right now I'm at risk of losing a whole lot more. Thank you for your help, but right now, I just need to be alone." And I turned and walked away.

Ask me why I did and the only thing I could say is that I had a devoted belief that a broken trust, like a cracked mirror, can never be properly repaired, that once a relationship is tormented in the way ours had been, even if we summoned the intense energy to put it back together, everything that would happen in that relationship would be viewed through the prism of its absolute worst moments. The good would always be tempered. The bad would seem that much worse. I wanted something fresh, easy, without the history, the miserable memories. And not to sound too altruistic—I thought she deserved better than what I had to offer. Who wants to see everything from the warped perspective of a tragic past?

So I kept walking. I stopped at Mongillo, who was still leaning on the bar with a couple of members of the band, and said, "You're an asshole for giving me up."

He looked at me and said, "Don't be a bigger asshole and walk out of here."

"Watch me."

After a few steps, I turned back around and told him, "We're on the 6:30 A.M. flight. We have urgent work to do together in Boston tomorrow morning. If you're not at the airport, I will fucking kill you."

And I headed for the door. On my way, I turned and looked at her through the crowd, standing in the exact spot she had been, looking back at me. We kept our eyes on each other's for a moment until finally I turned away, pulled open the door, and stepped out into the warm Washington night. As I flagged a cab, my cell phone rang and I looked down at it, figuring—all right, hoping—it might be her. But it was a *Record* number on the caller identification.

"Jack Flynn," I answered.

"Jack, it's Amelia Bradford, Paul's secretary."

Amelia, it's worth noting, is a perfectly preserved and uncommonly proper woman in her early sixties, unflappable by any measure. Because of that, her tone—something between concerned and panicked—seemed not so much surprising as alarming, especially when you factor in that she was calling at ten o'clock on a Friday night.

"Amelia, what's wrong?" I asked.

"Jack, I've found something. I've found something very strange and I don't know what to do about it. I know how Paul thought of you, so I think you should see it right away. Can you come down to the newspaper?"

"Amelia, I'm in Washington tonight, stuck here because of a cancelled flight. What do you have? I'll be in Boston by tomorrow morning."

"I think it's a clue, Jack. I found it cleaning out Paul's office this evening. It's something you should look at, but I don't want to go into it over the phone."

"Where will you be in the morning?"

"Here, in the office, continuing to box everything up and clean it out. It's so terribly sad, Jack, and it only feels worse with all this indecision."

I replied, "I'll see you tomorrow."

Would it be that life was that easy.

thirty-four

BOSTON'S COMBAT ZONE ISN'T what it used to be, which believe me, is very good news, because it used to be the seediest half dozen square blocks in all of New England—grimy streets lined with decidedly downscale strip clubs, porn theaters with sticky floors, and $2 peep shows with strung out whores begging through glass walls for $5 tips.

At two A.M. on a Saturday morning, with the rest of the city in its Puritan-induced slumber, the urine-stained streets of the zone were jammed with traffic, mostly with cars from the suburbs carrying a lone male driver on a journey one part hedonistic and two parts pathetic. Step into an alley, any alley, and you could get yourself a $20 hooker in mesh nylons and a chunk of crack. Just hope to hell that the hooker is a woman and the crack is actually some relative of cocaine, and hope even more that you can get yourself out of that alley alive.

No more, or at least not as much. These days, a glittering Ritz-Carlton Hotel looms some forty stories overhead, aside a second tower chock full of million dollar condominiums with extraordinary views over the historic Boston Common, the Public Garden, and the Charles River beyond.

The strip bars are mostly gone, but for one new upscale club and an inexplicable little holdout, The Glass Slipper, situated on a side alley where few people ever think to go. A better name for the joint might be The Orthopedic Shoe, given the age of the—ahem—girls who test their limited skills at the art of exotic dancing there. The movie houses have been boarded up or converted into Chinese restaurants and small

319

groceries. If the streets are jammed late at night, it's usually with couples coming into the neighborhood for some pork fried rice or chicken lo mein.

But like anything else in life, there are a few people who don't understand that the party's over and the rest of the world has gone home or moved on. Guys with mullet haircuts and Igloo coolers filled with cans of Budweiser still roll through the zone at any odd hour, because that's where they heard they were supposed to go. They are easy prey with easy money, looking for a few minutes of oral sex and a sniff of cocaine. Maybe someday they, too, will be able to let the 90s go. But for now, they make life that much better for the likes of Eric Glass.

Mongillo and I arrived at the corner of Essex and Harrison streets at about 9:15 on Saturday morning, fresh from our flight into Logan Airport, though fresh isn't a word I'd use to describe either the neighborhood or my current state. We could have split up, but until I got my police protection back, Mongillo didn't want to leave my side, and I wasn't about to push him away. No, he wasn't likely to scare off any would-be killer, but just the fact that he would serve as a witness might. Besides, that stunt with Elizabeth aside, I liked the guy, and life was better with him around.

We got out of the cab in a stream of sunshine and took a long, skeptical look around us. There were condom wrappers in the gutter. My eyes drifted toward a discarded hypodermic needle balanced on the grate of the storm drain. Trash floated by in the spring breeze. A homeless man wrapped in the remnant of a commercial rug staggered toward us, but just kept walking by, repeating to himself, "The cock-sucking ozone's going to kill me."

Mongillo took a long, hard sniff at the air, his considerable nose pointing up toward a robin's egg blue sky, and exclaimed, "Ah, the smell of commerce."

Actually, the smell was of urine, but that's okay. I dialed a cell phone number, and within a few minutes, a gleaming Lincoln Continental with heavily tinted windows pulled up to the curb. The driver and front seat passenger, two thugs in ill-fitting black suits, both stepped from the idling car and silently approached us. To the more cynical among us, this may have appeared to be a good old-fashioned rubout. To me and Mongillo, it's a way to make a living.

The men patted us down in absolute quiet, then the larger of them—tough as that distinction was to make—knocked once on the rear car window and said, "It's okay, boss." The door opened, and Vinny and I slid in next to a gentleman named Sammy Markowitz.

A word about Sammy: dangerous. Here's another: criminal. And some more: ruthless, conniving, depraved. But hey, he returns my calls, so I like him. Cops like to say that when you're trying to bust the devil, you don't rely on saints for inside information. For reporters, it's much the same deal.

Sammy, truth is, was an old source of mine, the provider of key information for a series of stories many years before that led to the indictment of a dozen cops in the city of Chelsea and the recall of the mayor. A little more than two years ago, he gave me key information while I uncovered a major Washington scandal. In Massachusetts, and seemingly in the nation, if there was crime, Sammy Markowitz's sticky fingers were somehow on it.

He was short and bald with a few day's worth of haphazard growth on his face, a clone of Don Rickles if Rickles wasn't quite as handsome as he is. He spent his days sitting in the back booth of his appropriately named Chelsea cocktail lounge, The Pigpen, playing gin rummy, sipping Great Western Champagne, and counting the day's receipts of one of the largest, most efficient bookmaking operations in America.

"Jack," he said, giving me an awkward hug, "I want you to know, you're becoming like another son to me, and if you call me at the last minute again in urgent need of help, I'm going to have you killed, just like you were my son."

I laughed. I think that's what you're supposed to do at these moments, though I've never really been sure. I introduced him to Vinny, who gave me a strange, sidelong glance.

Sammy said to Mongillo, "I've got a fat daughter, a big pig of a woman. I should set you two up."

Vinny didn't reply. I cleared my throat and said, "I wish I bedded all the women that Vinny does."

Sammy looked at me and said, "I don't like to be seen out here with you, you know? The cops are looking for you. There was a hired hitman looking for you. Christ, a guy could get hurt just being near you."

He handed me a manila envelope, looked up into my eyes and said, "This is what you need. Now listen to Sammy. Be careful now. And come by and see me sometime. We might be able to help each other out."

Maybe, or maybe not. Before I could decide, or even thank him, the back door opened again and the goon beckoned us outside. Vinny struggled out, and I followed. The door slammed shut, the goon got in the front and the car sped away, a glint and a gleam in the springtime sun.

I tore open the envelope and looked at two pictures, one a computer printout of a mugshot of Eric Glass, the other an apparent surveillance shot of Glass. He was an oddly good-looking guy, with light black skin, deep set eyes, his hair done in cornrows. The accompanying printout said he was five feet ten inches tall, 165 pounds, with brown eyes.

Also in the package was a photograph of an equally handsome guy, with short wiry hair, a chiseled black face, and a police uniform on—Michael Sweeney.

I had many questions to answer on this day, but one thing I've learned in this business is that it doesn't do any good to try to answer all of them at once. So here I was trying to find out what went wrong in that drug raid five years ago. Did Robert Fitzgerald publish a lie, and if so, what and why? What drove Hank Sweeney to abandon his retirement, risk his life, and come to my side?

With the aforementioned pictures in hand, Mongillo and I walked into a fabric store that fronted the corner. The signs on the dirty windows were written in both English and Chinese, the English ones reading, "Best selection in Boston," and "Buy ten yards, two free."

As the two of us walked into the shop, the door hit a bell and two startled elderly Chinese women turned and looked at us from behind a counter. One of them, no more than four feet six inches tall, came walking around the counter, right up to us, and said, "May I help you?"

I showed her the picture of Eric Glass and said in a voice that was entirely too loud, "Have you seen this man?" She held the sheet for a moment, brought it over to her friend, and exchanged words in Chinese. Well, I think they were Chinese, but how was I supposed to know? The store, by the way, was crammed full of enormous rolls of fabrics in every possible stripe, check, plaid, and solid color, not to mention other assorted patterns that included Thai elephants and what Martha Stewart might call "Meadow Flowers." This last one seemed to hold a certain appeal to Mongillo, because as I was following the shopkeeper to the counter, my compatriot had unspooled some of the fabric, held it across his large trunk, and said, "My next suit."

"Your next suit," I replied, "is going to be all white, with arm restraints."

The tiny Chinese woman came up to me, handed me the sheet, and said, "We no see."

How do you say *lie* in Cantonese?

I thanked them and led Mongillo to the door. We walked a block toward Boston Common and stopped at a morose looking bar with red paint peeling from the door and a dingy sign above proclaiming, "Something Fishy," followed by, in smaller letters, "Ladies invited." How nice. I'd have to remember to tell Elizabeth about it the next time we happened to cross paths.

We pushed the door open and went in. The stench of stale smoke hit us in the nose like a heavyweight champion's fist. I mean, there are West Virginia coal miners who would get sick in this place. It took a moment for my eyes to adjust to the dark and my olfactory systems to come back from their hyper-defensive mode, but when I did, I found myself looking at an establishment that might as well have been the set for the bar scene in *Star Wars*.

The bartender was, I don't know, coming along eighty years old, a toothless afterthought of a man with a shoulder holster that displayed a

Colt .45—and I don't mean the malt liquor. The room was long and narrow, taken up almost entirely by the bar. The first two stools closest to us were occupied by a pair of overweight transvestites in miniskirts that didn't—in fact, couldn't—cover nearly enough. They were smoking stout cigars, gulping Bud Light from the bottle, nattering on about a guy named Stork they both wanted to bed.

I heard Mongillo whisper to himself, "Holy shit. I don't even think I'd get a drink here." I heard the bartender say in a shrill voice, "Help you boys?"

"Two Buds," I replied. I don't think I'd drunk a beer this early in the morning since Paul Newman Day at Wesleyan College. You know, Paul Newman Day. The entire day, from the moment you wake up until the second you pass out, is dedicated to drinking a case of beer while going about your daily routine. In some parts, like my old college campus, it's considered a high holiday, at least when I was there.

"Glasses?"

Oh God, please no. "No thanks, they come in one."

One of the transvestites thought that was pretty funny, turned around and said in a gruff voice, "Hey sailor, not only do you have a sense of humor, but you're really cute."

I had the feeling that I had mistakenly wandered into the employee lounge at a circus freak show.

"Naw, you should see me when I'm out to sea," I replied. I don't even know what I meant, but now both transvestites were doubled over in laughter. They turned completely around in their stools to face us, and when one of them saw Mongillo, (s)he exclaimed, "Whoa there, you'd be quite a little handful."

I quickly scanned the bar, which looked like a regular Ellis Island of the depraved—blacks, whites, Indians, Hispanics, Chinese, mostly unshaven, huddled over cheap drinks made from watered-down rail liquor, barely talking to one another. It's worth stressing that it wasn't yet ten o'clock on a Saturday morning. Country clubs all over the region were packed with white, middle-aged, upper-class men giddy at the prospect of a round of springtime golf. Yogi Bear cartoons filled television sets all across the land. And here, free drinks for all my friends, as Mickey Rourke once said. Well, not free, but that's not the point.

"Buy you a drink?" one of the transvestites asked, the one, I might add, with the slightly less hairy legs.

"I just did," I replied.

They even thought that was funny. I was starting to think that this wasn't such a bad place, that maybe the University Club was overrated. Then Mongillo struck without warning. He pulled the envelope from my hand, showed them the picture, and said,

"You people know where I can find my friend, Glass?"

Their expressions quickly changed as they eyed the picture, then Mongillo, then me. The one with the hairier legs and the deeper voice asked, "You lawmen?"

"Only in bed, only with the right implements," I replied. The other one stifled a guffaw. I said, "I'm not. I'm just looking for a favor, and the guy in the picture is the only one I know who can give it to me."

"Well, don't tell him I told you this, but walk to the far end of the bar. He's almost always back there, on the end stool, sipping brandy and counting the night's receipts."

"Probably figuring out what his tax vulnerability is," I said, kind of casual, not wanting to look overeager and spook anyone.

The less hairy one couldn't contain his laughing now. He slapped a hand, polished fingernails and all, on his friend's shoulder and said, "Tax vulnerability. Get it?" I turned to Mongillo and said, "Let's go."

The two of us walked along the back mirrored wall—why, by the way, would an establishment like this, with the patrons that it has, want so many mirrors?—to the far end of the bar, where we saw nothing more than an empty stool with a mostly empty snifter glass. Mongillo put his nose up to it and proclaimed, "Drambuie."

We weren't there but ten seconds when a nearby door to what the people of the University Club would call the men's lounge, but the clientele here probably describe as the shitter, popped open, and out stepped a handsome black guy dressed in a crewneck sweater and a pair of khakis looking like he was about to head to theology class at Harvard.

I was so surprised I exclaimed, "Glass?" Mongillo hit me in the small of the back, but too late. Glass whirled toward me, put his hand up under his sweater like he was about to pull out a gun, and said, "Who wants to know." It's an old line, but a good one.

I said, "Jack Flynn. I'm a reporter for the *Record.* This is Vinny Mongillo, another reporter. We're doing a story. We need your help."

"I don't deal with no fucking reporters anymore." For the uninitiated, the word *anymore* was the most interesting one in that sentence. Then he said, "Glass don't deal with anyone he don't want to deal with."

I said quickly, "Sir, we need your help. Could you just hear us out for a minute. You don't want to help at that point, you just tell us. We'll go away. But I don't want you to say no until you know what the hell I'm asking."

He gave me an angry sidelong glance as he sat down at the bar, emptied his snifter, and hollered to the bartender, "Another Drambuie here, old-timer." The bartender, who apparently had no love lost for the charming Mr. Glass, wasn't exactly going to set a record getting down to him, but eventually he did, with a fresh drink.

Glass sat with his elbows on the bar facing away from Mongillo and me. We stood over either one of his shoulders. Every once in a while, someone would come by and slam the door to the shitter. When the toilet was flushed, the sound was so loud, so intense, you had the feeling of being in a Caribbean resort during a September hurricane.

"Remember a police raid five or six years back?" I asked. "Cops go to an apartment house in Mattapan. They knock down the outside door. They race inside and slam down the door of the wrong apartment. A minister dies, a cop dies. It's a disaster."

He didn't react, which I think was better than a denial. I think. So I said, "You were the police informant."

He swerved around on his stool, his fists clenched and his eyes white with anger. "I've never been a fucking police informant in my whole fucking life, you little puke. Get out of my fucking face before I shoot you in the balls."

Mongillo, God bless him, stepped forward, closer. I said, "Look, we're not here to argue over whether you were the police informant. We have the documents right here"—I waved the handy manila envelope—"that show that you were. If there's any question, I'd be glad to pass it down the bar and everyone can take a vote."

He continued to look at me, raging but quiet. I continued, "What we want to know is, did you tell your handler the drugs were in Apartment 11 or in Apartment 12?"

His rage turned to incredulity. He stared at me and said, "Even if I was an informant, which I'm not, you expect me to remember this all these years later, which apartment I sent them to?"

A valid point. Mongillo's phone rang and he stepped away to answer it. I shook my head and said, "It's easy. Do you remember at the time thinking that they went to the wrong place, or the place you told them to go?"

Now he shook his head. His rage had subsided. He said, "I'm not telling you I was even an informant. I'm just a guy trying to earn a living. You're not going to get anything out of me."

"The cop, your handler, might have been framed. His mother killed herself. His father's in mourning. I'm trying to figure out whether you gave him wrong information, whether you gave him right information and he made a mistake, or whether you gave him right information and someone else in the department screwed it up."

He sipped on his Drambuie. The toilet flushed and I all but pulled a copy of that day's *Traveler* off the bar and covered my head.

"The cop, your handler, is dead," I said. "His memory may have been violated. His family is ruined. You are the only sliver of hope." As I said this, I reached into the envelope and pulled out the second photograph, the one of Officer Michael Sweeney. I looked him flat in the face and said, "Not often enough can any of us give anyone hope. You can, to this guy's father."

He looked at the photograph out of the corner of his eye, then turned fully to face it. "Never seen him," he muttered.

"He was your handler," I said.

He quickly responded, "I said, never seen him."

I shook my head in resignation and slid the picture back into the envelope. Glass kept staring at me, surprisingly so. Rather than look relieved that this annoyance was retreating from his life, he seemed to appear interested for the first time in this brief conversation. He said, "You don't get it. I never seen that guy before."

I replied, "No, I do get it. You don't want to help. Fuck it. We're out of here."

Now he stared straight into my eyes. "I am helping. Your records say I was the snitch. You're saying this guy was the handler. I'm saying I never seen that guy."

Ding, ding, ding. Dawn breaks over Marblehead. Put it however you want. I asked, "Who would the handler have seen?"

My new friend, Glass, smiled a wry little smile and turned toward the bar. But rather than ignore me, he pointed to the front page of the *Traveler* that had been sitting there, and on the front page there was a small headshot of Boston Police Commissioner John Leavitt.

"Him."

"You worked with the commissioner?"

"Back then, he was a superintendent, the head of narcs and detectives. We had what you might call a relationship. I gave him information. He gave me money and room to run a business."

I looked him long and hard in the eyes. His gaze didn't waiver from mine.

"Did you tell him the right apartment."

"Oh, I absolutely told him the right apartment. He messed up. And a month after he messed up, he got himself promoted to commissioner."

"Thank you," I said. And without notice, I turned around, smacked Mongillo on the shoulder with the back of my hand, and mouthed the words, "I'll call you later." He was still on the phone as I bolted out the door.

And with that, all of life seemed to turn into one giant sleight of hand.

thirty-five

SHE WAS KNEELING ON the antique Oriental rug, boxes all around her and tears rolling down her alabaster cheeks, when I walked through the door of Paul's office and said in as calm a voice as I could muster, "Amelia, I'm sorry, I got here as fast as I could."

She looked at me with eyes that showed a depth of sadness that I don't think I've ever seen before. Amelia Bradford was more a Wasp than anyone I had ever met, in breeding, in demeanor, in outlook. Her family had lineage, manners, prestige—everything, in fact, but money, which is why she had been the secretary to the publisher of *The Boston Record* for the past thirty-four years.

"Oh, Jack, my God, look at you. You're bruised. You've been beat up. Oh God," she said, rising to embrace me and burying her cheek into my shoulder in another fit of tears. This isn't what any guy wants to be told, but I figured now was not the time to point that out to her.

She smoothed out her pants and took a seat at the desk chair that was askew in the middle of the bright room. I sat on a nearby loveseat.

She began to talk, but glanced over toward the open door and stopped. I got up and closed it and we resumed. The office, by the way, was silent but for the gentle hum of circulating air. The room was drenched in springtime sun.

"The police came the day of Paul's death and confiscated virtually every file," she said. "They were wheeling dollies in and out all morning. Most of the material they returned yesterday, but some I believe they still have."

I wasn't exactly in the mood for a long windup here, but didn't have it in me to prod Amelia along. So I sat on my tongue, so to speak, and let her go on. In this building, I guess we're all storytellers of some sort.

She continued, "They seemed especially interested in his computer files, particularly his electronic mail activity, and took his whole computer system with them. They took his datebooks, his desk calendar. They asked if he uses a Palm Pilot, which of course, Paul doesn't. He can barely figure out a Dictaphone." She talked about him in the present tense, which was more sad than anything else, but with this, a smile passed over the corners of her lips. She became serious again and said, "They even emptied his trash and took that with them."

Any moment now, a point. So I kept waiting, and waiting.

"But they were so obsessed with his email, wanting to know his address and his password, that they never asked me about good old U.S. mail, you know, stamps and the post office and the like. When he sends a regular letter out, I keep a copy in my computer system, from where I've made a printout. They didn't ask me for any files like that, and I was in such a state when this all happened that I never thought to offer it."

I think we were approaching what we in the business of journalism call news, so I leaned forward with my elbows on my thighs and studied her face as she spoke.

"I was going through some of this stuff last night, Jack. I just happened into the file and saw some of these old letters that Paul had sent to various people, and I just kept clicking on more of them, thinking of what a wonderful man he is, missing him.

"And then I came across this—" she reached toward the desk, picked up a sheet of paper and handed it over some boxes to me—"letter that he wrote. I'm embarrassed I didn't think about it before. This was written, as you see, a little over a week ago—just a few days before Paul was killed."

I took the sheet and began reading, but couldn't focus, so I looked out the window for a moment at the perfect blue sky and thought about Baker loping across a freshly mown field in pursuit of a brand new tennis ball, all firm and yellow. I returned to the page, my world in better order.

It was a letter from Paul to Robert Fitzgerald. The top of the page bore a stamp saying that it had been delivered to Fitzgerald's office by hand. In it, Paul wrote that a *Record* reporter—who I knew to be Vinny Mongillo—had approached him recently with concerns about the veracity of some of Fitzgerald's human interest stories. Paul said he had hired an outside investigator to re-report some of Fitzgerald's stories from the past two years, and many of the people quoted could not be found. He said he was aware that John Cutter had warned Fitzgerald that the integrity of some of his stories appeared suspect, but that the matter was put aside when he died. Now, he wrote, he would need to meet with Fitzgerald to determine his future.

"Robert," Paul wrote in his closing line, "you've been a major asset to *The Boston Record,* and consequently, to my family, for nearly half a century. Because of your work, your talents, and your dedication, my initial desire is to urge you to retire, and with that retirement, hope that this matter quietly disappears. But my principal reservation is that the transgressions have been so significant that we must take punitive action to restore the integrity of this great newspaper. Thus, I'd like to meet with you Monday morning in my office to review some options. I have sent you this letter both as a courtesy and as a request to begin pondering our respective futures."

And Monday morning, before that meeting occurred, Paul was dead. Five years ago, after John Cutter raised similar concerns, he, too, was dead, murdered, in a crime that had been concealed for all this time.

I stared at the letter until the black ink of the words faded into the white page and I was staring at nothing at all. I heard Amelia say, "Jack, are you having the same thoughts that I am?" But her voice sounded distant, like it was coming from the other side of a thin wall.

Let's hope it holds up.

That was Paul, Sunday morning, in the Public Garden, his words now having greater meaning than they ever had before. He knew. He knew. Not only was he headed off to work to wrestle back the Terry Campbell empire and save a family newspaper from the scourge of a down-market chain, but he had a fateful meeting scheduled the very next day in which he was most likely going to strip the most famous reporter in the history of Boston of his power, prestige, and reputation. By pushing Fitzgerald out the door, he knew he would be making it more difficult to keep Campbell from getting in, but Paul understood the importance of our reputation, the meaning of integrity, the preeminence of truth.

I looked up at Amelia, backlit by the morning sun. She was saying something to me, but what, I'm not really sure. Already, my shock was beginning to turn to anger, more an abrupt transformation than an evolution. Much as I liked the man, deep down, I was always skeptical of Fitzgerald's cozy relationships with politicians in Boston and Massachusetts. He had grown so tight with so many government figures, and so powerful in his own right, that he had become a part of the very establishment that our newspaper is supposed to scrutinize. Voice to the voiceless? Not anymore. Hell, maybe not ever.

I took a quick census of the damage caused, the people hurt. The roll of the dead was a brutal one: John Cutter, Paul Ellis, my neighbor Nathan. I had a sickening image of Hank walking into his tidy little house in Marshton one summer's morning and setting down bags of groceries on the kitchen counter while calling out his wife's name. And he'd wander through the unnatural quiet to find his Mary Mae covered in blood, a pistol in her hand, splayed across the couple's bed, unable to cope with the lies that Fitzgerald had effectively woven into a public truth.

And then I thought of Sweeney, sitting alone night after night in his easy chair, watching television, fingering the worn newspaper clips that contained those deadly lies. Now he lay in a hospital bed, a seventy-one-year-old man with a bullet in his gut trying to make things right but with no clear idea how.

We have a governor who might not be governor but for Fitzgerald's lies, a police commissioner who might not be commissioner but for a fabricated story of a bungled drug raid. My newspaper, the great *Boston Record*, might not be so great, so powerful, so widely read but for Fitzgerald's amalgamation of lies.

But did he kill? Was Fitzgerald a murderer? I started to think that perhaps he was.

Amelia was standing over by the desk, speaking to me in a voice I couldn't hear. Then I did.

"Jack, it's Brent Cutter. He's on the telephone. He saw you come in here and wants to speak to you."

She talked slowly to me, a little louder than would be the norm, as if I were Dorothy waking up in bed surrounded by all my farmhands who I thought were part of the enchanted journey toward the Emerald City. I started to say, "Tell him to . . ." but then couldn't bring myself to finish the thought with a woman as pristine as this.

She asked me, "You want me to tell him to fuck off?"

Another reason why I love Amelia. Her ancestor, Governor Bill Bradford of Pilgrim fame, was rolling over in his ancient grave. But Amelia is a devotee to current day practices and modern mores.

"That's exactly what I'd like you to tell him," I replied.

"Brent, he asks that you please fuck off." Never have I heard those words uttered with such exquisite grace and unfailing manners. I'd have to try that sometime.

Meanwhile, she hung up. I fully reengaged in the present tense. I had wrongs to make right, crimes to solve, even justice to administer, if I had to. And I'd have to do all this alone, because the police, led by Commissioner John Leavitt, were very well part of the problem, not in any way the answer.

Most of all, I had Fitzgerald to see, to complete the business that John Cutter and Paul Ellis were unable to finish over the last five years—that business, and so much more.

When I came out of Paul's office, the haze lifting from my head like the fog over San Francisco Bay, I ran flat into Brent Cutter, who was pacing back and forth in front of the reception desk awaiting my appearance.

"I thought Amelia provided you with instructions?" I asked, walking past him but not stopping, just as he did to me two days before outside the executive committee meeting.

He set off after me. Though his legs are roughly as long as mine, he seemed to have to run to keep up with my stride. "Jack," he said, "we need to talk, me and you, man to man."

I stopped short, such that he banged into my right shoulder. I whirled around, picked him up by his Zegna shirt, and slammed him against the corridor wall, narrowly missing the Pulitzer Prize plaque that Fitzgerald had won for local reporting in 1984.

"You son of a goddamned dick," I seethed at him, my face just inches from his. "Don't you ever call yourself a man after what you've tried to do. Don't you ever carry with you even a moment's expectation that I owe you a goddamned thing."

He was looking down at me like I was a maniacal crazy man, a creature wholly beyond comprehension. Of course, his hair was still perfect slicked back and the clothes I was about to rip probably cost about as much as my car.

"You're a little rodent," I said to him, still holding him firm against the wall. "You know what, forget that. Rodents have fur. They're too cute. What you are is a parasite, a little goddamned slimy slug trying to suck all the money out of the business that your family worked decade after decade to build.

"You are a piece of garbage, and you're lucky I don't break your pasty fucking greasy face."

And with that, I let him go. He slid down the wall, not all the way to the floor, but close.

He straightened up and tucked his shirt in, trying, but failing, to salvage some semblance of dignity. "I want to cut a deal with you," he said. "I was wrong to exclude you. I want to put this behind us."

I was starting to calm down, or rather, come down from my anger high. I looked at him and shook my head in resigned disgust.

He said with his typically arrogant tone, "If we sell to Campbell Newspapers, Terry will agree to a provision that the *Record* retains local control for five years. He'll agree to a further provision that mandates that I'm the publisher for the first thirty months, and you're the publisher for the second thirty months."

He paused, eyeing me warily, half hoping his offer was alluring, half fearing that I would slam my fist into the soft tissue of his nose. Truth is, I was somewhere in between.

"Jack, it's inevitable that this company's going to get sold. Old family businesses like ours don't work in this new economy. You'd have learned that your first week in B-school, if you had gone. The trusts are breaking up. The cousins don't want any part of it anymore, yet they still have a major say because of the shares they own. The economies of scale favor large chains. And the public is headed in other directions for news, like the Internet.

"So if we're going to get taken over, why not cut the best deal we can. What I'm offering is two-and-a-half years for you to be the publisher of one of the largest, most important newspapers in America. That's two-and-a-half years for you to leave your mark on the company, on journalism, to fulfill some goals, and to make a lot of money. Keep in mind, you have an equity stake in this company. You stand to make a small fortune in a buyout. And who knows. If you do well, maybe Terry keeps you on."

I looked at it slightly different. I saw it as two-and-a-half years to preside over the dismantling of a once great newspaper as a cutthroat, cost-conscious chain pares down what it views as the fat, also known as the newsroom. I saw it as two-and-a-half years of working for a militant conservative, not a real newsman.

Very recently, as in, earlier that week, the thought had occurred to me that Brent Cutter might be a murderer. Now I just thought he was a moron. But the worst part about what he was saying was that in some odd way he was starting to talk sense. Wouldn't it be great if life were that simple, if I could just sign on the dotted line, become an instant multimillionaire, order new furniture for the publisher's office, dine around town as one of the most powerful, eligible bachelors in the city, and not have a worry in the world. There's only one problem with that: history.

History says to me that John Cutter and Paul Ellis were murdered. History says to me that there's a good chance that someone within the newspaper killed them. History says to me that all those who came before me at this wonderful newspaper didn't bust their collective ass so I could cash in on some big payday.

Now I was starting to get mad again.

"Brent, I'm dealing with some issues right now—newspaper issues, moral issues—that your money-grubbing little brain couldn't even begin to comprehend. Here's something else you can't comprehend: this business is about more than the money. It's about more than our own personal ambitions. It's about more than holding the title of publisher. It's about a calling. You haven't heard it. I have. If you get in my way, I'll rip your fucking head right off your neck."

And I walked away. Poor Brent was sputtering something about negotiable deals as I punched through the double doors on my way down to the newsroom. I've never really believed in destiny before, but I had a date with it now in the form of Robert Fitzgerald.

Best as I could tell, the first impulse when you believe you've figured out who murdered two people you greatly respect—the very first impulse— is to call the friendly homicide bureau of your local police department. That didn't appear to be an option here, for a couple of reasons.

Reason A: If Eric Glass was to be believed, and at this point, this pimp and crack dealer seemed more believable than anyone else I knew, then it was John Leavitt who screwed up that bungled drug raid in Mattapan five years ago. It was Leavitt, back when he was a superintendent rather than the commissioner, who handled the informant, got the information, and directed the narcotics squad. And it was Robert Fitzgerald who blamed, in print, Sweeney's son. So forgive the living hell out of me for suspecting that Leavitt may have been behind the fact that John Cutter's murder evidence was rotting away in the basement of the coroner's office. He didn't want Fitzgerald to be caught lying, because he was a direct beneficiary of one of those key lies.

Reason B came in the form of a telephone call as I momentarily stopped in the familiar environs of the mostly empty newsroom just to clear my head.

"Flynn here."

A pebbly voice said, "Sweeney here."

"Hank?"

"Jack, listen up. Don't say anything until you hear me out. Don't come to this hospital. One of the police guards told me this morning that Travers found a partial fingerprint on the gun and matched it to a print of yours he pulled off your boat."

Sweeney paused here to wheeze a little. I heard him swallow hard, summon some strength, and continue. "He's got a police detail here waiting for you to arrive, and when you do, they're going to arrest you for leaving the scene of a crime.

"So son, just stay put and I'll call you later."

"Hank?"

"Yeah, Jack."

I wanted to tell him that I knew about his wife, about his son, about his anger and his loneliness and the injustices that made his life only a vacant shell of what it should have been. But I couldn't, not there, not then, not over the telephone. So I asked, "How are you doing? You holding up?"

"I'm an ornery old man with a bullet in his stomach, a doctor who says I'll be fine, and a wife who's ready to kill me after I get better." Pause, wheeze. "So yeah, I'm okay, Jack. I'm feeling better every day."

I was quiet for a moment, a silence born of sadness. He said, "You sound down. Don't be. We're going to solve John Cutter's murder, you and me. We're going to do that together. And when we do that, maybe we'll have Paul Ellis's killer as well."

I wanted to tell him that I think I already had, but I wanted to do that in person. Realizing that his phone was likely bugged, I knew I had to do it in person.

I said, "You're a great man, Hank. A great man with a great family."

And with that, he gently hung up the phone.

So wasn't this just terrific. My options were to find myself arrested, killed, unemployed (not to mention unemployable), or shamed. Or probably a combination of two or more of the above. Seems like just

Monday I had the world on a string. Now I come to find out that string was actually part of a noose.

As soon as I hung up the phone, Mongillo appeared at my desk, a fat roast beef sandwich in one hand and a pen in the other. He had a grin on his face that extended from the Sports to the Business section.

"Got it. Got it. Got it. I've got Randolph nailed. I have another example of him lying in his campaign literature—about a role he had prosecuting an accused murderer his last year as DA. It was a dual juris-diction case, and State Police are telling me that more of the work was done out of Middlesex County. They pushed the court proceedings in Suffolk only because they were shopping around for a more conserva-tive judge."

I looked at him, grim-faced, full of angst rather than excitement. He kind of bowed in front of me, just about did a little soft shoe, then said, "Jack, it's a hit. We might drive this clown right out of the nomi-nating process. This shows him to be a recidivist liar."

"Sit down," I said. And he pulled up a desk chair and sat near me. The room was mostly empty because it was still relatively early on a Saturday, meaning I could walk him through what I knew without fear of being overheard. I told him about my conversation with Randolph, about his accusations against Robert Fitzgerald, and his threat to go to the *New York Times* if we wrote about him again. I told him about Paul's letter to Fitzgerald three days before he died. I told him, essen-tially, that I wanted to run his story, that we would run his story, but we needed to buy another day. I apologized for keeping him in the dark. I told him that I just didn't know what else to do.

I couldn't go to the cops because they would either ignore it, arrest me, or kill me, or perhaps all three, in that exact order. When you're in newspapers, being ignored is as bad as being killed, and both seemed especially onerous right now.

So what I needed to do was to do what I do best, and that is to publish everything I knew in the pages of the *Record*—the fact that the police department's own toxicology tests show that John Cutter was poisoned, and the fact that two key officials—the governor and the police commissioner—had directly, professionally benefited from the lies published by a prominent *Record* reporter, Robert Fitzgerald.

But I needed to do this authoritatively, not accusatorily. I needed our stories to be the final, weighty word. I also needed them to be the first word. If the *New York Times* struck before we did, the *Record* would look as if it were engaging in nothing more than forced-fed damage control.

In order to do all this, I needed to sit down with Fitzgerald and coax a confession from him. I didn't expect for him to tell me he killed John Cutter and Paul Ellis. But I did need him to acknowledge that he had lied in print, and if he did that, we could avoid a messy string of he said/she said stories. Once I got Fitzgerald's untruths into the paper, the police department, put on very public notice that its practices would now fall under the glaring glow of scrutiny, would take over the criminal case of John Cutter's murder.

I explained all this to Mongillo. He sat in utter silence until he finally asked in an uncharacteristically timid voice, "Then what happens to the *Record*? Are we in such a mess that the board will just vote to sell it come Monday?"

"Good question," I said, glumly. "We can only control what goes into the paper. I don't think we can control right now what happens to it."

I called Justine Steele, the editor-in-chief, at home, and gave her essentially the same spiel, advising her to stay on alert. She said she'd come into the newsroom and be available that afternoon.

And then I picked up the phone and called Robert Fitzgerald.

thirty-six

MONGILLO PULLED THE NAVY blue *Record* delivery truck into the newspaper's enclosed loading port and shut the automatic garage door. He got out and we stood on the dimly lit dock together, both of us nervous but neither wanting to concede the same.

"If I do well driving this thing, maybe Campbell Newspapers will hire me in the delivery department," Mongillo said.

"A good thing," I replied, "because I think their drivers are paid better than their reporters."

Then I asked, "You know where it is?"

He gave me that look that implies—all right, outright states—that I'm an idiot.

"Just asking," I said.

I had an appointment with Robert Fitzgerald at six P.M. in his downtown office. I would have preferred to meet in the newsroom or the middle of Boston Common, or on the stage at Symphony Hall, where witnesses would inhibit the prospect of crime, specifically murder, but didn't want him thinking for a moment that I was harboring suspicions of anything untoward. He believed, I hope, that this meeting was a much needed morale-boosting session as I tried to save the newspaper from the grips of that miserable chain.

I had spent the better part of the afternoon typing up a story on John Cutter's toxicology tests, rehashing his murder, reviewing how those results were never made public and stood in direct contrast to his death certificate. I quoted Sam Brookstone, the Northeastern University criminologist, saying the results unequivocally indicate foul play. The story was ready to run when we were ready to run it.

After I finished writing, I went into the *Record*'s database of old stories, specifically looking at April 25—the day John Cutter was found dead at the Four Seasons Hotel five years ago. I plugged in Lance Randolph's name, along with Robert Fitzgerald, and got a hit: "Governor Proposes Stricter Gun Law."

The story, written by Fitzgerald, said that Randolph proposed tougher sentencing on Massachusetts' already tough handgun codes. That was mildly interesting, but it was the fourth paragraph that gave me what I needed. "Randolph unveiled his new proposals last night to an annual dinner gathering of party leaders and major political contributors in the main ballroom of the Four Seasons Hotel in Boston."

Bingo. What this showed was that on the same night that John Cutter was killed, Fitzgerald was downstairs in the hotel covering a political event. This likely explained why a tissue from the hotel men's room was found on Cutter's bathroom floor, because Fitzgerald brought it there and inadvertently dropped it.

None of this I could use in print, but still, it stoked my confidence, even anger, as I prepared to confront him.

Mongillo, bless him, had scouted out the front of the *Record* building and spied two unmarked Boston Police cruisers idling in the street, waiting, no doubt, to apprehend me as I came or left. My good friend, Luke Travers, had left three voicemails on my cell phone, the first asking me to call him, the second asking me to fucking call him, and the third asking me to fucking call him fucking right away. The poor boy needs some medication for his blood pressure. Maybe he's not getting any sex lately—I hope.

So here we were. I pulled up the rolling cargo door on the rear of the truck, walked into the cavernous, windowless freight area all gloriously smudged with ink and filled with the delightful odor of old newspapers, and took a seat on the floor against the side wall. Mongillo yanked the door shut behind me with a thunderous clap. I heard the sound of the driver's door open, then slam shut, the engine start, the garage door rise, and we were off.

He rolled open the door separating the cab from the freight and said in a low voice, "We're driving by an unmarked car right now. He's eyeing me, eyeing me, we're past him, no sign of movement. Bang. I think we're safe."

"As he's eyeing you, you ever think you might just want to shut up?"

"Everyone's a critic. Let me do it my way, Fair Hair."

We pulled up onto the Southeast Expressway on our way downtown. "Open and clear behind us," Mongillo announced. I stayed on my haunches trying to brace myself against the significant bumps.

Five minutes later, I felt him pull off the highway, cut hard left, then right, left again, and one more time, right. This wasn't built for what the nice people at Lexus like to call a "smooth, luxurious ride." We stopped at a couple of red lights. I heard him roll his window down at one stoplight, causing me to crouch down further. Then I heard him say, "No, no papers on board. Sorry, I really don't have any. Look, here's a copy of today's *Traveler*, just take this and get the fuck away."

Well, he certainly didn't have a future in customer relations. Distribution, he was still doing all right.

A couple of minutes later we glided to a stop, and he backed up a few feet with the beeper sounding. When we stopped again, he said quietly, "We're here. The window in his office is still dark."

I checked my watch—5:45 P.M. We were fifteen minutes early. I stood up with stiff legs and looked through the narrow door into the front cab and out the windshield. The sky was still a bright blue, streaked by the fading sun, but the street was covered in the deep shadows of a late spring afternoon.

"Stay in back," Mongillo said. "I'll watch for him."

I sat in the back of a *Record* delivery truck preparing for what was undoubtedly one of the most difficult, most important interviews I would ever conduct, ranking right up there with an election eve confrontation with a rather desperate president of the United States a couple of years before. I needed to make Fitzgerald understand that I knew, without even the remotest hint of a doubt, that he had fabricated multiple stories—and specifically, stories dealing with the governor's crimefighting record and the bungled Mattapan police raid. Then I needed to convince him to make it easy on himself, and in turn, the *Record,* by admitting the fabrications. This would provide a clean peg for a front page story. If I was on a streak, I could nudge the conversation toward the deaths of John Cutter and Paul Ellis, but this was far less likely. Most important, I had to get out alive.

"Still no sign," Mongillo said.

I checked my watch again—5:51. I felt around in my pockets and on the floor to make sure I had what I needed—a pen, a legal pad, and a microcassette. Maybe I needed a gun as well, but I'd already used one of those two days before, and the aftertaste wasn't something I particularly liked. My guile would be my most potent weapon. I think.

I thought of the first time I had met him. I had just started at the *Record,* just had my first front-page story, on how a Massachusetts congressman had accepted the free use of a Martha's Vineyard vacation house for an entire summer from a lobbyist representing Philip Morris, the tobacco empire.

He walked up to my desk, this tall, dignified man with the bow tie and the stately gait, more senatorial than most senators could ever hope to be. He held out his hand—I shook it—and he said, "Young man, you've already earned your pay for the year."

We exchanged small talk, and he invited me to come downtown to his office the following Monday—the beginning of our traditional, weekly meetings.

That first Monday I arrived, he sat in his rocking chair and pulled a tiny notebook out of the breast pocket of his checked sportcoat and carefully flipped through the small pages until he came to his intended notes. I thought it nothing short of completely charming that this great scribe, this legend, had invested the time in critiquing my work.

"How long did the story take you to do?" he asked. "When did you first call the congressman's office? Did you detail for the press secretary what you had?"

He nodded at my answers, guided me, corrected me, lauded me, always providing an anecdotal rationale for the way things should be done, but always sure to tell me there is no one precise way in this business to do anything at all. After we were finished with my stories, we analyzed the rest of the paper, the stories over the past week he liked, and why, the stories he didn't, and why not, the stories with potential that was never fulfilled. This is how it went every Monday from noon to one P.M., over coffee and bagels, and every Monday I left with the dueling sense of exhaustion and reinvigoration.

"Okay, I see him," Mongillo said, quietly. I moved up, such that I was sitting right behind his seat, within easy earshot. "He's alone. He's walking down School Street. Stopping, reaching into his pocket, pulling out keys, putting them in the door. He's not looking around, not acting suspicious. Opening the door, shutting it, that's it. He's inside."

I said, "Thank you, Bob Costas." Then, more seriously, I asked, "You don't think he's suspicious that there's a *Record* delivery truck parked across the street at a time when no newspapers are being delivered?"

Mongillo replied, "I'm backed into an alley. All he sees is the windshield, if he notices anything at all. And maybe we're out delivering the Sunday inserts."

Mongillo fell quiet, and I remained that way. He even had his cell phone set on mute—an unprecedented event. A moment later, he announced, "Okay, his office window is now lit up. Stay where you are, I want to see if he does anything odd up there, sends any code or signal out."

What is this, Robert Ludlum?

Another moment of quiet, broken again by Mongillo. "Nothing," he said. "He's done nothing to cause worry. It looks like he believes this is just a typical gathering between two longtime friends, the mentor and the demented."

Maybe that was funny, but I wasn't of the mind to laugh.

Mongillo continued, "I'm going to get out, walk around, open the back door, and let you out. I'll be waiting right here with my eyes peeled on the window. If you have the slightest problem or any fears, just appear in the window and hold a hand up. I'll get through the door myself and the State Police will be right behind me."

Fitzgerald himself once told me that when you scrape away everything else, your success in an interview often comes down to your demeanor, your comportment, your ability not just to express confidence, but to exude the notion that you are absolutely going to get your way. It's always worked for me before. I hoped to hell it would work for me right now. This is what I thought about as I stepped from the back of the *Record* delivery truck on a pristine Saturday afternoon in a dank alley in Downtown Crossing.

Be confident, get the story, make deadline. After that, everything else would work itself out.

thirty-seven

Seven years earlier

ONE EVENT DOWN, one more to go, Bertram Randolph—Governor
Bertram Randolph—thought to himself as he shook the last hand in
the line of construction workers outside the Coolidge High School in
Roxbury and looked around for his car.

The dedication had gone well. The speeches were short and
smooth. He thought he saw a couple of local reporters jabbing down
notes. And it would be a hell of a lot better than what he had next,
which was another damned fundraiser in a windowless banquet room
where he'd have to bare his political soul for a bunch of fatuous businessmen holding five-hundred-dollar checks.

He turned around and waved good-bye to the workers. His son,
Lance Randolph, the district attorney, suggested they walk back
through the school rather than across a dirt-covered construction site.
But he didn't want to get stopped again by every fawning teacher in his
path, so he said with a smirk, "Come on, kid. I always said politics was
a dirty business. Don't worry about your damned shoes."

They walked around a construction trailer in the gentle morning
sun, father and son, a political dynasty in the making. As they walked
side-by-side, Randolph turned to his son and said, "I'm thinking about
running for the Senate next year." Bill Gowan, the governor's State
Police bodyguard and driver, walked a few paces ahead.

Lance Randolph's eyes widened. He snapped his neck toward his
father and said, "You've got a lock on the governorship. Why challenge
an incumbent senator?"

346

"I've done this two terms already, son. I don't know if I have much left I want to do, or for that matter, can do. I'm sick of running every four years. I like the idea of playing on a national stage. And in the Senate, you can collect a thousand dollars at a time in contributions, cutting down on this bullshit fund-raising time."

The two were in the middle of a stretch of hard-packed dirt. Behind them were only construction trailers. To their right was the high, windowless brick wall of the school gymnasium. Straight ahead, about thirty feet away, was the school driveway and their shiny state-issue, navy blue Ford LTD sedan.

Lance Randolph was about to say something when a student walked around a far corner and called out, "Hey, Mr. Randolph." He was a strange-looking kid, with long, stringy hair. Stranger still was what he wore—a flowing white coat that looked like something he might wear in a science lab.

He repeated himself. "Hey, Mr. Randolph."

"Damn," Bertram Randolph said out of the side of his mouth. Ever since he got into this business twenty years before, he found himself constitutionally incapable of ignoring voters, whether they be young or old, black, red, or white, male or female. Some politicians were good at the gentle, dignified blow-off, but not him.

He said to his son, "Come with me for a second. We'll do this quick." And he veered toward the funny-looking kid.

They were but fifteen feet away when the young man reached inside the flowing coat and pulled out a short, semiautomatic rifle. Lance Randolph, the district attorney, froze, unable even to get the sounds out of his mouth to form a scream. Bertram Randolph, the governor, stopped, reached his hand out, and said, "Son, what you want to do is to give me that weapon right now before someone gets hurt and you get in big, big trouble. Give me that gun."

The kid looked at the governor as if he didn't understand. He then turned slightly to his right, took aim, and fired at Trooper Gowan, who was opening the passenger door of the governor's car. Gowan crumpled immediately to the ground. He never saw what hit him.

The teenager then calmly turned back toward the father and son. He took a step closer, the gun aimed straight ahead, and said to Lance Randolph, "You sent my friend to jail. Big mistake on your part."

And with that, Lance Randolph began to run. When he bolted, he was so panicked that he pushed off against his own father and mistakenly knocked him to the ground. The kid fired a long volley of bullets at the district attorney as he ran furiously toward the car, hoping to take refuge behind it. But every shot missed.

The prosecutor reached the car and dove behind the back end. The governor picked himself up slowly from the soft, filthy ground, wiped a smudge of dirt from his right eye, and stared at the young gunman, not wanting to show fear. Thoughts of the Brookline abortion clinic shootings, all the murderous rage that had become too commonplace in America. And here he was, face to face with evil.

"Give me the gun, son. I'm the governor of Massachusetts. If you give me the gun, I can help you out."

The elder Randolph looked out of the corner of his eye to the Ford resting about thirty feet away, wondering if his son was in the process of helping him, maybe pulling the gun from Gowan's holster to shoot his way out of this mess. But he didn't see anything, because there was nothing to see. Lance Randolph hid on the other side of the car, shaking too hard to act.

"Son, I'll help you, honest to God. But you have to give me the gun."

The kid gazed back at the governor, his face completely without emotion. His laboratory coat rippled gently in the morning breeze. His hair blew around the bottom of his neck. He took aim.

"No, son. No!"

And he fired.

The first shot slammed into Bertram Randolph's skull, knocking him back onto the dirt ground. The boy fired a dozen more times, the bullets ripping through the governor's gray suit and slamming into his flesh and bone with one sickening thud after the next.

The student stopped shooting. He looked curiously at the car and began slowly walking toward it. The district attorney hid behind the rear bumper.

Halfway there, the kid's face became contorted with a look of incomprehensible despair. He let out an almost inhuman moan, as if the reality of the moment, of his deeds, had just taken hold. He stopped, put the barrel of the rifle against the roof his mouth, and pulled the trigger.

As the boy lay dying on the ground, Lance Randolph emerged from behind the car, first tentatively, then confidently. He sprinted toward his father, dropped to his knees, and held him.

"Oh God, oh God, oh God," he kept repeating over and over again. He knew his life had changed forever in that one split moment with that one thoughtless reaction. He just wasn't sure yet how bad.

thirty-eight

THE WOODEN STAIRS LEADING up to Robert Fitzgerald's second story office seemed unusually high, but then again, so did the stakes. Perhaps the latter explained the former. Anyway, when I got to the top, I took a deep breath of the somewhat stale air and walked toward his open door.

Fitzgerald was standing behind his desk, his head down, shuffling through a pile of papers. I knocked once on the door by way of warning and walked inside. He looked up and flashed a bittersweet smile.

"Jack," he said in that deep, sonorous voice of his. "Jack, I've been thinking nonstop of you." He walked around his desk and shook my hand, placing his other arm gently around my shoulder. It would have been natural to fall into our old pattern, the teacher and his student, but I didn't because I couldn't. Calm and confident, those were the keywords, the demeanor that got me through so many interviews before.

"Sit, sit. We have much to catch up on." I took a seat in my traditional place, a brown leather club chair facing the windows. "How about a glass of port," he asked. "I've got some nice tawny that I think you'll like. It will soothe things a bit."

I nodded, figuring that alcohol could only help the situation on either side, emboldening me, loosening him. He poured two glasses and handed me one, then sat on the opposite side of the antique cherry coffee table in his Boston rocker. He wore a handsome spring sport jacket with a light checked pattern, an open-collared blue oxford cloth shirt and a pair of slightly rumpled khakis.

The room, by the way, was lit with low lamps covered in hunter green shades, giving what I'd best describe as a Locke-Ober feel or a

Somerset Club mood to the place, familiar, clubby, and refined. A single large blue Oriental rug covered much of the dark, parquet floors.

As we sat, my eyes drifted across all those photographs on his wall of fame—Fitzgerald with Henry Kissinger and John Glenn and Robert Kennedy and even Fidel Castro, not to mention every governor of Massachusetts and mayor of Boston in the last forty years. How many of these people did he lie for? How many of them illicitly benefited from the paper's blind faith in its star reporter?

There was also a collection of famous front pages framed and hung along the brick-colored walls, many of which included an analysis or story by Fitzgerald—the first moon landing, the assassination of Martin Luther King, the resignation of Richard Nixon.

Finally, I focused on Fitzgerald, who was, in turn, focused on me. "Jack," he said, "No one should be expected to withstand the pressures of the week you've just had, between Paul's death and the Campbell takeover bid. I hope you're being fair to yourself and will take some time off and get away soon."

I shook my head and said, "I can't even think in those terms yet, Robert. You know that."

He nodded and asked, "What do you hear in regard to the police investigation?"

I replied, "Nothing terribly encouraging. I don't get a sense that the cops are any further along today than they were on Monday, do you?"

It was a subtle first gambit, turning it back on him, testing his knowledge of the proceedings. He flashed a hint of being startled, and replied, "I think your information would be as good as mine, no?"

I didn't respond. It's an old reporting trick: Make him fill the void with something he might not have otherwise said.

Stunningly, he fell for it, showing me just how far off his game he was on this day. He got an anxious look on his face and added, "I don't know, Jack. It almost seems strange to think about—Paul dying, that old mariner on the waterfront getting shot to death, someone trying to kill you."

He lowered his voice as well as his eyes and said, "I don't know what to think."

I remained silent another moment to see if I could wring any other emotions or facts out of him, but he only sat staring at the floor. So I said, "This hasn't exactly given me great faith in Boston's finest."

He replied, "Give them time, Jack. Give them time. They're better than you think, and sometimes, breaks happen on major cases when you least expect them." Jesus, don't I know it.

We both fell quiet again for a moment. I heard a siren on the street directly outside and listened to see if it stopped at the front door, but it continued on for destinations unknown. Hopefully Mongillo didn't get excited at the prospect of a breaking story and follow it.

I took my first sip of port. It was silken on my tongue but raw against my throat. The taste, the sensation, jolted me into action.

I said in a strong, clear voice, "Robert, I have some unfortunate business to address with you." I swallowed subconsciously and stared him in the eye. His expression didn't change. He gave not an inch, showed no sign he had any expectation that anything out of the ordinary was coming his way. Outside, day was beginning to turn to night.

"We go back too far for me to beat around the bush, and I respect you too much for that, so I'll just be straight with you. I have hard evidence and credible allegations that you've fabricated information in at least two of your stories, and possibly many more."

He had been sitting cross-legged in the rocker, gently swaying. When I said what I said, nothing changed, nothing but the expression on his face, which turned from deadly serious—not to make trite use of such a strong phrase in this situation—and sincerely concerned, to a wry smile. It was an expression of understanding, of sympathy. It was, in a word, bizarre.

"Jack, son, people have been gunning for me since I got into this crazy business nearly half a century ago. You know that. Reporters are inherently suspect of success, even—no, especially—amongst ourselves. What are they saying this time?" He brought his arms up over his head, as if he was stretching, which I suppose was better than reaching into his pants for a pistol.

It was an interesting defense that momentarily caught me off guard.

I was expecting a tirade, shouted demands to know the identity of his accusers followed by an indignant reminder of all he had done for *The Boston Record* in general and me specifically. What I got was a superior attitude that said, *Poor Jack, you imbecile.* This was going to be even tougher than I first thought.

I said, "It's the governor, Lance Randolph. He says that back when he was district attorney, you lied about his conviction rate at the start of his first gubernatorial campaign, in an effort to help him. After that, he says, he was stuck with the lies, so he adopted them."

The smile got broader. For chrissakes, I think I saw his teeth, and no, they weren't fangs.

He replied, "So our youthful governor, in a desperate attempt to salvage his nomination as U.S. attorney general, blames a reporter for his inability to tell the truth. And Jack, you're accepting his story at face value?" He shook his head slowly, his gaze never leaving mine. "Son, I thought I knew you better. I thought I trained you better."

Obviously I had at least partially considered this defense. Obviously I had considered that if you're Lance Randolph, you're going to blame anyone even remotely suspect, and you'll spread that blame as far and wide and deep as it takes to cast any doubt in the minds of the reporters covering the story. But hearing Fitzgerald say it, hearing the words come out of his own mouth in that commonsense way in which he speaks, gave me sudden, though hidden, pause.

It's an odd sensation, making your accusations in an interview. It's as if the roof above you has been lifted, the walls around you removed, the trees outside defoliated. You are suddenly, completely, irrevocably exposed, with no reliable idea as to what might come next and nowhere to turn for protection. There was no turning back now, so I said, "That's not all. Roughly five years ago, in a story about a bungled drug raid in Mattapan in which a reverend and a young cop were killed, you blamed the wrong officer—the dead officer—for leading police to the wrong apartment."

He continued to meet my stare, squinting a bit as he thought back to the specific story, how he put it together, what he wrote. He said, "If

I'm remembering right, Jack, and this was a long time ago by our standards, the police gave me the information, on a not for attribution basis, on which officer committed the fatal error. If you have proof that I had it wrong, I think we owe the public a correction, even these many years later."

This I had thought of as well, but once again, stated bluntly by Fitzgerald, the evidence sounded so circumspect, or circumstantial. I exhaled slightly and felt myself slouching, fading into the leather chair, giving ground, losing confidence.

I said, "Robert, I've also conducted a detailed analysis of two years worth of your human interest stories. And in more than two dozen of them, we're unable to locate the people you quoted, or even prove that those people ever existed."

Now he seemed to be getting agitated. His cheeks flashed red and his eyes showed anger. He said, "Which stories? Which people? I don't sit in the newsroom like all these pseudo-journalists that come in these days, kids whose idea of reporting is making a few telephone calls over to Harvard and MIT, then writing their big think pieces on the direction of our society.

"I'm out there talking to real people on real streets, and often those people move on, live in different places, and maybe a few of them, out of self-preservation, even give me wrong names. Maybe."

He collected himself a bit, sat back in the rocking chair, folded his hands in his lap, and said, "Jack, you're better than this. Much better than this. The pressure of the week, of the future, must be getting to you, which is understandable."

He calmed himself down to the point that he almost seemed to be enjoying this, because he believed the outcome was preordained. But this wasn't some *60 Minutes* interview, or a Barbara Walters special on ABC, where attitude was paramount. In the ground game of newspaper reporting what mattered most was the information, not the emotion. So I fell back on an old Fitzgerald lesson: commune. Create sympathy, mutual interest, between the reporter and the subject. Involve him in your needs, in your life, in your story.

I brushed my hand through my hair. I looked at him in silence. I said, "I've been blessed in life, Robert, not by the success I've had in this business, in Washington. No, it's something more meaningful. I've been blessed by the people in my life. I've had three great and wonderful men, each of them a role model in their own distinct way—my father, Paul Ellis, and you."

I paused, probing him with my eyes through the descending shadows. My father died before he saw me become a *Record* reporter, though more than anyone, he taught me the importance of hard work and the glory of a career in newspapers. Paul Ellis died earlier this week. They were gone before any of their inevitable weaknesses were exposed to me, though if they were, I'd understand. Just as I knew they were great men, I also knew they weren't perfect men. They had flaws, each of them, some minor, others, I would bet, far more significant.

"And what I have left, Robert, is you, my journalistic mentor." My eyes drifted from his handsome Irish face to the window, to the darkening patch of sky beyond. "I understand you're going to have shortcomings. I understand that not even the greatest among us is as perfect as we would like to seem. And I also understand that those faults don't take away from the immense virtue and accomplishments accumulated over all these years, through the course of a life."

I slapped my hand softly against the rolling armrest of the leather chair. I stared at him so hard it's as if I was trying to bore into his brain. "Robert," I said, "I need you now like I've never needed you before. I'll be straight. The governor, Lance Randolph, says that if we write a follow-up to our story about him lying in his first campaign, he will go to the *New York Times*—the *New York Times*—with hard evidence that you, a senior *Record* reporter, aided and abetted him in that lie."

Fitzgerald tried to interrupt, but softly, not loud. I talked over him.

"He says that John Cutter knew about the fabrication. He sent him a note. He got a reply. He claims to have copies of both. He will, in essence, be accusing the late *Record* publisher of being part of an orchestrated lie—a great man who isn't here to defend himself."

I brushed my hand across my mouth. I was starting to work myself up, feeling angry, as I detailed the accusations.

"Robert, this comes as the board of directors of *The Boston Record* are about to meet to decide the future of a newspaper that has been in the Cutter-Ellis family for the last one hundred and twenty-seven years. One of their options, arguably their easiest option, is to accept the takeover bid submitted by a guy who you yourself call a huckster. And if they read on the front page of the *New York Times* that the controlling family was complicit in a crucial fabrication, they're going to take that money and run. Candidly, in that case, it's tough to even blame them."

I took a quick measure of the situation to see if I was having any discernible impact. Fitzgerald was leaning back in the chair, his legs crossed, one foot on the ground rocking ever so slightly, staring blankly back at me.

"You can try like hell after that to defend yourself, Robert. You can go on the talk shows and in print to salvage your name and reputation. The rest of the media will love the story. Lying reporter speaks out— film at eleven. But the upshot is, you will have effectively ruined the newspaper that made your career. The *Record,* as we know it, as we love it, as we respect it, will be no more."

He rocked with his head down, his eyes, if they were even open, staring into his lap. He said nothing, and in this position, he conveyed even less. I don't know whether it was a posture of disappointment, disbelief, regret, or perhaps all or none of the above.

I said, "Robert, I need your help. I need you to come clean, because by coming clean, you might save this newspaper and allow it to continue in its great tradition. You might also be able to save yourself and your own reputation. You don't want to be in the midst of a feeding frenzy, which you will be if this gets out first in the *Times.* Once that happens, we've lost control. The story's not ours anymore. You want to handle this within the family, on the pages of our newspaper, with readers who revere you and will understand, as I do, that even the greatest among us have faults. If we print it first, it's clean, it's concise, and then we move on."

I didn't think this was a bad little speech. Like I've said, I'm pretty good at what I do. But still, I got no reaction—not an eye flutter, not a syllable, not so much as a stalling cough.

Then I saw it. It was but a passing glint in the subtle light, the flash of a moment, so quick that had I blinked I would have missed it. It started near his face and ended on his left hand that rested in his lap—a teardrop, the most telling reaction of all.

He kept his head bowed. I went to the second prong of my attack. Fitzgerald himself taught me that in any adversarial interview, always project the aura that you're holding three aces, even if all you have is a couple of fours. Overplay your reporting hand in a way that you can never do in print. In fact, that may have been Fitzgerald's ultimate downfall—he overplayed on the pages of the *Record.*

"I have no choice," I said to him, my voice suddenly sounding strange in the gloomy silence of the office. "I have to go with something. I'm not letting Governor Lance Randolph and the *New York Times* control this story, and in effect, control the fate of our paper. My father worked here in the pressroom. The publisher sent me through college, offered me a job, and recruited me to come work in the front office."

He remained bowed, at least physically, though hopefully emotionally as well.

I continued, "I have enough. I have the details of the police raid. I'll use the governor's accusations, whether he likes it or not. Through my own reporting, our own internal investigation, I'm unable to find many of the people whom you've quoted in the last two years." I always like using whom, though I'm not sure why.

"It would be better to have a decisive, definitive story that includes you conceding error, the paper taking action, and then everyone moving on. But Robert, I have to do what I have to do. I will not allow Randolph to hold this paper hostage. I will not allow him to make accusations about us to another newspaper. I'll do this story with you or without you. And the paper will be the better for it."

I saw another glint in the light, another tear rolling off his lower cheek, falling through the air and landing with an imperceptible splash on the back of his hand. Still, he didn't move. He didn't wipe his hand. He didn't dry his eyes. It was as if he was frozen in thought, in despair, confused that a life so successful could ever lead to a moment of such profound tragedy. The gloom in the office seemed to have a sound to it, and that sound gradually, quietly, became stifling.

Without warning, he ran the back of his hand across both his eyes and lifted his head. He looked for the first time like a truly old man, like someone whose time had come and long since gone. When he spoke, his loud, sonorous voice was reduced to a tear-stained whisper.

"I lied in print, Jack. You have me. I made something up. I did wrong by the paper I love."

He spoke these sentences in rapid order. He stared at me, his face appearing as if it might dissolve into tears. I adhered to another lesson gleaned through years of experience: never get in the way of someone trying to tell their story. I sat there with my mouth shut and my expectations rising.

"But it's not the lie you think."

He paused here and looked at me, looked at me hard until his eyes slowly fell to the floor.

"Randolph's father, Bert, was a great governor and an even better man, a statesmanlike figure. He's the best politician I've ever known, and I'll admit, he became a good friend.

"When he was shot, when he died, his advisers panicked. They didn't want to relinquish control of the State House. The consultants didn't want to lose their cash cow. His son was the heir apparent. But politically, it looked awful that the kid was the lone survivor. He always had a reputation as being soft, living off his famous name rather than making one for himself. And the shooting just fed into the perception. Everyone's blood was shed at the high school that day but his."

He again stared down at the floor as he spoke, occasionally looking up and meeting my gaze. I reached quietly into my coat pocket, pulled out the cassette player, flicked it to record, and set it down unobtrusively on the coffee table between us.

"So that very night the governor was killed, they called me out to his house. Lance and his father's two top aides were there. They fed me a story about how the son tried to protect the governor against the assault, and how it was nothing more than raw luck that he wasn't killed as well. The kid told me that the shooter aimed the gun right at his face, but when he fired, his clip was empty. After he loaded another one in, he shot himself in the head."

Fitzgerald shook his head as he was finishing the sentence. When he resumed, he was looking into the far corners of the room, his voice far away, his eyes even farther.

"I knew it was a lie. They knew I knew it was a lie. When I got back here to my office that night, I made a call over to Boston PD, to John Leavitt, who was the head detective back then, and confirmed with him that there was no spent clip. But I put it in print anyway."

"Why?" I asked.

Fitzgerald suddenly focused on me as if he had forgotten I was there. He said, "Because Bert Randolph was my friend. I didn't think it right that his only son should have to suffer because, for whatever good or bad reason, he survived this ferocious attack. I wanted to preserve my friend's family name. And I wanted to make life better for that wonderful widow who lost her husband at far too young an age."

His gaze headed back to points unknown, and he added in that distinctly distant voice, "I knew it was wrong. But I thought in the back of my mind that it was the most human thing I could do."

His voice grew louder, but no less distant. "And I wondered, Jack, I wondered, can't we ever just be human in this business? Must we always lord the truth, like it's something far greater than any individual or all of us combined. Can't we extend a common courtesy? Can't we practice basic human decency? That's what I was thinking when I did this. Why must we, as journalists, always bask in human weakness, in the foibles of mankind?"

Good questions, all, some of which we had indirectly addressed in our weekly gatherings in this very room. You know the old saying: A plane lands successfully at Logan Airport every nine seconds and we don't write about it. The one that crashes—or is hijacked—is splashed on the front page. That's simply the nature of news—something new, something different. It can be an uncaring, unforgiving business.

With Lance Randolph, it wasn't necessarily news that he survived the attack. But his survival fed into a latent distrust of the man, that he was soft, not valorous, that he might have bolted from harm's way, even instinctively, and left his father to die. That suspicion could kill his career, much like the gunman killed his father. So he tried to overcome that perception by creating the news that he was in fact a hero. And that's where he, and Fitzgerald, went awry.

I asked, "So why, after that, did you continue to lie in other stories?"

There was a long pause. He stared at the floor, then looked up at me.

"Jack, I'm an old man trying to make my way in a young man's business, and the conceited fact of the matter is that it's not so easy being Robert Fitzgerald anymore. People have high expectations. I have high standards. I like to break news, be interesting, write fresh, and at my age, these tired legs aren't as fast and sturdy anymore."

Another pause, then he added, "After I lied once, they had me, and they knew it." He was gazing downward, again close to tears. The very act of speaking seemed to come as a relief, as if he was unburdening and didn't want to stop. I resumed my stone silence, not wanting to get in the way. "The ever-unseemly Benjamin Bank, his political adviser, held it over me that I had lied once, and pushed and prodded me to do it again. So I did, with the conviction rates. And then they began feeding me news, unveiling public proposals to me, giving me things a day ahead of everyone else. I became an addict, and in exchange for the news breaks, I treated them with kid gloves, and on occasions, when they needed it, I'd contort the facts."

He looked up suddenly from the rug, looked directly into my eyes. He said, "I tried to do the right thing. And in the end, it led to nothing but a pack of disgusting lies."

I asked, in a sympathetic voice, "What about Commissioner Leavitt?"

He chuckled, but it was a rueful little snicker, not anything funny. "He was there, at the school, right after it happened. He was the head detective then, a superintendent. Like I said, he knew there was no extra clip on the ground. He knew that Lance Randolph's story was an utter sham. So he blackmailed me. When he got into trouble on that botched drug raid, he called me and struck a deal. 'What harm,' he asked me, 'is there in blaming a dead kid for a raid gone inexplicably bad.'"

Here, I couldn't help myself. "The harm," I replied, "is when that dead kid's mother sticks a revolver in her mouth and blows her brains out because she knew the newspaper and the cops were lying about her only child, but there wasn't a damned thing she could do about it."

He looked passively at me and nodded. "Exactly as I've always told you, Jack. That every word we write will have consequences for people we don't even know and often can't even imagine. I lost sight of that one true thing."

I sat there in the dim light, exhausted. Fitzgerald leaned against the back of his chair and began rocking, partly in an attempt, I think, to soothe himself, partly just out of raw relief. Neither of us spoke for several long moments, until I said, "Robert, you know I have to go into print with this."

He replied, "I know you do. And for the record, Jack"—here, a slight smile crossed his lips—"I know it's nothing personal. The truth is just what we do, or are supposed to do."

More silence. If he was going to kill me during this visit, if he planned to pull a weapon from his pants or a desk drawer and shoot me in the head as Paul Ellis had been shot when he had the same information that I had now, then this would be just about the time. But he continued to rock, his head back, his hands in his lap, his eyes looking down at the floor.

I asked, "Robert, did you kill Paul?"

He didn't seem surprised by the question. He didn't even appear offended.

"No," he answered, still rocking, still gazing at the floor.

"Did you kill John Cutter?"

Again, no expression of surprise, not even over the assertion that

John Cutter had been murdered rather than died of a heart attack. He shook his head and simply said, "No."

He was lying. Or at least I thought he was. Or maybe I wasn't really sure.

At that precise moment, we heard the door open downstairs, the whoosh of outside air coming in, then the sound of someone padding up the wooden steps.

Fitzgerald looked at me and I looked at him.

"The Avon Lady?" I asked.

Then I saw the look of surprise that flashed across his face as he gazed toward the door, and I knew it would be nothing so simple.

thirty-nine

SPEAK OF THE GOVERNOR, I turned fully around in the leather chair to see the figure of Lance Randolph, who stood in the doorway, his arms crossed, looking blankly back at the two of us.

"Hello, Robert," he said from across the room. "And hello, Jack. The two of you come together to figure out how to cover up so many years of published lies?"

Quite the opposite, obviously, but I felt no compelling need to explain that to him, not now, anyway. Instead, just for kicks, I stood up and said, "Governor, this is a private conversation. Is there something we can help you out with?"

He began walking toward us. I'll confess, I didn't like the fact that he was alone. As the nominee to be the attorney general of the United States of America, he should have been accompanied by FBI body-guards. The fact there were none with him meant he had intentionally snuck out by himself for purposes that I think I was beginning to understand.

The other thing I didn't like was the gun that he pulled out of his belt, a smallish looking pistol that I suspected could still do a large amount of damage. My razor sharp mind scanned back to that speech he made at the Four Seasons five years back about stricter gun controls, and I wanted to remind him that he might be in violation of his own beliefs and perhaps laws. I didn't.

My jaw was somewhere down around the floor. Here I had been thinking, for every good and obvious reason, that Robert Fitzgerald was the cause of Paul Ellis's and John Cutter's deaths. But standing in front of me was a man with a gun who had every bit as much at stake—and arguably more—than the reporter who lied on his behalf. There's a lesson there in reporters and politicians getting too close, overly chummy, but at that particular moment, I'd be damned if I could figure it out.

Fitzgerald stood up and said, "Lance, put the damn gun away before someone gets hurt."

There were already four dead, not including Mary Mae Sweeney, and Hank Sweeney lay in critical condition in Massachusetts General Hospital. I think Fitzgerald was a little behind the times with his assertion, but again, I didn't bother pointing that out.

"Drop it, Randolph, or I'll break your fucking nose."

That, by the way, was me, feeling a surge of testosterone as I brought the disparate pieces of the puzzle into a clear image, and that clear image had Randolph as the killer of two publishers of my newspaper, two men I greatly admired.

Seven years ago, Randolph had directly benefited from a monumental Fitzgerald lie about his actions at the Roxbury school where his father died. Five years ago, he would have seen his career crash and burn if John Cutter had followed through on his apparent plans to publicly oust Fitzgerald for fabrications. Flash ahead to this week. Paul Ellis, like John, intended to fire Fitzgerald, and Paul, like John, was now dead.

It doesn't take the inventor of the Singer sewing machine to see a pattern here. In that pattern, I was apparently next in line. This was another classic Fitzgerald lesson come to life—there's always a story behind the story, and it's only the best reporters who can find it. Of course, Fitzgerald never told me that he was personally a part of the story behind the story, but no good would come of holding that against him now.

Randolph, still walking in our direction, glared at me and seethed, "Sit down." Fitzgerald promptly did as told. I mean, Baker could come over here and take lessons, he sat that quickly. I remained standing, glaring back at the governor.

He stopped five feet from me, pointed the gun in my general vicinity, and said, "Robert, what did you tell him? Did you fill his impressionable little head with more lies?"

Fitzgerald replied, "I told the truth, Lance. And the truth feels damned good."

Randolph laughed a shrill, hollow laugh. "The truth? What the hell do you know about the truth? You've been lying so long you don't know deception from reality anymore."

One of the knocks on Randolph was that he wasn't good off the cuff, that he appeared nervous at unscripted events. But I have to hand it to him, that was a pretty good line, and events don't get any less scripted than this one, or at least I hope they don't.

He looked at me and said, "I told you to sit."

I replied, still standing, "Give me the gun."

He screamed, "Sit down!" His words bolted through the dimly lit room and throbbed off the painted walls. I remained standing.

He continued to point the gun toward me, but turned to Fitzgerald and said, "Robert, if you had kept your mouth shut, everything would have worked out fine."

Randolph, by the way, armed with a gun, his cheeks flared red, his blond hair messed up, looked nothing like the self-entitled, spoiled frat boy that many of us in the Massachusetts press corps knew him to be. To the contrary, he appeared purposeful and determined—exactly what you want from your politicians, only without a gun in their hands.

Randolph said, "My old man told me that you can never control the press, but you should never let the press control you. Look at me. I've made both mistakes. But you people are vipers. You strike for no good reason. You love to make people suffer. You get your kicks out of watching people fall."

Yeah, what's his point? Actually, that's not what I was wondering. What I was wondering was how do I get that gun out of his hand, make my exit, and file for the Sunday paper. This might be one of the more trying deadlines I had ever encountered, assuming I would live to tell about it.

For reasons that were momentarily unclear, Fitzgerald stood up. I remained standing. Randolph looked from one to the other. He said to me, "By my count, you should have been dead five days ago." By my account, five days ago would have been Monday, the day the gunman tried to kill me in that Florida swamp. Another piece of the jigsaw falls into place.

We all stood there like awkward guests at an excruciatingly bad cocktail party. Of course, one of us held a gun in his hand, so it would have had to be an NRA reception. I caught a glimpse of my microcassette recorder, which was still on the table, resting on a short stack of *Columbia Journalism Review*—blending into the top cover. Never had I benefited so much from a magazine I thought too highbrow. The recorder, best as I could tell, was still recording, and I don't remember anyone in here saying that anything was off the record.

"So I'll do it myself," he said to me, his eyes showing fury.

At that moment, Fitzgerald charged at Randolph. Randolph swerved toward him and fired his gun. The bullet grazed Fitzgerald's shoulder and smashed through the window. And still, the old guy came. He slammed into the governor, who staggered backward and toppled to the floor.

Miraculously, Randolph held onto the gun, held onto it like it was a campaign contribution in the final weeks of a costly race. He held onto that gun like it was the only thing that mattered in his life, and at that moment, it probably was. Fitzgerald writhed on the ground in agony, grabbing his bloody shoulder. I jumped into the fray, because lately, that just seems like what I do. I got on top of Randolph as he rolled over and tried to get away. I had my right arm around his neck and my left arm on his gun hand as we both groped for control of the weapon. At that point, enter Vinny Mongillo.

There I am struggling in the middle of the office with the trigger-happy governor who would be the attorney general of the United States if he wasn't a murderer, and my colleague Vinny charges at us like he's a starting linebacker for the University of the Depraved. Randolph gave me a ferocious elbow to my Johnson or my Clinton, whatever it's called these days, causing me momentarily to lose my grip on his arm. He fired the gun at Vinny, the deafening sound immediately crashing into its own obnoxious echo.

He missed.

Think about that for a moment. Think about Vinny Mongillo, his sheer size, his proximity to the weapon, his straight path at the man at the end of it. And Lance Randolph missed. Granted, you don't have to take a shooting test to be the lead law enforcement officer in the United States of America, but maybe you should, and if you did, this errant shot alone should disqualify him. Vinny kept coming, Randolph was about to fire again, but I regained my wits and gave him a roundhouse punch to the temple, bringing him quickly to the floor, the gun falling aimlessly, harmlessly on the Oriental rug. Mongillo pulled up short just before knocking my nose somewhere into the back of my neck. I swooped down, grabbed the pistol, and pointed it at Randolph's head.

He lay on the ground, groaning and semiconscious, like a presidential candidate at the end of the New York primary. I handed Mongillo the gun, ran to the coffee table, and grabbed the tape player, which, much to my relief, was still recording. Somewhere, the gods of journalism shine down on me, even as they're about to take my newspaper away. I went over to Fitzgerald's desk to call 911, then hesitated with the receiver in my hand. If the wrong Boston cops arrived, all hell could break loose, or more accurately, all evidence could be contorted and concealed. I didn't want to call the FBI, because they're the ones that let Randolph out of their sights. Everybody's got an angle, and none of them seemed to help my cause.

So I said to Mongillo, "Let's put him in the closet."

"Put him in the closet? You can't just put him in the closet."

"Why not?"

Mongillo stood over him, gun in hand, his shirt untucked from the fit of physical energy. He shrugged and replied, "I don't know. Maybe we can."

I needed some time. I needed some time to get over to the newsroom, write a story detailing what happened that night, including the salient facts of Fitzgerald's lies and his firing, and get them in the Sunday paper.

Once the presses were rolling, let the cops come in. Let Commissioner

Leavitt arm Randolph with an Uzi submachine gun and set him free, for all I care. Everything would work out fine, because there's nothing better than enlightenment, no weapon better than public attention, a lesson I vividly recall learning from Fitzgerald so many years ago.

Speaking of whom, he saved my life, Robert Fitzgerald did, after almost causing me to lose it a couple of times before. He was sitting back on his rocking chair, holding his arm, watching the bedlam unfold with his jaundiced reporter's eye.

I said to him, "Drop you off at the hospital, Robert?"

He shook his head. "No, Jack. You're on deadline. I'll take a cab over. I'll be just fine."

You're on deadline. I love that answer. Once a newspaperman, always a newspaperman, even when you've strayed far across that sometimes smudged black line.

Mongillo picked up the governor, who was coming to, but not entirely there. I patted him down in search of more weapons, and found none. Mongillo placed him in Fitzgerald's coat closet and I wedged a chair under the doorknob.

Fitzgerald walked out ahead of me. I told Mongillo, "Don't move. I'll call your cell when I'm done. I'm going to need about an hour."

"What if he tries to escape?" Mongillo asked.

"Do what you always do," I replied.

He gave me a curious expression, his big eyebrows raised on his giant forehead. I smiled and added, "Shoot from the hip."

forty

Two weeks later

SO I'M SITTING AT a bar in a small town outside of Springfield, Massachusetts, when the man on the next stool wearing a Nomar Garciaparra tee shirt turns to me and says, and I quote, "The press sucks."

For originality, I'd give him a two, maybe a three, tops. For insight, something far higher.

"You know, I think you might be right," I said.

"What do you do?"

"I'm a reporter."

He took a big swallow of cold Budweiser and turned silently away to watch Evil Knievel's youngest son try to jump twenty-three motor homes, I think Southwinds, on the television above the bar.

Not that I can blame him—my fleeting friend, not the younger Knievel. All around us was the living evidence of his intuitive assertion. The traveling media circus, bored of the ruthless governor and lying reporter in Boston, had packed up their camera gear, their light poles, their immense makeup cases, loaded them onto their satellite trucks and driven a couple of hours west to the latest story of national import.

And this one was a rager—Hollywood starlet returns to her childhood home to visit her estranged mother for the first time in ten years, and said mother ends up dead of an apparent asphyxiation. You had celebrity, mystery, small-town values rubbed raw by big city problems. Plus there was nothing else going on, anywhere. For God sake, get me rewrite.

Before all this, the circus had been in Washington covering Chandra

Levy's disappearance, and before that, Monica Lewinsky, and before that, Boulder, Colorado, on the killing of that little girl who was far too young to ever be a model, and before that, Los Angeles and the O.J. Simpson trial, all along just giving the public what they want, or what we think they want, or what they don't know they want until they see it on TV or read it in print.

A guy came up to the bar. He had black-framed glasses on his under-sized head, a boy's regular haircut, and three pens in his shirt pocket. He waved a twenty in the air and said in a nasally voice that made him sound like he was a year shy of high school, "Bartender, bartender."

I turned to my bar mate who continued to ignore me and said, "A news producer, guaranteed."

When the bartender came over, the producer's cell phone rang and he picked it up and blathered incessantly, self-importantly, about satel-lite time and the night's standup and the glorious fact that the victim's sister broke down and cried in an impromptu interview.

Maybe Lance Randolph really was right. Maybe we are all vipers.

I ordered another beer and a bag of Chee-tos. The kid droned on into his phone. The bartender moved on to someone else. Another glamorous moment in the noble pursuit of news.

For the record, I made deadline that night two weeks ago. I made it by racing back to the paper in the delivery truck, bounding into the newsroom, and typing as fast as my lardy little fingers would carry my thoughts. Working with the body of the story that I had put together that afternoon, I wrote of Fitzgerald's myriad indiscretions, his admis-sions, his forced resignation. I wrote how he blamed the wrong cop for bungling a drug raid five years before, and how he repeatedly gave Lance Randolph more credit than he ever deserved. I described the unfolding scene in Fitzgerald's office with the governor and the handgun and the apparent reference to the shooting attempts of your faithful correspon-dent that occurred earlier in the week. Then I linked them all, artfully and carefully, to the murders of Paul Ellis and John Cutter that came before. And then, of course, I had an entirely separate story on the Cutter death and the evidence of murder that we found two days before.

When I finished, Justine Steele picked up a red telephone on the newsdesk. I'd never seen anyone so much as touch it before. I mean, the thing didn't even have a keypad, like the damned Bat Phone or the Hot Line in the Oval Office that links Washington to Moscow.

"Stop the presses!" she said. She listened for a moment, then barked, "Yeah, I said, stop 'em!" She hung up with an enormous grin that belied the new, grim reality of *The Boston Record*. Then she told everyone around her, "I always wanted to say that." This, ladies and gentlemen, is why she's a great editor.

Some people would say that we destroyed the newspaper that very night. Maybe I'm just a contrarian, but I'd argue that what we did was save it. We purged it of its darkest secrets, we made a stunningly public penance, and now we move on. Only time will tell the ultimate outcome, but so far, time has been very kind indeed.

The next morning, I took a fresh copy of the Sunday paper over to Hank Sweeney's hospital room. Last time I saw Sweeney, he was lying on his back on the dusty floor of an evidence archive with a formless circle of blood growing on the front of his black sweatshirt. Now, he was stretched out, sound asleep, with a collection of tubes and wires extending from each arm. He looked old, but he looked peaceful.

I was reading the *Record*'s sports section when he woke up. He blinked a couple of times, and I stood over him and said, "You're not having a nightmare, it's really me." I handed him the front page and pointed at the story that rectified the lies told about his only son. I watched him read, and then I watched the tears roll down his cheeks like a driving April rain.

"I have to tell this to Mary Mae," he said, reaching for the phone, his voice still weak.

I put my hand on his wrist and told him, "I know you do, Hank. I know you do. But I also know that Mary Mae is dead." And with that, he cried anew, tears of sadness and joy falling at the same time.

"And Hank," I added, "I don't want you going back to Florida. You're coming to live with me."

I was waiting for him to argue the latter point, but he didn't. So for the last week, Baker and I have had a new roommate to go along with the new apartment I rented on Commonwealth Avenue. I can hear him snoring two rooms away—Hank, not the dog.

After I wrote the story, after the presses were safely rolling, I paged my old cop friend, Tommy O'Brien, and told him to head over to School Street and arrest himself a murderer. The police didn't actually file charges against Randolph until the next day, when the paper was out and they had no choice, and even then, it was only for assault with a deadly weapon. The murder-for-hire charge for Paul's death came later that week, when it was shown that Kevin Clancy, a convicted felon, was paroled a few weeks before at Randolph's quiet urging, right about the time I started working on the inflated conviction rates story. After that, President Clayton Hutchins announced that he had "reluctantly" accepted Randolph's decision to drop out of the running. John Cutter's death is still being reinvestigated.

I miss Fitzgerald. I miss him like crazy, at least the Fitzgerald I thought I knew. Last time I saw him was when he walked out of his office, his face ashen, his arm dripping blood, his career in utter shambles. Since then, he's gone to that special, hellish place reserved for so many disgraced journalists and failed politicians. It's called talk radio. He hasn't begun his show yet, but the station is already advertising the hell out of him.

The police commissioner resigned the very day the story came out. Try as I might, I couldn't pin criminal wrongdoing on Luke Travers, though we essentially indicted him in the newspaper on multiple counts of being an excessive jackass and a complete incompetent. I think he's manning phones over at headquarters these days—and even then, I think he's over his pasty head.

The paper? Well, Terry Campbell abandoned his takeover bid. He was quoted in the *Wall Street Journal* calling the *Record* a "loony bin." The board of directors asked if I'd take over as publisher, and lead the newspaper through this tumultuous time. I said no. Justine Steele would do it better, I told them, and so far, she has.

She asked me to be editor. I, in turn, rewarded Vinny Mongillo with the job of senior political reporter, the one that Fitzgerald had held. "How," he asked me, "do I come in and fill the shoes of the guy who has written the most widely read prose in the city for more than a quarter of a century?"

"I haven't the faintest idea," I told him.

So why, you might ask, if I'm the editor of the *Record,* am I here at a roadside bar just west of nowhere on another gang bang of a story that no one in their right mind will remember a week from whenever? Because the Jack Flynn era at the *Record* lasted all of three days—the amount of time it took me to realize that the editor-in-chief spends the bulk of his or her time shuttling between meetings, deciphering budgets, and plotting personnel changes. Give me a Bic Click, a yellow legal pad, and a word processor anytime. The national search for a replacement is being conducted right now.

That just about covers everyone, except Brent Cutter, who I haven't seen since I shoved him up against the wall. I don't believe anyone's even noticed that he's gone.

I paid my tab, which came to $9.50 for four Budweisers and the bag of Chee-tos, and made a mental note to come here more often. I bade a warm farewell to my less than chatty bar mate, who continued to show me the back of his sweaty head. I started out the door destined for the Swirlington Ritz-Carlton, also known as the Motel 6. I assume they left a light on for me.

That's when I saw her. She was at a table right behind the bar, sitting there eating a plate of chicken wings with a Miller Lite and that day's paper spread out in her perfect lap.

"Hello, Jack," she said, licking the sauce off one of her own fingers, cocking her head slightly in that way she does, her long brown hair falling like silk to one side. She said it in a way that said she had seen me all along.

She looked as she always looks, which is gorgeous, tall, elegant, and so cruelly, inexorably familiar.

"Hello, Elizabeth," I replied. "I thought you'd left the business."

"Tried to, but couldn't. I'm stringing for the *Washington Post.*"

I stood there looking at her, and she sat there looking back at me. I wasn't sure what was left to say, but she seemed to have an idea. She said, and I quote, "I love you."

Well, that hit me harder than Kevin Clancy or Lance Randolph ever did. I felt my chest go light. I felt my throat close in. Somewhere in the near distance, I heard that lowlife of a producer tell someone in Atlanta that he had to fly tomorrow to Detroit. I heard the cut-in anchorwoman on the bar television say something about more indictments expected in the Lance Randolph case.

I loved her too. Always had, always will. I stared hard at her, sitting there looking so calm and confident. I asked, "Then what went wrong?"

She shook her head, her eyes never for a moment leaving mine. "Life went wrong, and we didn't try hard enough to right it," she said. "Maybe it's about time we did that now."

I looked down at the dirty linoleum floor of this bucket of blood bar. I didn't hear her get up. I didn't notice her walk toward me. When I lifted my head, ready to tell her something that I never quite got out and have long since forgot, her face was just inches from mine. And she kissed me—the most comfortable, most sensual, most familiar kiss I've ever had.

She pulled back a little, or maybe that was me. When she blinked, I felt her eyelashes on my cheek. She wasn't moving, and neither was I. She said softly, her breath on my face, "I'm never giving you up, Jack, so don't even think about trying to get away."

I asked, "Never means never, right?"

She looked at me, her face contorted into a smile born of endless relief, not sexy in this one moment, but stunningly beautiful, a smile that could define a life. And she kissed me again, hard, her arms wrapped around my neck. "Never means never," she said.

And with that, it was time to move on.

Acknowledgments

It never ceases to amaze in this crazy business of news how many ordinary people are willing to share their extrordinary experiences, their emotions, and their insights, all for the common cause of enlightenment. And the same generosity holds true, I'm finding, in the business of writing novels. Many people have given me their time, their encouragement, and their thoughts, and to them, I offer my humble thanks.

To Detective Sgt. Dan Keely, one of the great homicide investigators for the Boston Police Department, for his lessons on murder and the way they are solved. To Steve Taylor, a member of the family that founded *The Boston Globe* in the last century and sold it in 1993, for his keen insights into what it means to be part of a great family-run newspaper. To Rick Daniels, the capable and affable president of the *Globe,* for helping a mathematically challenged scribe understand the economics of newspaper publishing. And to Dr. Michael Miller, for his expertise and guidance on medical issues.

To Carole and Colleen, my two sisters, each of whom could have a career in book promotion if they weren't so successful in their other endeavors. Carole offers endless encouragement in everything she does; it's just her way. Colleen, a keen reader of fiction, knows more about what makes a novel work than I ever will, and prodded me toward completion yet again.

To Richard Abate, my agent and my friend, not necessarily in that order. He's relentless, and he's understanding, and for that I'll always be grateful.

To George Lucas, my editor at Atria Books, whose creativity, vision, and wisdom once more prevailed upon my modest offerings. Beyond that, he is also one of life's truly decent human beings.

To the great people of *The Boston Globe,* specifically to Michael

Larkin, the man who hired me long ago and still edits me now; to Marty Baron, a classic newsman in every sense of either word; to Matt Storin, retired but in no way retiring, who understands the business like no one else I've ever met; and to Richard Gilman, who continues to publish one of the country's most thoughtful newspapers, and allows us to keep our local identity, even as part of a national chain.